Duncan Lay is the author of two best-selling Australian fantasy series, the Dragon Sword Histories and the Empire Of Bones. He writes on the train, to and from his job as production editor of The Sunday Telegraph, Australia's biggest-selling newspaper. He lives on the Central Coast of NSW with his wife and two children.

Twitter: @duncanlay
Website: www.duncanlay.com
Facebook: www.facebook.com/duncan.lay

Also by Duncan Lay

The Last Quarrel: The Arbalester Trilogy 1

The Bloody Quarrel

Duncan Lay

First published by Momentum in 2016
This edition published in 2016 by Momentum
Pan Macmillan Australia Pty Ltd
1 Market Street, Sydney 2000

A CIP record for this book is available at the National Library of Australia

The Bloody Quarrel: The Arbalester Trilogy 2 (Complete Edition)

EPUB format: 9781760301644
Mobi format: 9781760301651
Print on Demand format: 9781760301668

Cover design by XOU Creative
Edited by Kate O'Donnell
Proofread by Melissa Kemble

Macmillan Digital Australia: www.macmillandigital.com.au

To report a typographical error, please visit momentumbooks.com.au/contact/

Visit www.momentumbooks.com.au to read more about all our books and to buy books online. You will also find features, author interviews and news of any author events.

To my friends Ronnie and Dimity, Jodi, Jason and Jen, who have helped me so much on my book tours

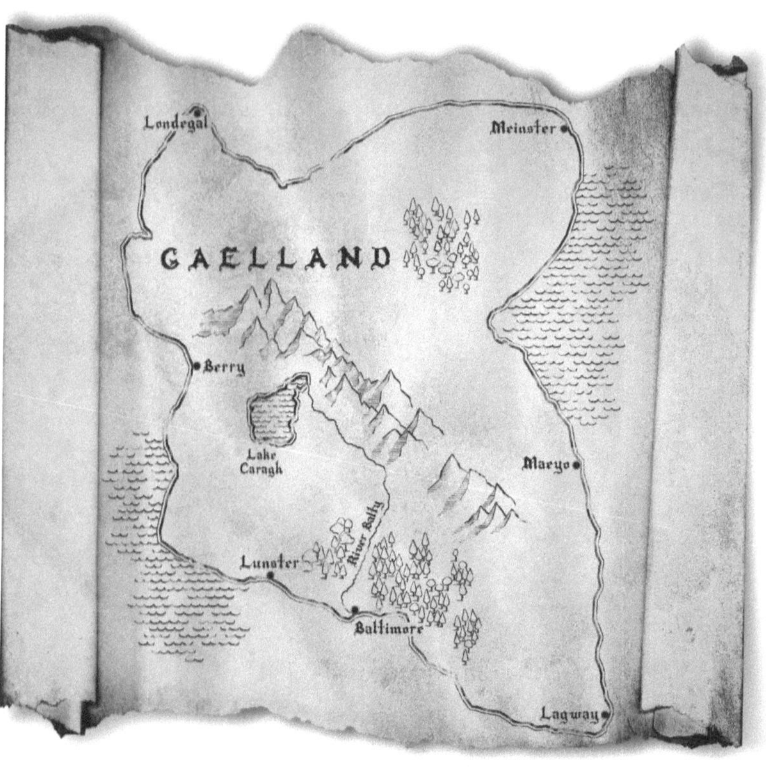

Londegal
Meinster
GAELLAND
Berry
Lake
Caragh
Maryo
River Bally
Lunster
Baltimore
Lagway

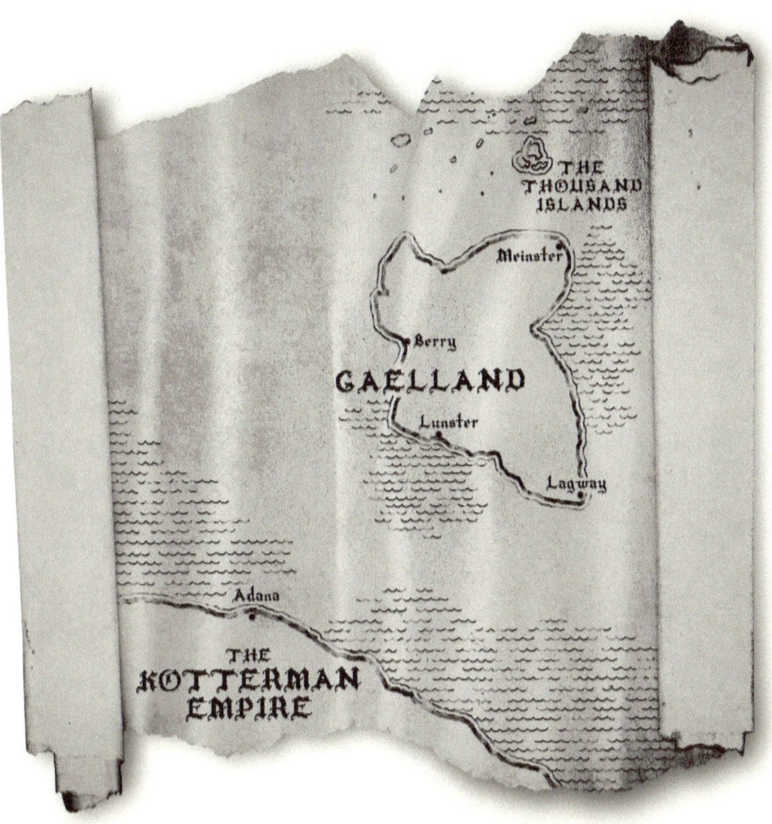
THE
THOUSAND
ISLANDS
Meinster
Berry
GAELLAND
Lunster
Lagway
Adana
THE
KOTTERMAN
EMPIRE

CHAPTER 1

Fallon stumbled backwards and fell, unable to tear his gaze from Cavan's dead body. His breath came in harsh gasps and his mind flew in crazed circles, like a bird trapped in a room. He scrambled to his knees and then vomited, the anguish and horror and guilt and fear pouring out of him. He wiped his mouth. He wanted to cry but his eyes only burned and refused to shut out the sight of the dead Prince.

Next moment, Brendan had grabbed him by the tunic and hauled him to his feet. "Why?" he asked, his voice a croak.

"Swane. The King told me it would be Swane!" Fallon managed to force the words out of his swollen throat. "It has to be Swane. Dear Aroaril, tell me this is Swane!"

Brendan just stared at him, his mouth open.

"No, this has to be Swane." Fallon turned his back on the dead Prince and appealed to Gallagher. "The King wanted me to kill Swane!"

Brendan opened his hand and Fallon fell to his knees, but Gallagher lifted him again.

"What did the King say to you?" he rasped.

"He was giving Swane a last chance to turn away from Zorva. If he refused to renounce evil, then I had to kill him," Fallon said, looking at Cavan and praying for him to stand up.

"Fallon!" Gallagher snapped at him, giving him a shake and stepping in front of him so he had to look into a friend's grim face instead of a friend's dead face.

"Think!" Gallagher hissed. "What did he really say?"

Fallon closed his eyes. "No, he never said it was Swane. Just his son. He made me think it was Swane," he said with a groan, putting it together in his mind. "He started talking about Swane and then after that only ever said 'my son'. I thought what I wanted to think."

Gallagher's hands tightened on Fallon's shoulders.

"What did he say to you?" Fallon whispered.

"We hadn't even got back to our rooms when that chamberlain Regan came rushing up to us. Said the King wanted to speak with Cavan about what would happen next. Of course Brendan and I came along but Regan said we had to wait in there while the King and his son spoke together. We couldn't hear what they were saying but saw Cavan get angry, then the King throw down his crown – and you know what happened after that."

Fallon groaned.

"The King must have been asking him to join them, to turn to Zorva. When he refused, Cavan was doomed. But why you? And what did he offer you to kill one of his sons?"

"Our families," Fallon said bleakly. "He promised they would be back with us if I did it."

Gallagher grimaced but did not say anything.

Brendan had been sitting down on one of the garden beds, head in his hands, but now he stood. "What do we do?" he asked despairingly.

"Swane is not behind this. The King is. And I don't know what to do," Fallon said. "I thought Cavan was our last hope. And he is gone."

The three of them stared down at the lifeless Prince. Fallon knew he should be crying but the shock was too great: it felt like everything had been knocked out of him.

"I know what you should do," a voice said behind them.

Fallon and the others whirled to see Regan standing there, his hands behind his back.

"You!" Fallon snarled and started forwards, only for Gallagher to grab him by the arm. For a moment he wrestled with his friend but Gallagher's grip was like iron.

"Don't be a fool. Can't you see what is above us?" Gallagher hissed.

Fallon glanced up and saw the walkway, where he had stood to shoot down his Prince, was now filled with Kelty's guards. And he knew only too well how exposed anyone down in the castle garden was to a crossbowman up there. But still he wanted to charge forwards. He was aching for a release, wanting to hit out, to try and wash away his horror and guilt in a tide of blood. Regan looked utterly calm, completely oblivious to his master's son lying dead on the path. Fallon wanted to smash that expression off his face. He remembered how King Aidan had written hurriedly on a piece of parchment and handed it to Regan.

"This is the bastard who led Cavan into the trap!" he snarled at Gallagher.

"Listen to me if you want to see your families again," Regan said evenly.

"I won't kill him. I'll just make him tell us everything." Fallon wrenched his arm free of Gallagher, only for Brendan to grab him.

"Let's hear it," the big smith said, holding Fallon easily.

"Very wise. Touch me and you will all die," Regan said evenly.

"Don't push your luck. Start talking or we'll take our chances." Fallon stopped shoving against Brendan, because it was like trying to push down a cliff.

"You once vowed to the King that you would do anything to get your families back. Hold to that oath and they will be returned to you. Break your word to the King and you will all die."

"Go on," Brendan said.

"You have killed the King's son and all earned a sentence of death. But the King is nothing if not merciful."

That was too much for Fallon and he surged forwards, but Brendan was an immovable wall.

Regan went on regardless. "Gaelland's true circumstances are beyond your knowledge. A critical time is approaching. Already wild rumors will be spreading about what happened in the city tonight. As far as everyone is concerned, and will be told, Prince Swane died in a treacherous attack."

"What do you mean, Prince Swane? That's ... not Swane lying there." Fallon pointed, unable to bring himself to say Cavan's name.

"Prince Swane will adopt Prince Cavan's duties and become the face of the Royal family. To prevent any distress, he will pretend to be Cavan at council meetings and elsewhere. You will escort Prince Swane as if he were Prince Cavan, as if nothing has happened," Regan said flatly. "That way, nobody will see anything amiss."

"If you think that will work, you are mad," Fallon said, panting, pushing at Brendan as though he could get anywhere.

"It does not have to be for long. Just until the Kottermanis arrive for their treaty discussion. Once that is concluded, you and your men will get your families back and can return to your homes. Simple."

"If you imagine we're going to sit down and eat with that Zorva-loving bastard Swane, you are madder than—" Fallon began.

"You will only see him at public functions. Nowhere else. And remember, you told my master you were prepared to do anything to get your families back. Anything. He believed you were a man of your word. Please do not disappoint the King. He hates that."

"And that gets our families back?" Brendan insisted.

"All of them. As if nothing ever happened," Regan promised. "Just serve the King until the new moon, when the Kottermanis arrive. And then you get your old lives back. You have King Aidan's promise."

"Shall I tell you what you can do with the King's promise?" Fallon roared, fighting to get away from Brendan, driven out of all control.

Brendan half-turned, shielding him from Regan, and tightened his grip around Fallon's upper body. It was like being slowly crushed to death and Fallon had to stop fighting to draw breath.

"Don't be such a bogging fool! You have killed Cavan, will you kill the rest of us and our families as well?" the smith hissed.

Fallon stopped struggling. "I never meant for this to happen," he whispered.

"Aye, I know." Brendan's grip slackened fractionally. "But it is done. And we still have to get our families back. This is our last hope."

"We cannot trust them! The King tricked and lied to me. We will go along with them and end up dead, or worse!"

"Do we have a choice?" Gallagher pointed out.

Fallon clenched his fists so tight, it felt like they would break.

"We'll say what they want to hear now and then grab the lads and sail away, take our chances on finding everyone in Kotterman. I would rather do anything than serve that bastard Aidan," he hissed.

Regan cleared his throat. "Do not make the mistake of thinking the King is a fool," he stated. "You are all living under a sentence of death and must prove yourselves every day to stay alive. The Duke of Lunster's ship will be returned to the Duchess and your men on board brought to this castle. You will be watched night and day and any attempt to leave or do anything that displeases King Aidan will see you and all your men killed. Is that clear?"

Fallon tasted bile and fought for breath. He had trapped everyone, put them all at Aidan's mercy, and there was no escape. Their only hope was that a proven liar would keep his word.

"Answer me!" Regan barked.

Fallon swallowed down his hatred. "It is clear. We will do nothing unless King Aidan asks for it; nor will we leave the castle," he said thickly. His mind was working furiously, but he could not concentrate. Every time he tried to pluck an idea out of the air, a way out of this mess, he thought of Cavan lying dead behind him and it was lost. The only thing he could cling to was a desire to defeat these bastards. He had to make amends for this, get his people to safety somehow.

Regan stared at them. "Return to your rooms now. I shall send word if you are required for anything else," he said. "And remember what I said. You face a simple choice. Death for all your men and your families, or their happy return to your sides. Don't pick the wrong one."

"Wait!" Fallon could not bear to leave Cavan there. "What about the Prince?"

Regan gestured behind them and they heard the rumble of an approaching cart. "The body will be taken out to the Guildhouse and join the others in the fire," he replied.

Fallon saw the guards approaching Cavan's body; he was being thrown away like so much rubbish. "Please, at least let me put him in the cart," he said.

Regan hesitated, then nodded. "Be quick about it."

Fallon had to force himself to approach Cavan's body. He went down on one knee and laid his hand on the Prince's head. He looked peaceful, for death had arrived so quickly, and it was almost possible to imagine he was asleep.

"I'm sorry, I am so sorry," Fallon whispered, but the tears still would not come. There was too much anger and bitterness swirling around him for the grief to have a chance. He took a deep, shuddering breath and forced the words out. "I swore to keep you safe and instead killed you. You deserved happiness; you deserved to be the King. And you never got any of it. I hope that you find the peace you wanted, and deserved, with Aroaril."

He remembered Cavan's secret plan to run away to his hidden island. "I'll make that come true," Fallon whispered. "We shall go there and get away from your brother and father and the filthy nobles." As he said that, he felt a little calmer. "We'll call the land Cavan and never forget you, my Prince. We will honor you every day."

He could not stand to see the bloody quarrel sticking out of the Prince's chest, so he rolled Cavan onto his side. He used his dagger to trim away the flights, which were pressed hard against Cavan's back. Then, grimacing at the thought, he grabbed the head of the quarrel, sticky with blood, and hauled on it. It was hard to get a grip and Cavan resisted the pull, his flesh holding on to the quarrel that had killed him. But slowly Fallon pulled it clear, until he had the entire blood-smeared shaft in his hand. For a moment he thought about casting it away, or even burning it, but instead he pushed it into his bolt bag.

"I will keep that bloody quarrel and look on it every day. And it will remind me to honor you," Fallon told Cavan gently.

He kneeled down and wrapped his arms around Cavan. Grunting a little with the effort, and wary of his back, he stood, holding the limp Prince.

"Let me help," Brendan said.

"No," Fallon said, his jaw clenched with the effort. Cavan was not a big man but he could feel the sweat pouring off him as he laid the Prince gently down in the back of the cart. There was a sheet there and he used that to cover Cavan's body.

The guards pushed him back then and he stepped away and watched his Prince being taken away to burn on a pyre, rather than be buried with honor.

"It should not end like this," Brendan said softly.

Fallon nodded, not trusting himself to speak.

"Time to go, Fallon. Remember my words and obey when I call on you," Regan said.

Fallon was numb now and allowed Gallagher to guide him back into the castle and up to their rooms. He felt like he was walking in a dream. He prayed he was. Because then he could maybe wake up and tell Cavan about the strangest nightmare he had.

But it was not a dream. And he had a horrible reminder when the men he had left on the Duke's ship, led by Devlin and with Kerrin in the center of the group, came walking down the corridor, a company of Kelty's guards following.

"Do you want to tell us what in the name of Aroaril is going on?" Devlin demanded. "And where is Prince Cavan?"

"Not here," Fallon said shortly. "We need to talk but it must wait."

Nobody looked happy about that but they followed him back to their rooms, Kerrin slipping through the ranks to be beside Fallon. He could not look down at his son, not knowing what he could say to the lad. The bloody quarrel in the bolt bag on his hip seemed to weigh him down, as if he carried around his guilt in there. And there was enough to crush him. Not only had he killed Prince Cavan but he had put them all at Aidan's mercy.

How was he going to get Bridgit back now?

CHAPTER 2

Bridgit and her friends had hurried after the young woman Ely, the helper Prince Kemal had given them.

The screams of Sean and Seamus, dying slowly out on the sand, followed them into the city. Even when they were surrounded by the hubbub of the port – even over the ensuing days as they settled into their new lives – Bridgit felt like she could still hear the men's cries accusing her.

Their house and prison was a large, plain two-story building with none of the bright tiles or decoration she had seen on Prince Kemal's home. Carefully they explored it. Inside it was cool and shady, with a large courtyard at the back enclosed by a high wall. There were plenty of rooms so they could divide the children up by families and ages, as well as keep one for themselves.

The only thing they did not have was a key. The walls around the courtyard were high, far too tall to get a small child over, and were topped with wicked-looking barbed spikes.

"We shall get out of here, but not that way," Bridgit murmured to her friends.

It became their custom to sit together at the end of the day, when the children had been put to bed, to talk about things they had seen and how that might help them with the escape plan they desperately wanted but hadn't worked out yet.

They were learning more about Kotterman in general and the port of Adana in particular every day. For instance, they were getting used to the call to prayers that echoed out at dawn, at midday and at dusk. Bridgit was impressed by the Kottermanis' devotion to Aroaril but also mystified as to how they could reconcile that with keeping slaves and treating them like animals.

Ely was living with them, working as their translator, and Bridgit was not sure if she was a help or a hindrance. The young woman spoke to the guards on their behalf when asked and negotiated for more food and supplies, but said little outside of that. She did watch everything that went on, so they had to be careful what they did and said around her. Although she was obviously a slave as well, for all they knew she was reporting back to the slave master Gokmen. But even without her there they had to be careful, for the children all had sharp ears and it would not take much for one or more of them to blurt something out in front of a guard.

Caring for the children was demanding, as well as tiring. The older kids helped out looking after the younger, but the little ones missed their mothers and there were many tears in the night: they failed to understand why they had to be there at all, of course.

Without Riona and Nola, Bridgit did not know how she would do it. For a small woman, Nola had a huge voice and was not afraid of using it. Where her husband Brendan was large in body and soft of voice, she was the opposite. Anyone who owed Brendan money for smithy work done had been far more terrified of Nola than of her giant husband. So now Nola was the stick that kept the children in line. Riona, like her husband Devlin, was a talker and a joker, and liked to keep the older children entertained. That left Bridgit free to sing and play with the ones who were missing their parents the most. Most of these were the ones she had adopted on the ship, and she was only too pleased to gather them into her arms and sing them to sleep.

If it was not for where they were, and for missing Kerrin and Fallon, she might have been happy. But they could never forget they were prisoners, and Bridgit could not get the image of Sean and Seamus out of her mind, nor the silent promise she had made to them and to herself to get their people home.

So the three took to talking at night, just whispering really, as they exchanged ideas and tried not to wonder too much about their husbands.

*

Bridgit jumped up when the crying began. She had a sudden fear that something, somehow that had been overheard: guards shouted in harsh Kottermani and children wailed in terror. She raced down to meet the Kottermanis, and found an angry Gokmen looking for her.

"I am here. Now please stop scaring the children," she said loudly. She knew how they responded to fear, so she squared her shoulders and kept her face calm, praying her voice would stay steady. She looked around and called for Ely, although she knew Gokmen spoke reasonable Gaelish, which was disturbing. Why would a slave master need to speak her language unless it was because he either planned to see many Gaelish slaves – or already had Gaelish slaves.

"What can I help you with, slave master?" she asked carefully.

Gokmen glowered at her. "Your people are not good workers. They do not understand orders to them. They make mistakes. Nobody will want slaves like that. They will not be ready to sell unless I do something."

Bridgit's heart sank at that. Anything he was likely to do would result in some of her people or, worse, some of her children suffering.

"You cannot expect them to understand your language," she argued. "Do you not have more like Ely, who can speak both languages?"

Gokmen shook his head. "There are too many of you, scattered across the city. We would need ten times as many guards who speak your words as I have now. No, you need to make them work."

Bridgit took a deep breath. She would do nothing that would hurt the children but neither did she want to be the one to make her people suffer. The noise of crying children calmed her mind. Gokmen's words about needing ten times as many guards gave her an idea, one that might solve two problems in one.

"You need to bring them together, not have them scattered across the city," she said firmly. "Have them in groups of ten, and not only can you have one guard there who can talk to them, you will find they work much better. My people are used to working together to get things done. Put two together and they will do the work of three. Put ten together and they will do the work of twice as many." *And it will make it much easier when it comes time to escape*, she thought.

"How is that possible?" Gokmen demanded.

"Because we work as a team, not as individuals," Bridgit said. "Try it. What do you have to lose? If, after a quarter moon, it has not worked, then you can try your methods."

Gokmen stared at her and she looked back, meeting his eyes coolly. Long years of pretending to Kerrin that she was happy and that there was nothing to worry about made this easy. She knew how to keep her face expressionless, so not a hint of what she was really thinking showed there. Talking to the slave master was simple by comparison.

"We shall try what you say," he grunted. "But you speak to them first."

"Agreed. Is there anything else?" she asked.

"They work slowly later in the day," he growled. "They are lazy!"

"They are not!" she stormed back at him indignantly, before calming herself as his eyebrows knitted together in anger.

"You are not managing them well. They are getting too hot and thirsty," she amended.

"How do you know this?" he asked suspiciously.

"Because it is twice as hot as we are used to. I need to see them, speak to them, and we need to come up with a better way to get a day's work out of them," she said briskly.

"I whip them until they work," Gokmen threatened.

"You will not!" Bridgit declared. "That will do nothing. Worse, they will work less and when Prince Kemal returns, he will punish you. Listen to me and I shall solve all your problems."

Gokmen muttered something in Kottermani, then nodded once. "We fix first thing tomorrow," he said.

*

Even with a hat to protect her from the sun, which had scarce risen above the horizon, the heat was still ferocious as she walked through the town. No wonder her people were exhausted.

The wasteland that had seemed to stretch in all directions from the slave house where they had first been brought actually only abutted part of the city. The other part, around the town and closer to the coast, was given over to fields. She could see the long lines of slaves toiling away and only had to have a quick look to see many of them had been burned by the sun.

"Listen now, I can make them work better, but you need to change what you are doing," she told Gokmen.

"Why? You are here to make them work better, not less," he growled back, looming over her, his big fist coiled tight around the handle of the whip he carried.

She folded her arms defiantly, which helped to disguise that her hands were shaking. "You can keep doing this but I tell you now, you will kill half of them. And what will Prince Kemal say to that? Or you can listen to me and they will be the best workers you have."

He stood over her for what seemed like forever but she locked eyes with him and refused to move an inch backwards, even though her mind was screaming at her to do so.

"I am the slave master and you will do what I say!" he thundered at her.

"Not when what you say is foolishness!" she said sharply.

She was dimly aware that all the slaves in the fields, not just the Gaelish but the others as well, had stopped and were watching them.

"It is up to you. But I will not be the one answering to Prince Kemal," she said, much softer. "Trust me. I can help us all."

Finally he grunted and took a step back. "What should we do?" he said finally.

Bridgit would have liked to smile in triumph but merely nodded. "Let's make a list," she said.

*

By the time she was able to walk back to the house full of children, she felt as though she had done some good for her people. After his initial anger and a series of not so subtle threats, Gokmen had agreed to everything she wanted. Instead of working through the hottest part of the day, the Gaelish would start before dawn, have more water breaks, rest for the hottest part of the day and then continue in the late afternoon and into the darkness. All would wear hats and clothes that covered their pale skin, while those already burned would have them treated with salves. They would also work in gangs of ten so there were enough Gaelish-speaking guards to have at least one with each gang.

It was still distressing to see people she knew being forced to work like animals, with men holding whips standing over them. But in truth the work was no harder than they were used to and the reaction of many of them to what she had done made her feel that standing up to Gokmen had been worth it. Men and women had taken her hand and told her how grateful they were and how they trusted her to first protect them and then get them out of this sandy, sweaty, revolting place.

It was a strange feeling, being responsible for so many people – it actually made her feel proud of what she was doing. If only her stomach was not so queasy with the strange food, she would almost be happy.

*

"What can you see?" Bridgit asked.

Riona did not turn her head from where she appeared to be watching a handful of children playing with their parents. "Dermot's group is being brought up from towards the docks," she replied. "I think they will be next."

"Keep an eye on them and see which way they go," Bridgit ordered. "But don't let Ely catch you watching like this. If she does, burst into tears and pretend to be searching the horizon for our menfolk in their ship."

"That's not as easy as it sounds," Riona said.

"Do it anyway," Bridgit told her, then hurried downstairs to where the first group of parents was being reunited with their children.

She had been unsure how Gokmen would organize this day, the first chance for the new Gaelish slaves to see their children. Would the children be brought back to the slave house outside the city gate, where they had spent their first few days?

As it turned out, the Kottermanis wanted to bring each gang of adult slaves there and give them just a turn of the hourglass with the children before being taken away. She knew the parents wanted more and if Prince Kemal had still been there then she would have asked him. But he had gone sailing back to Gaelland and all she had to work with was Gokmen. She wanted the first day to go smoothly and then she could use that to encourage him to give them more.

This was the message she spread to the parents, although none were happy about it.

"But you promised us a day with our children." Ena was one of many to protest.

"And you will get that, eventually. But we have to show we can be trusted, have to make them think there is no danger in bringing us together," Bridgit told her, although she made sure all the other parents nearby could also hear. "Or have you forgotten their idea for making us obey them? To kill two of the children? Would you offer yours up?"

"You know I would not," Ena said.

"Then enjoy the time you have been given," Bridgit told her. "And don't forget there are Kottermani guards both out the front and rear of here at all times."

Once she was convinced they were not going to protest any more, she turned to Ahearn. He did not have any children there but the Kottermanis had not bothered to ask, they just brought along two gangs of Gaelish.

"Have you seen any ships that could take us all?" she asked softly.

"There're a few. I recognize the one that brought us here, same sort of one that you arrived on, most likely. But will they have enough food and water on them? There's enough of us to feed on the long trip home. We can always try to fish but we don't want to run out of water with long days of sailing ahead of us."

"And then there's the pursuit. They won't let us go without a fight," Bridgit said. "And they know how to sail those big ships."

Ahearn nodded slowly. "There is that. We've all been around boats long enough that we'd learn quickly enough but we need the time to do that."

"So we need to get on board with enough water and plenty of food to last the trip back, as well as damaging as many other ships as possible, without the Kottermanis noticing," Bridgit said.

"When you say it like that it doesn't sound easy," Ahearn admitted.

"It can be done," Bridgit said with a confidence she did not feel. But he was her ally and had put his trust in her, so she could not let him see her fears. Just as if she were talking to Kerrin. "And when should we strike? When they make the call to prayers at dusk? Darkness will be our friend and they will be slow to react then."

"So they lock you up after evening prayers?"

"Aye. And they come for us before dawn."

"But it gives you the whole night to work on the locks," Bridgit pointed out.

Ahearn nodded again but his expression said he was doubtful they could break the locks that held them.

"Well, it gives us the chance to get out, for they are not watching us at night. If we can get a key then we can free you during the night. That will give us the time we need to get away and get a head start on the pursuit."

"There's a whole net-full of ifs, buts and maybes there," he said.

"But it gives us a start," she said firmly. "We just have to know where we are in the town and where you all are." She paused and looked around. "Will!" She spotted Riona's youngest running around. "Come here, lad!"

He raced over and looked up at Ahearn curiously.

"Don't tell me – this lad can pick locks?" Ahearn said with a smile.

"Not at all. But he will look as though you are talking to him while you tell me how to get from here to the harbor."

She drew a rough map on the tiles, using a finger dipped into water, knowing that the sun would soon wipe out any evidence. "And where are you compared to this?" she asked.

Slowly he took her through it, until she was sure she had it memorized.

"Are you telling me you can remember it all?" he asked. "Where we all are? Aroaril, we must be scattered across a score of places!"

"I shall draw this map for every group that comes in today and then draw it every night. You shall see, next week," she told him. "I told you I will get you all home and I will live up to my word."

Ahearn patted Will on the head with a smile. "You might at that."

*

As Bridgit had feared, by the end of the day, the children were more upset than they had been for ages, even the older ones wanting their parents back, and it took a huge effort from her, Riona and Nola before they settled down a bit. Telling them the next quarter moon would pass quickly helped a little but also reminded her of how fast time was slipping away and how long it had been since she had seen Kerrin and Fallon. One of the older girls was having her first red moon and Bridgit stayed with her for a little longer, comforting her. Although it also made her think about her own cycle, something that had never been far from her thoughts in Baltimore but swamped under the weight of other worries since then …

"I feel sick," the girl groaned.

"It will soon pass," Bridgit said, pushing a sudden fear to the back of her mind. She stayed with the girl until the lass fell asleep, then joined her friends.

"What did we learn?" Bridgit asked the other two.

"Some of them have been talking to the other slaves, although most don't trust them. I asked as many as possible to speak to them over the next quarter moon. Maybe they might learn more. But it will be hard – the other slaves don't speak our language. They can understand each other a bit, using sign language, but that is all," Nola said.

Bridgit bit her lip to hold back her disappointment. She'd had visions of a slave rebellion, with slaves going in all directions and creating more disruption, allowing them to get away. If dozens were running off into the wasteland behind Adana and sailing ships in six different directions, all the Kottermani attention was not going to be focused on them. "Well, it was worth a try, but I think we can forget about that. I am sure if we let them out they might cause some trouble for Gokmen but they won't do what we want," she sighed.

"I think maybe a third of our people are being held close to the docks. The others are closer to the fields," Riona said.

"That will make things harder," Bridgit said thoughtfully. "Anything else?"

"Only that Ely only came past me once and she never asked me anything."

"Again, does that make her friend or foe?" Nola wondered.

"We are going to have to decide soon," Bridgit warned. "If we plan to make our move then she either has to be helping us or we have to get rid of her."

"Get rid of her? How?"

Bridgit lowered her voice. "Kill her," she said.

Her friends stared at her in a mixture of shock and horror.

"It is either her or our children," Bridgit said simply. "I don't want to do it but I will, if I must."

"Aroaril, if I wasn't sitting here and watching you say those words, I wouldn't believe they could come out of your mouth," Riona said.

Now it was Bridgit's turn to look at her friend with surprise. The problem seemed so simple to her. To get back to Kerrin and to save these children and their parents, she had to remove every obstacle. By whatever means possible.

"Anyway, that is a problem for another day." Bridgit waved her away. "Nola, what did you see about the front door?"

Everything hinged on the front door. If they could get out and into the streets to scout around, then anything was possible, but the door only opened twice a day to bring in fresh supplies of food, and they weren't allowed near there then. Today, with groups of parents coming and going all the time, Nola's task had been to see what the guards were doing.

"There was only two men out there. No doubt they think that is more than enough to watch three old ducks like us and a flock of children," Nola said. "Each group of our people came with more guards, but that won't be a problem in the night. The doors are locked from the outside and they are big enough and heavy enough that we could not break through them. That means they are relying on the lock alone. If we can get the key, we are home and free."

"Maybe we could wait until they are praying at dusk, then lean out of the windows and drop something on them, then one of the older boys could climb down a rope we make by tying sheets together, get the key and let us all out," Riona suggested.

"That sounds like many things could go wrong," Bridgit said gently. "And there's still the little matter of finding all our other people and getting them to the docks, then getting a ship and getting out of here, all without raising an alarm."

"But we are getting closer to a way out, aren't we?" Nola asked.

"Piece by piece," Bridgit agreed. "But we have to be really confident. If it goes wrong, the punishment will be terrible. Death may be easier for all of us."

She could see their shoulders slump but reached out to embrace them both. "We shall find a way. We just have to keep our eyes open and our wits sharp. In the meantime we need to decide what to do about Ely. And maybe all this is for nothing. Fallon and the men could turn up at any moment. I have a feeling that they are getting close."

CHAPTER 3

"I need you all to listen," Fallon said heavily.

There was no room big enough for all of them, so they were crowded into the long corridor and clustered in doorways. He could not see everyone but at least they could hear him.

He could see Kerrin and Caley standing close, next to Padraig, and had to look away. What would his son think of him after this?

"Prince Cavan is dead," he said.

He waited while the shock rippled through them, only waving his hands for silence as they began to shout questions and demand answers. "We thought we had won when we captured Swane. But the King is the one really behind all this. When the Prince refused to keep quiet, Aidan lured Cavan into a trap and then tricked me into thinking I was loosing at Swane when it was Cavan. It was my crossbow bolt that killed him."

This time there was just shocked silence, until it was broken by a hoarse voice from the back. "Then we're dead men and our families are gone for ever."

Fallon could not deny that, although he could feel many of them willing him to. "We are prisoners here now and have to do what the King wants. If we cause no trouble, he has promised to get our families back."

"And you believe that?"

Fallon turned to face Sister Rosaleen. "We have no choice," he said roughly. "It is that or be killed."

Even as he spoke, they all heard hammering at the door.

"What in Aroaril's name is going on?" Brendan cried.

"I would say they are locking us in, so we can only leave when they want," Fallon said dully.

Devlin was the first to break the silence. "And if the King does not keep his word? Are we to sit here and wait for slaughter, like sheep in the butcher's yard?"

"They are watching us. If we try to break out, most of us will die," Fallon said. "Our only hope is to make them think we believe the King. Then we have a chance."

"That's it? Trust that a mad King will keep his word and not kill us all in our sleep?" someone cried.

"We're still alive now, aren't we? Regan could have killed me, Brendan and Gallagher in the garden, while Kelty's men could have brought Devlin and the others back dead, then hunted the rest of you through these rooms. They want us alive for a reason."

Rosaleen sighed heavily. "That is what I am most afraid of. If King Aidan has a secret purpose for us, then it cannot be good."

Fallon shook his head. "What else do you expect me to offer you? I cannot see a way out of this. If any of you can, then speak now."

He could feel their despair and frustration but none had a miracle way out of this hole he had dug them into.

"I am sorry. More sorry than I can say. I will do everything I can to fix it. But, until we can work out a way to freedom, we need to get some rest. There is nothing else to do."

"Nothing else to do? We should break out of here and take the ship back and get out of here!" someone shouted at the back.

"And how many of us would make it? They are waiting for that. We have to be patient. They made fools of us, made an idiot and, worse, a traitor, of me. Unless we can be smarter than them we shall end up dead. But while there is life, there is hope."

He hated the words and he could see they didn't like them either. But what could any of them do?

The men slowly shuffled into the rooms, moving beds aside to lay blankets on the floor for those who had come from the ship. Few looked at him, and then only to glare angrily. He took it all, knowing he deserved it.

Finally he was left with his friends, Kerrin and Caley, Padraig and Rosaleen. He patted Kerrin on the shoulder. "Head to our room lad, I shall be there soon," he said.

"What now?" Devlin asked.

"I need a drink," Fallon said, leading the way into Cavan's old room. It looked just like they had left it that day to go and see the Moneylenders Guild. It felt like Cavan could walk out at any moment and that was a knife to the heart.

While they pulled out chairs around Cavan's table, he poured them a glass of wine.

"To the Prince," he said.

As the others raised their glasses he drank his down in one mouthful, the thick wine burning the back of his throat. He poured himself another.

"Go easy on that," Brendan said. "You don't normally drink."

Fallon took another huge swallow and then brought the flagon to the table with him. "I don't normally kill Princes and friends either," he said, thumping the flagon onto the table. "So tonight I feel like drinking, what of it? Maybe I don't want to think about what awaits me in my nightmares."

His friends looked at the table, all except Padraig, who reached out and grabbed his wrist.

"Don't," Padraig said. "It is not your friend. I should know. Once you start down that path it is a long way back. And we need you now. Your son needs you and Bridgit needs you."

Fallon pulled his arm back, expecting to break the old man's grip easily, but Padraig held on doggedly. "You think we are the only ones playing this game? There is another side here, maybe more than one side, and they are all playing to win as well. So we have lost this round. We have lost the Prince and that is a bitter, bitter blow. He was a fine man and the hope of us all. But we are still in the game. At stake is not just our families but our souls, so for Aroaril's sake, Bridgit's sake and our sake, put down the wine my son and let's work out what we do next."

Fallon laughed harshly. "What do we do next? We wait and see if Aidan wants to kill us, or torture us first. We put our trust in a madman who's in league with Zorva. What else is there to do?"

Padraig dragged the goblet and wine out of Fallon's reach. "Think about why the King has kept us alive."

"It has to do with the Kottermani visit," Gallagher said. "They want us silent until then. And, I guess, all the people too."

"Yes,' said Rosaleen. 'The Kottermanis are said to be very religious. If the people of Berry realized Zorva had corrupted the King, there would uproar. If the Kottermanis heard that we were allowing worship of Zorva they might invade to stop it. They pray to Aroaril three times a day, not just once every quarter moon, like we do. To a Kottermani, Zorva worship would be a terrible threat."

"What does any of this matter?" Fallon demanded. 'Our families are trapped and now we are too."

"So we just give in to despair?" Padraig challenged. "You got us into the mess, true enough. But you can get us out of it as well."

Fallon shook his head. "How? You would be better off praying to Aroaril for answers."

He could not stand the pity in their faces. He would have welcomed anger but sympathy was more than he could bear.

"I am going to bed. Maybe the solution will come to me in a dream," he snarled.

Behind, he could hear them muttering. Probably blaming him. He left them to it.

*

Fallon pushed open the door to his room. The wine was sitting sour in his stomach, but the knowledge of what he had done weighed heavier. Although he might be able to throw up the wine, the guilt would never leave him. He wished he could close his eyes and have this nightmare all over, or at least get Cavan back again.

"Dad, what is happening? What was everyone talking about?" Kerrin asked, sitting on the bed with his arm around Caley.

Fallon could not answer. He had no words left. He looked down at Kerrin, whose expression said he knew his dad had all the answers.

He sat down next to Kerrin and wrapped his arm around his son's shoulders. Caley ducked her head under his other arm, nudging him in the chest with her nose, her tail swishing against his back.

"So Dad, what is your plan? What will we do now?"

He could not answer. He just buried his face in the top of his son's head and held him close, like a drowning man clutching onto a piece of wood.

"Dad, what is it?" Kerrin asked, his voice quiet but fearful. "Can I help?"

Fallon almost laughed then, a strangled grunt of a sound. "I wish you could. But nobody can help me, and nothing can fix the mess I've made," he said thickly. "Now we have to go to sleep."

"That's not true. You need to talk. That's what Mam would say."

So Fallon, as coldly and carefully as he could, explained how thoroughly they were trapped and how he had no idea of a way out.

He could feel Kerrin's eyes widen as he spoke but his son said nothing, only reaching around to hug him.

Fallon could not sit up any longer and laid back on the bed. Instantly Kerrin lay down beside him,

"I am sorry, son," Fallon said. "All my life I have tried to do the right thing, live by the laws and now I have killed our Prince, the man who was going to help get Mam back."

"It just means you have to get Mam back, not the Prince."

Fallon looked up at his son but Kerrin's face was completely serious. He sighed. How could he have been so stupid? How could he not see that was Cavan down there? Why did he trust the King? There were so many moments when he could have changed things, so many bad decisions he had made. If he had only seen what was happening, he could have sent his bolt through King Aidan and now Cavan would be King. All would be right with the world. Instead he had plunged them into chaos and darkness.

"You can do it, Dad, I know you can. You can do anything," Kerrin said.

That was the last straw.

The tears came. He cried for himself and his family, for Cavan and for Gaelland. He cried for the mistake he had made, for his foolishness, his arrogance, and because he hated himself almost as much as he hated Aidan.

"I am sorry, son," he said thickly. "I have let you down. I'm not worthy of you."

"Don't say that, Dad!" Kerrin begged, and Fallon saw his son's eyes fill with tears.

"It is true," he insisted. "Before this, when Mam was in charge of you, I didn't see you properly. There were many times I wished you were stronger or faster, or that your mam would let me do something to change you. Yet you did not kill your friend, the Crown Prince and the hope of this country. I am sorry, son. I let us all down, and it is my fault if we don't get mam back. You would have done better with another dad."

"No!" Kerrin cried, the tears streaming down his face now too. "You are the best dad and the only one I want. And we will get Mam back. We will! You made a mistake but you were tricked. You tell me all the time not to give up after one mistake. You can't give up. You can't!"

Fallon hugged his son close.

"Don't give up on me and Mam. We need you," Kerrin whispered. "And once you get her back, everything will be all right again."

Fallon feared that was no longer true. That nothing could be put right or go back to the way it used to be. But he closed his eyes and tried to find some sleep.

*

Cavan stood there with the crossbow quarrel jutting out of his chest, dripping blood.

"I am sorry! It was me. I was the bastard who killed you and I deserve to die. Let me go in your place – take me instead!" Fallon pleaded. The anguish filled him, poisoning him.

Cavan said nothing, just turned away with a sad look on his face.

"I will avenge you. I will. And I don't care what it costs! I will die to bring you peace!" The words seemed to release something inside and the anguish drained away.

Cavan disappeared from view and Fallon awoke with a start. His heart was pounding but he felt more at peace. The answer was obvious. He had to kill Swane and Aidan. And if it cost him his life, then it was no more than he deserved. With them dead, the others would be free to sail for Kotterman. Padraig would watch over Kerrin until they had Bridgit and all would be well. He closed his eyes again. He would see Cavan and beg his forgiveness, then take whatever punishment he deserved.

CHAPTER 4

"I think I'm pregnant," Bridgit said softly.

"Very funny, Bridge! We can always rely on you to say something to give us a laugh at the end of the day." Riona smiled. "I never knew you had it in you. You'll be giving Dev a run for his money before long!"

Nola chuckled too but Bridgit did not smile and, slowly, the grins faded off her friends' faces.

"What, you are serious?" Nola gasped.

"I am. But I wish I wasn't," Bridgit said, her voice barely a whisper. The fear had been growing within her, to the point where she had to say something. But saying it did not make it go away.

"Why do you think you are pregnant?" Riona hissed.

"Well, unless the moon has changed since we came here, I'm late. And I'm never late unless I'm pregnant," Bridgit said simply. "My appetite has gone as well and I cannot abide the sight nor smell of meat. That always happens too."

"You don't know that. You've never been in Kotterman before. This is not normal. We are not eating right and with everything else that is happening—" Nola said instantly.

"I know this is not Baltimore!" Bridgit snapped. "But I think I know my own body after all these summers!"

"Well, that might be it as well. You're not as young as you were," Riona said gently. "Maybe it is your change in life happening."

Bridgit shook her head. "Why are you working so hard to persuade me that I am mad and imagining things?" she demanded.

Riona and Nola looked at each other and then Nola reached out to take Bridgit's hand. "Because we know what you've been through before and what this could mean."

Riona took her other hand. "And because were relying on you to get us out of here and get us home."

Bridgit could feel the tears threatening to burst through the barriers she had put up after that fateful night back at Baltimore. Once she would have let them through. But she forced them back with an effort of will. "I know," she said. "I know what it all means and that is why I have been struggling to sleep these last few nights. They have churches here and they are always praying, but will a Kottermani priest want to save the baby of a slave like me?"

"You don't know you are going to lose this one," Nola said firmly.

Bridgit had to clench her teeth to stop herself from howling. "I have lost all the others. What makes you think I can keep this one?"

"Because you are not the same Bridgit," Riona said.

"What are you talking about?" Bridgit snorted. "Look at me, it is the same person."

"Not inside," Nola said. "We've all seen it. It's as if they left your fears or something behind when they took you."

Now it was Bridgit's turn to reach out and hold her friend's hand. "But I am afraid," she whispered. "Afraid I shall let you all down."

They embraced her then and again she had to work at keeping her tears in check.

Her friends drew back and she could see they were examining her closely. But it was as usual easy enough to keep her thoughts from her face. "Come now. Let's talk of something else. Like what are we going to do about Ely?"

"I wonder what her story is," Nola said. "How did she come to speak Gaelish? Does that mean there are more of our people here?"

"Who knows? But I can't trust her yet. The question is, did Gokmen put her in with us so we could talk to the guards or did Prince Kemal order her put in with us, to act as a spy and report back if we plan to do anything. I want to think they look down on us and see us as broken but I worry they are too clever for that. But you are right, we should at least pretend to be her friend: she might let something slip. And make sure the children try to play with her. Most people cannot resist children and that will tell us if she is a friend or not. If she ignores the kids or sends them away then we know she is not with us."

"And our plan to escape?"

"I need some more time to think about it," Bridgit lied easily. "Come on now. We need to get some sleep. Who knows when the crying will start?"

They lay back on the thin mattresses, which were stuffed with something strange and lumpy, and wrapped thin sheets around their shoulders. That was just one of the many strange things about this land. The idea of going to sleep without a fire or a blanket was strange, and yet neither of those things was needed there.

Bridgit made sure her breathing was slow and even, knowing her friends were listening for that. But her mind bounced from fear to fear.

Things had seemed so simple just a few days ago. She'd had terrible things to worry about, but they were all new worries and they could all be faced and fought. Now an old enemy had come from her past to terrorize her again.

This was a different battle from the ones she had lost against it, however. She could feel the old Bridgit trying to take charge, wanting to fall to pieces and knowing that she was going to kill the new life within her the way she had all the others before – with the exception of Kerrin.

But the new Bridgit was trying to fight back, saying that things would be different this time. During the day, when she was surrounded by children's laughter, the new Bridgit was able to win. But at times like this, in the dark and still, the old Bridgit was unstoppable.

She could see it all happening in her mind's eye. She would lose the baby, lose her life and never get to see Kerrin again. Worse, the children she was protecting would also be lost.

She tried to fight back, tried to tell herself that she could still rescue them and get back home, to where Sister Rosaleen could save the pregnancy, but she didn't believe herself. She wrapped her arms around her middle and prayed to Aroaril to keep the baby safe this time.

It had not worked before and she doubted it would work this time.

She wrapped herself in a sheet and murmured Kerrin's and Fallon's names. That was the one hope she clung to at times like this. That Fallon would come and rescue her.

"Where are you?" she whispered into the darkness.

CHAPTER 5

Fallon woke up slowly, his left arm and shoulder aching from where Kerrin was resting on him. Both his son and his dog were still sleeping so he rolled out of bed and massaged some feeling back into his arm. His head felt thick after just a couple of glasses of wine and he ruefully remembered why he did not drink much. He splashed a little water on his face but could not look in the bronze mirror. He was scared what he might see in the eyes looking back at him.

The knowledge of yesterday sat in his stomach like the heavy weights the fishermen used on their lines. It only started to lift when he remembered the decision he'd had made the previous night.

The more he thought about it, the more he was sure it was not a dream but a message from Aroaril. It had seemed so vivid and was so clear in his memory. His own death was the only thing that could wipe out the crime of murdering Prince Cavan.

"Hey, Dad, is there anything to eat?"

He forced his dark thoughts away and turned, contorting his face into something close to a smile. "Why don't we go and see?" he suggested.

He doubted there would be anything – there was no more Prince Cavan to give the orders. But they discovered everyone else enjoying fresh bread, cheese, cold meat and fruit.

"It arrived with a note from that chamberlain Regan. As far as the kitchens are concerned, Prince Cavan is still here, so they are sending everything up as usual," Devlin explained.

Kerrin filled his plate high, tossing chunks of meat to Caley, but Fallon just took a hunk of bread and a cup of water. He had to talk to Padraig and explain things to him. He was tempted to tell to his friends his plan but they might try and talk him out of it. That must not happen.

Kerrin reached out and grabbed his arm. "Dad, I have told Caley she has to stay with you now," he said softly. "You need her."

He shook his head but the dog stood by his side, even when Kerrin rushed off to find Padraig. He looked down at her as she stared up at him, her tail swishing from side to side. "You wouldn't look like that if you knew what I had done," he told her.

"Fallon!" Gallagher said sharply.

He looked up from Caley, trying to make his face look normal.

"Regan is here."

Fallon was on his feet before he knew it and hurrying down to the main door into their rooms, Caley at his heels. It was open, Regan standing at the threshold, being watched by Devlin and Brendan. As Fallon had suspected, there was now a locking bar on the outside, although the guards were far away down the corridor.

Fallon clenched his fists at that. They were so sure he was beaten that the chamberlain had walked into the heart of their company without so much as a dagger. Then he opened his hands. That was good. Just let him get near Swane and Aidan and he would show them how wrong they were.

"The King's greetings and you are to make ready for a meeting of the nobles in two turns of the hourglass. Prince Swane will be brought to the usual waiting chamber and you will escort him into the room, then stand behind him during the session. Afterwards, you will escort him back into the waiting chamber and he will be returned to his confinement," Regan said. "He will say nothing to you and you will say nothing to him, nor will you do anything to him. Is that understood?"

Fallon had to take a moment to hold back the surge of anger that filled him. "Understood. And agreed," he said through gritted teeth.

"There will not be many such occasions. But you must fulfill your end of the bargain in order for the King to live up to his," Regan said, this time with a hint of warning in his voice.

"We will do this. But we don't have to enjoy it," Fallon told him.

"Just so," Regan nodded. "Remember. The waiting chamber in two turns of the hourglass. Do not be late."

Fallon did not bother to reply and signaled to Brendan, who swung the door shut. He heard the locking bar being slammed into place and thumped the door angrily in response.

"If things were not bad enough, now we have to stand near that bastard Swane without ripping his head off," Brendan growled. "I suppose we shall have to go and get ready."

Fallon shook his head. "Not yet. Get Padraig and I shall explain."

"What is it?" Gallagher demanded.

"I have a way out of this," he said, then stalked back to Cavan's bedroom.

*

"What is going on?" Padraig asked. "Why the mystery?"

"I need a couple of volunteers, men with no families," Fallon said. "There is only one way out of this. I shall kill Swane and Aidan today." The others began protesting but he plowed over the top of them. "With them dead, you will be able to get out of here and sail to Kotterman to get back our families."

"They'll kill you!" Devlin said.

"That is a price I am willing to pay. I deserve it," Fallon said.

"And what about Kerrin?" Padraig asked coldly.

"You can look after him until Bridgit is back. I am no good with him anyway. He deserves better," Fallon said.

"Have you gone mad?" Padraig demanded. "That lad needs his father, not an old fart like me! Bridgit did not save him for this. And what if we cannot get her back? What of him then? Your duty to the living outweighs your guilt over the dead."

Fallon shook his head. "The answer came to me in a dream last night. I have to kill them to save my soul."

"Don't be a bloody idiot!" Padraig raged.

"What if it goes wrong? You will doom us all," Brendan rumbled.

"They will not stop me," Fallon vowed. "I cannot live with this guilt any more. I have to avenge Cavan and save you all from the nightmare I have cast you into. This gives you all a chance. Soon as that bastard Aidan is dead, break out. Make for the ship. I'll give you the nod when I am about to strike and you need to run in the opposite direction. By the time I am finished, Kelty and his guards will not know what to do."

They all protested then but he let it wash over him.

"I will not let you do it," Padraig declared.

"You cannot stop me. For if I am not there, the King will send his guards in to kill us all anyway. And you know this is the only way out of this pit," Fallon said, locking eyes with the wizard until Padraig blinked.

"What do I tell Kerrin?"

"The truth," Fallon said. "Tell him sorry. And tell Bridgit sorry as well."

Padraig smashed his hand on the table. "I shall do no such thing! My daughter sacrificed herself for that boy and now you are going to abandon him! If you are going to throw away her gift, have the courage to say it to him yourself."

Fallon shook his head obstinately. His head heard the words but his heart knew the truth. He would never be free of the guilt until he sacrificed himself.

"Don't do this, man," Devlin urged. "There has to be another way."

Gallagher and Brendan joined in, pushing him to think again, to come up with something else.

"I will lock you in here until you come to your senses," Brendan said.

"That you cannot do. For if we are late, it will be Kelty and his men breaking down the door," Fallon said.

He could feel their frustration rising as they argued more. But he just said nothing, until it petered out.

"Get ready. We cannot be late," he said. "And get out of it when I give the signal, because I'm going to take plenty of those bastards with me." He reached into his bolt bag and felt for the bloody quarrel. He would put that into Aidan's black heart and then he could face Cavan and look his Prince in the eye.

CHAPTER 6

Bridgit lay on her mattress and closed her eyes and ears to the noise around her. Every passing day made her more sure she was pregnant. She knew her body and attempts by her friends to tell her otherwise just annoyed her. Every day she tried to tell herself this pregnancy would be different but every day it was harder to raise herself.

"Bridge, we need you," Riona said. "It's a mess downstairs."

"Maybe later," she said and rolled over. After a while she could sense that Riona had left. She knew she should get up and help but even the needs of the children could not make her move. She wrapped her arms around her belly and held tight. To lose Kerrin and now to lose another baby ... it was not fair. What had she done to so anger Aroaril?

Footfalls told her Nola was approaching. For a small woman, she knew how to make an entrance. "Bridge, we need to talk about how we are going to escape," her friend said. "Everyone is going to want some answers soon and we have no idea how we are going to get out of here, let alone free a score of slave gangs scattered around this maze of a city."

"I'll think about it. I'll be down soon," Bridgit said, pressing her eyes shut.

"Are you sure you are all right?" Nola asked worriedly.

No, of course I am not all right! There is not one part of this that is right! she screamed inside her head.

"Fine," she said.

She could sense Nola wanted to stay and say more, but shouts from downstairs summoned her away.

Bridgit opened her eyes and stared dully at the mattress, seeing the lumps and bumps of the filling. Where was Fallon? Why hadn't he come for her?

*

"You have to come quickly! Something bad has happened!"

Bridgit came awake in an instant, her heart racing – something must have happened to Kerrin. Then she remembered where she was and lay back down.

"What is it, Ely?" she asked irritably.

The girl's eyes were wide and she was trembling with fear. Bridgit shed both her sheet and her inertia as fear ripped through her for one of the other children. "What is it? Is someone hurt?" she asked worriedly.

"It is Gokmen. He is furious. One of the slaves has done something and he demands to speak to you about punishment," Ely whispered.

Bridgit took a deep breath, fearing her heart would burst, it was hammering so hard. At least it was making her feel more awake than she had been for the last two days.

"Let him do what he wants. I am not the leader here. Who cares what I think?" she said.

Ely shook her head, tears rolling down her face. "You have to come. Or they will kill them, like they did before."

Bridgit shut her eyes, trying to close out the memory of Sean and Seamus. That could not happen again. "Right," she said, forcing her mind into action. "Come on."

She walked downstairs, Ely following nervously behind, to find a bristling Gokmen pacing around the entry hall, a pair of nervous guards hovering nearby.

"Follow me!" he snarled.

Bridgit stopped and crossed her arms. "Where?" she demanded.

Gokmen stormed across to her. "Do not question! Follow!" he roared.

She ignored his rage. "Not until you say where."

He turned away and she saw him clench his hands into fists, before beckoning to Ely and rattling off a long string of Kottermani.

"Through the city to the fields outside the walls," Ely translated.

"Then let me fetch a hat and water and we shall leave," Bridgit said calmly.

Ely's eyes were wide with terror and Bridgit added a little snap to her voice. "Tell him!"

Ely gabbled the message and Gokmen let out a roar of frustration, but Bridgit refused to be hurried. If she obeyed everything he said then she was handing all the power to him. And if someone had done something wrong, she needed every bit of help she could get. The memory of what he had done to Sean and Seamus would never leave her. But every time a thought came to the surface, her other worries dragged it back down into the depths.

Gokmen was nearly apoplectic by the time she was ready and charged off up the street. Bridgit set her own pace, which was much slower and resulted in another torrent of angry Kottermani.

"It is too hot for me to walk fast," she told Ely with a calm she did not feel.

It was of course also a chance to see as much of the city as possible. The place was a rabbit's warren and any chance to understand better how its streets flowed had to be taken.

None of this put Gokmen in a better mood by the time they got outside the city and into the fields, where a pair of Gaelish women were kneeling in the hot sun, surrounded by guards.

From the expressions on many of the guards' faces, Bridgit could guess what they thought the punishment would be, and she felt sick. She pushed that down ruthlessly. The women were not from Baltimore but she recognized them as mothers from Killarney.

"What is going on here?" she demanded. "Get them out of the hot sun! Do you want to kill them? They will be ruined as slaves if you treat them like that!"

But Gokmen had obviously had enough. "They tried to escape!" he roared, pointing at the two women.

"That cannot be so," Bridgit said, keeping her voice soft, and quiet. "They know what is at stake and that their children are at risk. Let me ask them what happened."

The two women turned towards her, hope and fear warring on their faces.

"We weren't running! We just needed a piss but the guards wouldn't let us go. We just wanted to go away from the fields, not on the crops," the younger said urgently.

Bridgit tapped Ely on the arm. "Tell him that," she instructed. "Make it clear that they were doing it to protect the crops and the people who would be eating them."

Ely nodded and spoke to Gokmen, before receiving a blast of Kottermani.

"He doesn't believe them," she said.

"They must be punished. They know the sentence. Five guards each," Gokmen said roughly. "No one will try it again once they see that."

Bridgit would never have taken that from Fallon and she was not about to accept it from another man, even if he was a slave master. Instinct took over. "Now listen here!" Bridgit stormed closer and jabbed him in the chest with her forefinger. "If you had already made your judgment, why call me out here?"

"To explain it to the others," Gokmen growled down at her.

Bridgit crossed her arms again. "You are wrong and you will not punish these women," she snapped.

Gokmen shook his head. "You are not in charge here. They will be punished and, if you argue, then you will share their punishment."

She took a deep breath. Part of her wanted to bow her head and agree, crawl away and go and lie on her mattress. If those men raped her then that would be the end for her baby. They could not harm her unborn child. That thought blazed through her head and the Bridgit who had hidden Kerrin and then gone out to fight took over. *They would not harm her child.* She had no weapon this time but her wits and courage. That would have to be enough.

"Wrong," she countered. "You will release them and escort me back to the children."

Gokmen looked over at Ely and Bridgit reached out without looking and dragged her translator closer. "Tell him that he will punish nobody, or punish us all," she hissed.

Ely looked as though those words might choke her but managed to say something.

Gokmen spoke swiftly to his guards and there was a cheer of laughter afterwards. Then he turned back to Bridgit, ignoring Ely, an unpleasant smile on his face. "You have been too long without a man if you want to share this punishment! So be it, you will join them!"

"Then Prince Kemal will have your heart torn out when he returns," Bridgit said loudly, anger roaring through her.

Gokmen shook his head. "Why would he do that?"

"Because I am pregnant," Bridgit announced, pinching Ely to make her shout the words in Kottermani. "And Prince Kemal is the father!"

Everything went very silent at that and the guards looked closely at her and then at Gokmen.

"That is not possible," the slave master said, but his voice was uncertain.

"Why else did he make me leader of my people? Why else has he shown me favor?" Bridgit snapped.

Gokmen looked over to his guards, at the women and then back to Bridgit, plainly unsure of what to do. "I cannot believe it," he said. "Prince Kemal has a young and beautiful wife."

"Do you want to bet your balls on it? Get it wrong and your last days will be spent screaming," Bridgit told him. Inside her mind she was yelling at herself, saying how crazy this was but on the surface she gave him nothing.

"I shall summon a doctor," Gokmen announced.

"Doctor?" Bridgit asked Ely.

"They can heal your hurts. But they don't usually deal with slaves," Ely whispered.

Bridgit felt her heart jump a little. Maybe the doctor could help the baby! "We shall wait for him in the cool. All of us. And bring water," she ordered.

Gokmen glowered at her then snapped out orders in Kottermani.

"If you are not pregnant then we are as good as dead," Ely muttered, her teeth almost chattering in fear.

Bridgit merely gave her a wink.

It was obviously a nervous wait for Ely but Bridgit was curious to see what this doctor was and if he was anything like a priest or priestess. He turned out to be an elderly man with kind eyes and soft hands, who handed her a clean jug to fill with urine. That was strange enough but then he sniffed it carefully and took a mouthful, rolling it around his mouth with a thoughtful expression before spitting it out and washing out his mouth. Bridgit did not know whether to be fascinated or revolted.

She watched as the doctor and Gokmen spoke quickly.

"He says he has more tests to do that will take two days to be sure but he believes you are pregnant," Ely said softly, relief in her voice.

"Can he tell if it will be a healthy babe?" Bridgit asked urgently.

"I don't know. I don't think so," the girl admitted.

Bridgit felt her heart slump a little at that but rallied as Gokmen approached.

"It seems you are telling the truth," he said roughly. "For now anyway. But I shall speak to Prince Kemal on his return."

"Ask him carefully, if you value your life," Bridgit advised. "For he listens to me."

"So what do I do with them?" Gokmen gestured towards the two frightened women.

"Let them go. They have been punished enough by a morning in the sun. And everyone knows what will happen if they do anything else. But you should tell your guards to let my people have a break for a piss now and again, with all the water they are drinking. And you can send that doctor down to come and see the children, as well."

Gokmen hesitated for a long moment and she had to quell a sudden shudder of fear that he would order her punished anyway. But then he began shouting at his men and she did not need Ely to translate to know the slave master had buckled to her bluff. The two women were freed, pausing just long enough to kiss her hand.

"Thank you! Bless you!" they said.

"The baby is Fallon's," she whispered, embracing them. "I lied to them, but we shall be long gone before they discover it."

They hid quick smiles, bowing their heads, before heading back to the fields.

"Now, escort me back. It is too hot out here," she said, hiding her triumph and wanting to sit down somewhere cool before she vomited in public.

*

Gokmen did not accompany them back, something for which Bridgit was heartily grateful. She was barely able to believe what she had done. Yet the way the guards kept away from her said it had worked. Of course there would be all sorts of trouble when Prince Kemal returned, so she had to be away by then. That was the only thing that would save her unborn child. The icy despair that had gripped her melted away in the heat of that knowledge. She looked around the city as they walked, trying to understand it.

"Ely, tell the guards we must walk back through the markets. The children are getting bored of the food they are given and I need to see what else is available," she said.

Ely looked back at her worriedly. "They will not like that," she said slowly.

"Tell them Prince Kemal's baby will become sick without it. And they will be punished when he returns and I tell him," Bridgit fired back.

Ely gaped at her and she shoved the girl towards the guards. "Quick now!"

The guards had argued briefly among themselves before agreeing, as she knew they would. It was a dangerous game, but now she was playing it, there was no way to stop. So Bridgit and Ely found themselves walking through one of the city's markets, the nervous guards about three paces behind. She doubted the guards could hear them talk and, even if they did, they wouldn't understand what was being said. They would be able to tell if there was an argument under way though, so she decided to keep things light.

"So, where did you learn our language?" she asked Ely.

"That is not important."

Bridgit heard the tone in Ely's voice and cursed herself. She needed to start this far more gently if she was going to win Ely over. She was a slave: of course she was going to be suspicious.

"Well, what do you think the children might like to eat?" She changed direction. "They are bored of lamb, flat bread and dates. You must have potatoes here?"

Ely shook her head. "It is the wrong season for them. They are grown in a different part of the empire, anyway. But maybe they would like to try oranges."

"And what are they? Some kind of animal?"

At this Ely burst out laughing, a surprised giggle that she covered with her hand.

Bridgit was torn between feeling foolish at having said something silly and relieved that she had made Ely laugh.

"No, they are a fruit. They are shaped like a ball and when you tear the skin off, there is sweet, juicy flesh beneath."

"I like the sound of that. Anything else? What was your favorite when you were a child? If you liked it, I am sure the rest of the children will enjoy it."

Bridgit congratulated herself as Ely thawed out gradually, talking about some fluffy grain that soaked up meat juices and gravy.

She was glad she had taken the time to speak to the young woman, for she drew involuntarily nearer to Ely when they entered the market. It took Bridgit back to the first day in Adana, when they had been overwhelmed by the smells and noises of the strange place.

She was thankful she wore the hood, for it allowed her to hide her surprise and her disgust at some of the things she saw.

The meat stalls were the worst. She had seen sheep and pigs and cattle butchered before, of course, but the strange, tall animals with the humped backs, were a revolting sight. Meat was meat but the lines of animal heads, tongues lolling out, flies landing on them, turned her already-fragile stomach.

The fish was a much more welcome sight.

"Can you ask the guards to bring us fresh fish for the children?" she asked Ely.

The young woman pulled a horrified face. "I would not do that," she said. "They will send us only the ones they cannot sell, that have been sitting in the hot sun all day."

Bridgit sighed. "Then the fish will have to wait for some cooler weather. I take it there is cooler weather here?"

"Not much," Ely warned. "In other parts of the Empire it changes but here the sun is always hot."

Bridgit thought about that. "How big is the Empire then?"

Ely chuckled. "I have been told that if you set off on a fast horse, you could ride around it in perhaps ten years. It goes on and on, takes in all different countries and people."

"Have you seen much of it?" Bridgit asked carefully, trying to approach the question she really wanted to ask in a different way.

Ely looked at her but then shook her head. "Hardly any."

Bridgit was tempted to press but decided to take it easy, instead. "What's that?" she asked, pointing to a stall full of strange nuts.

Ely showed her the fruit and the nuts and Bridgit made a point of trying as many as possible, encouraging Ely to do the same. At first the stallholders sneered at them but Ely said something to the guards and they instantly changed their tune, going from angry to fawning in a moment.

"The name of Prince Kemal carries much power here," the young woman explained.

There were many interesting things to try, but although Bridgit liked the strange nuts, she did not want to bring any back for the children in case they choked on them. The oranges were another matter entirely. Sweet and juicy, they made her tongue tingle.

"It was almost worth coming here just to taste them," she told Ely with a smile. "The children will love these!"

Some quick-fire Kottermani later and they found themselves returning to the house with sacks of oranges, and the promise of more to come.

Nola and Riona were horrified at the punishment Bridgit had averted, relieved that she had stopped it, happy that the decisive Bridgit was back and shocked at the way the children fell upon the oranges like a flock of seagulls onto fish scraps. Then the doctor arrived, carrying a bag full of strange powders and seemingly wanting to give one or more to every child.

All three were kept busy cleaning off sticky faces and fingers so the children were in a fit state to see the doctor, and Bridgit saw another way to work on Ely. "Ely! Can you clean up those three over there?" she called, pointing to where three girls sat, a pile of orange peel around them, licking their fingers and laughing.

For a moment she thought the young woman would refuse but then the girls held out their hands to her and she went across to them.

"Watch these ones," Bridgit hissed to Nola. "I'll go and talk to her again."

She hurried across to where Ely was trying to wash off the sticky juice with a little water. "Do you need a hand?" she asked gently.

"I think we have the last of it," Ely said, letting the girls race off.

"You are good with them. Do you have younger brothers or sisters?" Bridgit asked.

For a long moment she did not think Ely was going to answer. "I have a younger sister," she said in a whisper.

"You must miss her."

Ely nodded, a tear trickling down her cheek.

"I bet you wish your parents were free."

Ely nodded again, the tears falling faster now. "They are both dead now," she said hollowly.

"I am so sorry." Bridgit did not even think about what she did next. She just reached out and hugged the girl, bringing her into an embrace.

Ely stiffened and for a moment Bridgit thought she had made a terrible mistake, then the young woman dissolved into tears and sobbed into her chest. Luckily Bridgit had plenty of experience in looking after crying children. "There, there, you are safe now and among friends," she said softly, patting the girl's back.

But, inside, she was rejoicing. Surely she had found the key to escape here.

CHAPTER 7

Fallon carried his shillelagh, as normal, but also had both his sword and a pair of knives. Brendan had stripped the leather and wooden hilts off a handful of small daggers, making something that was pure metal and so immune to a Fearpriest's powers. They were unbalanced and Fallon doubted they would be easy to throw, but he needed as many weapons as he could find. Inside he was cold. His decision was made and he yearned for his chance to avenge Cavan.

His three friends followed a few paces behind. Nobody else had been willing to come with him but his friends had insisted. Yet he could not rob them of their chance to find their families or Gallagher of the chance of happiness with Rosaleen.

He was filled with a mixture of hatred and anger as he pushed open the waiting-room door with his left hand, right hand on one of the stripped-down knives.

"Right on time," Regan told him evenly. "I am pleased to see that."

Fallon did not bother to reply, he just stared across the room to where Swane stood with his back to them. He was dressed well, in what looked like the style of clothes Cavan would wear. His hair was cut like Cavan and, despite knowing that Cavan was gone, for a moment, Fallon felt his heart jump, for he looked so much like the dead Prince.

He took a step towards Swane before Captain Kelty and a dozen guards formed a barrier. If Aidan had been there too Fallon might still have run at them but he wanted them both.

"The nobles did not send for Prince Cavan to mediate for them in their meeting before they see the King," Fallon said, watching the way Swane was standing there, all relaxed, no shackles on him, as if he were mocking them.

"They did, but the Prince sent his apologies. I believe the Duchess Dina was forced to serve in that capacity," Regan said evenly, betraying no hint of surprise at the news the nobles had been meeting in secret. "Time to go in."

Fallon wanted to wait but decided it was better to look like he was beaten and then strike later. He forced his feet to take him closer to Swane as Regan opened the door into the meeting hall.

"My Lords and Lady! Prince Cavan!" he announced loudly.

Fallon could hear chairs scraping back as the nobles rose to their feet, then he led the way in, Devlin, Gallagher and Brendan falling in behind Swane. Fallon's back itched to have Swane behind him but nothing happened as he took up position where Swane would sit, marking where he would like to put his dagger. Time dragged before Regan opened the door again.

"His Majesty King Aidan the Second!" Regan shouted and the nobles applauded.

Fallon watched Swane clap along with the rest of them, appearing to be slightly bored by it all, and clenched his teeth and his fists.

"That's it. Just look like you usually do, as if there's a foul stench under your nose," Kelty whispered to him as he took up his position to Fallon's right, behind the King. Fallon was tempted to make his move then but Kelty was watching him like a hawk. *Patience*, he told himself. *Your time will come.*

"Let the meeting begin!" Aidan called, thumping the table.

Fallon let it all wash over him. He could only stand it because he knew what would come at the end.

Then he glanced down the table and caught the eye of the Duchess Dina. Alone of the others, she was not staring at the King, her expression rapt. Instead she was looking at Swane and up to Fallon. He saw her raise an eyebrow at him, then he broke eye contact, worried he might give something away.

She said nothing, however. At least, nothing about who was sitting in Prince Cavan's seat. When she did join in the conversation, it was to flatter the King and make him laugh and, usually, get him to agree with what she wanted.

She wasn't the only one doing it, but she was better at it than most.

On and on it went, until finally Aidan thumped the table. "I have one final announcement," he said loudly. "You know that my wife sadly died from a strange illness nearly fifteen summers ago. Since then I have remained unmarried."

The nobles all made sounds of sympathy but Fallon only remembered Cavan's story – how Aidan had beaten and raped his wife until she killed herself.

"I have been alone, without companionship since then," Aidan went on.

Again, the nobles murmured their support, while Fallon bit his lip as the image of the King raping the Count of Londegal's mistress filled his mind.

"But that is about to change. I can tell you, my dearest friends, I am to marry the Earl of Meinster's eldest daughter two moons from now, and hope to present you all with a new Prince or two by next summer!"

The table cheered wildly, nobles patting the back and shaking the hand of the beaming Earl of Meinster.

"Let that be the end! All business is to be held over until our next meeting!" the King announced over the general excitement.

"His Majesty King Aidan!" Regan shouted and the cheering nobles sprang to their feet, still clapping as Aidan walked out, Kelty leading the way with half the guards to push back the excited nobles.

Fallon glanced across and Regan nodded to him, so he signaled to his friends and led Swane out of the room. He felt his heart pound and he prepared to strike. First cut down two guards and then kill the King, before turning on Swane. It would be quick and bloody and confused, which was how his friends would escape. The King had paused to speak with the Count of Londegal, so the time was perfect.

He prepared to draw his dagger when a hand grabbed his arm. He turned, his free hand rising to strike down the fool who was about to stop him – to see Duchess Dina there.

"Don't do it," she said, her voice barely above a whisper and reaching his ears only. "Think of your son. Swane and Aidan are not worth it."

Fallon was about to tear his arm free when he realized what she had said.

"You know—" he began, his eyes darting behind, to where Swane had stopped, four paces back.

"That is not Cavan. They have killed him and are using you. But don't sacrifice yourself. There is a better way for revenge."

Fallon paused in shock. "How did you—?" he gasped.

"It was written all over your face. But look behind me and see that it was doomed," she said.

He glanced over her shoulder and spotted three of Kelty's guards had appeared on the other side of the table, all holding loaded crossbows.

"They can't stop me," he spat, pulling his arm free.

"Listen to me. I can show you how to kill them and still hold your wife afterwards," she said urgently. "I will come and tell you. Just don't do anything foolish."

Fallon hesitated, uncertainty clouding his mind for the first time.

"Think of your boy. He needs you," she said, then stepped back.

He looked at her, and back towards the King – to discover Aidan had disappeared into the waiting room once more. He rushed forwards, Swane and the others following, but a quick look inside the waiting room revealed that Aidan had vanished: only Kelty and guards remained.

"You did well, but we can take it from here," Kelty said, reaching out a hand towards Prince Swane.

Fallon felt sick with anger and disappointment and relief. "All yours," he said. He refused to look at Swane, although he could feel the man's eyes boring into him as he stormed out the other door. He did not know whether to be furious or grateful to the Duchess. There would be another chance but what of her words? Was there another way of killing them?

"What happened?" Brendan was the first to ask, once they were safely away.

"The Duchess knew it was Swane, not Cavan. She knew what I was going to do and stopped me," Fallon said shortly.

"Well thank Aroaril for that. What did she say?" Devlin asked.

"That there was a way to kill them both and still have Bridgit back."

"What is it?" Gallagher asked.

"She didn't say," Fallon grunted.

They walked in silence for a while.

"How could those bogging fools not know that was Swane sitting there, looking as if butter wouldn't melt in his mouth?" Devlin asked.

"They see only what they want to see, hear only what they are told," Gallagher said.

"And where is the Fearpriest?" Devlin asked.

"Aroaril willing, he's still rotting inside a cell with my fistguard in his gob and our iron wire cutting off his hands and feet," Brendan said.

"There's a thought to warm your cockles a little," Gallagher said.

"Nothing can make me feel better," Fallon said hollowly.

That quieted the others but Fallon did not care. He was torn between being relieved to still be alive and bitter that Aidan and Swane were not dead.

"Maybe the Duchess is going to tell us now what she meant," Gallagher said.

Fallon looked up to see her outside Cavan's rooms, Gannon standing like a rock at her left shoulder, a pair of other Lunster guards just behind. They were locked in a stand-off with Kelty's men Regan had placed there.

"Fallon, we need to talk urgently about what is happening in Lunster," she said.

"No visitors today," the guard officer announced. Fallon recognized him as the one who had panicked when Cavan had wanted to go into the village of Killarney. Quinn was his name. His eyes darted across to Fallon, carrying a warning with them.

"We have nothing to talk about, Duchess," Fallon said roughly, knowing this would get back to Regan. Besides, maybe she was secretly on the King's side and had stopped him to save Aidan's life.

He went to step past her, only for Dina to reach out a hand.

"I need your advice urgently on a problem in Lunster," she said loudly, then added in an undertone, "Then let me tell you how to get rid of that bastard Aidan and the foul Swane!"

Fallon looked into her eyes and saw what was blazing there, a mixture of indignation, anger and fear.

"I cannot help you. Please take your worries to the King," he said, nodding towards Quinn.

She rounded on the guards officer, her eyes flashing. "I am a Duchess of the realm. I need the advice of Captain Fallon for a quarter-turn of the hourglass. Do you dare forbid me? Must I go and tell the King that?"

Fallon almost smiled as he saw Quinn fold spinelessly. "Be quick then, Duchess," the guard said.

Dina smiled at him dazzlingly. "Thank you. And do not fear: it shall remain our secret. I shall not say a word."

Fallon opened the door and led the way inside, wondering what this would bring. The Duchess was all poised and polite until the door swung shut, then she grabbed his arm.

"Fallon, I am not your enemy," she said. "Fetch your priestess, get her to tell you that. I can see how desperate you are. Let me help save you. Fallon, Prince Cavan is dead, so you have no other friends and no other chance of getting your families back. You need me."

He did not want to trust her. What if this was a trap of Regan's? Yet the chance of perhaps finding a way out was irresistible. Without looking away from her, he pointed at Devlin. "Get Rosaleen and Padraig," he said.

*

Cavan's room was crowded. Dina's guards were outside, all but Gannon, who was standing behind the Duchess's chair.

"I know you must be suspicious and not want to trust anyone. But I am your friend, the only friend you have left in this court," she said evenly.

"Forgive me if I no longer trust the words that come out of a noble's mouth," Fallon said harshly and then gestured to Rosaleen. "Tell us, sister, can we trust her?"

Rosaleen reached out a little hesitantly.

"Don't worry, my dear. I want to prove myself," Dina said brightly.

Rosaleen took her hand and closed her eyes. "Tell us why you want to help," she said.

"Because Prince Cavan was the hope of Gaelland. When I saw Swane sitting there in his place, I knew he was dead. If I do nothing, I shall see myself banished back to Lunster. I want to stop whatever it is King Aidan is plotting. He has lied to me and I cannot forgive him, nor trust him."

"Well?" Fallon demanded of Rosaleen.

"She speaks the truth," Rosaleen said.

"I want to see Aidan and his foul son Swane dead and you get your families back. Maybe he has promised you your families but he breaks his promises, for he broke them to me."

"Again, I can feel no lies," Rosaleen echoed.

"Don't sacrifice yourself. Gaelland needs men like you and you cannot leave your little boy all alone."

Fallon glanced over to his friends, and to Padraig.

"You know she speaks the truth there," Padraig said.

"Confide in me and I will not breathe a word of this to the King, nor to Regan nor to anyone who would tell them," she promised.

"Truth," Rosaleen said. "She wants to help you, and will help you."

Fallon still hesitated. He distrusted her. She was a noble and only wanted what was best for herself. That's if she did not have some darker purpose. But Rosaleen had found only truth, not lies in her words. Maybe this was the chance they had been looking for. He wanted to wash away his guilt in Aidan's blood but then he thought of finding Kerrin hiding behind their house and how Bridgit had left him there and gone out to fight the Kottermanis to save their son.

"All right then," he said. He took her through what they had found beneath the castle, the link of Eamon to the Moneylenders, the King's obsession with the visit of the Kottermani Prince and then what had happened at the Guildhouse, the capture of Swane and his Fearpriest and the King's reaction.

Dina sat quietly through it all, occasionally expressing her shock or horror, while Gannon could barely contain himself, soft mutters and curses flowing out of him almost constantly.

Fallon had to grit his teeth before he could finish the tale and felt anew the burning at the back of his throat as he explained how he had been tricked into killing Cavan, forced to keep everything quiet until the Kottermani visit was over.

"Aroaril, what a horrible tale," Dina said softly, reaching out her hand and grabbing Fallon's forearm. "You must be suffering deeply. No wonder you wanted to sacrifice yourself."

Fallon bit his lip, unable to say anything in reply.

"It was not your fault," she said strongly. "You were tricked and betrayed by the King."

Fallon shook his head and she reached out, grasping his shoulder. "Stop blaming yourself," she said.

He looked at her and saw nothing but sympathy in her eyes. For a moment it almost felt like Bridgit was there.

"You have to let it go. You thought you had won and then Aidan fooled you. But what he did was madness – how could you expect it? I can see why you want him dead but true revenge is living happily ever after, having hacked off his lunatic head."

Fallon smiled, a little.

"Fallon, I want to help you," she said. "You know I can give you the nobles. You despise them, and rightly so, but there is great power there. Even the King is afraid of upsetting them too much, for if they ever banded together, they could remove him and replace him with another. And that other could be me. I was married to his cousin, after all, and am close to the throne by marriage. And if I took the throne as a regent, then my first act would be to restore your families."

Fallon stared at her, the others also reacting as well. "You want to take the crown?" he croaked.

"Fallon," she said firmly. "What else can we do? If Aidan was not bad enough, we face a future where the Zorva-worshippers have power. And, if by some miracle Swane does not take the throne, it will be a son Aidan has fathered on Meinster's girl Brona. It's revolting – the girl is younger than Prince Cavan was. And Meinster is nearly as bad as Aidan. He flogs his people and delights in punishing those who defy him. Aroaril knows what children they will produce together."

Fallon looked down at the table. Rosaleen said Dina spoke the truth. And she could not be as bad as Aidan. "How do we make that happen?" he asked.

"Get me the evidence that Cavan wanted. You need something tying the King to the Fearpriests, the snatchers, the witches and the selkies and to the Kottermanis. I present it to the nobles and they will act. Already they are afraid and angry about this marriage. They do not need much to tip them over the edge."

"Really? They looked delighted about it when the King spoke," Devlin interrupted.

Dina shook her head. "Have you learned nothing in your time here? To show your true feelings at a time like that would be a fatal mistake. But they are scared and furious. Nobody likes Meinster and he has just made himself the second most powerful man in the land. To those of us who have crossed him, defied him and thwarted his ambitions, it is a terrifying time. He never forgets and he never forgives. Oh, I can assure you that there are many nobles in Berry right now who are meeting and whispering nervously together."

Fallon glanced at Rosaleen, who gave the smallest nod of her head, saying she could detect no lies there.

"We have to be careful. We are being watched by Regan," he warned.

"And you are right to worry. He has a network of informants through the city, reporting back to him," she admitted. "But he cannot keep you in here all the time. You will get a chance. If you find anything, send word to me and I will find a way to meet. Apart, we can do nothing to stop Aidan. Together, we stand a chance."

Fallon glanced at Rosaleen and she nodded. "The truth," she said.

Fallon signaled and Devlin escorted Dina and Gannon out.

"Do you think—" Brendan began but Fallon waved him down. "Wait for Devlin," was all he said.

His mind was racing. He could see the possibilities in her words and part of him wanted to leap at the chance. But what of his dream? Was just killing the King enough or would he still be haunted if he did not sacrifice himself? Surely he needed to be punished as well ...

"Well, that sounded better than you throwing your life away and maybe ours with it," Devlin said as he walked back into the room.

Fallon looked around the table. "Is that what you all think?"

"It galls me to say it but maybe this is the best way," Padraig said. "The real question though, is can you accept that or are you still set on killing yourself?"

Fallon rubbed his eyes. What had seemed so certain that morning was now all mixed up. Could he have a life after killing Cavan?

"I need to sleep on it," he said, although it was only shortly after noon.

*

Kerrin wanted to go down to the crossbow range again. Anything was better than staying in these rooms. It had been bad enough when Dad talked to everyone and said the Prince was dead, but then it had got really scary when he started crying. Dad had never cried before, and he didn't know what to do. Then he had been strange again that morning, while Padraig had wanted to sit with him and hug him. That was even scarier. Grandpa had begun to talk about the two of them living together and maybe going to look for Mam. He had wanted to ask about Dad but had been afraid of the answer. Then Dad and the others had come back, Dad looking angry and his friends looking happy, which was even more confusing.

When Dad walked into their room and lay down on his bed, saying nothing, he watched for a little while and then could take no more.

"Dad, what is going on?" he asked cautiously.

"Nothing."

That was a lie, so he joined him on his bed. "Are you going away? Are you going to leave me?" he demanded, still afraid but having to know.

His dad stiffened, then sighed. "Maybe."

"Why? Was it something I did? I know I wasn't any good with the sword," Kerrin said miserably.

Dad turned over then. "It was nothing you did. It was something I did. I might have to go but grandpa Padraig will watch over you—"

"I don't want him! I want you!" Kerrin howled.

His dad sat up, startled, but Kerrin did not care any more. The memory of lying in that pit, knowing Mam was going, was never far away. He could not lose Dad as well. "Don't leave me!"

Dad reached out a hand and patted him but it did nothing. "I don't want to but I have to. I did a very bad thing—"

"Leaving me is a bad thing! How could you? You promised we would find mam together and you lied to me!"

Next moment he was hitting Dad, trying to punch out his anger, fear and frustration. He must have caught him by surprise, because it was some moments before he enfolded him in a hug, so he could not hit.

"I am sorry," Dad said. "You wouldn't understand but I did an evil thing, so I must be punished."

"Leaving me is worse," Kerrin said defiantly. "You always said you can make up for mistakes."

"I did. But this is the way I have to make up for what I did."

"And how will you make it up to me? You said you would never leave me – that we would rescue Mam. Breaking that promise is worse than anything you have done."

*

Fallon groaned, his son's words striking deep inside. In his mind's eye he saw a bloodied Cavan, looking sadly at him but, standing on the opposite side, a bloodied Bridgit holding a limp Kerrin. And her eyes were even more accusing.

"It's not so simple as making up for what I did by saying sorry," he said.

Kerrin got one arm free and began hitting him again. "Yes it is! You just don't want me around."

"Now that is not true," Fallon said angrily.

"Prove it. You swore an oath to me and you said a man is only as good as his word. Let's get Mam back together."

Fallon felt something tear inside him. The anger and self-loathing dissolved into fear and doubt.

He crushed his son to his chest. "Help me," he begged. "I feel like I am lost."

A sob convulsed the boy, who clung on as ferociously as Fallon held him. "Then let's find our way home together," Kerrin said, his voice a little muffled.

Fallon relaxed his grip and looked down at his tear-stained son. "I am not a good father," he said. "I am not even a good man any more. You deserve someone better."

"But I only want you."

Fallon felt his own tears trickling down then.

"Without you, we shall never get Mam back," Kerrin continued.

Fallon still wanted to atone for killing Cavan. But maybe he could have both. He closed his eyes. No visions came. This must be what Rosaleen was always talking about. You had to make your own choices.

"All right. Let's get Mam back," he said.

But he did not feel any better for saying it.

Then Devlin burst through the door. "Regan is here," the farmer said urgently.

Fallon felt his heart beat faster but did not want to alarm Kerrin. Was this the final message? Had they realized he wanted to kill the King? "I'll be right there," he said, forcing himself to sound casual.

Kerrin was reluctant to let go and he had to promise to come back before he could hurry out to where the chamberlain was waiting impatiently. Regan reached into his belt pouch and Fallon tensed but the man only produced a scroll from his belt pouch.

"The King wants to speak to you. In a turn of the hourglass. Here are the details. Do not be late," Regan said simply.

"Wait! What about?" Fallon asked as the chamberlain turned away.

"I do not know. Make sure you are on time."

Fallon watched the man stride away and broke the seal on the scroll to see it just repeated the words Regan had spoken.

"What was that about?" Devlin asked, as his friends joined him.

"The King wants to see me. To talk about something." Fallon showed them his scroll.

"Do you think this is it?" Brendan asked.

"No," Fallon said, although he was thinking the same thing. "If they wanted us dead, they would just storm in here."

"Well, you will know more in a turn of the hourglass," Gallagher predicted.

Fallon shuddered at the thought of seeing Aidan again, of sitting opposite him; he was flooded with the awful temptation to kill the bastard. Despite his promise to his son he did not honestly know if he could stop himself attacking the King.

"Don't do anything stupid. It will only be Aidan there. Swane is somewhere else. Kill Aidan and Swane will hunt us all down," Gallagher warned.

Fallon's mind cleared. It was both or neither. "Aye. I will just talk. But I'll find a way to go back into Aidan's rooms when he is in the throne room, surrounded by people."

"Why do you want to get yourself killed?" Brendan asked.

"If I am not going to kill him straight away then I'll get something for the Duchess to use. Let's see if the nobles can be trusted. If not, I always have a knife."

*

Kerrin sat on the bed with Caley, looking at the dog seriously.

"I think it is going to come down to you and me, Caley," he told her.

The dog tilted her head and chuffed a little in her throat.

"I couldn't save Mam and now Dad keeps going off. If we are to get her back, I think we will have to do it."

He didn't like the idea and he could tell Caley wasn't happy about it either. But it was taking too long to get his mother, and now Dad had said he might have to leave it to Grandpa Padraig. Well, that was not a plan. He had to be ready.

"We'll do the push-ups first and then try throwing knives," he told Caley. "When the time comes, we might have to save Dad before we can save Mam."

CHAPTER 8

Fallon sat brooding outside the King's rooms, having handed his weapons to the guards at the door. A pair of the King's guards had escorted him there and now all he held was the scroll. But how could he speak to Aidan and pretend nothing had happened? A vision of Bridgit came to him, of how he had disguised his anger when they had fought, because the more she thought he was angry, the longer it took to make up.

"The King is ready for you," a guards officer told him.

He stood, composing his face as he did so, then recognized the man. "Quinn. You are a busy fellow."

"That's right," Quinn said, his face betraying a sudden fear Fallon was going to say something about the Duchess.

Fallon said nothing more, just opened the door and stepped into the King's rooms. He forced the memories away of the last time they had been in there, thinking they had won and all that remained was for Swane to be executed for his crimes.

He did not know what to expect, because no one ever did with King Aidan. But, as he shut the door behind him, it was to see the King sitting back in a comfortable armchair, a second, somewhat less comfortable chair drawn up opposite. A pair of burly guards stood behind the empty chair, their purpose obvious.

"Take a seat, Fallon; let us talk," Aidan invited.

He felt a huge surge of fury just looking at the King but managed to force a smile onto his face and keep his voice even as he bowed.

"Thank you, sire," he said, sitting down and making his fists unclench, sensing the two guards relax as he did so.

"Fallon, you led an inspired defense when you were trapped at the Guildhouse. Surrounded, outnumbered, you used your head and your men to win," Aidan said, talking as if he were speaking about one of his favored hurling games, rather than a grim battle that had seen the cobbles awash with blood and guts.

Fallon merely nodded, not trusting himself to talk about that day.

"So I want to know, if the Kottermanis came here and attacked us, how would you defeat them?"

Fallon had to fight particularly hard to keep the surprise from his face. "Do you think the Kottermanis will attack us, sire?" he asked.

"Who knows?" Aidan waved a hand. "But I want to know what you would do if they did."

Fallon took a deep breath. There was a dangerous game going on. King Aidan might be unpredictable and evil but there was always some purpose behind his actions.

"We cannot match their ships, nor should we fight them in open country, for they have far more men than us," he said carefully. "They know they have far more soldiers than we could ever hope to put in the field and no doubt they are battle-hardened."

"Yes. The Empire is in a constant state of revolt. Every man they would send here would be a veteran. We would have a mixture of guards and the fyrd. One man of theirs would be worth two of ours, and they would have four or five times our number," said Aidan.

"We have to make them attack us here," Fallon said, his voice strengthening as he thought about it.

"Here? But if they take Berry then they have the whole country," Aidan said, his voice questioning, not accusing.

"It is the only city big enough for our purpose. We draw them into the streets and the alleys. That's where numbers count for nothing. The city is a maze but we know it all. We can use the roofs, we can use the back alleys and we can cut them to pieces, hurt them so badly that they never come again."

"Would it not be better to trust in our walls and try to hold them out?"

"They would destroy the countryside around us while they wait. And if they are always fighting then they would have ways to batter their way through stone walls. No, better to use their arrogance against them. They will march in here like conquerors, never expecting us to attack. Then we crush them."

"Attack them after inviting them in?" Aidan asked.

"You do not get prizes for fighting fair. We do anything we can to win."

Aidan clapped his hands together and laughed. "Excellent! The best answer I have been given by far. Most of the others all said we should use cavalry to destroy them on a flat field somewhere, for they could not bring horses across the sea. Yet they can bring enough bows to destroy any cavalry charge. Tell me, Fallon, would you think about being my war captain, if it came to it?"

Fallon forced down both his astonishment and his revulsion at the thought of serving this man. "You honor me, sire. But is there not someone better suited for the role?"

Aidan waved his hand in disgust. "Kelty? He is a perfect captain of guards but he is not a general. Who else is there? One of my nobles? Can you see the Earl of Lagway leading the men into battle? The Kottermanis would die laughing."

"I would be proud to serve you, sire," Fallon lied. He found it was getting easier to do, the more practice he had at it.

Aidan looked away then and seemed to be musing to himself. "It is worth looking at. A man who could make all the difference."

"Sire?" Fallon asked gently.

"That is all, Fallon. Thank you." Aidan was no longer looking at him.

Fallon stood and bowed, then used the opportunity to have a quick look around the King's room. There were many shelves there filled with scrolls. He would need plenty of time to search them all.

The guards outside, even the lieutenant Quinn, did not pay him any attention on his way out, instead watching the pair of fat

Guildsmen who were going to see the King next. Fallon picked up his shillelagh and left, thinking about the best time to come back and have a proper look around.

*

His return was met with heartfelt relief from all the villagers. They had barricaded themselves into individual rooms, ready to sell their lives dearly, only to emerge when Fallon returned. But none of them could understand why the King had wanted to talk to him.

"And that's all he wanted? To talk about the Kottermanis and offer you a job as his war captain?" Devlin asked in disbelief.

"Aye. I could barely believe it either. He only seems to be concerned with the Kottermanis at the moment. He doesn't seem to care about the witches and selkies any more. I know he always has something in mind but I don't know what it is. Maybe I can find out if I get into his rooms when he is passing judgment on some poor unfortunates."

"That's if he doesn't want us to watch over Swane while that is going on," Gallagher reminded him.

Everyone had relaxed and started to think about the evening meal, and some had even begun to complain about being stuck in these rooms all day, when Regan returned.

"Hide the weapons," Fallon ordered, as men jumped up in fear, "but be ready to use them."

But Regan merely had another scroll to deliver. "The King wants you to hand this to Duchess Dina at her townhouse," he announced.

"Are all his messengers sick or something?" Fallon asked suspiciously.

"The King asked for you particularly. You may take three companions and you need to leave now." He handed the scroll over. "Fail and the King will look on it as a breaking of your promise."

With that, the chamberlain turned and strode away.

"Could they have made this any more obvious as a trap?" Gallagher asked.

"But why go to all this effort?" Fallon growled. "Why not come in here with swords drawn?"

"Well, if it is a trap, we shall give them a surprise," Brendan said with relish.

"I should have killed the bastard when I had the chance." Fallon cursed and thumped the wall.

"There's many reasons to go back in time but no way to do it, so give it up, man," Gallagher said sourly.

"You can't go," Padraig said firmly.

Fallon patted Gallagher on the shoulder in apology. "Gall is right. We have no choice," he told the old wizard. "You heard Regan. We have to take the chance there is something else happening. Otherwise we are all dead. Look, use a bird to watch us and if something happens, you've got warning."

Padraig sighed.

Fallon embraced his father-in-law. "Just get Kerrin out. That's all I ask," he whispered. "I promised him I would not leave him and I will do all I can to return. But we are the King's pawns now and we must play his game."

Padraig winked. "That I can do. But make sure you get back. Bridgit would kill me if anything happened to you."

Fallon turned to his friends. "I am sorry, lads. You don't have to come. I can ask for volunteers—"

"We are your constables," Devlin said. "You're not going anywhere without us."

"Besides, a trap doesn't always work," Brendan said flatly. "All we have to do is break it."

*

But nothing happened as they walked through the streets. All four of them were carrying every weapon they could think of and the crowds were parting before them but they walked to the Duchess's house without anything happening.

"I wish they would hurry up and spring the trap on us. I am getting hungry and hate fighting on an empty stomach," Brendan grumbled.

"You might get your wish," Gallagher said. "Don't look now but we're being followed."

Instantly Brendan turned around.

"Could you make it any more obvious? If Devlin had turned, they might have missed him in the crowd but no, the biggest of us has to do it," Gallagher sighed.

"Six of them, it looks like. All wearing brown cloaks," Brendan reported. "Shall we take them now?"

"It's the ones I can't see that I worry about," Fallon said. "The Duchess's house is just there. Let's get inside and see if we can spot how many there really are."

The mysterious men made no move to attack them as they hammered on the door, which was opened. They were ushered inside to where the Duchess was less than pleased to see them.

"The King sent you here?" she gasped. "For Aroaril's sake, this has to be a trap!"

"We're being followed," Fallon agreed.

But, although they peered carefully out of the windows, all they could see was the same six figures.

"There's nothing for it. We'll have to go out there and attack them," Fallon said.

"Can we at least eat first?" Brendan asked.

But the Duchess had other ideas. "There is another choice," she said. "There is a back door. Those men will think you will be here for turns of the hourglass. Meanwhile you can be away and back at the castle while they still watch the front of my house."

Fallon was not sure about this but she was insistent ... and attacking men in the street seemed like a recipe for disaster.

"If you go now, they will never expect it," she said. "I shall make sure I am seen at the windows, pretending to talk to you."

She embraced Fallon quickly, which made him stiffen in shock, then she drew back. "Live," she said. "Do it for your wife and son."

The back door was opened and the alleyway behind scanned quickly. There was no sign of any watchers, so the four of them hurried onwards.

"Well, I feel much happier about this trap now," Gallagher said as they walked down a crooked alley, back towards the main road. "At least the Duchess seems on our side."

Fallon grunted. The houses were bigger and much nicer here than in the rats' nest of houses in the poorer quarters. Still, the smell was just as bad.

"At least there is no sign of those cloaked men," Fallon said.

"That's if we can find our way out of here," Devlin said as the alley took yet another turn. "Who designed this stupid city?"

"Fallon was right about it though. This is the place to fight the Kottermanis. We can use the roofs and places like this to destroy them," Gallagher said. "Imagine it, looking up, barely able to see the sun and not knowing if there was going to be a hail of spears or crossbow bolts from above at any moment."

Fallon looked up, as Gallagher suggested, then swore loudly.

"Get your backs to the walls. There's more up there!"

The four of them flattened themselves against the rough alley wall, eyes scanning above. But the roofline was empty.

"What did you see?" Devlin asked.

"Three hooded men," Fallon replied shortly. "Just for a moment, then they ducked away."

"The one from out the front? How could they have got here?"

"They didn't. These look completely different," Fallon said.

"Do you think this is the real trap?" Brendan wondered. "Did the Duchess push us into it?"

"Let's worry about that later," Fallon said.

He unstrapped his crossbow from his back and swiftly loaded it. Devlin and Gallagher did the same. Brendan just hefted his huge hammer but that was more than enough of a weapon in his hands.

They hurried down the alley, which led into a maze of others. No longer worrying about finding the way back to the main road, Fallon just led them left and right, looking to put some distance between them and whoever was above. He was horribly aware they were completely exposed but could not think who was after them. King Aidan had them at his mercy in the castle – if he wanted them dead then he would just send in his guards. The Duchess? But why not attack while they were inside her house? Obviously Swane wanted them dead but he was in a cell somewhere. And, anyway, they had killed his men. Or had they?

"Are they still up there?" Devlin asked as they stopped by a corner, all puffing hard.

"Can't see." Fallon craned his neck to check the rooftops. "But there's so many places to hide up there."

"Do we wait or do we go?" Brendan asked.

"I think these three might be the snatchers, the ones Cavan said he chased across the rooftops. The ones Eamon was protecting, the ones we weren't able to find," Fallon said.

Devlin stopped looking up and swung around. "The ones Cavan said had skin like wood that swords just bounced off?"

"But we don't look like children! Well, maybe Devlin if you put him next to Brendan," Gallagher said.

Fallon instinctively paused for Devlin to make some joke in return but nothing came.

"Let's keep moving," Devlin said instead.

They jogged down a series of alleys.

"Who builds these? There's not a straight line among them!" Gallagher protested.

Fallon caught a glimpse of the main road down a side alley. "There!" he cried and skidded to a halt.

The four of them raced down towards the bustle and light of the main road, strides lengthening as they sensed a way out of the dark maze.

But three figures emerged out of a doorway and formed a line across the laneway, long knives in their hands.

Fallon stopped immediately, his friends a step behind him. Unlike the cloaked ones who had obviously followed them to the Duchess's house, these were dressed all in black, with some kind of tight-fitting black hood over their face. They did not seem particularly large, but their silence and the long, curved knives they held in each hand were menace enough.

"Do we try to talk to them?" Devlin whispered.

"Bugger that," Fallon said, and raised his crossbow and sent a bolt thumping into the chest of the middle one, the sheer force of it knocking the figure back, spinning it around and sending it to its knees.

Fallon grinned mirthlessly at the remaining two as Gallagher and Devlin brought up their crossbows.

But his grin faded as the one he had knocked down bounced back to his feet and rejoined the others. He reached down and plucked the crossbow bolt out of his chest, tossing it away.

"Not this shite again," Gallagher breathed. "More of these boggers that just won't die."

"What do we do?" Brendan asked.

"Run!" Fallon cried.

They turned and tore back down the alleyway, even Brendan putting on a respectable turn of speed.

"Back to the Duchess's house!" Fallon called.

"Which way is that?" Gallagher cried as they turned down yet another identical-looking alleyway. "I can't get my bearings!"

Fallon glanced up but the sky was thick with cloud – no chance of seeing the afternoon sun. He looked over his shoulder to see the snatchers were chasing them. And not just chasing but gaining on them. The creatures they had destroyed in the Guildhouse had been slow-moving and shambling. These were the opposite.

"Hurry!" he cried.

The four of them sped up. They rounded a corner, bouncing off the opposite wall and using it to push themselves onwards, boots skidding on the rough and slippery cobbles. By contrast, the snatchers seemed to float across the ground.

Brendan was leading the way, arms swinging in all directions and his heavy hammer going with them. They had to stay a pace behind to avoid it. But while the other three could have gone faster, the big smith was built for power, not speed. Within a hundred yards, it was obvious they could not outrun the snatchers. Brendan was gasping for breath.

"Get out of it. I'll hold them off," Brendan gasped, slowing to a walk. "By the time they get past me, you'll be clear. Just look after Nola and—"

"Don't be a bloody idiot," Fallon said. "We don't leave you for anything."

He hauled back on his crossbow string, reloading swiftly as the three snatchers slowed down, advancing carefully, ominously, not showing any signs of exertion, knives held out before them.

"How can we kill them? They just keep coming!" Gallagher hissed.

"We'll hit them again. I'll take the center one, Dev take left, Gall the one on the right," Fallon ordered, snapping a quarrel into his bow.

"Loose!"

The three bolts streaked away. The snatchers were barely ten yards away and impossible to miss. All three bolts struck and all three went down – then bounced right back again.

"What now?" Devlin asked.

Fallon tossed his crossbow aside and produced one of Brendan's throwing knives from his belt. The big smith had stripped the leather and wooden hilts away, leaving something unbalanced but pure metal.

"Let's see if these things work," he said.

He took a step forward and hurled the knife, which spun once, thudded onto the chest of the central figure and bounced away.

"And now?" Devlin asked, his voice betraying his fear.

Fallon pulled out his shillelagh. "We fight," he said grimly.

He watched the snatchers advance slowly and could not stop thinking about Bridgit and Kerrin. It could not end like this. They had been ready for any normal attack but not this. He hoped Padraig was watching but could not spare the time to look up for a bird overhead.

The lead snatcher jumped high, covering the five yards between them in one effortless leap. Thoughts of his family vanished as Fallon reacted instinctively. He punched out his shillelagh, left and right, blows so fast they were hard to follow. Yet the snatcher swayed aside easily and swiveled, kicking out to sweep Fallon's legs away.

He flipped over and hit the ground with a thud and a groan and tried to roll away from the blow he knew must be coming.

But the snatcher never had the chance to deliver it. Gallagher waded in, a gutting knife in each hand, the pair of them even longer than the blades the snatcher held. He slashed right and left, high and low, forcing the snatcher to step backwards.

But the snatcher never looked in any danger, and his companions didn't move to support him – they stood motionless, just watching.

Gallagher's blows cut only air as the snatcher ducked and blocked with his own knives, deflecting Gallagher's away with ease. Then he sliced back, his hands moving blisteringly fast, and Gallagher had to throw himself backwards to avoid being cut open. His arms went wide and the snatcher pivoted on one foot to kick him in the chest and knock him flying. Gallagher hit the wall and dropped his knives before falling to the ground.

"Bastard!" Devlin had a sword and dagger and he thrust with the sword, only for the snatcher to melt away, knock his sword hand wide and stab back at his throat. Devlin threw up his dagger desperately and knocked the death blow aside, so it merely nicked his shoulder rather than burying itself in his neck. But if the snatcher was disappointed he did not show it. He just stepped inside Devlin's next thrust and rammed his elbow into his jaw, spinning the farmer around and down.

"Looks like it's just us," Brendan said, hefting his hammer.

He swung the huge weapon in a wide blow, forcing the snatcher to jump backwards. But then the snatcher darted forwards, trying to get within the swing of the hammer before Brendan could strike again. The big smith swayed back from a gutting blow of a knife and tried to bring his hammer around, but it was too big and slow and the snatcher was too fast. He raised his other knife and paused for a moment, as if enjoying the moment contemplating how to kill Brendan.

Then Fallon swept out his shillelagh at ankle level, not even trying to get to his feet, slamming it into the back of the snatcher's heels.

The snatcher stumbled but managed to regain his feet and spun, cat-quick, knives reaching out for Fallon. But he had turned his back to Brendan, who needed no second invitation. His hammer swept around in a massive blow that smashed the snatcher from his feet and flung him into the wall, his head flopping at a strange angle, his shoulder grotesquely smashed from the impact.

Fallon rolled to his feet and checked the other two snatchers, but they were still motionless, and reacted not at all to the collapse of their leader. Gallagher and Devlin got up too, picking up their weapons. Warily, the four of them approached the fallen snatcher.

Fallon jabbed him with the end of his shillelagh but there was no movement. He used the staff to flip the snatcher over, revealing a head flattened in and wobbling on a broken neck. There was no movement and the snatcher was leaking blood and brains through a huge tear in the black hood that had covered his face.

"Is it dead?" Gallagher asked.

"Don't know. But let's make sure. Hit him again," Fallon told Brendan.

The big smith took a step forwards and swung his hammer once more, flattening the snatcher's head and spraying the wall behind with blood, brains and teeth.

The body twitched but did nothing more.

Fallon faced the other two snatchers, still unmoving.

"So they're not like those other creatures. They can be killed without fire," he said triumphantly. "Let's get these boggers."

He thought the snatchers might run but instead they moved forwards, knives at the ready.

"Knock them over and we'll finish them off," Fallon told Devlin and Gallagher. "Use the crossbows."

As his friends frantically tried to reload their weapons, Fallon held his shillelagh at the ready, trying to keep the snatchers at bay. They had to be afraid of Brendan's hammer, he reasoned.

But these two showed no emotion at all, let alone fear, and were just as fast as the other one and twice as dangerous, because there was no playing with them. Fallon gave ground before them, using his staff to punch out at their heads, trying to stay away from their knives and feet.

They slashed and cut and sparks flew from the end of his shillelagh when they struck its iron tip and Fallon was horribly reminded of the time he had taken on Eamon and been humiliated. He did not have Hagen to save him this time, either.

But he did have Gallagher and Devlin. They reloaded and both loosed at the snatcher on Fallon's right. Struck by two bolts, the snatcher went down like a sack of potatoes. Instantly Fallon thrust his staff at the other's face, checking his advance for a moment.

It was all Brendan needed. He stepped out from behind Fallon and swung his hammer in a brutal arc at the fallen one. The snatcher was trying to get back to his feet but the hammer landed with a sickening crack on his back and sent him writhing to the cobbles. Brendan swung the hammer again and pounded the stricken snatcher's head flat, the iron head of the hammer ringing against the cobbles.

"Now there's just one," Fallon said, advancing on the final snatcher.

The figure backed away a little, crouching, and Fallon wondered if he would run for it – and how they could hope to catch him if he did.

Instead the snatcher jumped high in the air, foot lashing out towards Fallon's head. Fallon reacted instinctively, shillelagh whipping out to crack into the snatcher's knee as he slipped away.

The snatcher landed lightly, but then his knee buckled under him and he went down. Fallon slammed the end of his staff into the back of the snatcher's skull, bouncing it off the cobbles, then Brendan swung for a final time, almost ripping the head off with the force of the strike.

The four of them looked at each other and the three bodies, panting with the exertion and the reaction to the chase through the alleys.

"What the bogging hells were they?" Brendan asked, speaking for them all.

"Was it a trap or a test? It's almost as if we were being matched against them," Gallagher said.

"Well, if this is some game of Aidan's, let's change the rules," Fallon said. "Let's see how they were able to shake off a crossbow bolt."

He kneeled down by the first one and used one of Gallagher's knives to slit open the strange black tunic the snatcher wore. He swore softly.

"What is it?" Devlin asked.

Fallon tore the fabric open so all could see. "He has some sort of armor here but that surely can't be all, for there are rents in it." He probed the metal links with his borrowed knife. It felt different from chain mail, much finer, lighter and better forged, but no chain could stop a crossbow bolt at that distance. He ripped more fabric and then hauled up the vest of mail to reveal the snatcher's skin.

"It looks like wood or something," he said aloud, poking at it with the knife. Sure enough, it resisted the knife tip. It felt like he was poking at a piece of firewood. "What could do this to a man?" he wondered aloud.

"Nothing good, I'll warrant," Gallagher said.

"But why this elaborate scheme to have them ambush us? What game is Aidan playing? Does he merely intend to torment us until putting us out of our misery? And is Dina in on it?" Fallon growled.

"At least he let us out of the rooms for a while to get some fresh air," Brendan said with a shaky laugh.

Fallon snapped his fingers. "Aye. We are out. So let's use that. My gut tells me the snatchers have a hideaway around here. We check if there are any empty homes and go knocking."

"What if there're more of them inside?" Devlin asked. "And what of the men who followed us from the castle?"

"We'll use Brendan's hammer to do the knocking," Fallon said grimly. "And they learn there is something scarier than the snatchers out there. Us."

CHAPTER 9

Bridgit looked out across the city of Adana and unconsciously rubbed her hand across her stomach. Each day was getting slowly easier to deal with. Every time despair attacked her, she fought back by thinking about escape and returning to Kerrin and Fallon. A never-ending parade of children wanting attention helped as well. The nights were harder, but she had a plan to help there.

She had spent two days examining what Ely did and said, while taking every opportunity to speak with her, to see if she could catch the young woman out. But it all seemed as though Ely was the answer to their problems.

"Ely, tell us about the other Gaelish around," she said.

"There are more of us. I don't know how many but this is not the first time I have been used to translate for Kottermani with Gaelish slaves," Ely said steadily.

"Where are they now?" Bridgit asked, liking the way Ely called the Gaelish "us". "These other Gaelish?"

"A few would be in Adana, the rest scattered around the Empire. Most are not like you," Ely said.

"Few are, my dear," Nola said with a bark of laughter.

"No, I mean you are families and have children. The ones I have come across before, they are usually single men or women. The men tell me they were taken from fishing boats, the women were usually sold."

"Sold? Who would sell a woman?" Riona asked indignantly.

"The brothel who owned her," Ely replied.

Bridgit sighed. It sounded like the slaving had been going on for years – many years, if Ely was anything to go by.

"Did you ever meet a nobleman? He would have called himself the Duke of Lunster," she asked urgently. "He would have demanded to speak to a high-ranking Kottermani."

"I have never heard of anyone like that," Ely said with a shake of her head. "But perhaps he is elsewhere."

"He was the one who started all this. I think if we could but find him, we could get some answers," Bridgit said, with a touch of frustration.

"Let's worry about getting out of here first," Riona suggested.

"So what will happen when my people are put up for sale as slaves? Will they stay around here, so they can still see their children?" Bridgit wondered.

Ely shook her head. "That will not happen. They will be sent all over the Empire and will never see these children again. And once the children reach sixteen summers, they will also be sold and sent away."

Bridgit looked at her friends. "Then we have our time. We must get out of here before our people are scattered to the four winds."

"Bridge!" Nola exclaimed, pointing at Ely with her head.

Bridgit smiled. "She is coming with us. And will help us."

"Do what?" Ely asked.

"Escape, of course," Bridgit said easily.

She kept her eyes on Ely and saw the young woman's eyes widen, her face betray her surprise, before her usual mask fell back in place.

"How?" Ely demanded.

Bridgit smiled. "Now that is a good question. We have to get out of here, just after evening prayers. Now I think I know how to do that. But that just puts us into a city filled with people who hate us. We have to get onto a ship. How do we get the rest of our people out first?"

She saw Ely glance around. "How will you get the children through the streets? And have you thought what might happen if they catch you? Children will die."

Bridgit sighed. "I know the risks. But I cannot let everyone be sent away for a life as a slave, away from their children. And I certainly cannot raise these children to be slaves. It is worth risking anything to avoid that."

"But I thought your husbands and the rest of your village was coming for you?" Ely asked.

"I know they are trying. They will not give up. But we are running out of time. We cannot wait for them," Bridgit said, her hand stealing down to touch her stomach. "And if we can get back to Gaelland, we are safe. You will love it there. No more slaves. No more fear. You can live free." Even as she said those words she knew they were not really true. They were tied to their liege lord just as ruthlessly as slaves here were bound to their masters. And they had to work as hard to pay their taxes and feed their families. She pushed those thoughts aside, because they would not help here. And at least no Gaelish lord, not even Meinster, killed men as cruelly as Sean and Seamus had died.

"My mother told me many stories of Gaelland. But I have never been there. Would the people accept me? I don't look the same as you," Ely said nervously.

Bridgit reached out and held her hand. "We would accept you. That is all that matters."

Ely gave her a smile and Bridgit squeezed her hand one more time.

"You have been through the city. You know the way. Can you guide us? Can you help us think of a way to get the rest of our people out?"

"But how are we even going to get out of here ourselves?" Ely persisted.

Bridgit did not even have to glance at her friends to know they were staring at her and questioning what she was doing. But she had to know one way or the other about Ely. Tell her everything and then watch her like a hawk.

"We need to go out to the market again. We saw an apothecary stall where they were making up powders to help the sick. We shall tell them that some of the children are not sleeping and need a sleeping powder. Then we shall mix that up in the juice of some of those oranges to disguise the taste, and give it to the guards."

"It will not be strong enough. The powders for a child will not be enough to make a man sleep," Ely objected.

"True. But we shall give it to them in the afternoon, to give it time to work. They will be sleepy and slow, at the very least. So, we are outside: what then?"

"All your friends will be chained up and locked away," Ely said. "You will never get them out."

"We need files," Bridgit said calmly. "Nola here, her husband is a smith, and he uses files to smooth down metal. Where can we get one?"

Now Ely looked really alarmed. "What is a file? Is it a weapon?"

"No." Nola spoke for the first time, her voice scornful. "It is long and thin metal rod, with a rough surface. It might take them half the night but they can use that to break the chains."

"We could never get such a thing." Ely shook her head. "There is no reason for us to have them and no way for your friends to hide them all."

Bridgit gave Nola a smile. "It was a good idea," she told her friend.

"Well, we shall need something. Unless there's somebody else like Brendan who can bend metal," Nola said grimly.

Bridgit waved her hand at her friend. "Next time they are here, we shall ask them how they are tied up. I am sure we can work out something," she said.

The three of them turned to face Ely.

"Are you with us? Will you help us get home, and free yourself?"

Bridgit kept her eyes on Ely's face as she spoke and was relieved to see the young woman meet her gaze evenly.

"Anything is better than life here. I will help you," she said.

Bridgit winked at her friends. "Good. Because tomorrow night I am getting out of here," she said. It would be the perfect test for Ely. If the girl went near the guards, it would be the last thing she tried.

*

"Are you sure you want to do this?" Nola asked.

Bridgit glared at her. "Of course I don't want to do this! But I have to."

"It is so risky," Ely fretted.

Bridgit grabbed her by the shoulders and looked her in the eyes. "Stay strong and I shall be back. Panic and you will betray me," she said sharply. "All you need to do is keep calm, understand?"

Ely nodded unhappily and Bridgit pulled the hood up over her head, adjusting the scarf across her face so that only her eyes were showing. She had seen some women dress like that on her visits to the markets. Ely had explained these were usually women of quality who wanted to protect their faces from the harsh sun. The lower born, of course, had no reason to worry about their faces. That suited Bridgit's purpose, for women of quality were rarely bothered on the streets. She knew it was a fearful risk, and she was putting a brave face on while her stomach churned and gurgled with nerves. She had visited the privy twice already in the last turn of the hourglass and felt like going again – except this had to be done at the perfect time.

When the call to prayer went out, the two guards on the front door would turn to the east and begin to pray to Aroaril. That was their chance. She had watched them from the window several times and reckoned it was a clear count of one hundred before they returned to their watch.

"Ready?" she asked the others.

"We are," Nola confirmed.

They had spent the day before fashioning a long rope, using robes and sheets tied together. A group of fishermen's children had tied them together. Bridgit had been a little nervous to trust not just her own but also her unborn child's life to them, but they had grown up tying knots and repairing lines and nets for their fathers. If they failed, they went hungry, which was the best way to learn. Riona had tried each one, unable to loosen them despite her farm-bred strength.

"Still, lucky for you that you've lost some weight with this Kottermani food," Nola said with a half-smile.

Bridgit stepped up onto the chair they had placed by the window, slipping her foot into the loop made at the end of the makeshift rope. Nola, who had powerful shoulders and arms from helping out at Brendan's forge, adjusted the three robes she was wearing to pad her shoulders and then placed the rope over her right shoulder and braced herself against the window frame. This trailed back across the room and into the corridor beyond, where Riona, Ely and a dozen of the biggest and oldest boys and girls took up the slack, ready to slow her descent.

Bridgit looked down into the street, glancing both ways to see nobody around. That was to be expected, given all those around were expecting to hear the call to prayer and getting ready to obey it. But there was always the chance of something going wrong. At the front of the house, not ten yards away from where she was about to descend, the two guards were chatting together. Bridgit wiped sweaty hands on the front of her rope and adjusted her grip on the makeshift rope.

The trumpet call to prayer made her start and she watched with a mixture of fear and determination as the two guards immediately turned away from her, kneeling down and placing their foreheads on the ground, hands out flat before them, chanting the prayers. All around came the same noise and Bridgit signaled to the others, not making a noise. Ely slipped a mattress over the edge of the window so that their rope would not rub against the wood, then stepped back to take her place pulling.

Bridgit swung her legs out into space and slithered down the mattress, looking up to see the strain on Nola's face as the weight came across her shoulders. They had practiced this at the rear of the house the night before and it had gone well. But then there was only a tiny risk of discovery.

Bridgit tugged on the rope, then clutched tight as it began to descend, the long chain of teenagers and women walking towards the window, lowering her as they did so. She slithered down silently, hanging on for dear life and offering up a silent prayer to Aroaril that everyone else would continue with their own loud prayers. She was also counting in her head, so she had an idea when the prayers would finish and the guards resume their duty.

She glanced down and saw the ground rushing up at her and had to stifle a cry of concern. But her pace slowed right down and she touched down lightly. The use of colored robes had helped here, for they had worked out when a red robe was getting towards Nula's shoulder that Bridgit would be almost on the ground. She reached down with her left foot and stepped onto the cobbles, then slipped her right from the loop and tugged the rope twice.

Almost before she had finished the second tug, the rope vanished upwards, being whisked away at a fearsome pace. Without watching, Bridgit turned and strode swiftly down the street. The prayers were still going on and she was still counting, having reached fifty already. She had to balance silence with speed, and drove her legs hard, feeling her calves burn as the count went on and she strove to reach a corner.

She reached it as she hit a count of ninety, and turned to her right. She knew that way lay an alleyway they had used to return from the market and that it had usually been quiet at such times – but who knew what it would be like now?

She let out a gasp of relief when it proved empty and leaned against the wall, her heart pounding, while the prayers finished. She could hear the city slowly resuming its business around her but she stayed in the alleyway for a further count of two hundred, letting her heart calm down, before emerging and walking back slowly the way she had come.

The guards did not give her a second look as she strolled past, forcing herself to go slowly and not look up at the house, although she knew her friends would be watching for her.

After prayers, the city life was winding down, with people hurrying home and shops closing up for the night. The scarf and hood she was wearing not only marked her as someone who should be given room to walk – they also allowed her to look around without seeming to. This part of the city was worryingly busy now, although she hoped it would be much quieter when they attempted a similar trip in the dead of the night.

Still, seeing plenty of other women and children out on the street was reassuring. Obviously none had scores of children around them but they made it feel safer.

But this road came to an end and she turned left, heading towards the area where the field slaves were kept. Almost immediately the tone of the street began to change. There were fewer women and more men and unconsciously she lengthened her stride, aware that she was getting more people looking at her. Beneath the long robe she wore she held a sharpened piece of wood flat alongside her forearm. It was a chair leg the children had spent the best part of the day rubbing along stones to create a sharpened end. It was enough to make her wince if she jabbed her finger onto it but it was hardly a fearsome weapon.

On and on she walked, sometimes taking the wrong turn and having to make her way back, but it all looked possible. Late at night, when nobody was around, she was confident she could get the children through these streets safely. There were numerous little alleys where they could hide in darkness while others went past, and nobody had taken much notice of her.

It seemed as though Adana had been built piece by piece, bits added on all the time, rather than designed. Streets didn't seem to meet up and rarely traveled in a straight line. She turned and headed down towards the docks, where the rest of her people were being held. At first the streets were quiet and peaceful but the closer she came to the water, the rougher things seemed. There were certainly no more women of quality around. It felt like the village drinking hall at the end of a long day, when decent people were thinking of calling for Fallon to come and keep the peace.

Men were staggering out of whatever passed for drinking halls in Adana and leering at her. She couldn't understand what they were saying – and she was glad of that. Abandoning ideas of finding the last few places that held her people, she cut down an alley, hoping to get out of this area and find her way back to the house. Getting back in was going to be even harder than getting out, although requiring a little less timing. She decided she had had enough excitement for one night.

The alleyway was dim but a sudden spill of light showed what looked like a sailor, who staggered out of a doorway and then began to piss against the opposite wall. Bridgit let her chairleg-dagger slip down into her hand and stepped around him, walking even faster.

He must have felt her passing rather than seen it, but she heard the trickle dry up and then he called out something to her. Having no idea what he might be asking she decided it would be far safer to keep walking, and actually broke into something closer to a trot, hoping he would go back to whatever he was drinking.

But she heard footsteps behind her, getting louder, as well as another challenge, this one louder and angrier. The end of the alleyway looked too far away and she did not want to be attacked from behind, so she stopped and spun around. Her heart was thumping and her breath was rasping painfully in her throat, but the makeshift dagger was steady in her hand, hidden behind her back. She was under no illusions as to what was at stake. If she were discovered to be Gaelish, then rape would be the least of her problems.

The sailor slowed as he approached, a drunken grin on his face, and he kept talking. She could not understand a word but from his tone guessed he was bragging about what a great catch he was and why she should immediately go with him for a shag somewhere.

But when she said nothing his voice changed, becoming a little harder. He reached out a hand to grab her hood but she did not wait to find out what he would do next. She took a half-step closer, her left hand reaching out to grab his shoulder, her right whipping up with the full force of not just her arm and shoulder but all her fear and disgust. The sharpened chair dagger rammed up underneath the man's chin, ripping through the soft skin, into his mouth and up further, before striking and splintering on something hard inside his head. She tried to rip it back out but it was stuck and he was staggering back, trying to speak, but only a spray of hot blood was coming out.

She hesitated for a moment, seeing him futilely trying to pull the weapon out of his face, while he made strange grunting noises, his mouth pinned shut, his tongue pierced by her blow. Then he collapsed and she turned and ran for it.

She felt the hood flip back off her face and the scarf fall down as she raced away but she was more concerned about creating some distance before the man's friends found him. As she ran she wiped her bloody hand on the inside of her dark robe – not so much to hide what she had done but more because the hot, sticky blood made her skin crawl.

Bridgit emerged from the alleyway and slowed down instantly, flipping up her hood and adjusting her scarf. She did not recognize this part of town and she did not stop to get her bearings, instead walking swiftly and changing direction rapidly, to throw off any pursuit. Her heart had almost returned to normal when she finally walked back into the street that held the house that had become their prison. She could not have retraced her route if her life depended on it but she still counted it as a success. Now she just had to get back in safely.

There were two new guards in the doorway, sitting down and leaning back, one of them smoking a pipe, the other carving something with wood. She was pleased to see them so bored. No doubt guarding a house full of women and children was not a popular task for Adana's soldiers. That was how she wanted it. Carefully, because she did not want to attract their attention, she flicked a pebble up at the window she had escaped from only a couple of turns of the hourglass earlier. It vanished into the open window and she immediately hoped she had not hit one of the waiting children. A few moments later a pale hand waved out of the window and she continued up the street, as slow as she could go, keeping half an eye on what was happening at the door.

Almost immediately, there was a knock on the door from the inside and the two guards sprang up, pocketing the dice and unlocking the door to see what was happening. Instantly Bridgit changed direction and cut across the street, standing beneath the window as voices began to argue from behind the door.

Their makeshift rope dropped down at her feet and she slipped her foot into the loop, took a careful hold of it and tugged twice. She zoomed up the side of the building; and as she came level with the window, she looked into Nola's sweating face and grabbed the edge of the sill, to help herself tumble over the edge and onto the mattress.

"Stop pulling!" she hissed, as the older children continued to haul away, swinging her leg around.

From below, the sound of Riona and Ely talking to the guards was coming to a close.

"We did it!" Bridgit grinned up at Nola.

Her friend let the rope drop and reached down to pull her up, only to recoil when she saw the blood on her right hand.

"What happened?" she whispered.

"I'll tell you later. Not in front of the children. But know that we can do this," Bridgit said. "Now I need to wash. In fact it feels like I need to have a bath for a moon."

CHAPTER 10

Fallon did not want to leave the bodies in the alleyway, where Aidan could pretend none of this had happened. The easiest way to move them was in a cart, and he and Brendan found one swiftly. Its owner was less than happy at giving it up but found the sight of Brendan's hammer even more persuasive than Fallon's arguments.

The cart was small enough to get down the alleyway and they hurled the dead snatchers on to it before covering them with a canvas sheet. They looked strangely small and not at all threatening now. The six men who had followed them from the castle seemed to have disappeared, which made Fallon's neck itch. It reminded him of the time when he had joined a hunt with the Duke of Leinster. Beaters had been used to drive the game towards the hunters, where they could be killed. But now the hunters were dead, what would the beaters do? Go home or join the hunt?

"I reckon their hideout is around this corner," Gallagher said, leading the way to a boarded-up house in a quiet street. Fallon trusted the fisherman's memory, for he and Devlin had scoured the city for the snatchers on Cavan's orders. Judging by the nailed boards across the broken front door, they had been in there once already.

"When we go in, stay together. Nobody goes off by themselves for a look," he ordered, then loaded his crossbow. "If there's any more in there, get them down and Brendan'll do the rest."

"I hope there is," Brendan said wolfishly.

Fallon gave him a quick look but the big smith seemed serious. Fallon sighed again. How would everything go back to normal when Brendan wanted to smash in heads and Devlin would not make a joke? He shook that thought away. "Come on," he said, then saw they were attracting quite a crowd, although the sight of Brendan's bloody hammer kept the people at a safe distance.

"Stay back! We don't know what is in there!" he shouted.

It did little to deter them and he nodded to Brendan. Better to get in fast. Waiting just gave more people the chance to see what was going on.

Brendan's hammer shattered the door and Fallon led the way in, crossbow searching for anyone hiding in the shadows.

The house was dark and silent and Fallon quietly ordered Devlin and Gallagher to start knocking away the covers from the windows. Daylight poured in through grubby panes, revealing a large room with a small fireplace and a twisting set of stairs heading up into more darkness. There was nobody in sight and no furniture, nothing to indicate anyone had ever been here.

"Maybe it's still empty," Gallagher said.

"We'll look anyway," Fallon said. "Do you remember what is upstairs?"

"Do you know how many houses we broke into?" Gallagher said with a shrug. "More rooms, I suppose."

"Spread out," Fallon ordered. "And for Aroaril's sake watch the stairs!"

He eased closer to the fireplace, risked a look in there, but it appeared empty. Then he held up his hand and waved to Gallagher.

"What is it?" his friend asked, ghosting across the wooden floor.

Fallon stepped around the fireplace. He could hear faint voices, people crying, and he was reminded of the time when they had almost caught Swane and his Fearpriest, when the sound of crying children had lured him deep into the Prince's foul pit.

"Can't you hear that?" he whispered.

The others all froze also, everyone straining to pick up what grated on Fallon's ears.

"It's coming from around here." Fallon slapped his palm on the thick brick chimney.

"Is it next door?" Gallagher asked. "I can hear something but it's faint."

"Brendan, hit that wall," Fallon ordered.

The big smith shrugged, then swung his hammer at the rough plaster, except when it struck, it sounded like wood. Fallon waved the smith back and shoved on it. A chunk of a door fell away, revealing stairs leading downwards.

"That was not here when we came in last time," Gallagher said. "We never went down in any of those houses. None of them had a cellar."

"None that we could find, anyway," Devlin said.

The sounds of calling and crying people was getting louder now.

"Come on up! You are free!" Fallon bellowed down the stairs.

He waved and everyone moved back to the other side of the room, pointing their crossbows at the dark entrance to the cellar.

"What if it's more of them down there?" Devlin whispered.

Fallon did not think it sounded like child snatchers and was trying to work up the courage to go in there when the sound of feet on steps made him drop to one knee, bow aimed at the door.

"Don't loose! We have children!" a hoarse voice said, as a pair of dirty hands appeared from the doorway, followed by a thin man dressed in rags, blinking at even the dim light fighting its way in through the windows.

"Come on out," Fallon instructed.

The man shuffled into the room, his hands on his head.

"We have to hurry, the snatchers could be back at any moment," the man said urgently. "We need to get out of here before they do."

"How many are there?" Fallon asked.

"Three of them. They never say a word but they will kill a man as quickly as look at him," the man said, his eyes streaming tears. Fallon did not know if that was because of the light or because of what he had gone through. "We have to get out of here!"

"We killed all three. They are dead. We smashed their skulls in," Fallon said.

The man fell to his knees. "Praise Aroaril!" he cried. "We prayed for this moment but I thought Aroaril had turned His face from us."

"How many are you?" Fallon asked, lowering his crossbow.

"Many," the man said. "Come out now, it is safe!" he called, and other faces appeared at the cellar doorway. Small faces of women and children.

"Who are you?" Fallon challenged.

"I am Conor. My daughter was taken by the snatchers and we came to see Prince Cavan, who promised to get her back. But that night the snatchers came for us. They forced us to follow them or they would kill our children. This is the second house we have been in. They moved us at night and kept us in that cellar all the time, giving us bread and water once a day. Is it really true they are dead or am I dreaming?"

"Come with me and you can see their bodies," Fallon invited.

Conor wiped his eyes, tears pouring down his face. "Thank you! I shall never forget this," he vowed.

Behind him, other men, women and children were coming out of the cellar and filling the room. Fallon quickly counted nearly two dozen.

"Are you all prisoners of the snatchers?" he asked.

"We all lost children to them and were taken by them later," a woman replied, rubbing her streaming eyes with a dirty sleeve.

Fallon signaled Gallagher over. "We'll take them back to the castle," he said. "Let's see what the King says about this. He wanted to test us? Let's test him. But we'll have to put some of them in the cart. Make sure the bodies of the snatchers are pushed right up to one end."

Gallagher nodded and hurried out.

"We're going to get you some food, some clothes and the chance to clean up. And then you will probably need to tell your story to the King this time," Fallon said loudly. "But you are safe now. Nothing more will happen to you. The snatchers are dead."

"Have you found our missing children?" Conor asked eagerly.

Fallon turned back to the man. "I thought they were with you. I thought the snatchers had you all," he said.

"Not our children who went missing first of all. They were not with us," Conor said. "My daughter Becca. Have you seen her?"

Fallon remembered the sound of weeping children in Swane's lair and shuddered. He had to somehow look for them. "No. But we will find her, I promise you," he vowed.

He tried to urge them out and towards the front door but the first woman grabbed his hand and kissed it.

"Thank you! Aroaril bless you!" she sobbed.

Fallon smiled awkwardly at her, at the others who were all nodding and smiling through the tears. "I shall search the house for any sign of your children," he announced.

So while Gallagher and Devlin helped the women and children out, Fallon and Brendan checked the rest of the house out, finding nothing interesting, although the smith knocked holes in every wall.

He would have liked to spend more time checking but a look out a window told him the crowd outside was becoming bigger by the moment and he wanted to get off the streets before something else happened.

The smaller children and some of the women were loaded into the cart, the bodies of the snatchers pushed hard up against the headboard.

"We need to get Padraig and Rosaleen to look at these," he told Gallagher. "I don't know if it was wizard magic or blood magic but something had been done to those men."

The fisherman grimaced. "When I was moving the bodies, I saw they had had their tongues cut out," he said.

Fallon did not like the sound of that. It said, whoever these snatchers were, they took orders rather than gave them.

"Conor," he asked the man at the front. "Did you hear anyone speaking to them? Did they give you any idea of what they wanted with you?"

Conor shook his head. "We heard nothing. They did not like noise and we were scared to do more than whisper for fear they would kill our children. When they wanted us to do something, they grabbed a child and held a knife by their throat, then used hand signals to tell us what to do." His face twisted as he remembered and fresh tears appeared in his eyes.

Fallon patted him on the back. "You are safe now, away from them. And we shall do all we can to find your missing children," he promised.

Conor hugged his wife, looking incapable of talking any more.

Around them the crowd was getting restless, some demanding to know what was going on, others cheering as each family was brought out.

"What are we going to do with them?" Brendan asked.

Fallon looked around the crowd, guessing their numbers at over a thousand.

"Let's use them against the King," he said. "Give me a hand up."

The smith helped him stand on the side of the cart so he could see the crowd and also be seen by them. He waved his hands until they quieted down, wishing he had Padraig there to help him.

"We have found the lair of the child snatchers, the ones who have been taking children and blaming it on witches," he shouted, his voice booming off the houses and echoing down the street. "They are dead and you are safe!"

The crowd roared its approval in waves, those at the front passing the message on to those at the back, and he had to wait for them to quiet down.

"We have freed the families they had taken!"

Again they cheered him.

"Now we go to show them to our beloved King. Come along and hear how our great city of Berry is now safe!"

They bellowed their joy and, when Fallon jumped down, they fell in behind the cart and followed.

*

The crowd grew as they walked through the city, until there were thousands flowing in from the surrounding streets and filling the square in front of the castle. It seemed as if half of Berry was there and the guards on the gate looked terrified when Fallon ordered the cart stopped in front of them.

"What is going on?" their officer cried.

Fallon smiled to himself when he saw it was Quinn again. Kelty might have been a more difficult proposition. "We have killed the child snatchers and freed the families they had taken," he announced loudly. "The people need to see us present this to the King."

Quinn's eyes bulged at the thought. "Send them away! Or bring that cart in and let us shut the gates. The King will lose his mind if he sees this crowd gathered here!" he cried.

Fallon jumped down and stepped close to Quinn, seeing several familiar faces behind him, guards he had led into Killarney. But he did not reveal that. "The crowd has grown too big. We cannot send them away. But I have told them the King wants to tell them they are safe and the danger is over. They are happy and excited, ready to cheer King Aidan. Go and tell the King what is happening. If he is angered, then it will be my fault. But if you send them away, they will grow angry. And it will be your head on the block then," he said kindly, as if explaining something obvious to a young child.

"But I am ordered never to leave my post!" Quinn whimpered.

"I shall stand it for you. Do you not trust me?"

Quinn gulped and Fallon stepped aside, showing him the size of the crowd, which was growing every moment as more people rushed down to see what was happening.

"Go and get the King before it gets ugly," he advised. "You can tell him I ordered you to so do, using Prince Cavan's seal as my authority."

Quinn still looked reluctant, so Fallon grabbed his shoulder and turned him around. "Quick man! Before it gets out of control! Go now, while you still have a head on your shoulders!"

That was the final straw for Quinn and he raced away.

Fallon watched him go for a few moments and turned to the squad of men barring the gates.

"Bran, good to see you." He nodded to the black-bearded guardsman he had tricked and knocked down, then winked at Casey, the nervous young guardsman he had kept by his side at Killarney. "How have you been, lads?"

"Well, sir." Bran nodded with a smile. "Are there any places in the Prince's guard for the likes of us? We'd rather serve with you."

"I'll have to ask the Prince," Fallon said with a smile covering the pain those words gave him. "But I would be proud to have you lads under my command again." That part, at least, was not a lie. And if he could get at least some of Kelty's men over to his side, it could only help.

"Just say the word, sir, and we'll be with you," Bran declared, most of the other guards nodding their approval.

"Good work, lads. Now we'd better keep quiet. For the King will be here any moment and he doesn't allow talking on duty," Fallon said with a wink.

"Sarge, did you really catch the snatchers?" Casey asked.

"It's Captain now," Fallon said. "And yes, we caught them and killed them."

"How did—?"

"Better wait for the King," Fallon told him gently.

He expected it to be quite a wait but the King appeared, followed by a handful of nobles, Finbar, Kynan, an angry-looking Captain Kelty and a swarm of guards, including a worried-looking Quinn.

Fallon glanced across to Gallagher, who nodded. If the King planned yet more treachery then the crossbows were hidden in the cart and they could at least take the bastard with them.

He could feel his heart beating faster as the King strode nearer – but found himself relaxing when he saw the huge smile on his face.

"Captain Fallon!" King Aidan exclaimed loudly. "You have done what many said was impossible, caught these servants of the witches!"

Fallon had to stop himself taking a pace backwards, as the King showed no sign of stopping. More than that, Aidan walked up and embraced him. Fallon stiffened in revulsion as the King's arms went around him, then tensed, wondering if he was about to feel a knife going in, but the King merely patted him on the back and then released him.

"Show me these bodies, and the families you rescued," he said enthusiastically.

Bemused, Fallon took him over to the cart, where the children jumped down and awkwardly bowed alongside their parents. Aidan ignored them for the moment, instead wanting to see the bodies of the snatchers.

"Brilliant. You used staff and hammer to kill them, when no sharp weapons would work," he said approvingly. "I was right. You are the man for these times."

Fallon was not sure what he meant by that and was horribly reminded of the last time the King had wanted something from him.

But Aidan said no more, instead turning to the families and greeting them, shaking hands and patting shoulders.

"Thank you, sire," Conor said in a rasping voice.

"Don't thank me. You are safe now thanks to Captain Fallon," he told them.

Once he had gone down the line, he turned back to those who had followed him out of the throne room. "Finbar, I need to be heard by the crowd," he called out to the King's Wizard.

"You will now, sire," the wizard announced.

Fallon nodded to his friends. Anything could happen now. Gallagher leaned nonchalantly against the cart, right where their loaded crossbows sat, while Fallon let his hand fall naturally to the hilt of his dagger.

"People of Berry!" King Aidan called, his voice booming right across the crowd and silencing their chatter. "I have glad tidings for you! These servants of the witches, who had stolen children and families from their very beds, who had terrified you all, are now dead! Killed by Captain Fallon, the leader of my son's guards!"

Aidan paused as the crowd cheered, thundering their approval.

"Fallon has rescued the families taken by these servants of the witches and saved them from a terrible fate! He is a hero and I thank him!"

Again the pause for cheering and Fallon looked over at his friends. Gallagher shrugged, while Brendan and Devlin looked bewildered.

Aidan strode back to his side and raised Fallon's arm in the air. "Wave to them. You are the hero both they and I need," he said softly.

Fallon's head was whirling. What madness was this?

"Remember the name of Captain Fallon! He is a man to trust and a man to follow!" the King roared and the crowd shouted back their joy at him.

"You can sleep safe in your beds tonight, thanks to Captain Fallon! Now go home, tell your children and your friends what has happened here, and how you are free of the witches! Go now, spread the word!"

The crowd howled its approval, then began to slip away, melting back to whatever they were doing before.

"A very good day's work, Captain," King Aidan said, in a normal voice now, patting Fallon on the shoulder. "Not only killing the snatchers but freeing the families."

"Just doing my duty, sire," Fallon said, feeling he had to say something.

"It shows me I was right to choose you. And the people will remember what you did here. I shall make sure of it. Your men already do whatever you say. Soon the others will also," the King said, much softer this time.

Before Fallon could recover from his astonishment, the King turned away and strode over to Conor and the rest of the families. "Regan!" Aidan shouted. "Where are you, man?"

The chamberlain appeared at the King's side, seemingly from nowhere.

"Make sure these people each receive a gold coin," he ordered.

"Your will, sire," Regan said with a small bow.

"Sire, thank you," Conor said, taking a step forwards; Kelty took a step forwards of his own.

Aidan waved off the thanks.

"But sire," Conor persisted. "What of our missing children?"

Aidan paused. "You must prepare yourself for the worst there," he said sadly. "But, if they still live, then I am sure Captain Fallon will find them."

Fallon blinked at being brought in again, but Aidan said no more and strode back into the castle, Kelty at his shoulder, his face making it clear that the conversation was now at an end.

Fallon looked around the rapidly emptying square and wondered what to do now. Almost before he had finished that thought, Regan was in front of him.

"Good work, Captain. The King is very pleased with you. Quinn's men will dispose of the bodies and you are free to return to your rooms. If the King needs you again, he will call on you," the chamberlain said.

"These bodies need to be examined. Dark magic was used on them," Fallon said. "I want Padraig and Rosaleen—"

"We shall have Archbishop Kynan and the King's Wizard Finbar look at them," Regan interrupted. "They will report to the King."

Fallon saw Conor and the other families being given money and turning for their old homes and decided he'd had enough of this. There were many questions but here was not the place to discuss them.

"Come on, lads," he waved, "our job is done."

*

The rest of the villagers were waiting for them back in the rooms and cheered them in, Rosaleen rushing to see that Devlin was healed. Fallon took their congratulations and felt their relief and it was some time before they could get away to try and work out what had happened.

"What do you make of that?" he asked.

His friends looked back blankly, none obviously able to say.

"Aidan's mad, obviously," Devlin said.

Brendan grinned at his friend. "Good to hear you have your humor back, Dev!" he said.

Devlin stared at him. "What are you talking about? I was serious. The King is mad. Who knows why he does anything?"

"It is not that easy," Padraig said. "But it was obviously an elaborate trap. Or perhaps we should say test. Kelty's men chase you into the snatchers' arms but you turn the tables and return triumphant. Instead of killing you, he celebrates it. To me, it looks as if he is setting Fallon up as the man to lead an army against the Kottermani."

"But why Fallon – why us?" Devlin asked. "How could Aidan think we would do what he wants?"

"Aroaril knows. But if he does start a war, where does that leave our families? On the wrong side and not coming back," Fallon growled.

That silenced everyone.

"So what in Aroaril's name do we do?" Brendan asked finally.

"I won't lead an army for him," Fallon said. "I will not be remembered as a man who slaughtered more of our people than at the battle of Caragh Lake."

"But having an army that obeys you may be a good thing," Padraig pointed out.

Fallon rubbed his face. "Maybe. But I don't trust anything he does or says. I have to get into his rooms. We have to find out what he is doing. And I am going to try it during the next dinner he has planned with his nobles. We all know what they will be doing for most of the night."

"It is not safe," Rosaleen warned.

"Nothing is. But if we don't get to the heart of what is going on soon, we might as well cut our own throats before the King does it for us."

Nobody disagreed with him – and then someone knocked on the door.

Devlin opened it to reveal a grizzled fisherman called Donnchadh. "You're not going to believe this, but Regan's at the door again," he said apologetically.

*

Fallon took a seat across from the King, keeping his face as blank as he could. He felt like a puppet on Aidan's string – but until he got the chance to cut the strings and turn the knife on the puppet master, he had to play along. Regan had given him nothing but a scroll telling him to meet with the King at first light. Understandably he had not slept much and now his nerves felt scraped tight, as he prepared to hear what strange game Aidan wanted to play this time.

"Since your fight with the Moneylenders Guild I have been obviously hunting them down," Aidan said conversationally, leaning back in his deep, padded chair. "You will be pleased to know that most of their leaders have been arrested or killed and their funds have been seized by the Crown. In time a new Moneylenders Guild will be created and the rights to lend money auctioned off. But, for now, the Bankers Guild has taken over their duties, in exchange for a modest fee."

Fallon nodded, wondering why he was being told this. The Guild deserved to be punished for their treachery and alliance with Swane, but surely they were just operating secretly for Aidan?

"But that is not the real problem," Aidan continued. "We have discovered that the remnants of the army the Guild used to attack you have returned there. They now lurk there, perhaps as many as a hundred of them."

Fallon sat up straighter at that. The Guild bashers and thieves had been bad enough when they attacked but when some had been turned into undead monsters by Swane and his Fearpriest ...

Aidan nodded. "Yes, you see the problem as well as I. They are doing nothing, just sitting there. But what if they realize they have nothing to lose and start attacking the people? So we must destroy them before that happens. I want you to do it."

"Me, sire? But my men—" Fallon began.

"Not just your men. I will give you an equal number of my guards to lead in there as well. With your force doubled, then you will have no problem," Aidan continued. "Here are your orders. You may select your own men. Captain Kelty has been told to give you only the ones you ask for. Clean out this nest of vipers for me, Captain Fallon."

"Yes, sire," Fallon said stiffly.

"You will need all your men but I fear it will be too dangerous for your son. Make sure you leave him behind, with perhaps three or four trusted men to look after him," Aidan said thoughtfully.

Fallon bowed, to give himself the time to get his face under control. The message was unmistakable. Try to run away and Kerrin would pay. *Threaten my son, you bastard? I'll rip your bogging head off!* he screamed inside his head. But the guards were close behind him and he had no weapon.

"A sensible idea, sire," he said.

*

"So this is how he is going to kill us," Devlin asked.

"I don't think so. Or why would he let me choose who I took from his ranks?" Fallon pointed out. "It is another game of his. He might be testing us but we can come out of it alive. And, after today, I want those guards to fight for me, not for Aidan. He thinks we will just keep playing along with him. Not for much longer."

"Well, then get the city on to our side," Gallagher said.

Fallon pushed a smiled onto his face and waved to the crowd that was following them, a crowd that was still growing.

Fallon had picked out the guards swiftly, making sure he chose all the ones who went in with him at Killarney and getting Bran and Casey to help him select the rest, making sure that Kelty's favorites and the lazy and useless were left behind at the castle. Then he equipped everyone with crossbows, dressed his own men in surcoats and made sure half of them had barrels of lamp oil. If these renegade Bashers and thieves could not be killed in the normal manner, he would be ready.

Then he had divided them up into three companies of a mixture of villagers and guards, putting his three friends in charge of one each. Working all that out had to be done in the square outside the castle and the sight brought out the onlookers – and then led to the cheering.

"It's Captain Fallon, our savior!"

"Three cheers for Fallon!"

Fallon was filled with ice at the thought of walking off and leaving Kerrin at Aidan's mercy, to be watched by Donnchadh and a pair of others. He used his hatred to keep him warm. He had to fight to keep it off his face as he waved to the crowds as they marched through Berry.

Many of the crowd followed them all the way, while new people replaced those who stopped cheering. Fallon could see the effect it had on all the men. His villagers enjoyed the adulation, while the guards – more used to being jeered at – loved it. He had to call a halt when they came close to the square where they had fought the Moneylenders and Swane. He turned to the crowd, asking for Padraig's help so he could be heard by all.

"I can make you heard but anyone in the square will hear us as well," the old wizard warned.

"They must know we are coming anyway, and we can't risk having some of these people follow us in there."

"Go on then." Padraig gestured tiredly.

Fallon turned to the crowd and held out his hands. "No further. This could get dangerous and I don't want to see any of you hurt.

Go back to your homes now and leave it to us," he called, his voice echoing down the street and silencing the crowd.

They gave him one last cheer and then stayed where they were, keeping watch from a safe distance as he spoke to the men in his normal voice.

"Listen now," he said. "We stay close together. We think most of them are in the main Guildhall, but we will make sure there are no unpleasant surprises behind us. Gallagher's company will watch the main hall, crossbows at the ready. Brendan, you take your company in to the houses on our left, Devlin's company will go in to the houses on the right. If you see anything, fill it full of crossbow bolts. If it still tries to get up, then get out of there and we burn the houses down," he said. "There's no Fearpriest here, so I don't think they will be impossible to kill. But we take no risks, understand?"

He saw the smiles disappear from the faces of the guards at this. His own men were looking grim enough already, having been there once before.

He grinned at them. "Cheer up, once we are done here, we get to walk back through our adoring crowds again. I reckon we'll be so full of free beer and food by the time we get back to the castle, we may not make it!"

That brought a few smiles to faces and he broadened his own forced grin. "Come on. How often do you get to be heroes and save the city? Enjoy it!" He didn't like lying to them but he was happy with what he saw on their faces, a mixture of determination and pride, and he raised his crossbow. "Follow me!" he cried and led the way.

After being surrounded by noise all the way there, it was eerily quiet in the square. The center of the cobbled space was stained black and small piles of ash still marked where Aidan's guards had burned the bodies from the first battle, including Prince Cavan. That gave him a moment's pause and he reached in to touch the bloody quarrel. The men moved quickly, not quite silent but not talking, the loudest sounds their boots on the cobbles. Gallagher's company formed two lines and watched the main Guildhouse, while the other two companies split off. Fallon stared at the Guildhouse. The doors were hanging off the hinges and the ground-floor windows were still smashed, where the Bashers had tried to force their way inside. But otherwise it looked normal.

"Padraig." Fallon looked at the old wizard, who nodded.

"This is Captain Fallon. I have here a warrant from the King for your arrest. Come out peacefully and you will have a fair trial before King Aidan himself!" Fallon shouted, his words bounding off the empty buildings and sending pigeons flying in all directions.

"A fair trial like the women accused of being witches?" Gallagher muttered.

Fallon ignored him. "Come out now or we shall come and get you, with sword and bow."

His words echoed away and the pigeons fluttered back to their roosts. He watched them as much as he did the houses, trying to see if there was an area of roof that they avoided. But there was nothing. No movement and no shouts back. He waited further, letting the silence stretch out, then turned to his friends. "Go now," he said. "As we planned."

He took a few steps forwards, standing just in front and off to the side of Gallagher's company, crossbow tucked under one arm and eyes roving across the houses and rooftops.

There was a crash from behind as Brendan broke into a house and he turned to see what was happening there.

Brendan's company flowed into one building while Devlin had two of his men kick open another door and head in there.

Fallon watched and listened, his every muscle tensed, but they appeared quickly enough, waving their hands to show the houses were empty.

"Keep an eye on those rooftops!" he told Gallagher's second line. "Anything moves up there, loose at it and shout out!"

But nothing moved up there and nothing seemed to be in the houses, for Devlin and Brendan's men made sure the back end of the square was safe before starting on the ones down each side.

Fallon did not like the silence. It felt wrong, and he saw that Devlin and Brendan's men were getting further and further away from Gallagher's company now – far enough apart that they could be attacked in turn.

"Hold!" he shouted, his voice echoing off the buildings and startling a flock of pigeons away from the rooftops. "Back here, quick now!"

Neither Brendan nor Devlin argued, just turned their men around and jogged back so all three companies were together again.

"We were splitting up," Fallon explained. "Brendan, you start in the houses on your side again. Devlin, your men will watch them. Any trouble, fall back to us."

They nodded and began again, kicking in doors and searching through empty rooms. Fallon switched between watching what they were doing and keeping an eye on the Guildhouse. He switched back to the houses just in time to see some movement at a window on the first floor.

"Watch out!" he roared, then loosed his crossbow into the open space.

A man appeared at the window, a spear in his hand, preparing to hurl it down on Brendan as the smith was about to smash the door in, but Fallon's crossbow bolt flashed past his face and he leaned back, losing his balance because of the near miss. It was just enough. As he tried to lean out again and throw the spear down, Devlin's men loosed a ragged volley and he toppled out, struck several times, to crunch onto the cobbles.

"Watch him!" Fallon shouted, even as he hauled back on his crossbow string.

Nobody went near the body but it did not move. Fallon raced over there as Brendan's men formed a rough circle around the bloodied mess. Fallon raced right up to the fallen man, whipped out his shillelagh and used it to flip the body over. Between the bolts and the fall onto stone, the man was dead. And, although Fallon tried to stir him into life with a series of hits, nothing happened. It looked like these were indeed just men who had survived that filthy little battle and returned here because they had nowhere else to go, just as Aidan said.

"They are ordinary men," he announced, sensing the tension go out of his force at the words. "Now let's see if we can take a few prisoners."

"The windows!" Devlin called.

Fallon swung up to see more men appearing out of the shadows there, knives and spears in their hands. Without thinking, he dropped his shillelagh and grabbed the crossbow, loosing in one smooth movement. Devlin's and Brendan's men poured bolts into every window, while several knives and spears rained down on them.

Fallon saw a knife coming for him and ducked, feeling it whistle past his shoulder and bounce off the cobbles.

Three of his men were not so lucky, going down with spears or knives in them.

"Pull back! Keep loosing!" he ordered.

The wounded men were hauled away, although from the looks of a guard with a spear through his chest, he did not have long to live.

"Get Sister Rosaleen!" Fallon grabbed guardsman Casey and shoved him over towards where Gallagher was bringing his men across to help. "Reload and loose!"

With more than a hundred men loosing at anything that showed itself, the men inside the house soon stayed away from the windows, because any that appeared were quickly struck. Fallon checked the Guildhouse to see there was still nothing from there, then looked to where Rosaleen, bloodied to the elbows, was helping the wounded.

"Brendan, get the door open; Devlin, I want a barrel of lamp oil in there and a torch," he ordered. "The rest of us will make sure none of them even dare to come close to a window."

He had Brendan's company still loose as fast as they could load, while making sure Devlin's and Gallagher's men were all loaded. The building had a dozen windows, so he quickly sorted the men out so each window had at least eight men watching it.

"Ready? Go!" He signaled to his friends.

Using the already-cleared houses as cover, they eased down to the door, then Brendan's hammer smashed open the lock and a pair of guardsmen threw in small barrels of lamp oil, each one about the size of a man's head. Right behind them, Devlin tossed in a torch, and they ran backwards. Men appeared at windows but they were swiftly riddled with bolts, and only one spear was sent bouncing off the cobbles, well behind the running Devlin.

"Pull back further and pick off anyone who comes out," Fallon snapped.

Already smoke was billowing out of the lower windows and they could see flames through the open doorway. The furniture had been stripped out of these houses to fuel the pyre in the center of the square but the wooden floors and walls, splashed with lamp oil, were burning fiercely. That was a problem he would need Padraig to fix – but not just yet. Men could not survive for long in there and already they had to be wondering if it was safer to try to jump to safety or chance the flames.

A few moments later Fallon got his answer. A pair of men appeared at a first-floor window and swung themselves over, jumping down to the cobbles.

Even as they appeared, crossbows twanged, and they were followed all the way down by bolts, dozens of them, so they hit the ground riddled; the front of the building was scarred by repeated strikes.

"Gallagher's company only!" Fallon shouted but it was too late. Almost all his men had loosed.

"Reload!" Fallon shouted, furious at himself for not detailing only one company to loose at a time.

Next moment doors banged open and men began to pour out of the remaining houses. Dressed as a motley collection of Bruisers, they all carried some sort of weapon, from swords to axes to spears and staves. Without waiting to form up, they raced at Fallon's men.

"Loose!" Fallon shouted and no more than a dozen quarrels flicked out to knock over the lead runners.

More Bruisers were tumbling out of houses all the time but they had to get out of narrow doorways and were more staggered than a solid mass.

"Guards, drop crossbows and draw swords. Follow me!" Fallon bellowed.

He found himself looking forward to this fight. He was so full of anger about Aidan's threat to Kerrin, and full of guilt over killing Prince Cavan. He had to let it out somehow.

He laid down his crossbow and drew sword and dagger, then raced to meet the Bruisers without worrying to see if anyone was following him.

If they had brought shields he would have liked to form a line and throw these Bruisers back but, without them, it was better to run and meet them than stand there and wait.

The lead Bruiser was a tall man, his face dark with beard, his red tunic stained and torn. His face looked pinched and his clothes hung off him, suggesting he had not eaten much recently. But the sword he carried was bright and clean and that was all Fallon cared about.

Time seemed to slow as they got closer: Fallon could feel every breath, see every detail as the Bruiser rushed at him, right arm pulled back for a huge slash of the sword. The Bruiser's eyes seemed dull, uncaring, and Fallon even had time to wonder at that before they came together.

Time sped up again and Fallon stepped off his right foot, pivoting away to his left from the swing of the sword that came down diagonally with enough force to cut him in half. But it never landed, only swishing through air, as Fallon used their momentum to slip past. He stamped his left foot down and lashed sideways with his sword. The Bruiser had run on and Fallon's sword crashed into the back of his neck, tearing a huge wound and sending a spray of blood skyward. The Bruiser's head, barely attached to his neck, was flung forwards and he collapsed to the ground, twitching.

Fallon did not spare him a second glance because another was almost upon him. This one, dressed equally shabbily, lunged with a rusty spear at his chest. Fallon knocked it aside with his bloody sword and stood his ground as the Bruiser ran onwards, ramming his dagger into the man's throat.

Hot blood spurted over his hand and face and coppery gouts of it filled his mouth and nose as the Bruiser choked and gasped. Fallon ripped his dagger across, flinging the body away from him at the same time and snorted and spat to clear his nostrils and mouth of blood before the next Bruiser reached him.

He even had time to wonder if any of the guards had followed him as a howling Bruiser raced in, an axe over his shoulder. He stood his ground, then, while the man prepared a huge blow, flicked his dagger at the man's face. The Bruiser lost his swing as tried to avoid the blade, and before he could recover, Fallon stepped in, using the power of his hip and back to punch a sword thrust home into the man's chest. He twisted the sword inside the smashed ribs to free the blade and ripped it back with an accompanying burst of blood.

The axe dropped from nerveless fingers as the Bruiser reeled away, trying in vain to stop the spurts of crimson pulsing out from his torn chest.

Now Fallon did glance left and right, to see the guards crashing into the Bruisers with a series of shouts and screams. Right behind them was Brendan, swinging his huge hammer in enormous arcs. A running Bruiser was caught and tossed lazily through the air, chest stove in, by one blow, then Brendan reversed it and brought it down on the head of another, pulping it into scraps of bloodied bone.

Fallon retrieved his dagger and raced over to where a pair of Bruisers were threatening Bran. He hacked down with his sword, driving it into the Bruiser's lower back. The man screamed and dropped his sword instantly. Fallon twisted the blade again to break the suction of the flesh and tore it clear, as Bran beheaded the other Bruiser.

"Stand together!" Fallon roared. "Work together!"

The rush of Bruisers had turned to a trickle coming out of the houses and Fallon could see his men outnumbered them easily. Clustering together and working in twos and threes, they isolated and killed the Bruisers as they raced in.

"Watch my back," Fallon turned to Bran and the bearded guardsman nodded.

"I'm right behind you, Captain!" the dark man said.

Fallon blocked a wild swing of a shillelagh with his sword then stepped in and ripped his dagger across the Bruiser's eyes, feeling the tip tear through the eyeballs. The Bruiser cried out but did not drop his staff, so Fallon slammed his sword into the man's stomach, spilling his guts across the cobbles. Now he did drop his staff, crumpling slowly as his entrails coiled around his feet.

Fallon left him to die and looked across the cobbles, covered in bodies, blood, guts and shit, trying to make sense of what was happening – but there was no sense to be made. Normal men would have broken or run, yet these Bruisers kept coming. They had little skill and seemed to be relying on strength, although even that was lacking. By the time they had swung their swords or axes a couple of times, they seemed slow and weak, and easy to kill.

That had not stopped them from putting a dozen of Fallon's guardsmen down though, and the remainder showed no mercy to the last Bruisers rushing in, heedless of the slaughter of their comrades.

Fallon blocked one blow, using his sword and dagger crossed together, then Bran stabbed the man deep in the thigh, slicing open the big artery there. As the Bruiser staggered backwards, Fallon smashed him in the face with his sword, tearing away most of his jaw.

"Any more?" he bellowed, wiping his eyes clear of blood with his surcoat sleeve and looking around for new threats.

There were none. Some of the Bruisers – who looked to number forty or perhaps fifty – were still moving but only to twitch out their last in spreading pools of blood.

"Get the wounded over to Sister Rosaleen. And reload. There are supposed to be more of them than this," Fallon shouted, then hawked and spat, still trying to clear the tang of blood out of his mouth.

He patted Bran on the back and moved among the other guards, who were looking either dazed or ecstatic after what they had been through. The jubilant ones he quickly tried to calm down by making them reload crossbows and watch the rooftops. The shocked ones were different: he quickly spoke to them, offering them a pat on the back or quick jest, anything to get their minds off what they had been through.

He left Rosaleen looking after the wounded, although two of these had died before she could get to them and the rest, although healed, were too weak to do anything else for days.

The rest of the men were formed back into their companies and they watched as Padraig used his magic to put out the fire they had started. Then all turned to gaze at the Guildhouse.

"Do we go in there or check the other side of the square first?" Gallagher asked.

Fallon hesitated. Blood was drying black on the surcoats, hands and faces of most of his guardsmen, while he could feel it flaking off his skin every time he moved. "We check that first," he decided. There was something about the Guildhouse that did not feel right.

"Who do you want to send?" Gallagher asked.

Fallon glanced back at the men and saw their nervousness. The guardsmen had just gone through a nasty fight, and the villagers remembered the last time they had been inside the Guildhouse. Time to make sure they would follow him anywhere, even to stop Aidan.

"I'll do it," Fallon said, hefting his crossbow.

"I don't think that's a good idea," Devlin said immediately.

"Even so." Fallon grinned at them and strode forwards, approaching one of the windows from the side. He eased under the first window, keeping below the windowsill, aiming for the second. If there were anyone inside, then surely they would be watching the windows at the edges. He would, if he were inside.

There was still a faint stink of smoke and rotten flesh coming out of the building, while its torn and ragged window openings were a stark reminder of the earlier battle there. He crouched low, feeling his heart pound, telling himself it would surely be empty.

Then he pushed himself up, planning to duck back down again, quick as a weasel, once he had seen inside.

As he reared up, a ragged thief appeared right in front of him, directly on the other side of the window, a long knife in his hand, already bringing the blade down towards his face.

CHAPTER 11

Prince Kemal looked out over the water and sighed. Then he turned to look at his family, his wife Feray and sons Asil and Orhan, and smiled.

"What is it, my Lord?" his wife asked, her voice gentle and musical.

Kemal did not need to glance around to see if anyone was listening. His people knew better than to disturb his privacy. They were alone on the high stern deck, looking out over the endless ocean that divided Kotterman from Gaelland.

"I wonder whether we will like it there," he said. Many men, in fact most men, would not confide in their wives, let alone discuss matters of great import with them. But Feray was not an ordinary woman. He had married her because it solidified his father's grip on a vital part of the Empire, but he had swiftly fallen in love with her anyway. Their sons were eight and six summers of age and another source of joy to him, although they were less interested in what he was saying and more curious about a pair of dolphins that were swimming alongside the ship.

"How can we not? We will be representing your father and the great Empire of Kotterman, bringing a new province into its boundaries for the first time in one hundred years," she said.

He chuckled. "I know what we are supposed to do. I question why."

She cocked her head on one side. "Tell me, my Lord."

Kemal smiled and enfolded her in his arms. "Do you know why I have taken no other woman?" he asked. "Although my brothers believe an oath to Aroaril is no oath at all?"

"Because you know I would remove your manhood with a rusty knife?" she suggested with a grin.

"Well, that also. But the real reason is I could never find anyone with half as much sense as you. This business with Gaelland concerns me deeply. When my forefathers began to expand our Empire, they could not stop once they had started, because there were always enemies across the border who wanted our riches, as well as allies who wanted our trade. But we have no border with Gaelland and it is a huge distance from my father. And their King is a strange man. We talk to him because we must but he reminds me of a shark. It looks like he is smiling all the time, he even appears foolish on occasion, but then you catch sight of his eyes and you realize there is something evil there."

Feray shuddered a little. "But surely we have nothing to fear from him? There are too few of them and they are too poor to cause us concern."

"That is what my father thinks. But all he has done is read the reports on this King Aidan. He has never met the man. Although that is one thing about Gaelland coming under the Kotterman Empire. If we remove Aidan from the throne, it will actually help the people."

"Do you believe that?"

He smiled. "More than that, I know it to be true. Our agents have been meeting with people from the King's eldest son, Prince Cavan. Many of the nobles would like to see the end of Aidan's rule and the Crown Prince assures our agents they would welcome Kottermani rule if their positions are preserved and the lives of their people improved. Obviously I will need to meet with this Cavan myself, as well as the nobles he claims support him. It will influence my talks with King Aidan, although it is up to me to make my father's dream come true."

"What are you going to do, my love?"

Kemal kissed her on the head. "What I must. I can never forget that I have three brothers, all of whom would love to sit on the

Elephant Throne one day. As you say, Gaelland is the first new province to be brought into the Empire since my great-great-grandfather's time. My father lusts more for it than he has for any woman. He feels the touch of Aroaril on his shoulder and wants to leave his mark on the history scrolls. If I do not do this, then he will find another who will."

Her arms tightened around him. "I do not care if you are the Emperor or just a man. I would still be with you," she said against his chest.

He chuckled. "Let us never put that to the test!"

He might have said more, but his sons came running over then, the dolphins forgotten, wanting to show him how they had been learning the sword, brandishing their wooden practice blades.

"Come then, let us see how good you are!" Kemal challenged them, winking at his wife's indulgent smile as he defended himself against the children.

Asil, the older of the two, was slim and fast, while Orhan was younger but already stocky and solid through the chest and shoulders, and his blows had the same power as his older brother's, albeit without the speed.

Kemal fended the two of them off easily, his footing sure and quick, making them bump into each other and occasionally using his wooden sword to tap one of them, all the while telling them what to do better.

"Enough!" he cried finally, as Orhan abandoned his sword and grabbed him around the leg. "I am defeated by you!"

"Really, Baba?" Orhan asked, looking up at his father in delight.

"No!" Kemal laughed, grabbing them both in his arms.

Their laughter echoed across the ship as Feray called down to servants for refreshments to be brought up.

"What are you really concerned about, my husband?" she asked, while their sons sat and ate. "We have planned and prepared for this day, even learning their strange language."

Kemal grimaced. "Perhaps it is just the thought of living there for several years, away from the sun."

She chuckled. "Given you spend most of your time inside, that is unlikely to be what's troubling you."

He winked at her. "It is nothing I can place my finger on. I was led to believe the people were mere sheep, ruled by an evil shepherd. Yet there are some with spirit there. I have a strange feeling about what we shall find."

"Then it is lucky you have me to guide you," she told him. "Who are the ones with spirit you have found? The slaves you took?"

"The same," he said. "I left Gokmen to watch over their leader, a woman, but I wonder if the roles will be reversed by the time we return."

*

"The people talk of nothing but how you defied the Kottermanis and saved the women," Ahearn said. "They see you as a real leader."

"Well, I still need to lead them out of here. How strong are your chains?" Bridgit asked.

"Steel, tethered to a steel bolt that is sunk into stone," Ahearn warned. It was the day when the Gaelish could visit the children and Bridgit was back thinking of escape.

"What if you used lamb fat to grease it and tried to pull it out? You can't do it in one night but maybe over a quarter moon—" Bridgit suggested, then sighed. The men night be able to do it but how could the women hope to pull a bolt out of stone? And trying to break a chain with an axe or a hammer would take too long and make too much noise.

"Maybe we can get the keys from whoever is guarding you."

"And how will you do that? Your female wiles?" Ahearn asked with a smile, which took any sting from the words.

Bridgit did not smile back. "We shall have the knives and swords or the guards here. I will cut their bloody throats if I have to," she said.

Ahearn blinked. "Are you sure you can do that?"

Bridgit glared at him. "I know once we step outside those doors, we must succeed or they will kill some of these children. They will have to kill me first and, believe me, I am not ready to die yet."

She remembered what it had felt like to fight the Kottermanis in Baltimore and did not shy away from what she might have to do. If it came down to it, stabbing a man she had never met to save her unborn child and the children she had come to love had already been an easy choice. Something of that must have shown in her face, for Ahearn gave a wry chuckle.

"I think we did the right thing when we decided to listen to you, although those brothers from your village may not agree."

Bridgit shuddered at the thought. "Was the end quick for them?" she asked, not wanting to know but needing to.

"Well, if you call a day and a half quick. They weren't making much noise at the end," Ahearn said. "Like you with the children, it told us all the stakes we are fighting for. We know if we get captured again, some of us will pay the same price. I know I'll fight until my last breath to avoid that and so will most of the others."

Bridgit nodded. "We have perhaps half a moon before they send us to the block and scatter everyone across their Empire. We have to come up with a plan by then."

Ahearn smiled. "What are you going to do when you get us back to Gaelland?" he asked.

Bridgit had been watching the children play but his words snapped her head around. "What do you mean?"

Ahearn shrugged. "Just that it will be hard to go back to merely being a wife and a mother after you became our leader here. We all trust you with our lives. I can't speak for the others but that is not something I would do lightly. Aroaril, I wouldn't even do it for one of the nobles!"

He moved away, leaving Bridgit to think about that. Her mind had been clear. Get back to Fallon and Kerrin and get back to the way things were. But now she realized things would never quite be the same. She was not sure if that was a good thing or a bad thing.

*

"When are we going to escape? Look at what they are doing to us!" One of the women showed her blistered hands and her back, where the welts from a whip stood out red against her pale skin.

"You have to have patience. We cannot just walk out of here," Bridgit said calmly.

But the group of women were beyond calm. "It is easy for you. You sit here in the shade, playing with the little ones, while we sweat and bake out in the fields," another woman snarled. "We hardly get to see our children. And we are no closer to getting out."

Bridgit could feel the mood of the women and knew pleading for understanding was not going to work here. Besides, she had had enough of it. Every group of parents coming in had the same thing to say. She felt sorry for what they were going through but the alternative was far worse.

"Listen now!" she snapped. "If you want, I can go to Gokmen and tell him this is not good enough. Then he will kill the children he thinks are too young to make good slaves and put the rest of us on the block, send us all over their empire. You'll never see another Gaelish face again, nor speak your own language. And you know what happens to those who anger them. You all saw what happened to Sean and Seamus. Do you want that to be you?"

Her anger lashed at them and they wilted before her.

"But it is taking so long!" one of them muttered.

"Did you think we would walk out of here? You are chained up every night and even these children have armed guards. The Kottermanis are not fools. They know we do not want to be here. Only if they think us beaten will they relax. You want to get out of here faster? Stop complaining!"

She glared around at them and they did not meet her eyes. She softened her tone then. "I will try to get you all brought here at once. Then we can break out. I swear I will not see you sold off and I will not leave one of you here or I will die in the attempt. If that is not good enough for you, then say it now, so I can point you out to Gokmen and he can take you away to some Aroaril-forsaken spot in the desert to work as a slave there."

They were not happy but they were no longer complaining, at least. Their feelings did not worry her, which was strange. A few moons ago she would have been up all night worrying about what people thought about her. Now she did not have time for such silliness.

*

"Faster now! Come on, an orange to the one who does the best!" Bridgit clapped her hands.

She loved being with the younger children but, for once, she was working with the older ones, not one of them under fourteen summers, although none of them were over sixteen summers either.

The parents had gone after a long day of visits and quiet talks and Nola and Riona were with the younger children, trying to comfort them and calm them down. Bridgit wanted to be in there as well, but this was more important.

She had brought several lengths of fabric at the market on yet another visit with Ely and had now fashioned it not into replacement clothes but instead into several long slings.

None of the village children used crossbows but almost all of them had used slings before. They were a handy way of adding some extra food to the table, especially in autumn, when you wanted to save the salted meat and the smoked fish for when the snows came and dinner became truly hard to find.

She had seen the older children hit a running rabbit at twenty paces, or bring down a pigeon on the wing, and decided that sort of skill might be very useful indeed when it came time to break out.

Stones were hard to find but there were a few loose tiles around the house, as well as cracked parts, and these had yielded a small stock of missiles. Naturally she did not want any of the guards to see what they were up to but that was easy enough. After all, a strip of fabric became a cloth belt in a moment, while a stone was suspicious in the hand but innocent when lying in a quiet corner.

She put them through their paces, having them take turns to send a stone whistling into one of the children's mattresses. It made little sound but she was reassured to see how hard and fast they hit the target. The stones they were using did not look like much but they were the size of the top joint of her thumb and one of those in the head was going to make any Kottermani far less likely to trouble them.

"Good work. Listen now, make sure you keep practicing," she told them.

They smiled at her and she told them to go and hide the slings, then cuddle their younger brothers and sisters.

She went to join them herself when she ran into Ely. She felt guilty, caught out, as she did so, although there was no reason to be. Ely had not done anything suspicious since they had taken her into their confidence.

"Are you sure of this?" Ely whispered. "We are risking everything by trying to escape. We could stay here you know. The Kottermanis will bring back more of your people and you will have this job for many summers to come. I can stay here and work with you. It is not so bad."

Bridgit pulled away slightly. "We cannot stay here. My friends have children. Do you think they would stay to see them sold off into slavery? I have a family back home. I must return to them. It is natural to feel fear and to doubt. But you have to believe to get things done. And I believe we can make it home." She paused for a moment, amazed those words had come out of her mouth. Just a moon ago she could not have said such a thing and meant it.

"Listen, Ely," she said gently, reaching over and stroking the young woman's hair. "You have known nothing but Kotterman. You have only lived as a slave. Please, trust me when I tell you that life will change when we are back there. You will never need to work again, never have to live your life obeying other people's orders. I promise." She looked into Ely's eyes and was relieved to see the young woman smile and nod. "That's the way. Now, we need to speak to Gokmen tomorrow."

"Gokmen, why?"

"I need to persuade him to bring all our people here at the same time."

CHAPTER 12

Fallon ducked and triggered his crossbow in one movement. The bolt smashed into the thief's face, the force picking him up and flicking him backwards. But, behind that one, Fallon could see more of them, and some sort of barricade across the stairs. Another pair of thieves raced at him, knives in their hands, while a third threw a blade at him.

Instinctively Fallon ducked and covered up behind his crossbow, feeling the blade strike the stock and bounce away. Without bothering to see what else was happening, he turned and raced back towards his men. Crashing noises behind him said they were not going to let him get away that easily. He sensed, rather than saw, that at least a couple of them were after him but concentrated on getting back to the safety of his men.

"Down!" Gallagher shouted, waving at him, and he obeyed, sliding feet-first on the cobbles.

Next instant a score of Gallagher's company loosed their crossbows and the quarrels hissed over his head to thump into his pursuers. He turned over to see a pair of them jerking on the cobbles.

"I'd say they're all in there?" Brendan asked, offering a hand to help Fallon to his feet.

"Aye," Fallon agreed, brushing himself off and wincing at a bruised hip. "It looks like they copied us, barricaded the stairs. But they left a few to give any scout a nasty surprise."

"Luckily we sent in someone we could afford to lose," Gallagher said with a grunt. "What were you thinking of? What would we have told Bridgit?"

Fallon patted his friend on the back. "I agree. Next time I am an idiot, you can put a crossbow bolt into my leg to slow me down."

"The way you go, I'll be running out of bolts," Gallagher grumbled.

Fallon grinned and waved the others in closer. "This one will be tricky," he said. "We all know how hard it is to get up those stairs. And the floor is marble, so the lamp oil trick won't work, either. I want every broken door off every house over there."

"Why?" Brendan asked.

"We need shields and they're the only things handy," Fallon said.

While most of his men kept watch on the Guildhouse, the others used axes and swords from the fallen Bruisers to pull down a dozen doors: enough to make a solid wall of wood.

"We go in the front, sheltering behind these doors. Loose your crossbow, then hand it back and get a loaded one. We will pick them off until they either come down the stairs or there's so few left that we can go up," he instructed.

He chose his villagers as the crossbowmen, for he had seen them practicing and knew which ones could be relied on to hit a target – and who could reload fast. Each pair of guardsmen was given a door.

"Stay low and keep your heads down," he told them, selecting Bran and Casey to protect him. With him would be two other villagers, while more would form a chain of reloaders once they were inside.

"I thought you said I could loose one into your leg if you did anything else foolish," Gallagher said.

"This isn't foolish. It has to be done," Fallon stated. He ignored the looks from his friends and tapped Bran on the shoulder. "Time to go," he said.

He had a score of men from Gallagher's company on either side of the doorway and, at his signal, they loosed their bolts into the darkness beyond, trying to ensure nobody could hide to either side and surprise them.

"Go!" Fallon shouted and Bran and Casey hefted the thick wooden door and hurried in, walking hunched down, their heads well below the top. Fallon and his villagers were right behind them.

Someone thumped into the door and Fallon saw an angry-looking thief try to reach over, a long knife in his hand. He put a crossbow bolt into the thief's open mouth and Bran and Casey stepped over his body, carrying the door to the right, as arranged, clearing the doorway for the next team.

Fallon kept close to the door but could see a crowd of men up on the balcony, hurling down knives and rocks at them. Most either bounced short or thumped into the door but one rock hit a villager on the head, who went down instantly.

Fallon grabbed the fallen villager's crossbow and loosed into the crowd at the top of the stairs, making them duck away for a moment.

In that time, another pair of guardsmen rushed in carrying a door, going to the left this time, then a third came in and a fourth, until they had made a small wall of doors. All the time the thieves were hurling things down at them but they had no bows, which could have made a difference. As it was, without the door-shields, Fallon doubted any of them could have avoided being hit. With the doors, only one other man was struck, as he reared up to loose his crossbow and received a knife in the shoulder as a reward.

More doors came in, guardsmen now standing up to create a double-height wall, expanding it so they had a safe area protected right across the doorway area.

Behind this, villagers crowded in, to take their turn at loosing up at the balcony, ducking back to hand their crossbows out to waiting hands to be reloaded and getting another bow in return. Fallon picked off half a dozen thieves easily. They were clustered together, making them an obvious target. They were also running out of missiles to throw, for hardly anything was thudding into the doors now.

"Five paces closer!" Fallon shouted.

The guardsmen hefted up their door-shields and moved forwards, getting closer to the foot of the stairs. From there any that were foolish enough to show themselves were quickly killed, while the rest sheltered behind their own barricade, not even venturing out to throw things down.

Fallon searched for them with his crossbow but, when even he could not see anything to loose at, he waved for the others to stop.

"Three door-shields wide, we'll go up the stairs. The rest of you stay here and loose at anything that shows itself. Brendan, when we get to the top, we'll need you to bring down that barricade," Fallon ordered hastily.

Led by Bran and Casey again, they advanced in quick steps to the foot of the stairs, and began to climb. The rest of the men below kept watch, their crossbows threatening any that showed themselves – but none did.

Fallon tried to keep his head down and look up at the same time, which was not an easy task. But they inched their way up the stairs, the fine marble etched in fire and blood from their last fight here, until they reached the barricade. Just as they had done, the thieves had grabbed tables and chairs out of rooms to form a defensive wall at the head of the stairs.

"Brendan!" Fallon said.

The big smith signaled to the guardsmen protecting him and they raised the door they were holding up higher and he lashed out with his hammer, swinging it underneath, snagging tangled chairs and tables and sweeping them away. Nobody from behind the barricade tried to stop him, although Fallon was down on one knee, ready to loose at anyone who did. Three more strokes of the hammer and that part of the barricade was in tatters.

"Now!" Fallon roared and joined the others in putting their shoulders to Brendan's door and shoving what was left of the barricade aside. From below and outside, the rest of his men drew weapons and raced up the stairs, in a huge wave.

"And get them!"

Fallon turned to his right, loosed his crossbow and sent a haggard-looking thief flying backwards with a crossbow in the chest, then dropped his bow and drew his sword. There was a cluster of thieves at the barricade and they pressed forwards but they had seemingly thrown most of their weapons, for they merely had staves, nothing else. And they lacked the ferocity of the Bruisers, for their attack was slow, yet they still came on, refusing to surrender, although more of Fallon's men were pushing through the barricade with every moment.

Fallon waded into them, not wanting to lose another man. Behind him, villagers and guardsmen stabbed and cut and hewed, covering the floor in blood and guts and the foul stench of open bowels. Brendan swung his hammer like a man possessed, smashing heads and staving in chests, flinging bodies in all directions.

Yet the thieves fought on, hurling themselves at the massed swords. Even those brought down tried to grope for weapons and stab at the guardsmen, until swords ripped their lives from them.

Fallon slammed the last one in the jaw with his pommel and watched him stagger back to hit the balcony rail. "Give it up," he told the thief, Bran and Casey at his shoulders, both with blood dripping from their blades.

The thief hung there for a moment, blood pouring from his smashed mouth, then a strange smile twisted his face and he flipped himself head-first over the balcony, landing on the floor below with a sickening thud and explosion of brains.

"Aroaril! What would make you do that?" Casey asked, his voice thick with revulsion.

"I don't know, lad," Fallon admitted.

He looked around. The stench was appalling, while the only noise was the panting of his men and the gurgling as the last of the thieves died, drowning in their own blood. He was about to order them to start checking for any of their own wounded when a strange laugh cut through the quiet.

"What in Aroaril's name is that?" Gallagher asked, for all of them.

Fallon walked back along the landing, hearing the noise coming from one of the offices further down. Wordlessly he took a crossbow from one of the villagers.

On and on went the laugh, sometimes a giggle, sometimes a roar but always sounding like it was coming from a madman.

Fallon paused outside the office at the end of the corridor and pointed to Gallagher. "Get a barrel of lamp oil, a torch and Padraig. Just in case," he said.

As his friend rushed away he stepped into the room, crossbow at the shoulder.

"Welcome to my Guildhouse," chuckled a strangely familiar man, sitting on a chair in an otherwise empty room. He was empty-handed and dressed in the now-ragged but once-rich robes of a Moneylender.

It took Fallon a moment to place him. "Allen. The Guild master who promised to help Prince Cavan but then stood with Swane and sent in the Bruisers to kill us," he said. "What are you doing here?"

Allen laughed again, throwing his head back and wiping his eyes with merriment.

"You think this is funny? Your men threw themselves on our swords at the last, rather than be taken, and your precious Guildhouse is swimming in blood and shit. And you laugh?" Fallon spat.

Allen slowly regained control of himself. "If you knew what I know, you would laugh along," he said, shaking his head and smiling. "This is a game. All a game. I failed but I have done what I had to to make amends."

"Tell me what you know," Fallon said. "Make me laugh."

Allen shook his head. "You can never know. Not until it is too late. That's what makes it a jest, you see?"

Fallon snapped his fingers without taking his eyes off Allen. "Get Sister Rosaleen. She will get the truth out of him," he said.

Allen sighed. "Ah, you have to spoil my last moment of fun. But have you learned nothing in your time here? Your priestess failed to get answers before."

"What do you know about that? For Aroaril's sake, speak! We can protect you; we are here on the King's orders. Swane cannot touch you—"

Fallon's words were cut off by another burst of hysterical laughter from Allen. "You fools!" he told them. "This joke is at an end."

He reached into his robes and produced a small crossbow, less than half the size of Fallon's. He could hold it in one hand, for it had some strange grip angled down from the back. It also looked to have a small bolt, suspiciously like the one they had found in the Duke of Lunster's abandoned cabin, when this whole thing started.

"Put that down!" Fallon ordered, his finger tightening on his own crossbow trigger. "Where did you get it?"

Allen smiled. "Oh, you would love to know where this came from, wouldn't you? But now my game is at an end," he said conversationally, then raised the crossbow.

Fallon brought up his own crossbow, trying to dart to one side, then Allen reversed his own bow and opened his mouth, putting the tip inside, angling up.

"Stop!" Fallon roared at him, horrified, but it was too late.

Allen pulled on the trigger, his body jumping at the impact, and a point burst out of the back of his skull. His eyes rolled up, blood oozed out of his mouth, which was propped open by the bolt skewering his brain, then he toppled off the chair.

"Aroaril!" Fallon spat.

A few moments later, Gallagher, Padraig, Rosaleen and a pair of villagers carrying lamp oil arrived.

"It's over," Fallon said dully.

He locked eyes with Padraig and the old wizard raised his eyebrows expressively.

"Well done, sir," Bran said. "This is a great victory."

"Is it?" Fallon asked. "Because it doesn't feel like it."

"What do you mean, sir?" Casey asked. "We killed off the last of the Zorva-worshippers and made the city safe! The people will love us for this!"

Fallon forced a smile to his face. "Indeed they will, lad," he said. "Now we need to clean up this mess. Make sure our wounded all get seen by Sister Rosaleen. And stack the bodies of these bastards in the center of the square. We'd better have another pyre."

"What about their weapons, sir?" Bran asked.

"Collect them. We'll take them back to the castle."

"What about that one sir?" Bran pointed to the small crossbow in Allen's outflung hand.

Fallon did not hesitate. "I'll look after that one myself," he said. "Well done, both of you. I would be proud to fight with you again!"

"We'd follow you anywhere, sir," Casey said instantly. "We all would. There's not a man out there who would not die for you now."

Fallon smiled and nodded. *I might just need that*, he thought.

*

The crowd on the way back to the castle was even bigger than the one that had followed them on the way in.

This time they did not have to ask the gate guards to fetch the King, either, for he was waiting for them, flanked by an expressionless Kelty and the massed nobles.

Far better, from Fallon's point of view, was the sight of Kerrin up on the battlement over the gate, waving down with Donnchadh at his side.

Finbar was obviously there also, for the King's voice was able to boom out across the square and reach the thousands of people.

"Once again our city was under threat and once again it was saved by Captain Fallon and his gallant men!" the King boomed and crowd roared back at him.

"We can all sleep safe thanks to Fallon!"

On and on it went, until Fallon felt his face would crack from keeping the smile on.

Finally the King sent the crowd away, allowing Fallon and the others step away from the cheering people. But Aidan did not let Fallon go, instead beckoning him across to the side of the gate.

"You were everything I hoped," Aidan said seriously. "More than a hundred dead, for the price of two of yours. There's few who could have done better."

"I had nearly a score of wounded," Fallon said stiffly, although all of those would live, thanks to Rosaleen's work.

Aidan smiled. "Results are what matter. Who will remember the names of a couple of dead guards in a year's time? But your name will live on in the scrolls. The people will follow you and my guards believe in you."

Fallon bowed, not knowing what to say.

Aidan patted him on the shoulder and turned away. "All is ready," he said contentedly. "We just have to wait for the Kottermanis now."

Fallon dearly wanted to know what the King meant by that but he knew asking questions would be foolish and, besides, Kerrin was sprinting towards him.

"You're safe, Dad!" he cried. "I was going to give them one more turn of the hourglass and then I'd come looking for you."

Fallon smiled. "Were you now?" he asked.

"I am ready," Kerrin assured him.

"Well, that's good to see." Fallon grinned. "Let's get out of here."

*

The castle seemed to come alive with the knowledge there was a banquet for the nobles on again. Servants were working like dogs to prepare for it, while there was a never-ending stream of carriages arriving, disgorging brightly dressed nobles and their mistresses.

"Are they the same ones? Or new ones?" Brendan wondered, looking out of a window to the gaudy nobles below.

"The women? Why would you bring another one to such a night, after what the King did the last time?" Gallagher said gruffly.

"I don't think that bothers those bastards," Devlin said.

Fallon paced around the room, saying nothing. After days of Regan seemingly turning up every few turns of the hourglass with another mysterious test, they had been left alone to talk endlessly for the last couple of days about the King's plans and what he had in mind for them. They were no closer to the heart of it.

"Will you calm down and sit?" Brendan asked.

"Am I bothering you?" Fallon asked sarcastically.

"Yes, you are," Devlin said. "Go and spend some time with Kerrin. We'll send word if Regan arrives. But if he was planning to make us come along, he has left it late. We haven't seen him for days. Maybe he's forgotten about us."

Fallon glowered at them, then nodded. He felt like a bear with a sore head. The thought of going into the King's rooms filled him with fear and yet he could not sit there and wait for the maniac's next move, be a piece in whatever foul game Aidan was playing. He had danced to his mad tune for long enough. Now it was time to change the music.

He walked into his room, wondering what Kerrin would say this time. He still felt torn between wanting to kill Aidan and wanting to keep Kerrin safe. He did not know what he could say to the lad.

He found Kerrin throwing knives at a straw target, sending one after another into the red circle drawn in the center.

"What are you doing?" he asked.

"I told you, Dad. I am practicing. I have to be ready to rescue you and Mam."

"Do you now! How often are you practicing?"

"Every day. At least two turns of the hourglass," Kerrin said proudly.

"It's paying off," Fallon admitted, admiring the target. "You are a better thrower than some of the men!" He looked at his son. "And have you been doing anything else?"

"Loading the crossbow, push-ups and sit-ups, like you showed me. Every chance I get," Kerrin said. "If you get in trouble, like Mam did, I can save you. And then I can rescue Mam."

Fallon sighed. He was about to go off and risk his life once again. "Your mam wouldn't be happy with the way I'm looking after you," he admitted. "I'm sorry I haven't been the father you deserve."

"You are the one I want," Kerrin said stoutly.

"I have to go out again tonight. If they catch me I shall be lucky to get away with my life."

"But they won't catch you. You're too good."

"But if they do—"

Kerrin whirled and threw, the knife thumping into the heart of the target. "I shall get Mam back," he said fiercely.

Fallon hugged his son and felt his throat close up. "I'll do all I can to get back safely, I swear to you. I want us to be a family again more than anything I can say." He felt the new lines of muscle in his son's arms and shoulders and did not know whether to be pleased or sad. "How about we try a riddle while we wait?" he asked.

"Yes!" Kerrin cried.

Caley the dog was the first one to make it up onto the bed and Fallon finished with her on one side, Kerrin on the other.

"What sleeps all day, drinks all night, wears armor all the time but, if you stick a knife in its side, can give you treasure?" he asked.

Kerrin scratched his head. "What wears armor and gives you treasure? Is it a knight?"

"Think about it. What would drink all the time? Where would you be to keep drinking?"

Kerrin's brow, which was furrowed in concentration, smoothed over. "In the water! Is it a fish?"

"Nearly. What might give you a treasure when you open it?"

"An oyster!" Kerrin laughed.

Fallon patted his back. "That's right!"

"Tell me another!"

Fallon thought for a moment. "Why would the King make me into a hero and talk about fighting the Kottermanis in one breath, then say he is going to make a deal with them to get Mam back?"

"Is that a riddle?" Kerrin asked.

Fallon snorted a laugh. "It's one I am trying to work out. Now you think up a riddle for me while I go and try to find the answer to mine."

*

"Why do they not call their people to prayer like we do?" Feray asked.

Kemal chuckled. They were standing on the deck once more as their ship slipped into Berry's harbor. It had been a long journey and he would normally have been happy to see land, but the smell of Berry was enough to put anyone off. "They only go to church once every quarter moon and some do not do even that," he said lightly. "They are a strange people."

"Why do they not love Aroaril like we do?" she wondered.

Kemal slipped his arm around her waist. "You know, I think that is not true. They have priests and priestesses of Aroaril who can call upon the god's power and heal people. Our priests, for all the time they spend in prayer, cannot do that."

"Why should they need to? We have skilled doctors and apothecaries who can treat any with sickness."

Kemal sighed. "True, yet it is also disturbing. We look down on the Gaelish because we pray three times a day and they but once a quarter moon. And yet it is their priests who are showered with God's favor, able to save their people. So why is that? Is there something we are doing that Aroaril disapproves of?"

His wife shifted in his arms. "Well, the Gaelish do not keep slaves, as we do," she said gently.

He nodded. "That is true. But our whole society is built upon the slaves. They are the grease that keeps things moving. Without them, the desert would start to claim some of our cities and the water would begin to dry up."

"And, anyway, we do have doctors, while the Gaelish don't," she agreed, with a smile on her face.

Kemal chuckled. "That is not entirely a source of pride for us then. We have found a way to get around angering Aroaril."

"So perhaps all we need to do is pray once a quarter moon then?"

"Yes, I am sure that will do it!"

"When will you go to see their King?"

"There is no rush. He knows what my arrival means. We shall rest and then tomorrow I shall watch him bow down to me. Then my father will rejoice, for Gaelland will be ours."

She shivered.

"Are you cold?" he asked. "The sun is much cooler here. Do you need a shawl?"

"No," she said. "I just had the strangest feeling when you said that."

"Put aside all worries. We will soon be the rulers here."

CHAPTER 13

The sounds of music and laughter echoed faintly through the castle. Fallon found himself walking lightly and trying to stay close to the walls, although almost every servant in the castle would be down there, working hard and praying to Aroaril that they did nothing to offend one of the nobles. He wondered what Swane was doing and hoped he was suffering somewhere. Padraig had used his magic to send the dozen guards watching their door into a deep sleep, then to draw back the bolts from the other side.

"I can only hold so many asleep for a turn of the hourglass, so be quick," the old wizard warned.

That was ringing in Fallon's ears when the sound of footsteps on the stone flagstones made him stop and slip into a shadowed alcove, where he stayed while a guard strolled past, head down and not bothering to look what was happening around him. Fallon smiled to himself. Luckily the guards around there were not the most vigilant. But who would expect anything to happen in the heart of the castle?

Fallon waited until the footsteps had echoed away and then hurried off in the other direction. Unlike the hard leather boots that made such a noise on the stone, he was wearing soft leather slippers, which were almost silent. They were not good for running but he hoped that would not be needed this night.

The closer he came to the King's rooms, the more he thought everyone else could hear the hammering of his heart.

But there was nobody around and, a quick glance confirmed, no guards waiting outside Aidan's rooms. No doubt they were all downstairs and enjoying the night off. Or maybe ... He stopped himself thinking as he eased up to the door and tried the handle. If it was locked he had brought a set of lock picks, which Padraig had enchanted. He had never opened a door that way before but the old man swore they would be all he would need.

Yet the handle turned easily and he opened it slowly. The fire was still going, giving the room some light, but it had died down and was casting more shadows than brightness into the room. For a terrifying heartbeat, he imagined there was someone in the chair by the fire, but a second look revealed it was just a discarded robe. He stayed in the doorway for what seemed like an age as his heart slowed, then ducked into the room, shutting the door quickly but quietly, touching the wood to wood and then releasing the handle slowly and carefully.

He waited by the door, hands sweating, but no alarm sounded. He breathed a sigh of relief and then got to work, not wanting to waste any more time.

The first thing he checked was the desk. It was covered in scrolls and pieces of parchment and he glanced through them, seeing the expected tax tallies but also something a little more interesting: a note from each county on how many men they could bring in with the fyrd. It looked impressive and he knew ordinary people could fight, given some training and leadership, but he also knew few villages would have worked as hard as Baltimore. He shuddered at the thought of leading a mob of nervous farmers against a hardened Kottermani army.

He put those aside and went over to the shelves, where even more papers groaned and gathered dust. Just tackling some of the piles was daunting enough, and he worried he would put them back in the wrong order. He did not expect King Aidan to notice, for he knew he hated that sort of detail. But Regan would know every one of these scrolls as a father would his children.

Carefully he began going through them, looking for something to do with the Kottermanis. He quickly worked out that each shelf belonged to a different county and he moved on, looking for the shelf of Kottermani documents that had to be there. It was at the end and, worse, there were dozens of them. But there was nothing for it but to begin looking. His frustration rose with each scroll that he opened and hastily read. Regan's writing was small and, though it was neat, he obviously wrote for himself and not for another reader. They were lists of something but he could not work out what.

Then he started on a new pile – and paused. A name jumped out at him, or rather a series of letters. BLTM. It looked like nothing but he had seen it many times before, written to describe Baltimore. Against it were written a pair of figures. One looked suspiciously like the number of people who lived there, the other very close to the annual tax they paid to the Duke of Lunster. Looking down the rest of the list, he managed to work out many other towns and villages in Lunster, all with their population and tax take next to them. They did not seem to be in any order of size that he could see but there was one coincidence: the ones at the top of the list, including Killarney and Baltimore, had all been raided.

Fallon put that scroll aside and picked up some more. It looked like every county in Gaelland was listed there, in some strange order, with their population and taxes listed. But why should this be in the section for Kotterman?

Fallon felt paralyzed by indecision. He had not known what he would find but had hoped for some obvious letter from the Kottermani Emperor, not these lists that could mean anything and proved nothing. He replaced the lists and looked again at the wall of parchment. Would the King hide the truth there or was it somewhere else? Or had nothing been written down? He did not know what to do and hesitated, cursing himself for not thinking this through.

Then he heard voices and footsteps outside and his indecision vanished. He crossed to the door and pressed his ear up against it.

He could tell immediately it was no lone guard walking a bored circuit. There were half a dozen people out there and he forced himself to think, his heart pounding. He could not be found. But there was no other way out – or was there? Did the

King not use passageways to move swiftly between his rooms and the throne room?

He listened hard and realized he had no choice. From the sound of it, the banquet had been called short and the King was about to return. Aidan might have praised him to the crowd but that was not going to save him if he was found in the madman's chamber.

He needed some time, as much time as he could get, so he carefully clicked the lock into place. That would slow them down a little. Maybe even enough.

Leaving the door he looked around for where a hidden door might wait. The wall with the fireplace faced the outer wall, so could not be anything. The wall with the main door merely led out to the passageway again and it seemed pointless to disguise a door there. He wasted valuable time on the wall covered with cases holding the parchments but everything seemed solid so he turned his attention to the back wall, which was decorated with a series of hangings. He tested the first one carefully, seeing how it was attached and if there was anything behind it. It was firmly tied to the wall, which felt like stone.

"The King!" someone shouted outside and he abandoned his careful attempts to feel behind each hanging and instead thumped on them with his fist, feeling solid stone each time.

The sound of the door handle being rattled made him turn, a dozen excuses crowding into his head, each one as useless as the last.

"Where is the bogging key? This rutting door is locked! Get me the key or I'll have someone's head!" he heard Aidan roaring outside the door, kicking the wood and making it shiver.

Frantic steps told Fallon that someone was racing forwards in a desperate attempt to appease a furious King. Nervelessly he backed away, groping in his pouch for the bloody quarrel there. It might be time to try to use it on a second member of the royal family.

He took a deep breath, sent up a prayer to keep Bridgit safe and prepared to sell his life dearly. Then his heel hit something with the thud of wood, not the scrape of stone.

In an instant he whirled and shoved the hanging aside to reveal a door. He ripped it open and dived through, retaining the presence of mind to close it gently, even as he heard the rattle of a key in the main door lock. He shut it and held it closed, hardly daring to breathe. Behind him, steps circled down into darkness, the only light a dim line from underneath the door. Part of him was screaming to run down the stairs and get out of here but he had no idea where it led and what the stairs were like. With no light, he feared he would fall or, worse, stumble into some guardroom.

"Those bastard Kottermanis! Trust them to arrive at just the wrong moment! The night had barely started," he heard Aidan snarling. "Bring me some wine and make it fast!"

"Sire, they will not want to see you before morning. Their ship has merely arrived, that is all," Regan said reasonably.

"How can I enjoy myself knowing they are waiting to see me tomorrow?" Aidan growled. "I need a clear head for talking to their Prince Kemal. The arrogant prick. I look forward to wiping the smile off his face. He thinks us already on our knees to him. I will show him the price he will have to pay to laugh at me."

"I think we are all ready, sire. But what of Fallon and his men? Are they ready to play their part?"

Fallon leaned forwards, holding his breath as he waited to hear the answer.

"I believe so," Aidan said grudgingly. "I would have liked to make him take the final test first but he has passed everything we have set him so far. Fallon has proved he will do anything to get his men's families back. And his men have ability. Look at the way he got rid of the snatchers for us."

"Agreed, sire. I did not think such a thing was possible."

Fallon held back his anger. Did Aidan really think he would serve him faithfully? And what was this final test?

"What is your strategy, sire? Will you confront Prince Kemal immediately?"

The King paused and Fallon pressed his ear harder against the wood.

"Not on the first day. I want to hear what he offers us. Let him think he has us bent over a barrel and then the reversal will be even sweeter. I can see the look on his face now as he is forced to grovel to me!"

"Indeed, sire."

"Well, are we ready?" Aidan asked.

"I believe so, sire. But perhaps we should talk to your son, just to be sure."

"Agreed. Get him up here. And send a message to Fallon. He will need to be there tomorrow when we greet the Kottermani Prince."

Fallon would have dearly loved to stay and hear the conversation between Swane and the King. That would have told him all he needed to know. But Regan was going to arrive at Prince Cavan's rooms soon and he had to be there.

Ignoring the darkness, he began heading down the stairs, one hand pressed against the wall, toes feeling the way down each step. The stone steps curved down to the left and he prayed it would just simply end in a doorway. The little bit of light coming from underneath the King's door was gone now and he was in darkness, just the rasp of his own breathing and the patter of his slippers on the steps for company. Then his probing foot could not find the next step down. He swept his leg from left to right but could find nothing. He eased forwards, knowing that he was on flat ground again but not knowing what was around. What he would have given for the little light Padraig had created on top of his staff that time!

He swept his arms wide, eased forwards one tiny step at a time – then cursed as his knuckles found a door. He ran his hands over it until he found a handle, offered up another prayer that it was unlocked and turned it.

It moved under his hand and he blinked at the sudden light that came through the open doorway. He peered around cautiously to see he was in a small chamber that opened to the throne room. A couple of lamps threw a fitful light into the area but, after the darkness he had been through, it seemed as bright as day. He looked around carefully but, seeing nobody around, raced across the empty throne room to the door. There were surely guards around but he had to get out of the corridors. At least there he could make up some nonsense about going for a walk.

Hurriedly he opened the big doors and slipped through, hearing them close with a noise that echoed up and down the empty corridors. His worst fears were soon realized: he had barely taken a dozen steps away from the throne room when a handful of guards materialized out of a side room. He turned, ready to come up with some story, when he saw to his relief it was men he had led into Killarney.

"Captain Fallon, what are you doing here, sir?" Bran asked.

"Just out for a walk, lads," Fallon said warmly, nodding greetings to all of them. "How are you all? Drawn the night shift, eh? Can't be much fun."

"Could be worse. We could be outside," Bran said with a smile.

"Or chasing selkies and witches," Casey added.

"They're nothing to worry about," Fallon said breezily. "As long as you're with me, you'd be safe."

"Aye. But most of the time we're not with you, sir, more's the pity," Bran said softly, to general nods from the others.

"Well, we might see about changing that soon," Fallon said with a wink. He gave them a wave and hurried off, thanking Aroaril for such good luck.

"And where are you going, Fallon?" Quinn asked loudly.

Fallon cursed silently, then turned to see the officer had followed the others out and was now standing in front of Bran and the others. "I'm just on my way," he said. "Sorry I have to rush off."

"You aren't going anywhere unless you tell me how you got out of your rooms, and why the throne room door opened just now," Quinn said angrily.

Fallon smiled thinly. "But I outrank you, so I don't have to tell you anything."

Quinn took a couple of steps forwards and pointed at Fallon. "I will be making my report to the King and I will tell him of my suspicions about you. You may not answer to me but you will answer to him!"

Fallon smiled back while he cursed inwardly. His mind raced to come up with a plausible explanation but nothing was coming and, all the time, he feared that Regan was getting ever closer to delivering a message to him in a set of empty rooms.

Then his luck changed again.

"Captain Fallon is not saying anything because I asked him not to," Duchess Dina said sweetly, sweeping around a corner, dressed in full court finery, Gannon and another pair of guards at her back.

"Your grace," Quinn said, an oily expression on his face, as he bowed swiftly.

"Captain Fallon and I need to speak and I did not want the entire castle to know that. If you know what is good for you, I would suggest you don't mention it to King Aidan. He wants you to do your duty but you know how he is with those who exceed their orders."

"Indeed, your grace. Please, don't let me stop you," Quinn said hastily.

"Good work, my dear lieutenant. Keep it up. Now, please excuse us. Captain Fallon?"

"Right behind you, your grace," Fallon said, breathing a little sigh of relief.

Dina waited until they were two turns of the corridor away from Quinn before saying anything else. "What are you doing?" she hissed. "Thank Aroaril you survived the King's trap, but you cannot risk your life so recklessly."

"I was searching for the evidence you need, your grace," Fallon said instantly.

"And?"

"Nothing you could take to the other nobles," he admitted. "I did find strange lists of each county's population and tax take with other documents about Kotterman. But I could not bring it with me, for it could have been nothing."

He glanced across at the Duchess to see her face was blank and hard, her jaw set firm.

"That is a pity," she said. "But things have moved on from there. The King's revels were disturbed by news of the Kottermani fleet arriving in the harbor."

"A fleet, your grace? I thought it would be just one ship?"

"No, it is three ships. All of them bigger than anything we have in the water. No doubt they are packed with both soldiers and goods for sale. Anyway, the King has been talking of nothing else and all his usual thoughts of drunken debauchery were thrown away when he heard of their arrival," she said, talking out of the side of her mouth, her words barely reaching his ears. "It even stopped him talking about you."

"Me?"

"Nobody can talk of anything but your magnificent victory, getting rid of the last of Swane's men! Even if that filthy little toad gets free, he cannot do anything now," Dina said with satisfaction.

"To defeat so many so easily – not even Hagen could have done that. We will be glad to follow your orders," Gannon agreed, holding out his hand.

Fallon shook his hand but still felt uncomfortable. Not just at the praise for a victory that seemed, at the end, to be too easy, but because he hated the idea his old friend was the traitor who had betrayed them all to the Kottermanis.

"This puts us in a powerful position," Dina said happily. "What you have done has made yourself easily as powerful as any Duke or Earl."

"Surely not!" Fallon protested.

"True," she said. "I would say you are more powerful. For people only do things out of duty to their Lord, and because they fear being thrown off his land if they do not follow his commands. *You* they will follow out of love. I do not know why the King has chosen to make you such a hero but it has played into our hands. Together, you and I can bring down Aidan and see that Swane is punished for his foulness."

"Duchess—"

"Oh please, call me Dina when we are alone like this," she said warmly. "If we are to defy the King together, we need have no airs and graces."

"Dina," Fallon said, the word feeling strange in his mouth. "The King plans to attack the Kottermanis. He boasts of humiliating Prince Kemal and wants me to lead the people against them."

Her face creased in thought. "That could mean several things, none of them good," she said. "To threaten the Kottermanis risks everything. He would have to be very confident that we can beat them. Or he will never give up and will only yield Gaelland when the place is a smoking ruin. If he cannot have something, then nobody else can. Or it could mean he will pretend a defense and then blame it on a popular uprising, arrest the leaders and hand them over to the Kottermanis as a peace offering."

Fallon licked suddenly dry lips. "That would be me and my men," he said hoarsely.

"Exactly." Dina nodded. "So the first question must be, can we defeat the Kottermanis?"

"Yes, for now," Fallon said instantly. "Winter is coming and they will only have one chance to land an army. We cannot let them take a town like Lunster and settle in for the winter. We have to make them strike here, let them into the city and then destroy them by using the tight streets and rooftops against them."

"But they will arrive again in the spring, bringing more men next time," she said.

"Aye. But we have the whole winter to get ready for them. And, even in spring, we just need a week of storms and they will have to run for safety. They will see it will cost them too much to take us."

Dina shook her head. "We might defeat them a first time but not a second. They will bring three times as many ships and men as they need. But if we defeat them and then negotiate, we could win a much better deal for ourselves. This is what I fear Aidan plans. He will use you and then offer you to the Kottermanis to buy peace. You will be back with your families yes, but not in the way you imagined."

Fallon rubbed his sweaty hands along his tunic. "What do we do then?" he asked.

Dina smiled but there was no humor there. "We have to use a little patience. My fellow nobles are greedy men. They do not care who is ruling them, if the backside on the throne above them is Kottermani or Gaelish. But if they think they are going to lose their position, their power and their money, they will squeal like pigs in the slaughterhouse. We just need to present them with the truth and they will turn on the King. With your army and me to lead the nobles, Aidan will not stand a chance."

Fallon smiled at the thought but it faded as they rounded the corner to Cavan's rooms to find Regan arguing with Gallagher at the door.

"Ah, here is Captain Fallon now. Not asleep in his room after all," Regan said coldly.

"I am sorry, my dear Regan," Dina said instantly, her voice radiating warmth. "I begged Captain Fallon to come and tell me all about his exploits in defeating the scourge of Berry, those evil snatchers. As you know, the Captain served my husband's county all his life and he feels the old loyalty because of that. I did not want to embarrass him, or make my fellow nobles think I was somehow trying to use that old loyalty to influence such a hero, so I asked him to keep this quiet. Your guards were happy for me to take him for a quick walk."

Fallon glanced at the guards, who were very much awake and standing to attention. He knew Gallagher and Padraig had planned to wait and watch, and hoped they had woken the men up before Regan arrived. Although they had not given any such permission, the guards were all nodding their heads frantically in agreement. Fallon also noticed that even Regan was not immune to the Duchess's charm. She did everything but hold his hand and kiss his cheek.

"Please, do not punish me or Fallon for my silliness," she implored.

For a moment Regan looked cold, then he smiled. "Of course not, my dear Duchess. As always, it is a pleasure to see you."

"What did you need Fallon for?" she asked.

Regan produced a scroll. "Captain Fallon, you are required to attend the meeting with the Kottermanis tomorrow. You and four men will escort Prince Swane, as before, giving no indication he is not Prince Cavan. Afterwards, the King would speak to you."

Fallon merely nodded as he took the scroll. "I'll be there," he said.

Regan did not wait around but simply walked off, pausing only to give a little bow to the Duchess and a quick glare at the sweating guards.

"Thank you," Fallon said softly.

"It is the least I can do. He is a revolting little man but we have to step carefully around him," Dina said. "I shall see you tomorrow then. And, after you speak to the King, come speak to me."

"Yes, your grace," Fallon said, already wondering what he would hear from the Kottermanis – and what the King wanted. It seemed the more he tried to get out of the pit he was in, the deeper he fell.

*

"You need to keep Caley with you," Kerrin said firmly.

Fallon rubbed sleep out of his eyes. Darkness had been another bout with nightmares. "Thank you, son, but she is your dog. I couldn't take her away from you."

Kerrin ruffled Caley's fur. "She is not mine, she belongs to all of us, and she's here to help us," he said. "I don't need her as much any more but you do."

"I do, do I?" Fallon asked, amused.

"Well, you are the one having the bad dreams now," Kerrin pointed out. "I have talked it over with Caley and she agrees she needs to help you."

"Really? She is not just saying that because she wants to sleep on my bed?" Fallon suggested.

"Dad, this is serious. She helped me and now she wants to help you. When Grandpa did that thing to her, gave her a word to be quiet, he let her talk to me. She lets me know what she wants and she wants this. She knows you are missing Mam, just like I am, but she can also feel how upset you are over Prince Cavan."

Fallon leaned over and hugged both of them. He did not trust himself to speak. How could having a dog around wipe out the guilt he felt for killing the Prince he had sworn to protect – Gaelland's only hope?

"Please, Dad. Do this for me," Kerrin said.

Fallon looked at his son and saw the new lines of determination around his eyes and forehead. He had wanted his son to show some of that for many moons but, now it was there, he felt saddened.

"Then I will watch her, and she will watch me," he said.

"You need to shake on it," Kerrin said.

Caley obligingly held out a paw and Fallon took it, unable to keep the smile off his face. "Just as long as you don't hog the bed," he told the dog.

She chuffed at him in return.

"I have a gift for you as well," Fallon said.

"What is it?" Kerrin asked.

"It's a small crossbow, specially made for you. Brendan will make you up enough bolts so you can practice with it." He produced the bow they had taken from Guild master Allen, cleaned up and reworked by Brendan.

Kerrin ran his hands over it reverently. It was beautifully made, the actual bow some type of hardwood reinforced with horn, the stock more polished wood, with the strange grip that jutted downwards at a sharp angle. It was designed so you could curl your hand around it and still reach the trigger with your first two fingers.

Kerrin flung his arms around him and Fallon hugged his son back – only to push him away at the sound of fighting outside.

"Stay here!" he ordered Kerrin as he swept up his shillelagh. While Kerrin obeyed, Caley was at his heel, her teeth bared as he threw open the door and raced out.

But he slowed down as he saw it was a pair of his villagers wrestling with each other, rather than some sort of attack from Swane's agents.

"What in Aroaril's name are you doing?" he roared.

They appeared to be trying to choke each other, and he used his shillelagh to shove them apart, punching an end into each man's stomach, dropping them to their knees as a dozen other men came out of rooms to see what the fuss was about.

"Does someone want to tell me what is going on? Do we not have enough enemies as it is?" he spat.

"It was his fault – he was making sheep's eyes at the maid who brought breakfast," one of them gasped.

"So?"

"Well, she'd been smiling at me!"

Fallon shook his head. "I should give you both a whack over the head for stupidity! Not that it would hit anything vital, for Aroaril's sake! What has that got to do with anything?"

Gallagher cleared his throat.

"What?" Fallon turned on his friend.

"It's got nothing much to do with maids. But we're all on edge. I mean, it's been a long time since they last saw their wives," he pointed out.

"So everybody is on edge because nobody has had a shag in more than a moon?" Fallon looked up and down the corridor.

"Well, not just that," Devlin said. "But it has been a bloody long time. It makes you feel like every nerve is on a knife-edge."

"And it's not as if we know when we are going to get them back. We are just waiting around for the King to decide what to do with us," one of the men on the floor said.

Fallon tapped him on the head with his shillelagh without even looking. "We are getting closer," he said. "The Kottermani Prince is here now and we shall see him tomorrow. Then the King will finally tell us what is going on."

"But you keep saying that. And it gets bloody hard to stay patient," the other man on the floor said.

"And for some of us, it's just bloody hard all the time," Gallagher said with a wink.

Fallon could feel his own temper rising. He did feel some sympathy for them. Aroaril knew it had been a long time for him too and, while it should have been the least of his problems, it was still one that was difficult to forget about. But he was not about to admit that, not with Kerrin in earshot.

"You all need to be working harder. I'll make sure we'll be back training from tomorrow. You won't have the energy to do anything after I have finished with you," he growled.

"And how is that going to get our families back sooner?" one of the men on the floor complained.

"You just have to hold on for a few more days and all will be clear," Gallagher said.

"It's all right for you. You've got that hot priestess to keep you warm at nights," the man muttered.

"What did you say?" Gallagher growled, his long knife appearing in his hand.

Fallon cleared his throat and looked down the corridor to where Sister Rosaleen stood, her face stony.

"You should use the power of prayer to keep yourselves pure. What would your families say if they knew what was happening here?" she declared.

"An excellent idea, Sister," Fallon agreed. "I will run them around the castle until they pray for it to stop!"

*

"Highness, we have had no contact with the agents of Prince Cavan."

Kemal tugged at his beard thoughtfully. "And we have waited in the usual place?" he asked his agent, Abbas.

"Indeed, highness. But we dared not linger for fear of questions being asked. The rumors around the marketplace say there has been trouble, and fighting, in the streets. Prince Cavan is being kept safe in the castle," Abbas replied. He looked like a plump, prosperous merchant, one of dozens who kept Gaelland supplied with the latest in luxuries from across the sea. But behind the round face and twirling moustache was a mind like a steel trap.

"Do you think the King suspects his eldest son has been speaking to us?"

Abbas spread his hands wide. "Who knows what goes in the mind of that mad king, highness? But there is a new name on the streets: a captain of the Prince's guards. His praises are being sung by both the commoners and high-born and even in their churches they speak his name."

"And who is this new hero of theirs?"

"His name is Fallon, highness," Abbas said. "We have never heard of him before but then he is said to have come out of nowhere to defeat the darkness that has plagued Berry's streets."

"There is no darkness on the streets," Kemal said irritably. "We both know what is behind that."

"Apologies, highness. I was merely reporting what the people are saying. They worship this Fallon—"

"What?" Kemal sat up straighter in his chair, the repetition of the name cutting through the many thoughts crowding out his head. "Who is he?"

"Fallon? We do not know, highness. He seems to have appeared out of the backwoods of Gaelland to rise quickly. It is said he saved Prince Cavan's life."

Kemal leaned back, not even looking at Abbas. Could it be the same man? A touch of disquiet struck him. The Gaelish woman Bridgit had spoken of her husband many times and he had even laughingly suggested he would seek out the man Fallon on his return to Gaelland. But could it be the same Fallon? Perhaps it was just a coincidence. But better to be safe than sorry. "I want to know everything about this Fallon. Especially his hometown. Get it to me as fast as you can," he ordered.

Abbas bowed floridly. "Your will, highness. I shall have it for you within the day."

Kemal watched him go. As soon as the door was shut, Feray stepped out from behind a curtain, where she had been sitting silently. For all his skills, Abbas would have been uncomfortable at delivering his messages in front of her, while Kemal wanted the benefit of her good sense.

"What do you make of that?" he asked.

"I don't think you should go to meet the King," she said immediately. "Not until you know what is really going on. It feels too much like a trap. Why have Prince Cavan's agents stopped talking to ours? And this Fallon is another concern. All of a sudden this hero comes out of nowhere. Why now? You should send a message to the King, saying you are tired from your long sea voyage and cannot meet him for a few days."

"And if we are unable to discover anything by then? Will I keep on making excuses? No, this is not a negotiation. We are here to give him terms. I cannot show even the slightest weakness: King Aidan must realize he is but a King in name only and I am the real ruler here," Kemal said firmly.

"One day is nothing. At least try to make contact with Prince Cavan's agents," she urged.

He sighed. "Your words make good sense but I must ignore them for now. I must show Aidan his days on the throne are numbered."

"You should be careful, my love. Desperate men can do foolish things," she said.

Kemal smiled. "I will take more than enough guards. We planned to keep several hundred here to keep an eye on Aidan over the winter as it is. He will get a taste of our power and that will knock any thoughts of foolishness out of his head."

*

King Aidan gathered all those who would be attending the meeting with the Kottermani Prince together before they entered the throne room.

"The rules of this meeting are simple. Nobody is to say anything. I will be the only one who talks. Anyone who breaks this rule will wish they had never been born," the King declared, staring around the room carefully.

Fallon felt the burning intensity of the King's gaze, then, when it swept past him, glanced around the room. Everyone was dressed in their finest clothes, though nothing Kottermani. It was Gaelish outfits only. These were not nearly as rich and colorful but, as the King was making abundantly clear, it was them against the Kottermani.

He had received a detailed list of instructions from the chamberlain Regan and had no doubt everyone else had been given something similar. Even Swane had lost his customary mocking look, replacing it with a blank face. He locked eyes with Fallon for a long moment, before looking away slowly, as though he were not worth the effort. Fallon restrained a surge of anger only because he knew he would not have to hear the bastard's voice.

With Fallon were his friends, as well as six of the biggest villagers. All of them were dressed in mail shirts, with Prince Cavan's surcoat over the top. The mail was heavy, especially on the shoulders, and they had to wear tight leather belts to try and bring some of that weight off their shoulders and onto the backs. He also had Caley by his side, the dog unwilling to leave him.

With so much weaponry in their hands, Fallon was tempted to strike at both Aidan and Swane. But Kelty had three score of his men on the balcony above, all armed with crossbows, with another score of them lining the walls. Even the nobles wore swords, although many of them looked ridiculous as they tried to walk without being tripped up by unfamiliar scabbards.

He stood behind Swane, imagining ramming his shillelagh into the bastard's face.

All seemed ready – until Regan raced into the throne room and up to the King's side.

"Sire, Prince Kemal is on the way, but there is a problem," he said softly, his voice nevertheless carrying easily to Fallon in the silent throne room. "The Prince is bringing an army with him. The people are cheering the display but the Kottermanis are equipped for war."

"How many?" Aidan demanded.

"At least three companies, sire," Regan replied.

"Then let us go see this. All of us," Aidan commanded.

There was something of a crush at the doors, as nobles tried to be close to the King and Kelty tried to surround him with guards. Swane took his place at his father's shoulder and Brendan's bulk kept some space around them, at least.

Swiftly they all filled the battlements above the castle gate, where they could hear the approaching Kottermanis. The sound of drums and trumpets was echoed by the thump of marching feet and overlaid by cheers of the people, who were obviously enjoying the sight.

"Why has he brought so many, do you think?" Duchess Dina whispered, moving in close to Fallon's left shoulder.

Fallon was very aware of Swane just a pace away.

"He wants to make a point. I am not sure what it is though, Duchess," he said carefully.

There was no time for anything more, for the Kottermani vanguard stamped into the square facing the castle. The front rank all carried bright silken banners, while many down the sides of the column also waved colorful flags. The soldiers were in perfect formation, each rank taking a step at exactly the right moment, thumping their boots into the cobbles in perfect time.

Fallon watched them carefully, trying to see how they would fight. Their armor was far different from the gray mail he was used to seeing. Instead it seemed to be a series of overlapping leather patches, each one studded with small metal squares to make a coat that looked something like a fish's scales. The leather was brightly colored too, a mixture of red, black and blue, so each company looked the same, yet different. They carried no shields but they all had long, curved swords at their sides. Their helms were different as well, conical and rising to a point, with a metal tail of chain mail that covered their necks. None of them carried crossbows but one of the companies, the ones in black, had a quiver at their hip and over their shoulder something like a hunter's bow, the long, straight piece of wood that only a handful of Gaelish knew how to use, except the tips of these ones curved strangely. The men with their strange armor and swords held little fear for him. He was confident his crossbows would wreak havoc among them. But the strange bows were another matter. A hunter's bow could release six arrows in the time it took to reload a crossbow.

He thought about that as the procession formed up into three squares, with much banging of drums and sounding of horns. With all the flags, the colors and the noise, it looked like a festival, and the people of Berry were treating it as such, waving and dancing and cheering.

Finally, with a last flourish from the drums, the flags were dropped, the soldiers stamped to attention and the Kottermani Prince, decked out in the same armor except that the leather showing beneath his mail was gold, stepped to the front of his men.

"Prince Kemal, welcome to Berry. And please thank your men for such a wonderful display!" Aidan shouted down. "But I am afraid we do not have a room large enough to hold all of them! Perhaps you would care to enter with merely an honor guard?"

Prince Kemal signaled and half the men in red marched forwards to form a new square.

"Would you like to send the rest back to your ships? I am afraid I am unable to offer food and drink to so many," Aidan called down.

"That is not necessary. They will wait for me for as long as it takes," Kemal called back, his voice deep and his Gaelish only slightly accented.

Aidan waved. "Bastard," he said softly through his smile. "Regan, escort him in."

Fallon took one last look at the Kottermani soldiers. They all looked strong and disciplined and the thought of taking them on in a straight fight made him uneasy.

*

The throne room was crowded with men.

On one side was the Gaelish nobility, as well as Fallon and his friends, while the other side was taken up by the immaculate ranks of the Kottermani soldiers. Up close, they looked even more impressive. Fallon would have liked to inspect their armor closer still – while it could not hold out a crossbow bolt, he wondered how effective it would be against a sword. But he could see there was going to be no chance to find out. The tension in the room was thick enough to cut with a knife.

It was not helped that the balcony above was filled with Kelty's guards, but the real reason was King Aidan's obvious anger. Usually that meant something bad was about to happen and, with only a handful of guards actually on the throne room floor, the nobles clearly did not like their chances of getting out of there if Aidan did explode.

But if Prince Kemal and his Kottermani soldiers felt the same tension, they showed no sign of it. They did not even seem concerned by the number of crossbows above them. They might as well have been in their own capital.

"We welcome Prince Kemal and trust he had a good voyage," Regan announced.

To Fallon's eyes, it looked as though Aidan would have been happier if they had all drowned on the way over.

"We return the warm welcome of King Aidan," Prince Kemal said, his voice even but still reaching into every corner of the silent throne room. "It is a pleasure to see so many noble faces here to greet me."

Aidan looked, if possible, even sourer at those words.

"Thank you again, Prince Kemal. King Aidan now invites you to join him for a private discussion, with just our personal attendants," Regan said, bowing low.

Prince Kemal inclined his head in acknowledgement. "I would be pleased to do so, as long as Crown Prince Cavan is there."

The throne room went very still and Aidan's face glowed red. "This is a discussion just concerning you and me," he said through gritted teeth.

If Kemal was affected by Aidan's obvious anger, he did not reveal it. "It was not a request. It was a requirement. We do not talk unless the Crown Prince is there."

For a moment Fallon thought Aidan was going to explode with anger and he nodded to his friends, thinking this could be the time to make sure Aidan and Swane did not survive the vicious battle that surely had to erupt between the Kottermanis and Gaelish.

Then the King bottled up his anger with a visible effort. "So be it," he said. "Cavan, bring two men only."

Swane did not look around but Fallon knew it had to be himself and Brendan, or people would know something was wrong. As Swane strode after his father, Fallon nudged the big smith and they followed.

Fallon was actually delighted he would be there to hear what was happening. And he was not the only one. A hand plucked at his sleeve and Duchess Dina looked meaningfully at him, then towards the massed nobles, each of whom was looking like a small child being deprived of its favorite toy.

He nodded to show he understood she wanted him to be her eyes and ears in there, then hurried to catch up with the others.

In contrast with the packed throne room, the audience room was much quieter. A table and chairs had already been set up, with jugs of water and wine and glasses ready. But there were fewer people than chairs. Apart from the King, Swane and Kemal, there was a plump Kottermani with a huge moustache, Kelty and a hulking guard and a pair of Kottermani bodyguards.

Fallon was fascinated by them. Each was as big as Brendan and they both carried huge swords strapped to their backs. Aidan and Swane sat down on one side of the table, Kemal on the other. Regan hovered behind the King and the plump Kottermani waited behind his prince. As to Fallon, Brendan, Kelty and the other guards, they lined the wall on their respective sides of the table.

"What was the meaning of speaking to me like that in my own throne room?" Aidan growled before Regan had even had the chance to offer anyone a glass of wine.

Kemal looked almost bored in the face of Aidan's obvious anger. "I said it because I can. You no longer have the power here," he said coldly.

Aidan's meaty fist thumped onto the table. "Is that any way to start a discussion between our two countries?" he snarled.

"No," Kemal agreed. "But then this is not a discussion."

Before Aidan could say anything else, Kemal held out his hand and the plump Kottermani chamberlain placed a thick scroll into it. Kemal then rolled it across the table, where it came to rest against Aidan's fist.

"We have lived up to our part of the bargain that was struck the last time we were here," Kemal said. "Now it is time for you to live up to yours. Inside are the conditions you must comply with."

Aidan ripped open the scroll and began to read, his face losing its ruddy color almost immediately. Fallon craned his neck and leaned to his left in a vain attempt to see what was on the scroll. Whatever it was, it was having a powerful effect on the King. He would have loved to know where Aidan planned to place that on his shelves – and what the Kottermanis' part of the bargain had been. He silently urged Aidan to rage and demand answers, so more could be revealed.

Instead, the King rolled the scroll up and tapped it on the table. "All of these?" he demanded. "What if we were to—?"

Kemal held up his hand. "Again, you misunderstand me. This is what you have to do. There will be no discussion and no changes possible."

"And if I am not happy with that?"

Kemal shrugged. "That is no concern of mine. But if you attempt to break this agreement then you will face the full force of the Elephant Throne. As it is, I will stay here with nine companies of my men for the winter, to await my father's arrival in the spring. We shall then take over this castle. You and your court must move out."

Then he stood. "Send me your reply when you are ready, and specify whether you require me to also address your nobles.

But do not leave it too long. I expect a reply within two days, or I shall come back to find out why."

Aidan did not even bother standing; he just waved the scroll in Kemal's direction.

Swane, however, stood and Kemal paused for a moment.

"Crown Prince Cavan," he said. "I do not recognize your new bodyguards. Won't you introduce them?"

Fallon glanced at Aidan but the King was slumped at the table and not seeming to pay any attention to what was going on.

Swane looked at Fallon and then back to Kemal. "These are my Captain Fallon and my bodyguard Brendan," he said, his voice soft and without its usual mocking tone.

Fallon found himself almost nose to nose with Prince Kemal. He locked eyes with the man and found it strangely disconcerting. Kemal seemed to be weighing him up, as if he were some sort of prize animal. And Fallon did not like the calculating look in the Kottermani's eyes.

"Is this the Fallon we have been hearing so much about, who has inspired all Berry?" Kemal asked conversationally.

"The same," Swane confirmed.

Kemal nodded, a slight smile playing around his lips. "You seem smaller than I expected," he said. "And a little older."

Fallon bristled instantly but Kemal turned aside from him to place a hand on Swane's shoulder.

"Prince Cavan, send your agents to meet mine tomorrow, the usual place," he murmured, his words just reaching Fallon's ears.

Fallon kept his eyes on Swane, who bowed his head.

Kemal nodded, then looked at Fallon and smiled slightly, a secretive smile that Fallon did not like at all.

"Until I hear from you then, King Aidan," he said, then signaled to his bodyguards.

The Kottermanis walked out, leaving the Gaelish standing alone, except for the King, still slumped over the table.

"Sire?" Regan asked tentatively.

"Get those rutting Kottermanis out of my home before I do something I will regret!" Aidan snarled. "Go!"

Regan scuttled off and Swane cleared his throat. "Father?" he began.

"Leave me!" Aidan thundered. "Kelty, take my son back to his room. Fallon, you and your man wait there for a moment."

Fallon stopped still as Kelty waved Swane out through a different door from the one Kemal had used. He tracked Swane with his eyes but the prince did not even glance in his direction. Fallon had not found out nearly as much as he wanted from this meeting but he had at least one nugget of gold. Back when Cavan was alive, Gallagher and Devlin had followed a group of Kottermanis to a secret meeting with Swane's agents. It seemed Swane's men had been pretending to be Cavan's agents, because Cavan had certainly never asked them to do that. Now Kemal wanted to talk secretly with the man he thought was Prince Cavan. That gave Fallon an idea and maybe a way out of this trap.

Aidan waited until the door was shut before looking up at Fallon. "So Fallon, are you ready to defeat the Kottermanis for me?" he asked brutally.

Fallon squared his shoulders and hid his misgivings about what was going on. "Of course, sire," he said. "I will need more men though. And I will need to start training them again."

The King nodded slowly. "Fallon, you have earned my trust, lived up to your promises," he said. "I respect that. Trust earned is rewarded. I shall have the guards removed from your door and the locks as well. You are free to come and go as you need to get men ready to fight the Kottermanis. And there will be more men coming."

"And, sire, what about our families if we start a war with the Kottermanis?" Fallon asked, knowing it was a risk but unable to walk out of there without an answer.

Aidan paused for a moment. "They will be part of a peace treaty. I give you my word," he said.

Fallon saluted. "Thank you, sire!"

"I shall call for you again when it comes time to explain how we shall crush the Kottermanis. For now, you are dismissed, Fallon," Aidan waved his hand.

Fallon nodded to Brendan and the pair of them hurried out of the room, although he could see Brendan was not happy.

"What do you mean by agreeing with that man? Making our families part of the peace treaty? That wasn't the plan!" he growled.

"I know," Fallon said. "We have to act ourselves. Let's get everyone together and I'll explain."

CHAPTER 14

"I learned more from what the King did not say than from the things he did say," Fallon told the others, looking around Cavan's table, gathered to plan as they had many times before. But this time Duchess Dina and Gannon had joined them. He had made sure Rosaleen was sitting next to them, with instructions to reveal if they were attempting some sort of trickery. It made things feel strange, having them there, but he could feel the pressure of what he was about to do and knew he would need all the help he could get. The rest of the rooms were empty. The rest of the men were out practicing with the crossbows. The King's promise had obviously spread to Regan because both the locks and the guards were gone from their door.

"He made some sort of bargain with the Kottermanis. We don't know the details but the price of what they want is too high for the King to pay."

"Aye, you should have seen it," Brendan put in. "That Kottermani Prince treated Aidan like he was a fat dog turd – and the King just took it, as well! Let the man insult him to his face and swallowed it down like it was nothing!"

"Surely not," Rosaleen put in.

"I never thought to see the like. If anyone from Gaelland had attempted to do that, they would have been rewarded with their head decorating the castle gate," Dina declared.

"It is no tale," Fallon confirmed. "He treated Aidan like a rude child. But while the King might have taken it in the room, he is planning to give it back. He wants me to destroy the Kottermani force the Prince plans to leave here over the winter."

"And our families?" Padraig asked.

Fallon sighed. "You were right, old man. He merely told me they would be part of the peace treaty. But, after the way the Kottermani Prince treated him, I can't see them agreeing to any of his demands anyway. You should have heard it. 'This is not a negotiation,' he tells the King. 'I will take over your castle.' And all this right to his face!"

Padraig grunted. "Believe me when I say I take no pleasure in being right."

"So what was the bargain the King made with them? What did they do for him that they demand such a high price in return?" Gallagher asked.

"That is the real question," Fallon admitted. "To me, it *has* to have something to do with the families being taken. We always thought it was the Kottermanis behind that, but why would that be the result of a bargain with the King? What did he get out of it?"

"We'll probably never know. But, for Aroaril's sake, what are we going to do now?" Devlin asked.

Fallon rapped the table with his knuckles. "To business then. And we had a real stroke of luck in there. The Kottermani Prince thought that Swane was indeed Cavan. And, better yet, it seems Swane's men have been meeting with the Kottermanis in secret but claiming to be from Prince Cavan. That was the purpose of the meeting Dev and Gall discovered last moon, when they followed Kottermanis to a house in Berry."

"What?" Dina exclaimed.

Fallon smiled grimly. "Even better, the Kottermani Prince whispered to Swane that he wanted his agents to meet with the Prince's men tomorrow. There must be something he is after and we can use that to get at him. Especially as the King has decided the Kottermanis are the real threat. He told us we are free to come and go as we wish."

"Can we trust that we are not being watched?" Padraig asked.

"Not entirely. But if we are careful, we can do what we wish."

"How do you mean?" Dina asked.

Fallon pointed to Devlin and Gallagher. "Can you describe the house where you saw the Kottermanis meet with Swane's agents?"

Gallagher grunted. "Yes, but we don't want to go near it. It will be watched. It is an obvious trap."

"I wasn't thinking of going there," Fallon said, unable to keep a smile off his face. "Instead I am going to give Prince Kemal a message myself, saying the house is being watched and instead to come to the townhouse of the Duchess Dina. And there we shall strike. Once we have him, we shall force him to return our families."

He sat back and waited for their reaction.

"What if he doesn't agree to give them back? He didn't strike me as the sort of man who will back down quickly," Dina asked.

"I will make him," Fallon promised. Inside, all the frustration, the fear and the anger of the past moons were surging to a peak. If he could but get his hands on that Prince Kemal, they would all be returned.

"And what then? It doesn't change what is going on between Gaelland and the Kottermanis," Dina argued.

"Ah, but we have—" Brendan began, only for Fallon to kick him under the table. He needed Dina's help but he did not want her to know about their plan to sail away to Cavan's island. She thought they would aid her grab for power, and he reckoned she needed that incentive to help.

"Once we have their Prince, the Kottermanis will be forced to negotiate," Fallon said. "And part of the deal could be a change of ruler for Gaelland, to someone better suited." He nodded to Dina. "And, of course, we would make the return of the Duke of Lunster, your husband, part of any deal."

Dina said nothing for a long time, then she nodded. "Yes, I can see how that could work," she said quietly.

"So you will stand with us?" Fallon pressed.

"Of course," she assured him.

He flicked a glance across to Rosaleen, who nodded fractionally.

"But Fallon, why are you sending them the message? Wouldn't it be safer to send someone else?" Gallagher asked.

"Prince Kemal knows me now; he met me with Cavan and thinks I am trusted. If we are to trick him, we have to do it this way,"

Fallon insisted. *Besides, I want another chance to meet this Prince. There is something between us, something I do not like.*

"Then this is how we shall do it," he said, slapping his hand on the table.

*

"And what did the Gaelish King say?" Feray asked.

Kemal smiled lazily. "He looked as though he had swallowed a wasp! But he has no option but to agree to everything. He cannot stand against us and he must know that, for all his arrogance."

"I still think it is a risk, threatening a man like that. From all I have read on him, and everything you say, he is not a rational man. He has been pushed into a corner and could do anything to get out. Men like that are truly dangerous because they do not care who or what they hurt. Do you think he cares how many of his people he sacrifices to preserve himself? Look at the insane bargain he negotiated with you last time!"

Kemal tugged at his beard, before realizing what he was doing and stopping. "That reminds me," he said absently. "Ali and his men have not made contact with us. Abbas must find out what is going on with them. I wanted them to report in detail what they have been doing at King Aidan's bidding. The story of Fallon freeing the streets from darkness. I hope that does not refer to Ali and his men. Or Aidan will have more to answer for."

"My love, please listen to me. I have a bad feeling about this place. It stinks, and not just of unwashed Gaelish. There is something rotten here – I don't think your father knows what he is getting by trying to bring Gaelland into the empire."

He shook his head. "It does not matter what you or I think. My father has decreed it, so shall it be. And Aidan will do his best to slip out of the bargain he has made but he will find it impossible to move with us inside his castle."

To his surprise, she did not take that as the end of the discussion and looked ready to keep arguing, except there was a knock on the door. He gestured towards the curtain that covered the stern window and she darted there, vanishing from sight in an instant.

"Enter," he commanded.

One of his guard captains hurried in and bowed low.

"Highness, there is a Gaelish man here. He says his name is Captain Fallon and he has a message for your ears only. He refuses to speak to anyone else."

Kemal was instantly intrigued, on several levels. "Is he armed?"

"With a sword and some sort of strange staff."

Kemal nodded absently, his mind racing. "Bring him in, but make sure he has given up all his weapons. And have two of your best men escort him in, ones who speak no Gaelish."

"Your will, highness." The captain bowed and hurried away.

"Is this the Fallon you were telling me about?" Feray asked.

"Indeed. And now he comes with a message. Presumably it is from his Prince Cavan. Perhaps he warns us of the King's intention. In any case, it should be fascinating," Kemal said with relish.

He only had a short wait before a pair of hulking warriors escorted Fallon in.

If Fallon were worried by the armed men on either side of him, he was not showing it. Instead he looked straight at Kemal, his face devoid of emotion.

"He merely has a scroll, which he refuses to give to anyone but yourself, highness," one of the guards rumbled.

Kemal nodded his understanding and then switched to Gaelish. "Welcome, Captain Fallon, to my ship. What brings you here?" he asked pleasantly.

"I bring a message from Prince Cavan. He could trust nobody else. The former meeting place is watched and the King's eyes are everywhere. Prince Cavan's words will explain all," Fallon said, holding out the scroll in his left hand.

"Bring it to me," Kemal ordered one of his guards in Kottermani.

He kept an eye on Fallon as the guardsman took the scroll but Fallon did not move a muscle. Once he had it in his hands, Kemal broke the wax seal and read swiftly. The words merely echoed what Fallon had already said, begged forgiveness for changing things but pleaded for the Prince to come in person to the house of the Duchess Dina, who would not be suspected by the King.

"Why does he ask for me in person? All this time, we have only exchanged words through agents," Kemal said, tapping the scroll into his free hand.

"The stakes are much higher now," Fallon said. "Prince Cavan wants to speak to you himself. He does not want any confusion or any chance of misunderstanding. If his words speak directly into your ears and yours into his, then he can be sure you are in agreement."

"Why has he not spoken to us before now?" Kemal demanded.

Fallon smiled briefly. "King Aidan is not a foolish man, for all his shouting and screaming. He misses little and he has plans you want to hear. Plans that would identify Prince Cavan as a traitor if they were ever read by the King's men, so he cannot risk writing anything. Plans that only Prince Cavan can fully reveal to you, for he is the only one the King has told. That is why I am here now. He dare not trust anyone else. And I hardly need remind you of the stakes involved."

Kemal believed the words but he knew what Feray would be thinking, and he had her voice in his head, saying that he should not take any risks.

"You must know something though. If you really are as trusted as the King says," he challenged.

Fallon nodded. "I don't know how he plans to do this but the King has already asked me to kill your men."

"What?" Kemal snarled, coming out of his seat.

Instantly his guards, neither of whom spoke Gaelish, drew their swords and pointed them at Fallon's throat.

"Stand down!" Kemal told them irritably and the guards reluctantly sheathed their blades. "Why you?" he asked Fallon.

At this, Fallon smiled a little and shrugged. "In truth, my Lord Prince, I do not know. One day I was a mere village sergeant and now the King wants me to lead his soldiers."

"How would you go about defeating my men?" Kemal demanded.

Fallon chuckled. "My Lord Prince, I do not know yet. I have not seen them in action and I fear the bows they use, which I have not seen before."

"You are right to fear them," Kemal said with satisfaction.

"But there are thousands of us and your men have to eat, and sleep," Fallon went on.

Kemal was about to reply angrily when he saw the truth in those words. "So your Prince has an answer to this?"

"He does. If you are willing to hear it from his lips."

Kemal could almost hear his wife's voice from behind the curtains, warning him not to accept this. "Why can the Prince Cavan not come here?"

Fallon smiled. "The King's men watch this ship all the time. I can slip through the crowds unseen; he cannot. For him to turn up here would be as good as saying he intends to betray his father. And how would that help both your causes?"

Kemal acknowledged the point but he still had to convince his wife. "How will we find this house?"

"I can guide you there," Fallon offered.

Kemal gestured to the two big guards. "And you know they will be either side of you, ready to take action if you play us false?"

"I would expect nothing else," Fallon said. "Bring as many guards as you feel comfortable with. The Duchess's house is large indeed."

"And what if I was to order you taken below, where my men would make sure you told the truth?"

"Torture me? You would not discover anything new and you would lose the chance to have the Prince as an ally," Fallon said evenly.

Kemal stroked his beard to make it look like he was considering things but, in truth, he had made his decision already. "Then it is agreed. I shall bring a company of guards."

"Perhaps a few less might be better, if we are to avoid the attention of the King's men," Fallon suggested.

Kemal nodded agreement. "Before you go, Fallon, which village were you from?" he asked.

"Baltimore, my Lord Prince."

Again Kemal made a show of pretending to think. "Did I not hear of some disasters befalling that part of Gaelland? Something about being attacked by strange creatures – called selkies or something? Was your family safe?"

For the first time he saw a reaction from Fallon.

"The families were all taken from that village, including my wife," he said, his voice rough where before it had been smooth.

"That must be terrible. You must be devastated," Kemal said, watching the man's face carefully.

"Prince Cavan has promised to do whatever it takes to get our families back," Fallon said.

Kemal nodded. "So your loyalty is tied to a promise to see your wife again?"

"It is. I would do anything for that day," Fallon said, his voice throbbing with intensity.

Kemal smiled gently. "That is good to know. My men will return you to the docks. I shall see you tomorrow and we shall meet your master then."

Fallon bowed and left, escorted out by the guards. Again, the door had not even closed before Feray was out.

"You should take the man below and put him to the knives, to make sure this is not a trap," she said.

Kemal shook his head. "The man is right. Were I to do that, then I will have lost the Prince and the best hope of this new province of ours coming peacefully into the empire. Fallon is right – King Aidan will do something foolish. Cavan is a reasonable man and the people love him: all our agents say that is so. With him on the throne, Gaelland will submit peacefully. We should have dealt with him from the start, rather than striking that ridiculous bargain with the King. No, I have to do this. Besides, Fallon will be beside me tomorrow. If it is a trap, he knows he will die first."

Feray sighed. "I hope you are right. But why did you have to tease the man like that? You know where his wife is; you have spoken with her many times."

Kemal grinned. "I wanted to see if he was the man Bridgit said he was. I don't think so. That man would have already sailed for Kotterman."

"And died hopelessly. While this one is beloved by both the King and the Crown Prince."

Kemal walked over to embrace his wife. "If anything happened to you, I would move the moon and all the stars to get you back again.

Besides, I learned a valuable thing. If we want him to betray his people, we have but to offer him Bridgit. You heard him, he would do anything to get her back."

Feray shivered. "Do not talk of such things," she said. "It makes me feel as if a ghost has walked over my grave."

"That is the Gaelish weather giving you the shivers," he said with a laugh. "Come, let me warm you up."

The door was unlocked and he took a moment to fix that. He did not worry about his men but his children were another matter.

*

"He has our families," Fallon declared.

"Are you sure? Did he actually say that?" Devlin demanded.

"He didn't admit anything. But there was something about the way he acted. As if he knew a secret joke about me," Fallon said. "It was all I could do not to punch the bastard and choke the truth out of him."

"What did he say?" Devlin asked.

"He was rabbiting on about selkies," Fallon said. "But I could tell he was holding something back. It was almost as if he knew Bridgit. Maybe he was even the one to sack Baltimore."

"Bastard," Gallagher said.

"And he had his wife there. He hid her behind a curtain but I could see two cups on the table, and every time I said something, the curtain shivered. He must think we are fools."

"But is he going for our trap?" Dina asked.

"He swallowed it easily enough. We guessed right. I gave him a little bit of truth and he gobbled it up, like a fish with the bait."

"Obviously he didn't try to get some more out of you with a pair of hot irons then," Brendan said.

"He threatened it, but I talked him out of it easily enough. I'll lead him right into the trap. Once we have him, we'll take him to the old Moneylenders' Guildhouse. We won't be disturbed there and if he starts screaming, there'll be nobody to hear him."

CHAPTER 15

"We have a few problems," Ahearn reported.

"Only a few? Then things are improving," Bridgit said drily, deftly grabbing young Will as he tried to run off and getting him to sit down in front of them.

Ahearn leaned down and patted Will absentmindedly on the head. "Sean and Seamus are long gone, but their cousins, the two big ones from Killarney, are causing trouble."

"How? They are slaves, for Aroaril's sake!"

"I hear things from other gangs of slaves. They are muttering about escape and how they will be the leaders once the chains are gone. Not only are they going to be a handful if we do get out but it can only be a matter of time before the guards overhear them."

Bridgit was about to swear, then she remembered Will was sitting there with them.

"I'll have to find a way to go and talk to them," she said heavily. "I owe them for what happened to their cousins. And they are the biggest men we have here. They will be invaluable in an escape."

"They might be more trouble than they are worth," Ahearn said warningly. "Maybe it would be better to have a word with Gokmen and see them staked out as well. What they are saying about you is not pretty. They blame you for what happened to their cousins and they want revenge."

"I can understand why they hate me. But they must see that destroying our chances of escape only hurts them. I will give them a chance first," she said. "But if they are risking all our lives, I will sacrifice them to Gokmen."

Ahearn looked doubtful. "I respect you, Bridgit, but I fear you are letting your guilt cloud your judgment. They are a pair of right bastards and we'd be better off without them."

She shook her head. "I have to give them a chance. Please, trust me on this."

He smiled. "I can't stop now!"

*

The big cousins did not have any children in the house nor indeed family in Kotterman. Bridgit reflected it would be a foolish woman indeed who married a large drunk who liked to use his fists. Of course, if they were rich or even good providers then she knew it could be another matter entirely but their laziness ensured they lacked even that attraction. But, like all the Gaelish, they were brought to the house and given a turn of the hourglass there. The last time they had spent it sleeping and stealing food but this time Bridgit was watching for them.

"What do you want?" Blaine, the shorter and fatter of the two demanded.

"A word with you," Bridgit said firmly.

"You've got some nerve, woman!" Carrick, the taller one, spat. "You had Sean and Seamus killed. Do you know what it was like, having to see them slowly die out in the sun? They could not even scream by the end. Why would we want to talk to you?"

"Because your lives depend on it," she said flatly.

"Are you threatening us?" Blaine growled.

"No, just showing you the truth," she said simply. "Do you want to return home or be a slave here for the rest of your life?"

They glowered at her but did not answer.

"I think I know which one it is," she said. "But, if you talk too much, they will know what we are about to do. At least one of the guards on your gang speaks Gaelish."

"It's all very well for you to sit here in comfort, out of the sun, with plenty of food and talk of escape. But the quarter moons slip past and nothing is happening, while we sweat in the fields," Carrick grumbled. "Do you even have a plan for getting us out?"

"That I do."

"Well, what is it, woman?"

Bridgit crossed her arms. "My name is Bridgit. You would do well to remember it. Keep your gobs shut for the next quarter moon and I will tell you. Keep flapping your lips and I'll be talking to the slave master instead. We are getting out of here, with or without you. Now I have sworn to the shades of Sean and Seamus that I will get you home and I would like to keep my promise. It is up to you."

"Why, you little bitch! How about we—?" Blaine snarled and started forwards, only for Carrick to hold him back.

"Easy there," he rumbled. "Attack her and we'll never escape."

Blaine subsided angrily and Carrick looked sharply at Bridgit. "We want out. But you had better know what you are doing."

"I do. I will get us all home," she promised. "I have a plan."

"Then we have a deal," Carrick agreed and, after a few moments and a swift blow to the ribs, his brother nodded acknowledgement.

None of them offered to shake hands.

Bridgit walked away, leaving them to lie down in the shade, and breathed a sigh of relief. It was just as Fallon had said. They were cowards and, when pushed hard enough, they would always give in.

*

"How could you let us take that shite from her?" Blaine demanded.

"For once in your life, keep your gob shut," Carrick told him. "We swallow shit now, because there's nothing else for it. She has the Kottermanis in her back pocket. But we are getting out of here, one way or another. And then we will be getting revenge on her. She had Sean and Seamus tortured to death. She deserves nothing less."

"That day will be worth waiting for."

CHAPTER 16

Fallon waited for Prince Kemal. Kemal's guards were already there, dressed in dark cloaks. They had different armor from the day before. It was still a series of overlapping layers of leather stitched to a leather jerkin but it lacked the metal reinforcement. It would offer protection but Fallon could see it would be far lighter and obviously not shine so much and attract attention. He also took the opportunity to look at their swords. They were long and curved, with a strange hilt. Where Gaelish swords had quillons to protect the hand if an opponent's blade slid down it, these ones lacked any crosspiece. The hilt got slimmer the closer it came to the blade, so that the hand would be flat with the blade, but that was it. That grip looked like it would be better suited for slashing and cutting than defending yourself. It was an interesting thought to keep.

Kemal had organized about 30 guards, all of them older men, all with scars and the faces that said they had fought before. Fallon had a pair of throwing knives on his belt and three of them in the small of his back, where they were hidden by the cloak he wore, while his shillelagh was in its usual place on his back as well. But his most dangerous weapon was the knowledge of the streets where he would lead them. It was the same maze where he had faced the gang of child snatchers and he had walked it endlessly yesterday evening with Caley, until it was fixed in his mind. Even Regan no longer seemed to care where they were going or what they were doing, which was fine by Fallon. He had made a point of telling the

Chamberlain that they were planning a mock battle in the streets, in case word got back to Regan, but even that had not seemed to interest the man.

The way Kemal had behaved the day before had him burning with anger. He had been tricked and lied to and betrayed and deceived at every turn. Today that would end. Kemal knew what was going on and he would drag the truth out of him and then use the bastard to get back Bridgit and the others.

He allowed himself to imagine what that reunion would be like for a moment. His friends probably thought that without Kerrin and him, she would surely have fallen to pieces. Fallon feared that could be true but he held firm to the belief that she could find the strength within her that he knew was there. The way she had hidden Kerrin and then taken on the Kottermanis made him hope that was true.

"Are you ready?" Kemal asked and Fallon glanced up from his daydream to see the Prince join them. He was wearing drab clothes and a simple cloak. At his signal, most of the guards slipped off the ship in twos and threes, wandering away into the crowds.

"They will meet us soon. I have another party of men, with one dressed in my gold armor, leaving now," Kemal said, pointing to where that group was attracting plenty of interest leaving another Kottermani ship further down the docks. "So now, with the interest of the King's men focused on them, we shall go."

They slipped over the side and hurried into the crowd, Kemal's giant bodyguards falling into place behind them, another pair of hulking men moving in front.

The Prince said nothing as they made their way through the crowded docks, although Fallon noted dark-cloaked guards shadowed them, joining up once he led them down a side road and into quieter streets.

"Tell me something about Prince Cavan," Kemal invited.

Fallon had been braced for a sneering comment and this one caught him off guard. It took him a few steps to recover himself and push away the pain that simple question triggered. "He is the hope of Gaelland. He wants to make his people's lives better, not treat them like animals, the way his father does. He wants to break the power of the nobles and the Guilds," he said. "Everyone who meets him loves him, and feels he will be this country's savior."

"Excellent," Kemal said. "When he speaks, the people will listen. That is what we need. But you must have got to know him well, as his captain of guards."

"Aye," Fallon said, his throat suddenly swollen again with grief. *If only Cavan were really here, we would have some hope for the country ...*

"That is good. I can see the emotion you feel for your Prince. It makes me think he is a man I can trust. Unlike his father!"

Fallon grunted agreement. "This way," he said.

"When Prince Cavan is on the throne, things will be better for your country. I promise you that," Kemal said. "It may be a hard thing for you to accept but it is what I hold to. Life will be better for the ordinary people."

Fallon was only dimly listening now, for this was the start of the maze and it would not do to miss a turn. This route was not going to end at Duchess Dina's house. But, if he lost his way, it was going to end badly.

He led them left and right, feeling a surge of relief as the little items they had placed to help him remember the way came into view. His memory held true and he threw in an extra flourish, leading them a quick circle before heading back to the planned route.

There was nobody around now and the Kottermanis were in a tight group, the only sound the echo of their boots on the cobbles.

"This place is like a rabbit's warren. How can you be sure of your way?" Kemal whispered.

"Practice," Fallon said. He did not want to say any more, for they were very close now and adrenalin was coursing through his body.

"I could almost swear I saw that alley earlier," Kemal said. "Are you sure this is the way?"

"Oh yes," Fallon promised, glancing up and seeing a figure move into place on the rooftops above. The entrance to another alley was just ahead and he did not want Kemal's men to take a look inside there, so he stopped.

"How long to the meeting place?" Kemal demanded.

"We are here," Fallon said.

Kemal turned in surprise. "But this is a filthy alley! Explain yourself!" he exclaimed.

Fallon slipped his hands into the small of his back, looking as though he was stretching but really drawing a pair of throwing knives.

"Now!" he roared.

*

"Do we loose?" Craddock asked, as the Kottermani guards filled the alley below.

"Not until we get the word," Gallagher hissed back. He had two score of the villagers up on the rooftops, half on each side of the alleyway, just waiting for the chance to let loose on the Kottermanis below. Fallon was out ahead of them, a cluster of guards around him and the Prince. He was probably five yards ahead of the main body of guards, which looked too close from up there but should prove enough – if everything worked as it was supposed to. And Gallagher desperately wanted it to go as planned. Not just because that was his friend down there, risking his life. With everyone but him suffering the loss of their family, he felt he could not pursue Sister Rosaleen at a time like this. Yet she filled his thoughts, the way his wife once had, before she had been stolen away by childbirth. He wanted nothing more than to declare what he felt and hope she returned his feelings – yet he could not. Not until the families were home. That was the deal he had made with himself and he was not about to break his word.

"Something's happening!" Craddock hissed, breaking his thoughts.

Sure enough, the Kottermani Prince was berating Fallon, whose hands were at the small of his back.

"Ready!" Gallagher said softly, bringing his crossbow up to his shoulder. His words raced down the line of villagers, while the men over the other side of the rooftops saw their friends prepare to loose and raised their own weapons.

"Now!" Fallon shouted, his voice booming up.

"Loose!" Gallagher shouted in response, aiming at the main group of guards. He knew he was not half the shot with the weapon that Fallon was but, although they were three stories up, the alleyway was so tight and the guards so many that it was impossible to miss.

The first release was out of time, Gallagher's side going first and then the men on the opposite side loosing a few heartbeats later as they realized.

But the effect was dramatic. A dozen guards fell instantly, spitted by the quarrels that sank into their leather armor and the flesh beyond as if the protection was not even there.

Kottermanis shouted and screamed and dragged themselves along the cobbles, or clutched at shafts that were buried deeply in their bodies. Instantly the cobbles were awash with blood and brains.

The survivors drew swords and hugged the alley walls, keeping low and trying to make themselves into small targets. But with villagers on either side reloading as fast as they could and picking off the guards one by one, there was nowhere to shelter.

One brave guard rose up and raced at Fallon's back, sword raised high.

Gallagher cursed, trying to get a quarrel into his bow fast enough to get it around and spit the man but saw he wasn't going to be in time. Then Craddock spotted the danger too, swiveled and put a bolt through the guard's head, exploding the skull and spraying the wall with blood and brains and chunks of skull.

"As good as Fallon!" Gallagher shouted.

Craddock grinned at him as he hauled back on the crossbow string. "I was aiming for his back!" he confessed.

Gallagher laughed and looked for a new target. The guards were pinned down. Now it was down to Fallon.

"Stay alive, my friend," Gallagher whispered.

*

As the two big bodyguards turned towards Fallon, he brought out his hands. The pair of them were so close that, even had he not spent many turns of the hourglass practicing this with Kerrin, he would have found it hard to miss. He flicked one out to his right in a back-handed throw that sent the solid metal knife whistling into the Kottermani's throat. The man stopped instantly, blood pulsing out from around the wound and he sank to his knees, fighting desperately for breath past the steel blocking his windpipe. Moving smoothly but not rushing, Fallon transferred the second knife from left hand to right, then pivoted on his heel and whipped the second knife out in an overhand throw that slammed the blade into the right eye socket of the man on his left. This guard went down like a sack of potatoes and Fallon reached down to his belt again for the two knives at his sides, even as the Kottermanis at the front turned around, the choking noises of the dying guard alerting them to the fact something was wrong. Fallon did not even look behind him, for those guards were not his problem.

Again he threw overhand at a guard and watched the knife punch home in another throat. The guard reached up and tore the blade out of his flesh, but the spray of blood that followed painted the wall as he staggered backwards. As the fourth man moved in, Fallon changed knives and threw again – but this time the guard was ready for it and ducked, the blade slicing a wound across his cheek but failing to strike home.

Cursing, Fallon forgot about the knives and whipped out his shillelagh.

"Stop! What are you doing?" Kemal yelled at him but Fallon ignored him, focusing only on the angry guard, blood streaming down his face and long sword held back over his shoulder.

Behind him he could hear shouts and screams as his men loosed crossbows into Kemal's guards, but he had not time to worry about that.

As he had predicted when he first saw the sword on the guards' belts, the Kottermani swung it extravagantly, a swing that would have cut him in half had it landed. But he merely stepped back and let it slice harmlessly through the air.

Kemal shouted something at the guard in Kottermani. Fallon had no idea whether he was encouraging the man or suggesting he surrender, for the guard seemed to hesitate over his next strike.

Fallon had no intention of giving him the chance to make a decision and jumped forwards, the shillelagh punching out.

Again, as he had hoped, the long Kottermani sword was too slow to come around in a block and the end of the shillelagh thumped into the guard's nose, snapping his head back. Shifting his hands along the staff easily, Fallon slammed the end into the man's jaw, sending him flying backwards to crash into the wall and slide down into a limp heap.

A hand grabbed at Fallon's leg and he looked down to see the first guard, blood still dribbling out from around the knife deep in his throat, trying to hold him back and say something to his prince at the same time, although there was no way he could get any words past the length of steel in his neck. Fallon reached down and ripped his throwing knife free, hot crimson spraying over his hands. The guard let go.

Again Kemal shouted, pointing behind Fallon, and Fallon spun to see what was happening there.

As he had planned, and hoped, the villagers on the rooftops were pouring down a vicious storm of crossbow bolts into the narrow alley. The Kottermani armor was no use against the heavy bolts, and they slammed into heads, chests, bellies and legs. The guards were trying to find shelter against the walls of the alley but there were villagers on both sides setting up a deadly crossfire, and there was nothing to hide in or behind – except the bodies of the already dead men.

Half were down already and the rest were cowering but, at the cry from their Prince, they rose to their feet and raced forwards, heedless of the quarrels still flying down.

Fallon did not wait for them to arrive. He jumped at the furious Prince Kemal, shillelagh at the ready.

Kemal had a dagger at his belt but he did not try to draw it, instead he turned and ran, calling his guards on.

Fallon felt himself grin in triumph, although guessed it must look terrifying with the blood of the dying guards painted across his face. He tore after the fleeing Prince, with a dozen guards in hot pursuit of him. "Devlin!" he shouted.

*

"Should we go now?" Brendan hissed anxiously as the first shouts and screams echoed down the alley to where they were hiding.

"Stay! Stick to the plan!" Devlin snapped. "Fallon has to get out of there before we go in."

"But what if he—?"

"He knew the risks. And the plan was his," Devlin said harshly.

They still waited and Devlin could feel his resolve slipping away. Was that Fallon screaming his last out there? He was about to order the men out when the Kottermani Prince raced past. A few heartbeats later, Fallon tore after him in pursuit.

"Now!" Devlin shouted.

At his signal, a score of villagers in armor and carrying shields and swords stormed out, Brendan at their head with his fearsome hammer over one shoulder. Behind them came Devlin and a dozen more, all of these with crossbows.

Brendan's men formed a two-deep line of shields. The Kottermani guards raced onwards, shouting their defiance, then Devlin and his men leveled their crossbows and loosed as one, the devastating volley turning the charge into a bloody horror.

"Get them!" Brendan roared, bursting through his own line of shields. The villagers hesitated for a moment, then Devlin dropped his crossbow and drew his sword.

"Follow him, you fools!" he howled and charged after the big smith.

Brendan reached the first guard before Devlin's blade had even cleared its scabbard but the smith did not need any help. The hammer swung down, brushing aside a feeble sword parry and slammed into the side of the guard's neck with a hideous crackle of breaking bones, throwing the man through the air.

With the backswing, Brendan came down low, crunching out the next guard's legs and turning them into bloody fragments, the skin pierced in a dozen places by shards of bone.

Then Devlin was beside him and, an instant later, the rest of the villagers. Devlin ducked a sword blow and rammed his blade back. The guard's leather armor resisted for a moment but Brendan had put a wicked edge on all their blades and it punched through the leather and deep into the flesh. Devlin felt the steel grate on bone and twisted the blade viciously, provoking a howl of agony from the guard and a fine spray of arterial blood that painted his arm and face. He ripped the sword out and the Kottermani reeled away and fell.

After what Brendan had done, Devlin expected the last handful of guards to surrender, or run. But they still pressed on, seemingly determined to get to their Prince. Villagers surrounded each one, ganging up in twos and threes. A villager would block a blow with his shield then the next one would strike. Devlin hacked his blade into the back of a guard's neck as he hammered at a villager's shield, making the man fall in an instant, his head barely hanging on by a chunk of skin and cartilage at the front.

Brendan swung his hammer up in a huge blow, striking the last guard's lower body and lifting him three feet into the air with the impact, his ribs turned into a scatter of splinters.

"Is that it?" Devlin demanded, wiping his face clear of blood and looking around.

The alleyway looked like a slaughterhouse and stank like one, with blood, brains and shit covering the cobbles. Kottermani guards rolled in their own gore, moaning and screaming, or begging in their own language. None was able to get to his feet.

"Where's Fallon?" Brendan asked, painted in blood, his hammer encrusted with pieces of men.

"We'd better find out," Devlin said. "Follow me!"

*

Fallon sprinted after the fleeing Prince Kemal. He trusted his friends to finish off the guards but all that was for naught if their prize got away.

Kemal was showing quite a turn of pace and Fallon pounded doggedly after him, not narrowing the gap but at least keeping him only about five yards in front. Surely the man must tire soon – he had been stuck on a ship for half a moon or more!

But Kemal's pace showed no sign of slacking – until a pair of villagers stepped out from a doorway to bar the way, shields held low.

Fallon expected the man to back off but Kemal actually increased his pace. Fallon stretched his own legs, suddenly fearful his careful plan was about to come apart.

*

Kemal ran easily, conserving his energy. Surely a trap prepared so cunningly as this one would not allow him to simply run away. But he had to get away – and then come back with a full army. These Gaelish would not get away with treachery, he vowed. He could not allow the sacrifice of so many good men to be in vain.

He was tempted to turn and take Fallon with him, at least, but the man held that strange staff and had shown uncanny skill with it earlier. If Kemal had his sword he would have been delighted to match his skills against the traitorous Gaelish but, with only a knife, he dared not risk it.

Then he saw the final act of the trap, as a pair of men stepped out of a doorway, barring his escape and blocking the way ahead with shields. Kemal did not hesitate. Behind him were only dead and dying guards and more pursuers. Ahead was the only way out, but maybe they would not expect him to realize that. He lengthened his stride, angling towards the one on his left, hauling out his dagger in the same move.

That man ducked down beneath his shield, bracing himself for the impact. But Kemal did not try to ram his shoulder into the wooden shield. Instead he jumped high, using his left foot to drive the shield down and push the man away and also catapult himself back across to the right. The man there tried to turn and get his shield around but Kemal was coming from the wrong direction and he was able to drive the knife over the top of the shield and into the man's chest. The mail stopped the blade from driving in but the force of the blow sent the man staggering backwards, gasping for breath.

Kemal let go of his blunted knife as he landed and kicked out again, his foot slamming into the shield of the first man, sending him staggering back across the alleyway and opening the way to freedom.

With a flare of triumph he turned to run, ready to sprint for freedom, when something smashed into his legs.

*

Fallon watched in horror as Kemal took apart his two men and gave himself a chance to escape. He was still a couple of paces away but did not like his chances of running down the fleet-footed Prince. Maybe ten years back but certainly not now. So he drew back his arm and hurled his shillelagh, sending it spinning towards the Prince's legs. The staff hit Kemal's right leg and the Prince stumbled, keeping his feet only with the greatest of efforts. By the time he straightened, Fallon was upon him.

In desperation, Kemal grabbed the shillelagh and swung it like a club, trying to knock Fallon out. But Fallon simply ducked beneath it, letting the staff pass over his head, then drove forwards, ramming his shoulder into the Prince's midriff. The breath whooshed out of Kemal and he folded over Fallon's shoulder as Fallon kept his legs pumping, picking Kemal up and back-slamming him to the cobbles, driving him down with the full force of his weight.

Already winded, the Prince could only manage a strangled croak as he hit the ground and lay there dazed.

Fallon glanced over his shoulder, breathing heavily, to see his villagers regain their feet, one of them cursing loudly at the huge bruise he had growing under his dented mail.

"Come on, let's get him away from here before someone comes looking," Fallon puffed.

He felt exhausted and his legs were trembling in the aftermath of the fight but he was filled with exultation all the same. All the answers he needed were right there, lying at his feet.

CHAPTER 17

Bridgit stepped back into the shadows, drawing the hood further down over her face, so that there would be no pale reflection of skin in the light of the torches the guards carried.

She had slipped out of the house at prayers again, using the same trick and rope as before. This time, however, she was not trying to memorize a map and find the places where her people were being held. She had accepted that was too difficult and the risks of capture too high.

The plan of freeing one group at a time had been thrown away. Instead her idea was to gather everyone together and then get out. That was hard enough but would only get worse once they were in the city. Tonight she was looking around the harbor and particularly the defenses it held. After seeing the huge bows on the land wall of Adana that had put paid to the foolish plans for escape of Sean and Seamus – and, also, their lives – she had been worrying about the same thing happening as they tried to sail out of Adana. Those giant crossbows could cause havoc on a ship packed with people.

The docks were quiet at this time of night but she was wary, all the same. The last time she had roamed through the city, she had been forced to kill a man. Once again she had a sharpened chair leg as her only weapon and she prayed she would not need to use it.

The patrol walked past, two men talking to each other and not even looking around. She waited until the sound of their footfalls had echoed into silence and then slipped out of her hiding place behind a pile of barrels and headed along the harbor wall that stretched out into the sea and protected the ships in the port. This was in two parts, a short, straight arm and a long, curved one that would force all ships to turn almost on themselves as they passed it to reach the open sea. It reminded her, with a pang, of the shingle hook at Baltimore. But, as she feared, this wall had several of those giant bows, all placed where they could strike at ships coming in or out of the port. There were no guards actually manning the bows and she was able to go right up to one, see the huge bolts, each one the size of a spear, which sat in barrels, ready to be loaded in. The weapon was unloaded but it would be a slow sail out of the harbor and guards would have more than enough time to reach these weapons.

At the far end of the harbor wall, lights burned and men were moving around. But they were more than a hundred paces away and she took the time to feel and test the cord that had to be drawn back. It felt like animal hair, twisted and spun to form a cord as thick as her wrist. It would take a fearful effort to draw that back but, without it, the weapon was useless. On the night they left, a group would have to come along here and cut these cords while the children were loaded on board. Or it could still end in disaster.

A loud laugh from further up the wall made her hurry back, keeping to the shadows. The good news was, there were few guards around the ships and certainly not enough to stop a band of desperate Gaelish. Now she just had to get back safely and get the rest of her plan moving.

After endless nights of talking, she had decided the way to do it was to gather everyone together a few nights before the adults were to be sold off as slaves. She would ask Gokmen for a farewell celebration, and hope the slave master would give them that, at least.

She knew there would be plenty of guards, but they had the sleeping potions to slow them down, while the slings were prepared and ready, as were a few other surprises.

It would be risky but there was no other way she could see.

"What about the lads? Fallon, Brendan and the others?" Nola had asked.

"We cannot wait. If they arrive in time then we shall be ready but I will not stake everything on that."

"You realize this could end with us all dead, or wishing to be dead?" Riona asked gently.

"Better dead than slaves," Bridgit said. "But I still think we can do it. Trust me."

"We will," the others agreed.

CHAPTER 18

Feray was watching her sons practice their swordwork, trying to keep the fond smile off her face, when there was a huge commotion on the deck. She tried to watch it out of the corner of her eye while keeping her face impassive, but could feel her control crack when Abbas approached, his face gray. She sent her sons below with a quick word.

"Highness, we have terrible news. Your husband and our Lord was attacked and captured by the Gaelish. His surviving guards told me they walked into a trap and were attacked from above."

"How do they know he was captured?" Feray asked immediately, proud of the way her voice was steady, despite the turmoil inside. She had known this was a trap! There had been something about that Captain Fallon that she instinctively distrusted ...

"Several of them saw him being dragged away by the Gaelish. What are your orders?"

Feray thought swiftly. "So they wanted him alive. That means they have a purpose in mind for him. Arm every guard we have and get them ready, swordsmen on the dock, archers on the ships to give them cover."

"Highness, should we not flee and alert the Emperor? We can return with an army and demand his return or slaughter every one of them," Abbas suggested.

Feray shook her head fiercely. "No," she said. "We do not return without word from him. They want something from him.

Once we know what that is, we shall decide whether to pay the price, go and get him, or go and get the army."

"Pay the price, highness?"

She glared at him. "We will give them any amount of gold they want. For we can come and take it back in the spring. But getting him back is the only thing of importance. Or do you want to be the one to tell the Emperor how we left his son in the hands of the Gaelish and fled to save our own skins?"

"I shall prepare the guards, highness," Abbas agreed. "Do I send someone to talk to King Aidan and demand my Lord's return?"

"No. We say nothing and ask for nothing. Act as if nothing has happened. See to the wounded and hide the dead."

"Your will, highness."

"And send out every agent you have. Let them know I will give them their own weight in gold for news of my husband," she told him.

*

Fallon watched as the hood was yanked off Kemal's head and the bruised Kottermani Prince blinked at the sudden light. He let the Prince look around him, see the chair he was tied to was the only furniture in the room and that it sat in the middle of a huge dried bloodstain. He grudgingly admired the way the Prince did not react, merely staring at Fallon coldly.

They had hooded him and then hustled him through the backstreets until they reached the Moneylenders' Guildhouse. Most of the villagers had returned to the castle then, leaving just Fallon, his friends and a handful of others to keep a careful watch. Fallon had thought about killing the wounded Kottermani guards so no word could reach Kemal's people of what had happened, but instead loaded the dead and wounded into a cart and let the dazed survivors take them back to the docks. There was plenty of evidence of a fight but nothing for Regan's agents to take back to the King.

Fallon said nothing, wanting Kemal to feel the tension and fear in the air, let his imagination go to work. After all, he had been a pampered Prince, used to his every whim being obeyed. This had to be making him uncomfortable. Finally, Kemal could obviously take it no longer.

"Release me, return me to my people immediately and I might be able to overlook what you have done," he snarled.

Fallon smiled down at the Prince, his arms folded across his chest. There was no humor there. Even if this was not the man who had attacked Baltimore and carried off their families, he could get them back.

"Don't you realize what you have done?" Kemal demanded. "You think this is clever? I know what you have done. Your Prince Cavan has been pretending to be with me against his father when all the time he was with King Aidan. But fooling my agents will avail you all nothing. Harm me and my father will take this country apart. We would have left one of your own to sit on the throne and able to make some decisions. But that chance is slipping away with every heartbeat you hold me."

"You are the one who has been fooled, Prince Kemal," Fallon said harshly. "Your men have been meeting with the agents of Prince Swane. Prince Cavan is dead."

"You fool," Kemal scoffed. "I know the evidence of my own eyes. I embraced Prince Cavan not a day ago!"

"That was Swane, made to look like his brother with the use of dark magic," Fallon said. "You think you are in control of Gaelland? It is an even bigger trap than the one you walked in to with me."

Kemal just sneered at him. "Why should I believe anything you say? You have already proved yourself to be a liar."

Fallon whistled and Caley trotted in.

"This is my dog and she hates Kottermanis. You can be her dinner if you like," he told Kemal.

The Prince watched Caley warily as the dog caught the smell of him and began to growl, thick, vicious noises that made the hair on the back of the neck rise.

"She'll tear you into pieces," Fallon warned. "Tell us what we want to know and I'll call her off."

"Let her do her worst," Kemal invited.

Fallon brought Caley a little closer but she would not go within three paces of the Kottermani. She hated him, that was plain enough from the way she was growling and snarling, her lips pulled back and teeth bared. But she seemed to be more concerned with protecting Fallon from Kemal than attacking the Kottermani. He sighed. It had been worth a try but she was not the sort of dog to attack anyone.

"I wouldn't want her to be poisoned by you," he told the Prince, then whistled Caley away. She slunk out, still growling.

"What now? What else do you plan to threaten me with?" Kemal asked mockingly.

Fallon pulled the bloody quarrel out of his pouch and held it before Kemal's wary eyes. "This is the quarrel I used to kill Prince Cavan," he said. "He was not only my Prince, he was a friend. I was tricked into killing him by King Aidan. Now I pretend to stand by Swane in public because King Aidan has promised he will get our families back from you if we do."

Fallon caught the flicker in Kemal's eyes and stepped in closer, holding the bloody quarrel under Kemal's nose.

You know all about that, don't you?" he said softly. "You were the one who led the attack on Baltimore and carried our families away. Why?"

Kemal looked up at him, eyes glittering hatred. "This is about your families? You fools, they will die in the most terrible ways imaginable after what you have done to me." He raised his voice, shouting his next words out. "You think to use me as some counter to get their release? You will only buy their deaths. Rather than release your families in exchange for me, they will start to skin your children alive until you beg to hand me back. How long do you think you can defy my father while the screams of your sons and daughters echo in your ears? I will make sure they work on Bridgit first. Her screams will haunt you for the rest of—"

That was enough. Fallon felt a red mist descend.

He stepped in and began to punch Kemal, snapping the Kottermani's head back with the force of the first blow and whipping the blows in from left and right, rocking the Prince from side to side, trying to beat away his own anger and the Prince's arrogance.

"Stop it! You'll bloody kill him!" Gallagher and Devlin grabbed him and dragged him backwards.

Fallon fought them for a few heartbeats then subsided, wincing at the pain in his knuckles. But, looking at Kemal, that was nothing.

The Prince raised his head slowly, blood oozing from his nose, from his mashed lip and from a cut on his left cheekbone. His left eye was already swelling shut and he spat again, a frothy mixture of blood that landed on the floor.

"Get control of yourself, you stupid bogger! We need him alive!" Devlin growled.

"You heard the bastard! He took our families! And he bloody knows Bridgit's name! How does he know her name, eh? He must have seen her. Maybe he's already killed her!" Fallon snarled.

"They have to be still alive, or why else is he threatening us?" Gallagher said reasonably.

Kemal looked up at them. "Anything you do to me will be paid back on them tenfold," he said, his voice thick with blood. "I will tell you nothing. Release me."

"He won't talk, eh? We'll see about that," Fallon said. "Brendan, give me your hammer."

Kemal watched them as Fallon brandished the huge hammer, its head still stained black with blood, and brown with other things none of them wanted to think about.

"You are just trying to scare me. You dare not hit me with that, for it would kill me," Kemal said.

"He's right," Gallagher whispered. "He's not like those thieves that you bluffed back in Killarney to get answers for Prince Cavan."

"Who says I'm bluffing?" Fallon asked. "Brendan, take off his left boot."

The big smith looked at him uncertainly but Fallon gave him a shove. "This is for Nola and the kids. This is for all of them," he hissed.

Brendan pulled off Kemal's boot and held the Prince's leg immobile, foot on the floor, just as he would do a horse for shoeing.

"Are you going to talk to us about our families?" Fallon demanded.

"Go and rut yourself," Kemal told him furiously.

Fallon hefted the hammer and swung it down, crushing Kemal's two smallest toes.

The Prince screamed and writhed on the chair, his eyes bulging and the tendons on his neck and arms standing out. A thin line of bloody spittle dribbled from his lips, landing in his lap. His chest heaved as if he had run for miles and it looked like he had bitten into his already cut lip.

"Are you ready to talk now?" Fallon asked him.

He locked eyes with Kemal and was astonished to see no give there. The Prince's eyes were full of pain but all that was behind there was anger.

"I will give you nothing!" he spat.

Fallon swung the hammer up and crushed the other three toes.

Kemal shrieked with pain, eyes screwed shut, breathing in short, hard gasps. Fallon glanced down to see the ruin of the man's toes. They were a mixture of blood and flesh, the skin torn away and pieces of bone poking through.

"Ready to talk now?" Fallon repeated.

Kemal's eyes snapped open and Fallon saw the fury and the agony in there.

"I will never talk to you, bastard! Nothing will stop me peeling the skin from your body. The rest of you, I shall let you live if you deliver both Fallon and me to my ship right now!"

Fallon tapped Brendan on the shoulder. "Get his other boot off," he said.

Kemal tried to fight but, tied to his chair and in the face of Brendan's huge strength, he stood no chance. "Do what you want to me. I will give you nothing!" he raged.

"Let's see if you still talk like that when we break every finger you have and cut off your prick one inch at a time," Fallon said coldly.

"My answer will still be the same." Kemal spat a mixture of blood onto Fallon's boots.

"And I will keep hurting you until it changes!" Fallon swung the hammer up again. Kemal glared at him, nothing but anger and hatred in his gaze. Not even a scrap of fear.

Fallon let the hammer drop and stepped away.

"Maybe we can use Sister Rosaleen, the way she got into the mind of Swane's servant that time?" Gallagher suggested.

Fallon shook his head. "That's only half the battle. We don't just need what's in his head. We have to break him, so he does whatever we want and gives our families back." *Besides*, he added silently, *I want the pleasure of making him pay for what he did to us.* "We will need Rosaleen to prove he is telling the truth later, but we need something else first. Get Padraig."

They waited while the old wizard was fetched from below, watching the Prince battle the agony of his crushed toes. Fallon felt nothing.

"Aroaril, what are you doing?" Padraig gasped. "Have you gone mad?"

"I am mad," Fallon agreed. "And sick to death of every bastard tricking me and using me."

"What do you want? I will not use magic to hurt this man," Padraig warned.

"Even though he took Bridgit? Even though he threatened to make her screams last an eternity?"

"Even so." Padraig drew himself up. "I will not sink to that."

Fallon grabbed his shoulder. "Well, I will. But luckily we need you to do something different," he said. "He wants to use our families against us. Well, let us use his family against him. Let's see if he is so brave if his wife and children are here, hot irons close to their eyes."

Kemal's head snapped up and his voice took on a ragged edge. "I invite you to try," he said. "You will never get close to them. They will kill you."

"Fallon, we are going to steal his wife and children?" Padraig asked in horror.

"This is the only way!" Fallon told them. "We won't hurt them unless he makes us. It is all down to him." Yet even as he said that, he knew it was a lie. He would break this man and nothing was going to stop him. "I know what to do. They will be watching the land. We shall come from the sea. And this is how we shall do it—"

"Taking women and children from their beds? Fallon, are you truly sure of this?" Gallagher asked.

Fallon looked around at his friends. "They took our families that way. And with his wife and any children in our hands, he will do what we say." He glared around at them and, one by one, they all nodded.

"Let's do this," Devlin said.

"Aye. I am in," Brendan agreed.

They looked back at Kemal, who sneered at them. "You will be begging for mercy soon enough. Mercy that will not come if you go near my ships!" he cried.

"Let's do it," Gallagher said.

CHAPTER 19

Feray looked out over the darkened bay and shivered. It was not a cold night but there was a definite chill in the air, a reminder that this was not home. The window for sailing was closing. Soon the winter storms would begin and trap them there.

There had been no message from either the Gaelish nor Abbas's agents during that long day. The worried spymaster had his men scouring the city, but there was no word and no clue what had happened to her husband.

"Perhaps we should ask King Aidan for help, highness," he had suggested. "I have thrown a golden net over the city. Most of these Gaelish would sell their own mothers for a silver piece and I have offered them gold. If they cannot find him for us, then we need to search elsewhere."

Feray had held on to her temper only with the greatest of difficulty. The thought of asking the Gaelish for help made her skin crawl. The only compensation was the thought that whatever price they wanted for Kemal's return, he would avenge.

"We have to give it until noon tomorrow," she said finally. "If you have been unable to find him by then, I shall see King Aidan personally. I want you there to write down exactly the price they demand for his return, so we know what to punish them with in the spring."

She let the frightened Abbas go and keep his agents searching through the night while she walked around the deck. Their sons were asleep in the cabin and she would have to join them soon, even though she knew she could not relax, not with Kemal lost somewhere in the city.

It was strange, she had never thought she could feel so much for her husband of a political marriage. Her family had once ruled a huge land to the south of Kotterman. Hundreds of summers ago they had their own empire but then had come the Kotterman army and they had been swallowed up into the greater empire. But her people still respected her family and the Kottermanis were shrewd enough to allow them to always be visible in the ruling of their old lands, even if they lacked true power. Her marriage to the Crown Prince had been both to cement the ties and stamp out the first flickering of a rebellion among her people.

She had expected to be a political pawn only but soon found that Kemal was not like that. Two of his brothers would have been but he was different. First she liked him, then she loved him and now she could not imagine life without him.

"Where are you, my love?" she asked aloud.

She glanced over to the docks, where companies of angry men stood, swords drawn and arrows in hand. Anyone who tried to come near the ships was going to get a very unfriendly greeting. The guards were in an ugly mood, after more than a score had been killed and another dozen terribly wounded. The two doctors they had brought with them had been working all day to try and save at least some of them.

Satisfied that nothing needed her attention, she stepped down into the ship and their quiet cabin, which took up the whole stern of the ship. The boys would be asleep but she had to see them, kiss their brows and gather some strength from them. Perhaps a cup of herbal tisane might allow her to close her eyes for a turn or two of the hourglass.

Wearily she pushed open the cabin door – and then her eyes snapped fully open as she realized there were two men standing there. One of them the traitor Fallon, who had lured her husband into a trap!

She opened her mouth to shout for the guards but he held his finger to his lips and pointed to where the other man stood, a vicious-looking knife held above her sleeping sons.

"What do you want?" she asked, her voice a croak.

*

Fallon smiled wolfishly as he saw Kemal's wife shut the door behind her and sag back against it, her eyes betraying her terror for her children.

So far it had been easy enough. Thanks to Gallagher, they had stolen a small boat and paddled carefully across the water from the docks to where the Kottermani ships were moored. Approaching from the darkness, the guards on the docks had not been able to see them, for their eyes were dazzled by the light of dozens of torches and lanterns. Gallagher brought them in under the stern of Kemal's ship and held them there while Padraig went to work. Thanks to him, they were able to throw a rope upwards that fastened itself to the window and, again thanks to him, Fallon and Gallagher had climbed up it with little more difficulty than going up a set of stairs. Without the magic, it would have been too difficult to even dream of attempting.

Once inside, it was just a case of waiting for the Prince's wife to come back in. Finding the two sleeping children there had been a bonus.

"Your husband sends his greetings. He has sent us to get you," Fallon said gently. "We were betrayed and attacked this morning but your husband and I escaped. He is in hiding." He had no idea if she would believe these lies but it was worth a try. If she thought they were being taken for torture, she might just shout for help and take her chances.

"Then why the knife near my children? Why threaten them?" she demanded, her voice low.

"We cannot risk being heard. Come with us and all will become clear," he said.

"Why did you not bring my husband with you instead?" she challenged.

Fallon did not like the way her voice was getting louder. They needed to be away from here unseen.

"He is in the boat below. Come and see," he said, stepping away from the window and signaling for Gallagher to put away his fearsome knife.

Kemal's wife looked suspicious but he held out his hands, palm out, and she edged across to the window, leaning out to see the boat below. Instantly he struck her on the temple, pitching her unconscious to the padded seat along the rear wall of the cabin.

"Aroaril! Fallon! Hitting a woman?" Gallagher gasped.

"That is the least I will do," Fallon said. "Come, help me get them down."

*

Kemal tried to block out the pain from his crushed toes. He did not even want to look at them, for they made him feel weak. The throbbing agony was making him feel sick but he would have sooner given up his birthright than let those bastards know how he was hurting. He almost welcomed the pain from his crushed lips and bruised face, for it distracted him from his foot. He balanced on his heel, not wanting to put any pressure on what was left of his toes, and every movement sent a fresh surge of agony through him.

He clung to one thought, that he would escape and get his revenge. They would not defeat him. Whatever happened, he would never bow to this peasant. As long as he held true to that, they could not truly hurt him. Pain would pass. Injuries would heal. And he would have proved he was stronger than them.

The door banged open and he looked up swiftly, squinting through his bruised eyes to see Fallon stride in. The man walked over and squatted down right in front, his face calm.

"You have my wife. You have my friends' wives and children. I tried to give you the chance to help us, to admit your mistake and give them back. But you refused to talk. So I have decided to give you a taste of what we have been going through. We now have your wife and children," he said, his voice low and reasonable.

"You are lying!" Kemal sneered. "They are too well protected. If you think I am going to fall for that, then you are an even bigger fool—"

He felt his voice trail away as two of the Gaelish, the giant and the short one, dragged Feray and his sons Asil and Orhan into the room. His heart seemed to stop, then leap up into his throat and, instantly, the pain in his foot and face was nothing to worry about. Not compared to seeing his family in the brutal hands of these Gaelish. His careful control, which he had tried to maintain even in the face of torture and humiliation, dissolved in an instant.

"Let them go! They had nothing to do with this! I swear, if you harm them, I will make you suffer in ways you have never imagined!" he screamed at them, tearing at his bonds with all his strength, heedless of the surges of agony this flared in his foot.

Then Fallon leaned in and slapped his face, nothing hard, more of a tap, something you might give to a child who was lost in a screaming tantrum. It silenced him, as well. "Now you know how we feel. Now you know what we have been going through since you took our families from us," the man said. "You know what I am prepared to do. Don't make me hurt them. Tell us what you know."

Kemal looked over at his family, seeing their terror and feeling it strike deeper than the hammer blows that had smashed his toes. But he was the Crown Prince, the heir to the Elephant Throne. This man was a peasant and, besides, his friends and accomplices were visibly unhappy at using a woman and children. They would not go through with this. It was all a bluff. He just had to hold his nerve and Fallon would give up. Victory would be his and then he could make promises, win their freedom – and take a terrible revenge. He just had to hold strong.

He looked at Fallon and shook his head.

"Do you think this is a game?" Fallon snarled at him, then whirled and strode over the room, where he grabbed Feray by the arm and dragged her over, forcing her down to her knees so she was staring right into Kemal's eyes, the pair of them close enough to touch if their arms had not been bound.

"No. Let her go," Kemal ordered, trying to put all the power and authority he had into his voice. "You do not want to do this. Once you harm her, you have crossed the line. There is no way back from there." He locked eyes with Fallon. Everyone else melted away, even Feray and the boys. It was now a test of wills between them. And his will would prove the greater.

*

Fallon saw the iron in Kemal's eyes but the man's words were soft as wool. Crossed a line? He had killed Prince Cavan! He was so far over the line, he could no longer see it. Only one thing mattered: getting Bridgit and the other families back. Even if he were as good as destroyed himself, at least his friends and his son would have some chance of rebuilding lives they could bear to live, of healing from the terror of the past moons. This arrogant bastard was all that stood in the way of that, and nothing was going to stop Fallon now. The prick was bluffing. That might work with his wife there, who looked like she would back him up. But not his sons.

Fallon dragged the wife away, then he grabbed the younger of the two boys and hauled him over, putting him right in front of Kemal's face. He locked eyes with the Prince, seeing the man not even look at his obviously terrified boy, instead keeping up his defiant stare.

The Prince said something to his son in Kottermani, probably some sort of encouragement, so Fallon backhanded Kemal, rocking his head away, and then drew his knife and held it in front of the boy's eyes, letting him see the edge, roughened from all the sharpening. The boy's eyes grew wider than ever and his breath was coming in short, urgent gasps.

"What if I take his eyes?" Fallon asked conversationally, putting the tip of the knife right in front of the boy's nose, making it seem massive.

The young boy, who was surely not more than six summers, was shaking like a leaf in a winter breeze and then his bladder let go with fear, urine puddling around his feet and some of it washing towards Kemal's wrecked foot, making the Prince move his injured toes away with a hiss of pain.

"Or what if I take his fingers? Has he learned to feed himself yet?" Fallon asked harshly. He grabbed the back of the boy's head and made him look down at his father's broken toes. "Or maybe I'll smash his feet, like yours?"

He reached down and began to tug on the boy's damp boot, making the child scream with fear, his terror muffled by the gag.

Behind him Fallon could hear the mother going crazy, but she could do nothing against Brendan's huge strength. She was shrieking something in Kottermani and Kemal said something back, his voice cracking a little.

Yet he refused to give, still meeting Fallon's eyes.

"Don't make me do this." Fallon glared at him.

"You won't do it. You can't!" Kemal spat back, eyes burning with hatred.

Fallon snarled at him and showed him the knife. He bent and sliced it lightly across Kemal's lower leg, drawing a thin stripe of blood and pooling it on the blade.

"This is your doing, not mine," he hissed, then placed the blade on the boy's cheek.

The lad shrieked at the touch and Fallon turned the blade, not cutting the skin but allowing some of Kemal's blood, which was already on the blade, to ooze down.

He looked into Kemal's eyes as he did so, saw the defiance begin to crack. The boy was sobbing helplessly now, his brother and mother screaming.

"I will peel him and you will watch. I will skin him and wear him like a cloak!" Fallon spat.

His eyes were locked to Kemal's and, although the man was trying to hold strong, Fallon could see it was breaking apart. He took all his own anger and guilt and agony and fear and let them show through in his eyes.

"You know I will do it," he whispered.

For a moment more Kemal held him, then his eyes snapped shut and a tear trickled down his face. "What do you want?" he asked, his voice a broken murmur.

CHAPTER 20

"Here, have a drink." Fallon poured a cup of water for Kemal. "You have a lot of talking to do."

"Where is my family?" Kemal demanded. "How are they?"

"They are safe. My wife's father, Padraig, is with them now. He is a wizard and is no doubt showing them small magic tricks and telling them jokes, which, if they could understand them, would horrify them," Fallon said briskly.

"I need to see them."

Fallon shook his head. "It doesn't work like that. They stay somewhere safe. You talk, or they come back and start screaming."

He watched Kemal sip the water and nodded to his friends. The moment Kemal had cracked, he had hustled the wife and sons out of the room, where the youngest boy could be cleaned up and the three of them could recover a little. Sister Rosaleen had arrived, Gallagher having gone to get her while Fallon used Kemal's wife and children to make the Prince talk.

The Sister had been horrified at what they had done but she still used her powers to heal the Prince's wounds. She was now sitting beside Kemal, her face like stone. Fallon had braved her disapproval and insisted she be there. He did not trust the Prince not to try and offer a few lies mixed in with the truth. And he'd had enough of being lied to. More than enough.

"Sister Rosaleen will be testing the words you say. Aroaril has given her the power to tell truth from lies. Lie to us and your family will be punished, understand?" he growled at the Prince.

"I understand," Kemal said softly, glancing at Rosaleen.

She held Kemal's hand, which seemed to calm him, and had her eyes closed, mouthing silent prayers. Fallon was not sure what Rosaleen was praying for and suspected it might be punishment for him. But he was past caring about that. She would prove he had made Kemal bend to his will and then he could be sure the man would return their families. The truth was no longer enough, but it was a good start.

"Our families. Are they safe?"

Kemal nodded. "They are all together. They are at the port of Adana, the closest point to Gaelland. Your wife, Bridgit, is their leader."

Fallon felt his head whip around so fast to look at Rosaleen that he swore his neck cracked.

She nodded that this was the truth, her eyes wide.

"How is Bridgit the leader?" Fallon demanded.

"She fought back at your village, took down three of my men, and then began demanding better food and conditions for the children. It just grew from there and now she is their leader. She and two of her friends are caring for all the children while the rest of the adults work, preparing for their new lives as slaves."

"What were the friends' names?" Devlin demanded.

Kemal screwed up his eyes as he thought. "I can't remember," he admitted. "But they were chosen by Bridgit."

"Nola and Riona. It has to be," Fallon said.

Devlin leaned back in his chair, staring at the roof and blinking his eyes rapidly, while Brendan buried his face in his hands.

"They are safe and will be well treated. They are valuable property," Kemal said.

"And they are all still in this Adana?"

"For now. They will be sold off around the Empire within a moon."

"Well, that is not quite true. But more of that later. Now tell me why you attacked our villages?" Fallon asked.

He watched the Prince slowly sip his water, wincing as the cup touched his lips until he realized there was no pain from them since

Rosaleen had healed up his facial injuries too. Fallon sighed and ostentatiously laid his knife on the table.

"It was a bargain with your King Aidan," Kemal said tiredly.

Fallon leaned back in his chair and glanced over at Rosaleen. She nodded slightly and he pressed on.

"Tell us all," he said.

"For years we have traded with your people, but always we have been looking you over, seeing if Gaelland was worth bringing into the Empire. My father, the Emperor and ruler of the Elephant Throne, decreed it was time for Gaelland to become part of the Kotterman Empire. He sent me, his first-born son, along with a small fleet of ships, to inform King Aidan of what was to happen and to allow him to prepare his people. We did not want to bring you into the Empire with blood and fire. We would be far happier for Gaelland to see the benefit of being part of the Kotterman Empire."

"And it would mean you wouldn't need to waste money rebuilding all the towns you sacked," Fallon said sourly.

"Of course," Kemal nodded. "King Aidan was at first furious, then he calmed down and accepted what I said. He offered us a bargain. We would help him prepare his country to become part of the Empire and he would ensure a peaceful handover. For the first year or two I would be here, to make sure all was going smoothly but, after that, he would merely have a Kottermani administrator at his shoulder, checking and approving all his decisions and ensuring the correct tax was being paid back to the Elephant Throne. A few companies of Kotterman soldiers would be stationed here but, once he had proved he would obey all orders from Kotterman, things would go on much like before."

"What was the bargain? How would you prepare us for being Kottermani?" Fallon demanded.

Kemal took another mouthful of water. He looked tired beyond belief but his voice was still strong.

"King Aidan said he needed to use his people's superstitions to terrify them and make them think that becoming Kottermani was the only way to keep their children safe. At his request, we gave him three of my father's bodyguards, men trained to run and fight and hide and move silently. Aidan was going to use his wizard, Finbar, to help them kidnap children and hide them away, tell his people it was witches taking them."

"And really they would be shipped to Kotterman as slaves?" Fallon asked.

"No! What would we want with children? They cannot work properly. They would be worth little to us." Kemal sniffed. "No, the King would hide them and then release them when the country came into the Empire, thereby proving that the people were now safe."

Fallon looked immediately at Rosaleen, who slowly nodded. He glanced around at his friends, who were also looking horrified. There were many more questions here. Why had King Aidan wanted them to kill the snatchers if they were really working for him? It was obvious this was not all the answers: just half of the story. But the really important part was still to come.

"And our villages?"

"King Aidan wanted to use another legend, of seals that come to life as men and commit evil in the night. Your selkies."

"Aye," Gallagher said sourly.

"Yes. He gave us a local guide and we used our ships and men trained to dive deep under the water to catch lobsters, to instead take men from fishing boats and isolated houses. And from two villages, one small and one large," Kemal said.

"And were these people to be returned after we all became Kottermani?" Fallon interrupted.

Kemal shook his head. "No, these were slaves. The first payment of many to come from Gaelland and a deposit on the bargain we made with Aidan, a sign of his good faith."

"They were our wives and children, you bastard!" Brendan thundered.

Kemal faced him without flinching but Rosaleen put up her hand in warning and the big smith subsided.

"The local guide? Who was he?" Fallon demanded, thinking of his friend Hagen and wondering if the man really had been a traitor, or just forced to do it by the King – and then killed by the King's agents for his trouble.

"I do not know. We would meet them by boat every other day and be given a list of places to avoid and others to hit."

Fallon clenched his fists together. He dearly wanted to know the truth about their betrayal. "And the Duke of Lunster? Was he taken because he disagreed with the King?" he asked, remembering Hagen's warning to him.

Kemal looked down at the table. "I never attacked the Duke of Lunster's ship. The biggest boat we took was a fishing boat with ten men inside," he said.

Fallon shook his head. "I thought we understood this was only to be the truth?" he snarled. "We saw the Duke's ship! It sailed right into our village, stripped empty, and there was a bloodstained quarrel in the Duke's cabin, one just like the ones you used when you attacked our village!"

"As I told your wife when she asked me, I don't know what you are talking about. If the Duke's ship was attacked, it was nothing to do with us. In any case, we were only taking those approved by the King," Kemal replied, his voice rising in pitch.

Fallon did not need to glance at Rosaleen to confirm what he already suspected – Kemal was speaking the truth.

"When did you speak to Bridgit about this?" he demanded.

Kemal shrugged. "She was asking about the Duke, wanting to know why he was not the leader of your captured people. I gave her the same message. The King demanded that his nobles be protected. None of them were to be harmed. We were to only take ordinary people as our slaves."

Fallon rubbed his hands through his hair. Something at the back of his mind was jumping up and down, demanding attention. He closed his eyes for a moment and then it swam out of the depths of his memory. The scroll he had found in the King's rooms, detailing the counties and villages and their tax take, filed in the Kotterman section, now made sense.

"What else?" he asked harshly.

"On my return, I was to deliver the final terms to the King, which I have done. He has until the next full moon to formally sign over Gaelland to the Kotterman Empire, or we shall come back in the spring and take it by force. I am just awaiting his acceptance."

"And the meetings with Prince Swane? Or men you thought to be from Cavan?"

Kemal shrugged. "We always knew that King Aidan was going to be a difficult man to deal with. He is unpredictable and volatile. It seemed sensible to meet his heir. We were approached by men claiming to be from Prince Cavan and, after a series of meetings, we had agreed to him replacing King Aidan. That was what was in my scroll to your King. The final act of his reign is for him to hand over his power to Prince Cavan and to take no further part in running Gaelland. It was the justification I used for taking your country. At least it would be governed properly and we would see that life improved for the ordinary people."

"Really?" Gallagher asked sarcastically.

Kemal glanced over at him. "We have done this before, many times. Once we tried to keep the nobles happy but we learned that was not enough. The nobles can do nothing without the support of the people. Get the people happy and they will cause no trouble."

"Except for the ones taken away for slavery," Devlin added.

"What, do you think we are going to keep storming into homes and tearing people away? That was for your King's benefit, not ours. We would take slaves, yes, but they would be criminals. The penalty for thievery, rape and murder would not be flogging or hanging but the rest of your life as a slave far from home. Everything we have learned about Gaelland told me there would easily be two hundred men a year to fill that quota."

Fallon had to agree that was probably true. He looked across at his friends. Something had changed in the last few questions. It was as if Kemal were getting his confidence back.

"So what was Swane's plan? Why have these meetings?" Fallon asked.

Brendan, Gallagher and Devlin all took turns to shrug.

"It may have been to test us. Or me," Kemal said into the silence.

"What do you mean?"

"When I first came here, it was to promise King Aidan that he could remain as a figurehead. Orders from Kotterman would have to be obeyed, of course, but he would still have power, and respect. Soon after that, the request to meet with Cavan – sorry,

Swane's men – came to my agents. Perhaps King Aidan was seeing whether we could be trusted."

"He's certainly playing his own game," Fallon said sourly. "We killed your father's three men and rescued many of the people they were holding. But there has been no sign of the lost children they took."

"You killed them?" Kemal asked. "I did not think they would die easily. They had been trained since birth in fighting."

"And they had been given some magical help as well," Devlin added.

"Now the King has many questions to answer," Fallon said, then pointed at the Kottermani. "But first we need to deal with you. This is what is going to happen. You are going to return to your ships, this night, and sail for Kotterman. Once there, you will release our families, put them on a ship and return them to us. And to make sure you do, your wife and sons will be staying here with us. If our families do not return, or if you come back with an army, I can promise you that your family will die in ways that will give you nightmares for the rest of your life. But, as soon as our families are back, your wife and children will go back on the same ship, unharmed."

"How can I believe you will just let them go? How do I know you will not try to keep using them against me, or give them to the King to do the same?" Kemal demanded.

Fallon held out his hand to Sister Rosaleen. "I will swear on anything you want," he said. "All we want is our families back. Once we get them, then your family is no longer needed."

"But you will be trying to live in a country ruled by me, or at least by my father. Surely you must be thinking that I will return to take a terrible revenge on you, unless you have something to use against me," Kemal insisted.

Fallon stared at him. "We shall not be staying here. As soon as our families are back, we shall be leaving here and sailing away from Gaelland and away from you. We will live free, and live in peace, and you will never find us."

Kemal looked thoughtful. "I wish I could believe you," he said. "But this is my family's lives we are talking about."

"Prince Cavan discovered a deserted island, big enough for our village, hidden amid rocks and sandbars," Fallon said. "I would show you but I do not plan to have any visitors once we are there."

"Why do you not come on your ship with me? We can exchange families at sea," Kemal suggested.

Fallon shook his head. "That would put us in your power," he said. "It would be too easy for you to surround us. No, this is the way we will do it. And I will swear an oath before Aroaril on Bridgit's life that I will protect your family as my own until ours are returned."

Kemal tugged at his beard. "And how am I supposed to get your families away from Adana? I cannot just walk in and set them free. Questions will be asked. Money has already changed hands."

"Think of something! Pretend it is a new deal with King Aidan! Lie! You are the Crown Prince, for Aroaril's sake!" Gallagher growled.

"Word will still get back to my father," Kemal warned.

"We don't care. Anyway, this is not a discussion," Fallon said with finality. "You will do these things or your family will suffer. Terribly."

Kemal shook his head, lowering it. When he looked up, Fallon could see tears in his eyes. "I will do what you say. But I swear to Aroaril that if my family is harmed, I will devote my life to hunting every last one of you down. You will all die screaming if a hair on their head is out of place. I don't care if I have to search every cursed island out there!"

"You have nothing to worry about. As long as our families come home," Fallon said.

Kemal shuddered. "Can I at least say farewell to them?" he begged.

Fallon hesitated, but only for a heartbeat. "You can say your good-byes. Which was far more than you gave us. With a good wind, you will only be apart for a moon. Go on, the Sister and Brendan will take you. But be quick."

*

Kemal had to force himself to not limp, for he was so sure his healed foot would hurt that he flinched when he put it down, even though the priestess had repaired the hideous damage. But the imagined pain from his wounds was as nothing to the burning shame he felt inside. He had broken and let Fallon beat him.

But he forgot all about that when he stepped into the small windowless room where his family were huddled together. The old man who was sitting with them stood with a smile and stepped outside, shutting the door behind him. The moment the door was shut, Kemal rushed over to enfold them in his arms.

The four of them clung together, Kemal letting the tears trickle silently down his face as his wife and children sobbed in his arms.

"It is over. They will not try to hurt you. You are safe," he said softly, putting all the reassurance into his voice he could manage.

"Baba, I am sorry, when I saw you and when that man was yelling—" Orhan said, his voice muffled by his sobs.

"You have nothing to be sorry about. It is I who is sorry, for putting you in this danger. Do not blame yourselves: we could all do nothing more. The ones to blame are the Gaelish out there and the fools who allowed you to be taken from our ship. Both will pay for what they did," Kemal told them, unable to keep the anger out of his voice.

"They were in the cabin when I returned to check on the boys. But I do not understand how they managed to get in there without being seen or heard," Feray said.

"I suspect magic. The old wizard there has it, as does that priestess of theirs. No wonder my father hates it so much," Kemal said.

"Baba, can we go home now?" Asil asked softly.

Kemal took a deep breath. "Not yet," he said. "I must return home and free their families. That is the price they demanded."

"And us?" Feray whispered.

"You must stay with them until their families return."

As soon as the words were out of his mouth, his sons began to wail, until he silenced them with a glare.

"They promise to take care of you like their own children and they know that if a hair on any of your heads is harmed, my revenge will be terrible. They want me to just return their families and wait for you to arrive in Adana by ship, but I will escort their people back with a fleet. We shall exchange you and then it will be time for revenge," he said.

"But, Baba, I don't want to be here! Don't make me stay with these stinking Gaelish!" Asil begged.

"This will be good training for you both. I had you taught Gaelish, so you will be able to talk with them. We will rule here by next summer and it will give you a good insight into these people. Asil, you will one day follow me onto the Elephant Throne, and it will help prepare you for that. Now, have I ever broken a promise to you?"

The pair of them solemnly shook their heads.

"Well then. I promise that I will be back for you within a moon. Are we agreed?"

The two boys nodded again, just as solemn, then they both stepped forwards and flung their arms around him. Kemal held them back, not wanting to let them go, but knowing there were things he needed to say to Feray. He kissed them both on their heads and then gently pried their arms away.

"I need to speak to your Ana now," he said gently. "But I promise you that I will be back. Promise me you will be strong."

They both drew themselves up, Asil rubbing the tears away from his eyes.

"We will, Baba," Asil said, Orhan echoing his words a moment later.

Kemal reached out to place a hand on each of their shoulders and squeezed gently. "I know you will," he said.

They stepped back, going over the other side of the room, and Feray reached out to brush his check. "My love, your face – it has healed," she exclaimed. "Your foot as well?"

"I am as I was before," Kemal confirmed, although he knew the words were a lie.

"Can we trust these Gaelish?" she asked.

Kemal kissed her hand. "We have to," he said. "I have put you at their mercy because of my weakness. I am so sorry, my love. Maybe if I had been stronger, they would have had to let us go—"

"You cannot blame yourself," Feray said instantly. "Fallon is a monster and he would have hurt our boys and then me. You are far more of a man than he is."

Kemal cradled her hand to his cheek. "I wish I felt it. I swore to keep you safe and failed. But I will regain my honor and my manhood, get you back and wreak vengeance on Fallon and his foul accomplices."

"Be careful, my love. I will happily put my life in your hands, but freeing so many slaves cannot go unnoticed. Your brothers will bring it to your father's attention. I would not see you lose position—"

"Silence," he said, leaning in to kiss her lips gently. "I don't care about the Elephant Throne. An eternity sitting on its cold stone is not worth a moment in your warm arms."

She smiled gently. "You were blessed with the gift of flattery but it is a welcome gift. And do not worry about us. I will keep the boys safe."

"I will be back before you know it," he told her. "But I should go now. I do not want them to come in here and tear me away from you. I do not want that to be the boys' last memory of this day."

She nodded, tears rolling down her cheeks and he kissed them away, tasting the salt on his tongue.

"Come, give your father a farewell embrace!" he called and the boys rushed over.

Kemal closed his eyes, feeling their arms around him, then forced his eyes open and let the feel and smell and sight of them fill his senses, so he would have something to keep him strong over the next moon. Whatever it took, however long it may be, he would see Fallon dead for this.

*

Fallon watched the little Kottermani flotilla sail away into the darkness, feeling hope stir in his chest, the way the sun was just beginning to rise over the horizon to the east.

"Can we trust him?" Brendan asked, when they had returned to the Guildhouse and gathered in the entrance. Their captives were upstairs, held by Donnchadh and a few other villagers.

"He was prepared to do anything for his wife and children, just as we are. He will come back with Bridgit and the others," Fallon said confidently.

"Can he trust us? Are you thinking of keeping his family after we get our people back? They would make a powerful bargaining tool," Padraig said. "You can make Prince Kemal do anything for them."

Fallon glanced at the old wizard. "I will keep my word, as I said I would," he said shortly. "I don't know about you but I have had enough of betrayals and politics to last me a lifetime. We will get our families back and then sail for Cavan's island. Kemal will hunt for us but never find us."

Padraig nodded and gave him a small smile back in return. "That is good to hear, my son. I would not want Bridgit to return to find her husband was here but his spirit was lost, replaced by a lesser one."

"It sounds like she is changed herself. Leading the people! Apart from the likes of those numbskulls Sean and Seamus, there's all the dimwits at Killarney and a bunch of others as well. To lead them is no easy feat," Gallagher said.

"Aye," Fallon admitted. "It sounds as if she has found her strength again." Thinking of her made him groan aloud with longing. He wanted to see her again so badly! And not just see her. Just thinking of her made his groin throb.

"What now?" Devlin asked, cutting in on those thoughts.

Fallon had to take a moment to tear his mind away from a naked Bridgit.

"We will keep Kemal's family in the Guildhouse. People stay away from that, so any agents the King has prowling the city won't find them."

"Won't the Kottermani agents be more of a worry? I am sure Kemal left some of his men behind, with orders to find and free his family," Gallagher said.

"Those too," Fallon agreed. "Keeping his family away from people will stop any word from getting out. As to watching them, we need to move a dozen of us in here. Get blankets and food out of the rooms and bring them along. We'll rotate the men through here."

"Don't forget the city's still looking for those missing kids. If people nearby hear screaming children, they're going to come in for a look," Gallagher warned.

Fallon grimaced at the thought. "We might bring Kerrin down here and have him play in the square, so passers-by see a local child about the place. Aroaril knows he has been stuck with nobody but us for company for long enough. But only during the day, mind you, and only with me to keep an eye on things. I don't trust that wife of Kemal's. She'll have her eyes open for a chance to get out. If she grabs Kerrin, things could get ugly."

"And of course they have been going so well up to now," Padraig said.

Fallon rubbed gritty eyes. Dawn was not far off and none of them had slept. "Well, Aroaril willing, we will only have one moon more of this nightmare."

CHAPTER 21

"The King wants to see you now," Regan said.

Fallon rubbed sleep from his eyes. It felt like he had just closed his eyes when the chamberlain turned up. "What is it?" he asked.

"He told me to fetch you, not answer pointless questions," the chamberlain said testily. "Get cleaned up and hurry down to his office."

"Does he just want to see me?"

"He didn't say. Perhaps bring a few, if you wish, and they can wait outside. If the King wants them as well, then call for them. Again, I would advise you to hurry. It is luncheon in less than a turn of the hourglass and the King will not want to be kept waiting."

Fallon splashed water on his face, pulled on clean tunic and trews and collected an equally sleepy Gallagher and Brendan. Had the King somehow discovered what they had done? Regan was said to have a network of informers in the city. Had one of them seen something? But he had to leave his friends outside while he went inside.

Fallon had to be careful to keep his face calm. Kemal had given him even more reasons to hate the bastard. Aidan was the one behind the Kottermanis taking Bridgit and the others, as well as stealing the children. His blood boiled as he thought of all the money people had had to pay to protect themselves from make-believe selkies. And then to blame witches and selkies and to burn innocent women at the stake, all the time knowing the truth ...

He had to fight the urge not to smash his fists into the King's face; he contented himself with the thought that Aidan's time on the throne was limited and in a moon's time Fallon would be gone from Gaelland, never to see the undoubtedly humiliated King again. All he had to do was keep out of Aidan's way until then. He plastered a small smile over his fury and disgust.

But the King showed every sign of being delighted to see him. "Sit down, Fallon, we have much to talk about and little time," he said cheerfully.

Fallon did so, trying to look interested.

"The Kottermani fleet has sailed for home," Aidan said, leaning back in his padded chair. "Do you know why?"

Fallon hoped his face looked mildly confused and not guilty. He made a show of thinking. "No idea, sire," he said.

Aidan considered him for a few moments, then sighed. "It is a shame Prince Kemal did not wait a little longer, for I had a surprise for him, which would have wiped the sneer off his face. No doubt he plans to return in the spring, with more men, so we shall have to be ready for them then."

"What is the surprise, sire?" Fallon asked, careful to keep his voice respectful.

Aidan smiled. "Ah, I would love to tell you but that would spoil it! Perhaps in a little while ... Yes, I think I can tell you soon. I do so wish that Kemal had stayed. It has been a long time coming. I was all set to unleash the surprise on him when he returned to the castle to demand my answer. What I would have given to see the look on his face then! His smug arrogance would have been wiped off in a heartbeat! I wonder why he left so suddenly though. Perhaps he heard something about the surprise, through all his agents running around my city, curse him!"

"You know about his agents, sire?" Fallon asked, eager to get the conversation away from reasons why Kemal left.

"Oh yes. I had my son meet with them, so we could mark who they were and then keep an eye on them," Aidan said dismissively.

Fallon nodded thoughtfully to disguise the tremor of fear that rippled through him. If the King's men were watching the Kottermanis and got wind of Prince Kemal's family ...

"But while I wish Kemal were here to swallow his bitter medicine, it seems we shall have to ram it down his throat in spring," Aidan went on. "And this is where you come in."

"Sire?"

"Tomorrow you will train me an army."

Fallon felt his mouth sag open and closed it quickly. "Sire, where am I going to get the men from? And the weapons? We would need thousands of swords, shields and suits of mail. If every blacksmith in the land worked from dawn until dusk, we would not have enough," he said carefully.

Aidan waved a hand. "You will soon see that we have more than enough," he said, with a broad wink. "I have been planning for this for moons now. The first shipments will begin to arrive in Berry this moon and there will be plenty more to come between now and spring. Train me the men and I shall see them fitted out to face the Kottermanis."

Fallon nodded slowly, swallowing his horror. "But what men should I train, sire? We do not want to use up all the valuable workers and take them away from their jobs."

Aidan patted the table with his left hand. "See? I knew you would be the right man for this job. It will be an army of the young, sons aged between sixteen and eighteen summers. They will be eager to learn as well, once they know the famous Fallon will be leading them into battle."

Fallon wanted to argue more, to try and protect these young men from what was coming, but the King's face was alight with enthusiasm and he knew there was no chance of an outright refusal. Not without creating more problems than he could handle.

"I shall need some extra trainers, sire. The more expert men I have working with them, the faster the training and the better the soldiers at the end of it," he said.

King Aidan immediately pulled a scrap of parchment towards him and scribbled quickly on it.

"I shall tell Kelty that you can have one hundred of his men. Along with your own men, that should give you plenty," he said.

"How big an army do you want, sire?" Fallon asked, shocked at the numbers.

"Several thousand," Aidan said casually.

"Are there enough young men in the city for that, sire?"

"I doubt it. But there will be plenty more arriving from the counties. They are already on their way here, or I shall want to know why not."

Fallon nodded, his mind whirling. More than ever, he felt as though he were a twig, being swept along by a river to parts unknown. One thing was obvious. Aidan would have an army, with or without Fallon. And Fallon reckoned having the army loyal to him, rather than to Kelty or that seasick idiot Quinn, was by far the best plan. If he controlled the only army around here, then the King would be at his mercy. Besides, his training might just save a few of their lives.

"I shall start at dawn tomorrow, sire," Fallon said, standing and saluting.

Aidan handed him the written orders and smiled. "I am sorry that Prince Kemal left so soon. My final gift was to demand the return of your families. I am sorry that has been delayed but, once we have destroyed the army they send against us, I promise you it will be my first concern!"

Fallon made himself nod and offer a small smile. "Thank you, sire," he said, not having to make up the hoarseness in his voice.

"No, thank you Fallon. I shall not forget the service you have done for Gaelland. It was chance that brought you into my plans but I am truly thankful it was so."

Fallon met the King's eyes and felt, strangely, that the King was being completely honest. He saluted again and turned away, unable to stand looking at Aidan any more. His hatred was just as strong but there was another layer of confusion over the top. What else was the King playing at?

*

He collected Brendan and Gallagher and the three of them went in search of Kelty, to give the grim captain the news that he had to hand over a company of guardsmen. They found the officer out the front of the storage block, supervising the unloading of a dozen wagons.

Fallon headed straight for Kelty, the orders in his hand, but stopped when he saw what was in the wagons. Swords, spears, shields and crossbows were being dragged down by the barrel-load. "Where did these come from?" he asked, watching sweating servants carry them inside, past where Regan stood, making notes on a long scroll.

"All over," Kelty said with a shrug. "These ones have the badge of Londegal on them."

"But how? It must have cost a sack of gold!" Fallon exclaimed. "Where did the money come from?"

Kelty said nothing but his look said it all. Fallon remembered the last time he had been there, when Kelty had been selling off part of the tax tithe to the local merchants in exchange for coin. And then there had been the selkie tax ... The more he learned, the more it seemed King Aidan had been planning this from the start.

"Which men do you want?" Kelty said.

Fallon turned back from watching a bundle of spears being carried in carefully, the leaf-shaped heads looking shiny with grease. "How did you know I wanted men?" he demanded.

"I know what you have to do. And I told the King you would need help to do it," Kelty said with a shrug.

Fallon handed him the orders and Kelty's scarred eyebrows rose a little. "A whole company, eh? Which ones?"

That was easy for Fallon. "The men I led against the Moneylenders."

Kelty handed back the orders. "I'll have them ready at dawn tomorrow in the square outside. I already have a company of men taking the King's orders out around the city. Looks like you'll be in for a busy few moons."

Fallon nodded. "By Aroaril, don't I know it!"

Kelty gave him a strange look and then turned away so Fallon waved to his friends and went in the other direction.

"This is all coming together now," Gallagher said softly as they walked away. "Looks like Aidan has bought the weapons stores from Londegal. No doubt he has done the same with the other counties. That would have cost plenty of coin. The sort of coin you could only raise through a selkie tax, say. He's probably had every smith in the country working for him for the past moon."

"If he hadn't sold out our people to do it, I could almost admire him for it," Fallon whispered back.

*

"What do you mean, he did not attack my husband's ship?" Duchess Dina demanded.

Fallon shrugged. "What I said. Somebody else did it, most likely the King. After all, he tricked me into killing his own son, so having his cousin murdered does not seem like it would bother him."

"But surely he was lying!" she protested. "He must have wanted to hold on to his most valuable slave!"

Fallon sighed. "Sister Rosaleen was sitting beside him and told us everything he was saying was true. Besides, he knew we had his wife and sons under guard elsewhere. We had broken him: he was giving us everything he knew. I know you were hoping that your husband was being held in Kotterman somewhere but it looks like he was killed and his ship sent into my village to give the King some sort of evidence to proclaim the selkies were behind the disappearing people."

Dina looked away for a long time her hands over her eyes and, when she turned back, those eyes were red and watery. "Then I must accept it," she said. "We need to bring this to the attention of the other nobles, get them to denounce King Aidan at his next meeting. The fact he sold off his own people and kidnapped children, blaming it on witches and selkies, is disgusting. But what will really outrage them will be the news the selkie tax did not need to be paid!"

Fallon coughed lightly. "It may not be as easy as you think to get some outrage going. It looks like he is using that money to buy weapons from every county. I saw wagonloads arriving from Londegal just this day."

Dina looked at him for a moment and then cursed. "I thought it was just for Lunster," she said disgustedly. "All our weapon stores purchased and then enough money to pay the local smiths to replenish the stocks. Of course I have not only lost a husband but had hundreds of gutter scum from Berry dumped into my county.

For the others, it is different. They will just see the gold flowing to them and forget about everything else."

"But you have to get them to stop him," Fallon said firmly, thinking of what would happen after he left for Cavan's island. "I don't trust him. His plan to make an army will see thousands of people slaughtered. I think the Kottermanis will see Berry as the key to Gaelland and the easiest way into Berry is the harbor. But even if we defeat them inside the city walls, the ordinary people will pay a huge price."

Dina laughed, but there was no humor in it. "Have you ever seen him change his mind?"

"If all the nobles are telling him the same thing, he has to listen to them," Fallon insisted.

Now it was Dina's turn to sigh. "I shall try. What of your relationship with Prince Kemal? Can you use it to get him to negotiate? Perhaps we can do a deal for me to take the throne."

"Perhaps," Fallon said guardedly. "But I don't think he will be looking too fondly on anything I say."

"Well, I shall try with King Aidan and you try with Prince Kemal and perhaps we can save Gaelland between us," she said with a smile.

"Meanwhile, can I borrow Gannon and a squad of your men? If I am to train these poor lads then I need all the help I can get," Fallon asked.

Dina smiled widely. "Of course. He is getting bored here, anyway! You know, Prince Cavan would have been so proud of you. What you are doing will make a real difference to the people."

Fallon bowed his head.

"If we can remove that bastard Aidan from the throne and his weasel son Swane as well, then Cavan will look down and smile upon us," she said.

"I would like to think of that," Fallon admitted.

*

Fallon was thinking about seeing Aidan replaced by Dina as he slipped back into his rooms. Maybe he could not make that suggestion to Prince Kemal, but he could make it to the man's wife.

After what he had done, he knew full well that Kemal was not going to listen to anything he said. But planting the idea in his wife's head might work even better.

"What are you thinking, Dad?" Kerrin asked.

He patted his son on the shoulder and felt the solid muscle there appreciatively. All the hard work Kerrin was doing with the throwing knives and crossbows had changed him. He was not coughing now, not even when he ran. There was another change in him as well, something in the eyes, a hardness and determination that had not been there before. Again, after wanting to see it for so long, now it was another painful sign that things were changing.

"How would you like to help me?"

"Sure, Dad. What are we doing?"

"I need you to play with a couple of Kottermani boys," Fallon said with a smile.

Kerrin looked up at him, puzzled. "But what about my training?" he objected.

Fallon squeezed his shoulder. "Your training is going very well. But if there is one thing I have learned, life is more than training. I want to see you laugh again."

"I will laugh when Mam is back," Kerrin said fiercely.

"And this will help bring her back," Fallon promised. *Kerrin needs this even more than I thought.*

*

Devlin was delighted to see them as they slipped into the Moneylenders' Guildhouse.

"I know you said she must speak our language but all three of them have just been chattering to each other in Kottermani. Won't say a word to us," he said, jerking a thumb over his shoulder, up the stained and burned stairs to where Kemal's family was hidden.

"Has anyone been around?" Fallon asked. "Anyone suspicious?"

"There was a couple of strange-looking men who came sniffing around earlier but I sent a pair of the bigger boys out there and they disappeared right quick," Devlin said.

"Watch out for them," Fallon said bleakly. "Not only have the Kottermanis got agents out all through the city but the King let slip that he has men following the Kottermanis. If either were to get wind of who we have here, we could end up in the shite right quick."

"A comforting thought," Devlin grunted. "So are you just here to cheer me up?"

"Not really," Fallon admitted. "Me and Kerrin are here to try and cheer them up."

"Well, good luck with that!" Devlin said with a snort.

Fallon led Kerrin up the stairs to the large office where Kemal's family was being kept, the door guarded by a pair of villagers, whose grim faces broke out into smiles at the sight of Kerrin.

"Have they been making much noise?" Fallon asked.

"A bit of singing. Nothing more," Craddock replied.

Fallon nodded his thanks and pushed open the door, Kerrin at his shoulder.

"What do you want? Get out!" Kemal's wife said, the moment he was inside the room.

She was seated on the large mattress they had provided, one arm around each of her sons.

"I wanted you to meet my son, Kerrin," Fallon said, stepping aside slightly to reveal Kerrin.

"Why?" she sneered.

"Because he misses his mother, just as your boys must be missing their father," Fallon said, leaning against the wall. "So you have something in common."

"We have nothing in common!" she snapped.

Fallon ignored that, watching instead the way the two boys kept their eyes on Kerrin.

"When your husband's men came to our village to steal away all the women and children, my wife hid our son, our only child, then went to fight them armed with only my training sword, which was blunt. She sacrificed herself so that he would have a chance at getting away," he said conversationally. "Would have you done any differently?"

This time she did not answer and he took that to be a good sign.

"Kerrin, what was it like without your mam?" he asked his son.

Kerrin looked up at him in surprise and he nodded slightly.

"I cried myself to sleep every night. If I hadn't had my dog to help me, I don't know how I would have got through it," Kerrin said.

Fallon nodded towards the two boys. "They will probably feel the same. But perhaps the chance to run around in the sun might help them."

"They do not need your help! You are the one who put them in this place, who was about to hurt them!"

"Yet I did not harm them. For better or worse, we shall be seeing much of each other over the next moon," he said. "Trust me, I want to see you returned to your husband, your boys to their father, because that means my wife will be back with me, given the chance to hold our son again and hear how she saved him. The next moon here will seem long and boring for your boys but perhaps with a playmate, it might go faster?"

"They want nothing to do with you!" she said sharply.

"Perhaps not now. But they will want to get out of this room and run around a little," Fallon suggested.

Again, she said nothing to this.

"You know our names. I am Fallon and this is Kerrin. Will you at least let us know your names?" he continued.

For a long moment he thought she would spit anger at him but she glanced at Kerrin and then seemed to relent a little. "I am Feray and this is Asil and Orhan," she said.

"And do they speak any Gaelish?" Kerrin asked.

Again she hesitated but Fallon could see while she might have refused his question, she obviously did not see as much danger in replying to Kerrin. "They both speak it, a little. They expected to live here, after all."

"How did you learn to speak our language?" Kerrin continued curiously.

"We had a teacher. A young woman who spoke it," the older boy, Asil, said.

Fallon tucked that away in the back of his mind for later. If a young woman spoke Gaelish then she was either a slave who had been taken earlier or the child of a Gaelish slave. That said the

Kottermanis had been taking Gaelish slaves for a lot longer than just the bargain with King Aidan.

"Would you like to kick a ball around tomorrow?" Fallon offered.

"They have never done anything like that," Feray admitted.

"That's all right. Kerrin hasn't done it much either," Fallon said, reaching down to pat his son's shoulder.

"We can teach each other," Kerrin said.

"Perhaps," Feray said.

"Then we shall see you tomorrow," Fallon said. "Good night."

He was pleased to see Kerrin waited until they were not just out of the room but halfway down the stairs before asking questions.

"Do I have to play with them?" he asked.

"Yes," Fallon said firmly.

"Why?"

"Because we need to get them liking us before her husband comes back with Mam," he said, not adding the other reason: that Kerrin needed to laugh again.

CHAPTER 22

Prince Kemal looked across the sea and wished Feray were there. He could not bear to think of her, nor of his boys, suffering under the hands of that bastard Fallon. All he could cling to was the thought he could get them back. Any other ending was impossible to consider. A tiny part of him raged silently, promising to turn the whole of Gaelland into a land of stinking corpses if his wife and children were harmed, but he had to keep that locked away tight. Partly because it would mean giving in to despair and those black thoughts but mostly because it made him understand Fallon and what he had done to get his wife back. And he only wanted to feel hatred for Fallon.

Freeing the slaves was not going to be easy. There would be many awkward questions asked, and news of it would reach his father. Anything to do with Gaelland interested the Emperor. But he would explain it away as part of the bargain that had to be made to bring the country into the empire without much bloodshed.

He did not care about what his father would do or say, nor about how his brothers would try to use it to undermine his position. At least two of them lusted after the Elephant Throne, that kind of sick longing that would never end. He had already been told by several of his father's more trusted advisers that he would need to have them killed the day his father died, or face civil war and rebellion.

Kemal's over-riding thought was to get Feray and the boys back. But it was not his only thought. He had to prepare not just for things going wrong with the families being handed back but with the handover of the country. King Aidan could not be trusted and he had to return to Gaelland with a huge force.

He drove the crew unmercifully, stripping extra sailors from his accompanying two vessels and leaving them to follow at a slower pace while he pushed his ship to the edge.

"As soon as we are within the limits of our messenger birds, I want to be told," he instructed the frightened ship's captain. "The men can rest once we reach Adana. I want to be there tomorrow. Or sooner. How soon we get there will determine your payment. Either more gold than you can carry or a slave's collar."

As soon as word came that he could use the message birds all Kottermani ships carried, he would release them for Adana. The words they carried were the same: *Assemble me an army.*

He had never used his power so brutally before, terrifying men around him. If Feray had been here, she would have chided him, gently suggested a better way to do it.

But she was back in Gaelland, so he merely sat in his cabin and brooded.

He replayed that day and night over and over in his mind. First he obsessed over a way he could have got out of the trap, but that was just a taster. The main dish was the battle of wills between himself and Fallon. He remembered every look on the man's face, every word he said. He longed for the chance to go back and do it again. This time he would stay strong and it would be Fallon who cracked and begged for the return of his family. Every time he closed his eyes, he saw Fallon's face and he relived that scene in his mind, always finding new ways to stay strong and save his family. He had left Feray, Asil and Orhan back in Gaelland but it felt like he had left more than that. And until he took back his pride from Fallon, he would always feel lost.

*

Fallon stared at the mass of young men in disbelief. The square out the front of the castle had been slowly filling during the night and dawn had revealed at least two thousand men. They stood in little groups, instinctively seeking others they knew, from their own village or street but, when Fallon had emerged from the castle, followed by a mixture of guardsmen and villagers, the recruits had begun to cheer and chant his name.

"Can you help me talk to them?" Fallon asked.

Padraig nodded slowly. "Aye, but we need to be careful," he said. "Aidan might have let us off the leash but he is going to be listening to what you say over the next few days. You are about to become one of the most powerful men in Gaelland. The King only has about three hundred guards, of whom about a third would rather follow you anyway. Make these lads loyal to you and Aidan will be helpless against you."

"I look forward to that day," Fallon said softly.

"But who takes the throne afterwards? The Duchess?"

"Well, she would be better than Aidan."

"Aye, but so would what I left floating in my chamber pot this morning! Now do you want to talk to these lads or not?"

Fallon smiled. "Better than talking to you, old man!"

Padraig slapped him on the shoulder and nodded once, to let him know his next words were going to be loud enough to be heard across the square.

"Men of Gaelland!" Fallon called, his voice echoing off the houses at the edge of the square. "You have come here today to protect your families, your friends and your country! Children will look up to you, women will swoon over you and men will want to shake your hand! Listen to me, listen to the warriors who will teach you and you will become Gaelish heroes, blessed by Aroaril!"

They cheered again, roaring their enthusiasm.

"Now divide yourselves into groups of ten! Stay with men you know, for you will be living and fighting alongside them. They will be your brothers, as I will be your father!"

Again they cheered, but this time they began to shuffle around, dividing themselves up.

Fallon pointed at Padraig and the old wizard gave him a wink.

"Right, how many weapons have we got for them?" he asked, turning to the men he had appointed as his lieutenants. It did not feel right, not having Devlin there, but he had a more important task.

Brendan loomed over Gallagher, Gannon and Bran, the bearded guardsmen looking somewhat uncomfortable. Gannon at least had been commanding Duchess Dina's guards but Bran had merely been an ordinary soldier, pushed around by officers like Quinn, the man who had been too scared to lead them into Killarney. Now he had the same rank as Quinn and Fallon had to hide his smile when he saw Bran sneaking a look at the new crown sewn onto his tunic's shoulder.

"As soon as we make a count, another line of carts arrives from a county and it all changes," Brendan said. "But we have maybe three hundred swords and getting on for a thousand shields, which should be enough for today."

"Good; you all know what to do?" Fallon asked. "Your men are all ready?"

"I think so, sir," Bran said stiffly.

Brendan slapped a big hand onto the guardsman's shoulder. "He's only Fallon, man. You don't need to call him sir!"

Bran's eyes widened and then grew some more when Kerrin strode up, crossbow over his shoulder and Caley at his hip. The boy stamped to a halt and saluted while Caley sat down by Fallon's side.

"I'm ready to help, Dad," Kerrin announced.

"Now you do need to call him sir," Brendan rumbled, slapping his other hand on Kerrin's shoulder.

Fallon winked at his son, then grinned at his new officers. "Remember, what we teach these boys today might keep them alive tomorrow. Go to it!"

The recruits were divided up by the simple expedient of the trainers gathering the first groups they found together until they had enough men for the equipment they had. Bran and Brendan had about half of them, splitting those up equally, giving them both shields and teaching them to form a wall of shields while Brendan tried to use his size to break through. Fallon had the ones with the swords, taking them through the basic cuts and blocks he had learned as a recruit more than twenty summers earlier. Gallagher, with most of the villagers and Kerrin, worked with about fifty of them on crossbows.

Gannon and his men, on the other hand, took the rest of them on a run through the city, followed by a string of other exercises that had them sweating and puffing. Fallon strode through the recruits, nodding as they saluted excitedly or cheered him, even when they barely had any breath left. Caley did not leave his side and they cheered her too.

He smiled as he saw Kerrin demonstrating the crossbow. "This is my son. I taught him everything I know and he is going to teach you, so listen to him," he announced.

"If I can do this, then you can," Kerrin told the recruits and Fallon saw them redouble their efforts. He looked up at the castle and wondered whether King Aidan was watching. A moon of this and he would be ready to lead them into the castle.

*

"How goes the training?" King Aidan asked.

"It went well for the first day, sire," Fallon said carefully.

They were standing atop the wall over the castle gate, watching the exhausted recruits slowly setting up awnings for shelter. Servants from the castle were bringing out huge pots of stew for the hungry young men, followed by endless cauldrons of potatoes. Fallon could not imagine what all this was costing the crown. Even the selkie tax might not be enough.

"How will you fight them?" Aidan asked, looking out over the makeshift camp.

"Well, we can use the shields to block up our tight streets, sire. Then from above we can use our crossbowmen. We shall lure them into an endless series of ambushes. Victory will not come cheap but it will be certain."

Aidan slapped him on the shoulder. "There!" he said triumphantly. "That is the sort of thinking I cannot get from my nobles. You understand that sometimes you have to sacrifice to win, and no victory comes without cost."

Fallon forced a smile onto his face. Strangely, having the King so friendly towards him was worse than seeing him shouting and screaming. Aidan made his skin crawl and it was all he could do not to shudder when the King patted him on the shoulder again. "I want to hear how the training is going every second day," he said. "I must see how my new army takes shape."

Once he was sure the King was gone, Fallon hastily spoke with his new lieutenants, getting them ready for tomorrow. The recruits had to be run until exhausted, and the ones who had not worked with swords that day given the chance to use them.

"I'm not like the King," he told them. "If you have an idea to make these lads better, I want to hear it."

"Maybe we should only train the best of them with the sword. It is going to take moons of work to get some of them even able to work out which end of the blade to hold. And even then, they will be taken apart by the first Kottermani they face," Bran said, his words spilling out in a rush.

"Well, we can't leave them to die," Fallon said, trying to be careful not to shut the guardsman down.

Bran nodded. "Most we can teach to use spears. That way we can have the biggest men at the front with the shields and then others behind, with spears, who can reach over their shoulders."

"I like it," Fallon said immediately. "We just have to show them how to use a spear without sticking it in someone's ear."

"And why don't you pick a company to use the shillelagh? We've all seen you with it and the Kottermanis have never faced it before," Bran continued.

"Still, you would need a big set of balls to go into battle armed with little more than a staff," Gannon said.

"What would you use the balls for?" Kerrin asked. "Kick them at the enemy?"

Fallon cleared his throat. "Maybe just stick with the spears," he suggested. "Now, get some rest: we need to work them even harder. Aroaril knows when the Kottermanis might come, or how many men they could bring."

"Are you thinking that Kemal might bring his army back earlier than expected?" Gallagher muttered.

Fallon nodded, even as he waved to the guardsmen who had been training his recruits. "Aye," he said out of the corner of his mouth. "That is what I would do. Give our families back and then come and take them."

"Will these lads be ready by then? He'll be back within a moon and that'll be his last chance to get an army here before the winter storms hit," Brendan said warningly.

"Aroaril knows. All we can do is our best," Fallon said, then patted his friend on the back. "How're the bruises? I saw you throw yourself into enough shieldwalls for one day."

Brendan chuckled. "They took one look at the dried blood and brains on my hammer and were running away before I even got there!"

"Well, tomorrow they can't do that. They have to stand," Fallon said.

Brendan stretched. "First, I need something to eat. I swear I could swallow a horse and chase the rider right now!"

"You do that. I'll go and wander around the shelters out there for a while, then duck out and see what has been happening with Devlin and Kemal's wife Feray."

"You have more energy than me. But then again, all you did was wander around and wave as people cheered you," Brendan said with a wink.

"Now that's the sort of joke I'd expect from Devlin," Fallon grunted.

Brendan sighed. "He doesn't laugh any more, that lad. I hope he can again when Riona and his kids are back."

"Aye, that makes two of us," Fallon said heavily. "I hope he'll laugh his head off."

Brendan shrugged and held up his battered and bloodied hammer. "And I never thought I could kill a man, either. But what we have done has changed us all. Maybe we can never go back to what we were."

"Aroaril, man! Any gloomier and I'd be calling you Padraig!" Fallon snorted. "Now off with you and get some food in your stomach – that'll put the smile back on your face."

He just needed to get them away from here and off to Cavan's island. Then things could get back to normal and they could forget all about this nightmare.

"Today was great, Dad. Can we do the same tomorrow?" Kerrin asked.

"Maybe. I'm thinking I might need you to work on those Kottermani boys tomorrow."

Kerrin pulled a face. "That won't be any fun," he complained. "I have to keep training. If I need to save you or Mam, I have to put the work in."

Fallon felt a pang at the thought. How many times had he wanted to hear that from a younger Kerrin? Now he would give anything to have the lad go back to want to play with his soldier figures, rather than practice to be a soldier.

"You have done plenty. But I need you to work on those Kottermanis for me. That is the best way to help Mam," he said, hating the way he was using that lie to make Kerrin do what he wanted.

"All right," Kerrin said reluctantly.

"Come on, talk to the recruits with me," Fallon said, hoping that would make Kerrin smile again.

The recruits were certainly delighted to see them both. Fallon still found it strange to have them cheering him and saluting when he walked past. But it was important that they knew he cared for them, for that was the only way to get them to fight and die for him.

"Had enough to eat?" he asked at a score of shelters, which always brought a smile.

Having Kerrin throw a knife into one of the poles holding up the shelter, or loosing a bolt from his one-hand crossbow into the potato that was sitting on someone's plate made them roar with laughter, while asking where they were from gave him both an idea of how many more might be coming in from the counties and also how this was a cross-section of Gaelland.

"Get some rest, lads," he told them. "Because tomorrow the real work starts!"

That always brought a groan and, after the twentieth time he said it, he signaled to Kerrin and the pair of them slipped away, Caley at their heels.

*

"What is this for?" Feray asked with disdain.

Fallon bounced the ball, an inflated pig's bladder reinforced with leather.

"It's for a game. We use it to keep fit and have fun," he replied.

"But why have you brought it here to us?" she demanded.

Fallon tossed it to Kerrin, who caught it on his second attempt.

"I thought your boys might like to get outside in the fresh air and stretch their legs, run around and have fun," he said. "Kerrin and I will be playing out there. You are welcome to come and watch. Or even to join in if you like," he said casually.

His attempts to win over Feray were going nowhere. Extra food, even Kottermani delicacies, from the palace kitchen was treated with cool distaste. He had known it was not going to be easy, for he had tricked and abducted her, tortured her husband and threatened to do the same to her son. But time was slipping away and he had to try if he was going to use her to influence Kemal, even unwittingly.

"We're going now. You might like to enjoy a little sun, while it is out," he said, putting his arm around Kerrin's shoulder and walking away.

There was a quiet plea from one of the boys in Kottermani and then he heard the footsteps as they followed him.

The little square outside the Guildhouse was empty, although Fallon had left a couple of villagers in the entrance, to keep an eye on anyone who might be coming near and to stop Feray and her sons if they had the idea to run.

Fallon had no intention of playing out in the open, where they could be seen from the street beyond, but over to the left side of the square, the part without the bloodstains etched into the cobbles, there was room to run behind the shelter of the houses lining the entrance. He and Kerrin began by kicking the ball to each other, the bladder bouncing over the cobbles, while the two Kottermani boys watched, Feray holding the hand of each.

Fallon had not played in years, although it was a common enough game among young guardsmen rather than among children. Like the game of hurling, which the nobles loved to bet on, Gaelish football was less of a game and more of a training exercise for guards, so they could get fit and learn to work with each other as a team without risking serious injury.

The old skills came back and he found himself forgetting about training an army, about winning over Feray, even about missing Bridgit as he chased the ball around with Kerrin. He missed a catch and saw that the Kottermani boys were watching avidly. So next time Kerrin kicked it, he deliberately let it bounce past him and right to their feet.

"Kick it to me," he invited.

The taller of the two boys, Asil, swung his foot and sent the ball bouncing back over the cobbles.

Kerrin raced to get it and kicked it to the other boy, Orhan.

Two kicks later the two boys had torn their hands free of their mother's and were joining in, the three of them trying to keep it away from the chasing Fallon. Fallon deliberately missed the ball a couple of times to keep the game going but then had Orhan, the boy he had threatened to torture, cornered, Looking at him, he could not believe he had been prepared to use a knife on the lad. It felt like a tale told to scare children rather than something real.

But as he approached, arms outstretched, it stopped being a game – Orhan too remembered all too readily. Abandoning the ball, he raced back to his mother.

Fallon picked up the ball and cursed himself, although was careful not to let anything show on his face. "That feels like enough for today," he said brightly, puffing a little himself and seeing that the boys were sweating. As Kerrin was also sweating, at least it meant it was not fear making the Kottermani boys perspire.

He tossed the ball back to Asil, who was also edging towards his mother.

"Keep it to play with. Perhaps we can have another game tomorrow," he suggested.

Without saying anything, Feray hurried her two sons inside. But Fallon noticed they took the ball with them.

"Did that work, Dad?" Kerrin asked.

"We'll see. But at least we had fun!" Fallon said, turning away and heading back to the castle with his son.

*

"They are not picking up the sword fast enough," Bran said. "They have forgotten what we have taught them by the time they take another turn with the swords."

Fallon looked around at his other lieutenants and they all nodded. "We are trying to find the best three hundred and concentrate on them but that is easier said than done," Gannon agreed. "We can all agree on the best one hundred, perhaps the best two hundred, but then it gets difficult."

Fallon leaned back against the castle wall and forced a smile to his face. "Look happier," he said out of the corner of his mouth. "Some of them are watching us."

As the others straightened up and took the sour looks off their faces, he nodded approval. "Then we only take two hundred for the swords. Work them every day."

"What of the others?"

"Spears," Fallon said instantly. "I want them drilling with spears. I don't know if the Kottermani armor will stop a sword blow but it will not be able to block a spear. I want to fill these streets with long spears, like hedgehogs. Lines of them. A first rank with swords and shields. A second rank with regular size spears, the height of a man, a third rank with spears half a length longer and a fourth rank with spears twice that length. If the Kottermanis want to get through, they will each be facing three spears trying to impale them, just to get to the men with shields."

"Where are we going to get spears like that from?" Brendan asked.

"We have the spearheads already. Just cut longer poles. See the shipbuilders down by the docks and get the poles they use for pushing ships out, as well as ones they use for oars. All they have to be taught to do then is stand firm and don't thrust it through the man in front."

"A spear twice the height of a man will be fearsomely heavy," Bran warned.

"Then we find the strong ones. Surely that is easier than finding the best swordsmen," Fallon said encouragingly.

"Aye," Gannon admitted.

"Then let's not waste any more time. Who knows how much we have?"

*

Fallon wandered through the square, keeping a close eye on what was going on around him. One of Gannon's men was screaming at the recruits and he tapped the man on the shoulder, leading him a few paces away.

"They are not men who are doing this for money. They are going to fight for their country. We have to build them up, not break them down," he said in a whisper, keeping a light smile on his face. "We don't have the time to do it the normal way."

The guardsman nodded sullenly and Fallon patted him on the shoulder, keeping the man there with a forceful hand.

"You might be thinking I'm too soft on them. That men who are about to go into battle have to obey without thinking. Yet they will not be standing in a big line with everyone else. They will be split into small groups, fighting alone in streets, not knowing if they are the only ones left. They have to trust you, not fear you, or you will be left to face the angry Kottermanis all alone," he said.

The guardsman nodded uncertainly and Fallon let go of him, turning instead to the group of ten who were wrestling with the longer spears and nearly hitting each other.

"Men! Come closer!" he called and they stood straighter, delighted to see Captain Fallon taking an interest in them.

He made them stand shoulder to shoulder, physically moving men in until they were touching each other.

"You've got to be closer to the man next to you than you are to the women you are shagging," he told them.

"What if you're not shagging anyone, Captain?" one of them asked nervously.

"Oh, you will be soon enough. Just tell them you were one of Captain Fallon's men and they'll be falling over themselves to get close to you," he said, making them laugh.

"That's the way," he said, inspecting their new line. "Remember that. And remember I am proud of you. All of you!"

He gave them a cheery wave and nodded to the guardsman.

"Dad, what were you talking about?" Kerrin asked.

"Just a silly joke," Fallon said hastily. Sometimes he forgot Kerrin was there ... Now that Bridgit was on her way back, he would have to be careful what he was saying. It would just be his luck for her to get back and find Kerrin swearing like a drunken sailor. That fear made him strangely happy. For the chance to see her again, he would happily endure any number of tongue-lashings. And worrying about her return was far better than worrying about her never returning.

CHAPTER 23

"What do you want?" Gokmen demanded grumpily.

Bridgit smiled thinly. Since she had fooled him into thinking she was carrying Prince Kemal's child, he had treated her warily. That had changed to something close to respect after the doctor had confirmed she was pregnant. The slave master had even let the doctor keep visiting her and the children once a quarter moon, making sure that all were healthy. His earlier bluster and shouting was almost gone – she could sense the prospect of an outraged Prince Kemal demanding revenge hovered over him at all times.

"Before my people are sold away, they must be brought here, so I can speak to them and they can spend a last day with their children," she said briskly, making it sound as though there was no choice in the matter.

"Why?" Gokmen growled. "Why can they not see the children as they have been doing?"

"If you want them to be good slaves, then you will do this. They need a proper day together, not just a turn of the hourglass. It makes far more sense to have them all here at once, then they all leave at once."

Bridgit paused while Ely finished off the translation. Gokmen understood most of what she said but not all and she wanted him to know exactly what she was asking.

"Why do they need this?" Gokmen asked.

"You want them to be good slaves? Then they need this. Or you will find some of them causing trouble – and it will be you who pays the price," Bridgit said sternly.

"If they try to run, they know the penalty," Gokmen said remorselessly. "And if they do anything worse, I will kill some of the children."

Bridgit bit back her fury. "I shall speak to Prince Kemal when he returns. He knows that I alone can make my people into good slaves for you. You will be the one facing the whip if this does not happen," she threatened.

His eyes widened in anger and, for a moment, she thought she had gone too far – then the familiar wary expression crept over his face. He obviously felt he could not risk the Prince's wrath.

"But when the Prince returns, when I tell him of how you have helped, you will be well rewarded," she added, softening her voice.

Gokmen tugged at his beard. "Why here?"

"Here is familiar to the children. Here they are happy," Bridgit said simply. "This is one final day of happiness, before their parents leave for a life of slavery. Place guards outside the front door and we shall be just as safe as any other day of visits."

Gokmen considered this as Ely translated it into Kottermani. Bridgit hoped the young woman was saying all the right things.

"There must be no trouble. If there is, the children will pay for it," he said finally.

Bridgit hid her relief. Without this, her plan to get the people out of Adana was doomed to failure. "They will arrive after morning prayers and leave after evening prayers," she said.

Gokmen scowled at her but obviously could not see anything wrong with this. Again she kept her face still. The whole plan was based around giving the guards a series of drinks through the day so that by the evening they would be drowsy and even more bored than usual.

"And there will be plenty of food and drink for them," she added.

Gokmen grunted. "Agreed then. It will happen next quarter moon. Prince Kemal will be back soon, perhaps even by then."

"I shall tell him how you have been a good and faithful servant of his and helped my people adjust to their new life," Bridgit said, then her brain caught up with what Gokmen was saying. "Prince Kemal is returning early?"

"He is," Gokmen confirmed. "You will be pleased to see him?"

"Oh, most pleased," Bridgit lied. "But how did you hear these glad tidings?"

Gokmen pointed upwards and rattled off a string of Kottermani.

"What is it? A special wind at this time of year?" Bridgit asked Ely impatiently.

"Birds," Ely said. "Messenger birds, trained to fly to their home. It seems one of them arrived today from Prince Kemal, as he sails back to Adana."

"My joy will be complete then," Bridgit said with a broad smile that got nowhere near her eyes. "Did he say why he returns?"

"He has ordered a muster of soldiers and for a fleet to be ready. He will return to Gaelland with an army," Gokmen said. "You will have more of your people to look after soon, I think."

"That will be another thing to look forward to," Bridgit lied brightly. "Thank you, slave master Gokmen."

He nodded, she bowed and then left him, her mind racing.

*

"Why does he want an army? Does he seek to take Gaelland, make us part of his filthy empire?" Ahearn asked.

"Well, if he does, we have to get back as fast as possible. If nothing else, we need to warn them what is coming," Bridgit said.

"How can they stop a Kottermani army? We have no army of our own, just a company or two of guardsmen with each noble and the fyrd, which is us, armed with whatever we have," Ahearn said. "We have seen their soldiers in armor and those huge bows that they have on the wall. What can we do against them?"

"More there than what we can do here," Bridgit said crisply. "And once we are there, who knows? There are men who will fight, men like Fallon."

Ahearn grunted. "You told us that he would come for you and the rest of your village and that has come to naught."

Bridgit bit her lip at that thought. She had been so sure Fallon would come. It would be the sort of idiotic thing he would do. Having seen Adana and its defenses, she knew that any attack he made would have been doomed to failure. But surely he would have tried anyway?

She shook her head. Now was not the time for such thoughts. They had to get home before they thought about anything else. "That is by the by," she said. "This is the plan."

She looked around at the ring of worried faces. This was the fourth group of adults who had come to visit the children that day and none of them had appeared excited about her idea. But none of them could come up with anything better and, try as she might, she could not either.

She took them through how it would work, from drugging the guards, to luring them in and overpowering them, taking their weapons and heading to the docks. Once there, a small group would have to cut the cords on the giant bows while the others hurried onto a ship.

"I have been through the city twice just after prayers and it is quiet," she said. "But if we do meet some guards, we shall have to put them down quickly and silently. We need time to get to the ship, make sure there is enough food and water on board and secure those giant bows. And the children are not going to be able to run fast, either. We cannot have a panic where some are left behind in the rush for the ship."

"I can lead the men to take out the bows," Ahearn offered.

Bridgit shook her head. "We need you to captain the ship. You are too valuable. We cannot take the chance of losing you."

The other men looked at each other and she sighed to herself. None of the other groups had volunteered either. It sounded like it was going to be a death sentence for whoever was going and the fact she had just stopped Ahearn from going was hardly encouraging them.

"I will lead you. I just need six strong men who can cut through horsehair ropes," she said, glaring at them.

Ahearn grunted. "You sit back while a woman offers to lead?"

The other men half-heartedly agreed to come along and she felt a trickle of fear along the back of her neck. The chances were they would be cut off and forced to jump into the harbor, swim to the ship and try to climb up a rope to get to safety. She wanted to tell them that she was too important to risk on such a dangerous mission but could not. It had to be done and, if nobody else was willing to take it on, she had to step up. She knew that from Fallon. A leader had to do the things everyone else was too scared to try.

"Rest at night. Eat and drink as much as you can, especially on that day," she said, changing the subject to something they would be happier to talk about. All were looking leaner as a result of their moon as slaves. The food was generous but the unrelenting work had trimmed them all down. "We shall have extra food and drink and we need to eat and drink all we can, for who knows how much food we will be able to take with us? You may be feeling fear, worrying too much to want to eat but you have to force yourself to."

They did not look much happier at that idea and she had little else that was pleasant for them to hear.

"Ahearn, you must not pick up a weapon and instead go in the middle of the column, with the children," she continued. "You are the most valuable one among us. Without you, we will not be able to navigate back to Gaelland. We cannot risk anything happening to you."

Ahearn muttered something under his breath at that but nodded slowly. "You realize we shall be lucky if any of us get to those ships?" he asked.

"No, we shall all get to the ships," she said crisply. "That is my worry. You worry about getting us home. That is your concern."

He grinned then. "By Aroaril but you have the heart of a lion! You can count on us."

"I always knew I could," she lied with a smile. "Just be ready to follow me on that day."

*

"There is a problem with two of your people," Gokmen said angrily. "You must solve it or I shall be forced to."

"Take me to them and I shall talk sense into them," Bridgit said briskly, covering her fear. Surely all of them knew what was at stake now? They had been told to act cowed, to be as obedient as possible, so the guards would think them broken, and relax. Maybe not all had believed her when she said she would get them out, they just had to be patient, but they had understood what they needed to do. She did not want to see anyone else suffer the same fate as Sean and Seamus or, worse, have her plan wrecked by one idiot.

The walk through the city down to the docks gave her time to calm down and clear her head. Ideas were already forming as to how to get them out of there and she had to let this pair know that. Or maybe it was a couple of mothers or indeed fathers who were missing their children. They would be easy to reassure.

Then she saw the pair surrounded by Kottermani guards and her heart sank. Blaine and Carrick. For a moment she thought about leaving them to Gokmen's punishment but the thought of watching Sean and Seamus scream out their last on the boiling sand made her shudder. She owed it to them to at least try to save these two.

"Leave them to me," she told Gokmen, then strode onwards.

"What is happening here?" she asked briskly, gesturing for the brothers to move a little away from the guards.

"You need to talk to these guards, make them leave us alone. We need all our strength to make the escape," Carrick declared.

"Don't be fools," Bridgit snapped at them. "And for Aroaril's sake keep your voices down!"

"They can't understand us. But you need us, so make it so we can rest this afternoon. We are sick of working ourselves to death," Blaine complained.

The pair of them loomed over her but she stood her ground, poking Blaine in his large stomach. "You stupid bastards. We can't let them suspect we are doing anything! For Aroaril's sake, get back to work!"

"You need us," Carrick said, flexing his arms. "And you owe us for what you did to Sean and Seamus. Just tell them we are sick and need to rest. We deserve that at least."

She stared at them in disbelief. "If it was just your lives then I would not care," she told him. "But you put at risk every child the Kottermanis took. You would have seen them playing around Killarney over the years. Would you like to see them die?"

"Without us they won't get away. We deserve a little special treatment," Blaine growled back.

"You want special treatment? I'll get you special treatment!" Bridgit snarled at him, stepping closer and forcing the bigger man to step back. "I just have to say the word and you will be tupped by every guard here, used like a woman by all those men."

"You are saying that to scare us," Carrick complained.

"You should be scared!" Bridgit hissed at him. "They will make your every waking hour a living hell! Now, I should be happy about that. I should be helping pick out the guards who want to rut you like you would a sheep. But because of what happened to your cousins, Aroaril rest their souls, and because you could be useful, I have sworn an oath to get you home safe. Don't make me break that."

She glared at the two of them and they quailed a little before the fire in her eyes.

"But we'll be too tired to help the escape," Blaine muttered.

"Grow up and act like a man. At the very least, die like a man. Or," Bridgit pointed out one of the bigger guards, a man as tall as Carrick, "if you don't want to be a man, I'll have him use you like a woman."

The guard, who obviously did not understand any Gaelish, nevertheless leered at the two men and smoothed his bushy moustache.

"Now, who's going to work? You on the docks, or the guards on your arse?" she demanded.

That was seemingly enough for the two of them. They both turned and picked up sacks, putting them over their shoulders. She turned, although she could feel their stares burning into her back.

"You won't have any more trouble with them," Bridgit assured Gokmen.

He nodded at her, offering a hint of a smile.

But will I have more trouble with them? she wondered.

CHAPTER 24

"Faster!" Fallon roared at the men.

After a quarter moon of training the men solidly with their weapons, he was moving on to the next stage. They still worked with weapons in the morning but, in the afternoon, he drilled them through the city. The Kottermani confidence was a weapon he hoped to use against them.

"Stand your ground then, at my order, run as if you're breaking. Then reform the line!" he bellowed at the group of fifty he was working on.

At his orders they formed a line bristling with spears, four deep, which filled the road. If the Kottermanis tried to break that, they would be shredded by the massed iron points. But if they stood back and tried to use their bows, his men could not stand. There would be crossbow parties up on the roofs but they would be no match for the Kottermani bows. No, the only way to beat them would be to make the Kottermanis think they were breaking. A soldier's first instinct on seeing a running enemy would be to chase them. That should bring them onto the spears – and make their advance more ragged as well.

"Duck down!" he roared and the four ranks tried to shelter behind the one line of shields. It was a pitiful protection and he knew they could not hope to withstand an arrow attack like that.

"Now run! Like you mean it! Look scared!"

The group broke up, the tight ranks dissolving, men looking over their shoulders as they ran, some of them stumbling, others nearly colliding with the wall or with each other.

"They are all keeping their spears. That could make the Kottermanis suspicious," Bran said as he watched with Fallon.

"A second time, yes," Fallon judged. "But the first time they witness this, they will see what they want – men running from them."

Bran nodded and they watched the chaotic retreat down the street.

Fallon cupped his hands around his mouth. "Form the line!" he shouted.

It was a clumsy thing compared to their earlier attempt but they shuffled together and the spears came out and soon there was an impenetrable line across the road once more.

"Would you like to break through that?" Fallon asked as they walked down the road.

"Not really, no," Bran agreed. "But can they do it without you yelling at them?"

"They'd better," Fallon said flatly.

"Can't we get the wizards to help us? Surely some magic could help defeat the Kottermanis?"

Fallon grimaced. He had already had that conversation, several times, with his friends. "I don't trust those bastards," he said. "Risk all our lives on the Guilds? We rely on ourselves and nobody else!"

*

"How heavy are those?" Fallon inspected the special ladders Brendan had designed. Each of them was more than three times the height of a man and had hooked ends at both top and bottom. They also had close-fitting rungs as, unlike normal ladders, these were designed to get crossbowmen from one roof to another without them having to climb down.

Brendan picked up one with a grunt, but only just. "Two men can move them. Three would be better though," he said.

"And if they have to dump them?"

Brendan bent to demonstrate. "Pull these iron pins out of the middle and it's in half. Then you can just kick it off the roof," he said.

Fallon patted the big smith on the back. "How many have we got?"

"This is the fourth. But we'll have the rest done by the end of tomorrow."

Fallon admired the device. It was an idea straight from the child snatchers who had terrorized Berry for moons. The three hundred crossbowmen he had would be split up into ten companies and given these ladders. They could then move across the rooftops, retreating or advancing as necessary to keep raining bolts down on the Kottermanis. From up high they could stay out of the way of the Kottermani bowmen as they reloaded – and also make themselves smaller targets.

"It feels strange to making all these preparations, knowing we will be long gone by the time the Kottermanis get here. I wonder how these lads will go without us," Brendan said softly.

Fallon nodded. "I know. But for Aroaril's sake don't say it too loud!" he hissed.

Brendan hit him on the chest lightly. "Here comes the King," he muttered.

Fallon was about to hit him back harder and mock him for such a lame attempt at a jest, when he heard the footsteps and turned hurriedly to see King Aidan approaching, Kelty and Regan at his shoulders, a handful of guards behind.

"How is my army progressing?" the King asked brightly, waving them up as they sank to one knee.

"Well, sire. These are the ladders our crossbowmen can use to move from roof to roof, staying one step ahead of the Kottermanis." Fallon stepped aside to show Aidan the work.

"Excellent! And where will you be during the fight?"

Fallon did not hesitate. "I will be on the roofs, so I can see what is happening. I shall have a few guards with flags and several trumpeters, so they can signal down to the different units. We shall have one of these ladders, so we can quickly get from one point to another. Our whole strategy is to split up the Kottermanis and prevent them from using their numbers. We want them to be confused, for we know what we are doing."

King Aidan smiled broadly and rubbed his hands together. "Perfect. I cannot wait until we visit slaughter on those bastards! And then you can drag Prince Kemal before me and we shall so terrify him that they will never again cross the sea to threaten us!"

"How will you do that, sire?" Fallon asked innocently, hoping he would get an answer.

But Aidan merely held up his hand. "That is for another day," he said with a half-smile. "But, tell me, where is your son? I hear he has been helping inspire my new soldiers!"

"Indeed he has, sire." Fallon bowed his head. "But he is with friends today, taking a break from training men."

"A wise idea," Aidan agreed. "Truly, it was a lucky day for this country when you walked into my court! Well, don't let me stop you. Keep going: I know there must be a hundred things that demand your attention, Captain!"

Fallon and Brendan bowed as the King walked away.

"There's another who is in love with Captain Fallon," Brendan muttered.

"I look forward to the day when I break his heart," Fallon said coldly.

*

That thought accompanied him through the streets as he headed off to the Moneylenders' Guildhouse, where Kerrin had spent the day with Asil and Orhan. The boy had not wanted to miss a whole day of training but, for the first time, Fallon sensed he was actually happy to play with the Kottermanis. While it was good to see the recruits adopt his son as one of their own, it was even better to see him running around like a normal little boy, rather than a grim recruit, always doing extra running. He had actually been woken one morning by grunts and groans as Kerrin worked out fiercely in their room, even though he would face a whole day of training. Just what had he turned his son into?

The streets were still full of groups of recruits, most of them coming back to the square after training, and he greeted each one, taking their cheers and salutes until it felt as though his face would crack from smiling so much.

He wondered if he might be able to bring them with him. Leaving them to fight the Kottermanis without him seemed like cowardice. There were plenty of ships in the harbor, after all. But then he thought about all their families as well – and the prospect that Cavan's secret island would not be able to support so many. Even taking down King Aidan and leaving the Duchess in his place was not going to be much comfort, but he could not see another choice.

He checked around carefully before hurrying down a side street to bring him out near the Moneylenders' square. Even though Berry was overcrowded, this place was quiet, thanks, no doubt, to all the battles and bloodshed scaring people off. But he was always looking over his shoulder as he got close, and liked to double back down an alley or two, just in case. He could never forget that the Kottermanis had agents searching the city for Feray and her sons and the King had his own spies scattered through Berry as well.

Once he was sure he was alone, he slipped into the square to see a ball game under way: the three boys raced around, laughing.

He smiled at that and then tensed as a pair of villagers appeared at his side. "Anyone come around?" he asked.

"Nobody," they confirmed. "But some of that laughter might be getting a bit loud."

"I'll speak to them," Fallon promised, although he liked to hear Kerrin laugh. It had been a rare enough thing lately.

He walked over to where Feray watched the game, calling out advice. Devlin was about ten paces away, leaning up against a doorway, and he waved to Fallon. Fallon was about to go over to his friend when an impulse made him go and stand near Feray instead, where he clapped as Asil made a particularly fine kick.

"They have learned fast. They are very skilled," he said, thinking that every mother liked to talk about her children.

She glanced at him and for a moment he thought she would turn away and he would have to go and speak with Devlin instead, but she was distracted by Orhan making a strong catch.

"That was even better." Fallon applauded.

"They have only trained with swords before, not really played these games," Feray said reluctantly.

"Well, they have quick feet and hands and good eyes; you must be proud," Fallon said, keeping his eyes on the boys, looking sidelong at Feray.

"I always was," she said.

He took a deep breath. He could either keep going with these harmless statements or say something of worth. "I am sorry about what happened and about keeping you here," he said softly. "More than you can know. Believe me, I never wanted any of this to happen. But your husband came to our village in the night and took all our wives and children. He may have had the permission of our King but we knew nothing of it until we returned home to find our homes empty. As soon as our families are back, you shall return to your husband, I swear to you."

She said nothing and he just kept watching the game, wondering if she was going to pretend not to have heard anything.

"But can I believe you?" she asked. "Without us, you have no hold over my husband and no way to stop his vengeance."

"I give you my word," Fallon said. After all, they would not be staying in Gaelland and Kemal would never find them.

"Words are easy. Did you not swear you were telling the truth when you lured my husband into your trap? Would you offer Kerrin's life on your word? Pledge for Aroaril to take him if you lie?"

Fallon hesitated. That was far more than he wanted to commit. Kerrin's life was the one thing he could never, would never risk. Feray snorted in derision and he thought of the men he was training and how this woman might be able to save their lives by persuading her husband to make a peace deal with a new ruler of Gaelland.

"I swear on Kerrin's life," he said heavily. "And that is the strongest pledge I could ever make. As my wife saved him, as we battle now to save her – that is how I will fight to see you and your boys back with your husband."

*

Feray heard Fallon's words and hated him for them. Each one was worming its way inside her defenses, inside the wall she had put around her to survive this. When you hated your captors, it was easier to survive each day, for that warmed you and thoughts of revenge enabled you to get through whatever was needed to make the time pass. But her boys had begun to enjoy playing with Kerrin, to look forward to it as the one bright spot in each day. She could not deny them that. Yet with it had come sympathy for these people. As much as she tried to hold on to her anger, she could see herself and Kemal in what they had done. If anyone had stolen Asil or Orhan, she would have torn their throats out with her teeth, let alone threatened to hurt their loved ones.

If Fallon had still been angry and mad, the crazed man who had held a knife to Orhan's eye, it would have been easy to despise him. But it was harder to stop herself talking to this man, the one who spoke easily about the children.

That was dangerous. She knew Kemal would come back with Fallon and his men's families. He would not risk anything happening to her or the boys. But he would also come seeking revenge for what Fallon had done and she could see the day when Fallon, his wife and son were under Kemal's power and she would be forced to watch them being tortured.

"I cannot do this," she said, the words torn from her.

"What's that?" he asked, his voice still light.

"You think that this will be over when my husband returns? I can understand what you did, even if I hate you for it, but he will never accept it. It will never be over," she said fiercely.

Fallon turned to her. "But surely, understanding each other is the first step," he said. "I understand your husband as I know myself. We are alike in what we feel for our families. Surely if we can find common ground there, we can find common ground for our people, our countries?"

"It doesn't work like that," she said irritably. "And while he might understand you, he will never forgive or forget. Can you?"

"If my wife and my men's families are returned to us, then yes, we can," he replied.

"Then you will never be able to rule a country, like my husband."

"Really? I thought being a leader was putting aside your own thoughts for the good of your people?" he countered. "Look at our sons playing. Does that not say we can find a way to live together?"

She looked at the boys playing and shook her head.

"Well, it does not matter overmuch. I will be gone from this land, as will the rest of us," Fallon said. "He can take his revenge against Gaelland but he will never find us."

She sighed. "This was never about revenge. We hoped to help Gaelland, to see it freed from the rule of a mad king. With my husband controlling the country, life for many would get better."

"Except for those sent to work for the glory of your empire," Fallon said. "You have felt what it is like to be kept against your will in a strange place, away from those you know and love. Would you wish it on others?"

She bit her lip, knowing she had no answer. Things that seemed so simple back on the ship, or in the first few turns of the hourglass after being kidnapped from the ship with her sons, were now more complicated.

"Where will you go, if not to live back in your old village?" she asked instead.

"To an island far from here. Where we will never be found. We have had enough of fighting."

"But what of your country? Will you just let it be taken?" she demanded. "You are the King's man: how can you turn your back on him?"

He chuckled then, a harsh sound. "I will never be his man. He had me kill my Prince, my friend. And what I have seen him do ... There is no man in his court fit to follow."

"How about a woman? Or do you think we should wield no power?" she challenged, interested to know more about the Gaelish nobles from one who did not care for them. She had read the reports from Kemal's agents, of course, but those were all colored by the quality of the informants.

He laughed again, but this time it was genuine. "If you ever meet my wife, Bridgit, you will see that I know a woman can easily wield power!"

"And are there any like that at court? Do you Gaelish allow women to have power?"

"There is one," he said. "The Duchess Dina. Your husband would do well to speak to her, although I warn you, her husband disappeared at sea, thought taken by the Kottermanis. Your husband denied doing it but she does not believe it so. Convince her, or return him, and you will have an ally here."

She pondered that. Having an ally among the nobility would be a real help. But she was sure no noble had been taken. The deal had been for ordinary people only.

"We shall see," she said. She wanted to add that it had been good to speak to him but did not want him to know that. He was friendly enough now but that could all change. "We had better stop these boys playing before it gets dark!"

*

Fallon watched her walk over to her boys and summon them reluctantly away from the game. He smiled to himself. The ice had been broken at least and the idea about Dina had been planted. Now he had to sneak over to the Duchess's house. She had sent him a message through Gannon that day, which the sergeant had passed on carefully, looking all around him. But what she could be concerned about, he had no idea.

CHAPTER 25

"How is your army coming along?" Dina asked pleasantly.

Fallon lifted his goblet of fresh pear juice to his lips but paused. "It is not my army, but the King's," he said before drinking. He was seated at a gorgeous Kottermani table, surrounded by beautiful Kottermani furniture and ornaments, in a room that was big enough to house a family in Berry's slums and that family could have lived happily for the rest of their life on what it had cost to furnish it. He felt uncomfortable there, afraid to leave a mark on the table or even lean back on the polished chair.

Dina chuckled. "Let us be honest about these things. Have we not been through enough to have reached that?"

Fallon put down his goblet and smiled acknowledgement.

"Good," she said. "It is your army. Who is the King to them? Do you think they will die for him, the way they will die for you?"

"No, I do not," Fallon admitted.

"So when will we be ready to seize the throne? Together we can rule Gaelland and bring Prince Cavan's dream to life!"

Fallon looked at her, his mind awhirl. The training was coming along but he was not willing to risk them against Kelty's guards yet. A pitched battle in the streets could see hundreds of ordinary people slaughtered as well, or even the King barricaded in his castle and Fallon trying to force him out before the nobles rode to Aidan's rescue. Then there was Kemal and Feray. He could not trust her to support the Duchess yet, while if Kemal arrived here to find him ruling, then he would want revenge from the whole country. But he could not reveal all that.

She leaned forwards, her face alight, and reached out to touch his arm. "It will solve all our problems," she said. "You already have the loyalty of a third of Kelty's guards and your own men, plus the recruits. You could take the castle in a heartbeat. I will take the crown, with you as my captain. I can bring the nobles into line and we can finally punish Aidan and Swane for what they have done. We will find the missing children and then we can negotiate properly with the Kottermanis, so that our people are protected and your families are brought home."

Fallon took a big swig of juice to try and moisten his dry mouth. "But you are talking about Aidan," he said. "He will not go quietly. And what do we do with him after we have taken his throne? Every noble who wants more power will march to his aid. We'll be fighting the whole country."

Dina shook her head. "He sold off your families to the Kottermanis! He was behind the child snatchers and then burned a score of women at the stake, claiming they were the witches behind it. He has whipped and killed a dozen servants in the last few years alone, to say nothing of the maidens raped and the families destroyed. Then he murdered the Crown Prince – and, as for his remaining son, he has been consorting with Fearpriests! Do you think he deserves to be rewarded? Once the people know what they have been doing, they will never support them. You can leave the nobles to me. As to the Guilds, as long as they make money, they don't care who is on the throne."

"But even if we show the people all he has been doing, he is still the King. He controls all the courts. What would we do with him?"

Dina patted his forearm. "You would sentence him. You are an officer of the crown first. What is the penalty for his crimes?"

Fallon closed his eyes for a moment. "Death," he whispered.

"Indeed. And with him and Swane dead, the way is clear for this country to know peace."

Fallon moved his arm out of reach and pushed his goblet away. It was dangerously tempting… but he had made so many mistakes. Each time he had acted, sure he was doing the right thing, it had gone horribly wrong. He had once trusted his instincts, now he doubted them. Everything within him cried out to see Aidan dead but he could not take any risks. Bridgit and the other families were on the way back. Best not to rock the boat. What if things went wrong and he got many of his men killed? How could he face their families then?

"We're not ready yet," he said.

She reached out again for his hand. "Get them ready. How many times have you spoken of your regret for loosing the bolt that killed Prince Cavan? How many times have you said you want to atone for that? This is your chance! We can make his legacy live again. He may be gone but his dream will live on. You can tell your son that you made the country a better place. You know we can do this! The Kottermanis will go away after a year or two and we shall be left to run Gaelland the way we want, to make it better for everyone!"

Dina sat back, triumphantly.

"I just want my family back, and all the other families," Fallon said.

"Don't be a fool!" she snapped. "You have the chance of a lifetime here, Fallon! You have the fate of our country in your hands: you can't let it just fall from your grasp and walk away!"

He sighed. "But that is exactly what I want to do."

She stood and began pacing around the room, nearly knocking over half a dozen rare Kottermani vases as she strode about the expensive furniture. "You need to think about this," she said impatiently. "Gaelland can come out of this so much better than before. We can come out of this as heroes!"

"My mind is made up," he said, his voice firming. "I will exchange families and that will be it."

"Don't be a fool! Do you think Kemal will leave it there, shake your hand and tell you that you played a good game? He will demand revenge and come hunting for you. A Kottermani ship will return to Baltimore but this time it will rain fire and death upon you! Only by taking the throne can you protect yourself."

He shook his head. "Where I am going, he will not be able to find me."

She stopped suddenly, the wind of her passage setting a delicate vase to trembling on a small table beside her. Without looking she reached out a hand and settled it. "You think to leave here?" she said quietly. "What will happen to Gaelland then? To your army? To me and your other friends?"

Fallon spread his hands helplessly. "I can think of no other way to protect the country from Kemal's revenge. If I am not here, he has nobody to threaten."

She smoothed her hair, flicking it back from her face, then walked over until she was right in front of him. "Listen to me," she said gently. "You are making a terrible mistake. I won't say any more to convince you now. You have to listen to that small voice in the back of your head. Talk to your friends, think of what Prince Cavan would have wanted. And then come and tell me your decision. But do not leave things too long. We have to act soon."

Fallon pushed back his chair carefully, not wanting to damage it, and stood.

"I will," he said, knowing his own decision but thinking he had better humor her, or she would never let him out of there.

"Good," she said softly and took his hand. "We can do this, Fallon. We can change this country and make history. You just need the courage to join me."

*

"The King needs to see you now!"

Fallon turned away from the recruits with a groan. This was becoming wearying. At first the reports to the King had been formal enough but, as the men got better and word spread around Berry of the training, King Aidan was becoming more and more enthusiastic.

"Keep working, I'll be back as soon as I am able," he told them, signaling for Gallagher to take over the lesson.

The King was not in his private rooms but instead in the throne room, a score of nobles and double that of Guildsmen standing around. As soon as Fallon walked in they broke into applause.

"Here he is, my champion!" Aidan announced, standing up and walking through the crowd towards Fallon. Instantly the nobles and Guildsmen redoubled their efforts to cheer him and roared their approval as Aidan strode right up to Fallon and embraced him.

Fallon stood awkwardly. He was becoming better at hiding his revulsion, at least.

The King drew back and raised Fallon's right arm into the air.

"This is the son I never had," Aidan announced, his voice thick with emotion.

Fallon glanced towards the King, fighting to keep the shock and horror from his face. How could the man say something like that, after ordering his eldest son killed? But Aidan was not looking at him, instead addressing his audience.

"My lords, I commend him to you! The man who will lead the defense of Berry and help our men create an empire, one to rival the Kottermanis!"

The cheering redoubled and Fallon forced a sickly smile to his face. An empire? From where? Holding off the Kottermanis would be victory enough.

Aidan shook his arm in the air and patted him on the back. "He has done more than I hoped, more than I imagined. He has proved that we were right to defy Kotterman and that we deserve not just to be free but to stand above all other countries!"

Fallon thought that some of the nobles were looking tired from all the enthusiastic applauding they were doing, but none dared to slow down.

"Whatever he needs, give it to him, for he speaks with my voice!"

Fallon nodded and bowed his head, keeping the smile fixed on his face.

Aidan patted him on the back once more. "Now, come and tell us how training progresses," he said.

"Sire, I really need to get back to watching the recruits," Fallon said. "Could I not just tell you tomorrow, at our regular meeting?"

There was a collective gasp of breath from around the room and the applause faltered.

For a moment Fallon thought he had gone too far, then Aidan smiled and nodded.

"Indeed, my champion. Every moment is precious! Please, get back to work and we shall relax, knowing you are there to be our shield."

He embraced Fallon once more and again Fallon had no idea what to do, except bow and back out of there once he was released.

As the doors shut behind him, he breathed a sigh of relief. This was getting stranger by the day.

*

"What are you going to tell the Duchess?" Padraig demanded. "Are we going to get rid of Aidan?"

"Aroaril knows I would love to. The man is now talking about creating an empire! He's utterly mad! But it's too risky. I'm just going to avoid her, tell her I need more time, or that I am too busy training the army if I meet her," Fallon said.

The old wizard scratched his belly irritably. "I don't like this much," he said.

"Well don't do it. It looks disgusting as well, your hand under your robe like that," Fallon told him with a smile.

But Padraig did not grin back. Instead he took his hand out from underneath his robe and pointed at Fallon.

"I think we need to move Feray and her boys Asleep and Otherhand."

"Asil and Orhan," Fallon said patiently.

"Whatever. But I don't like the way the Duchess's mind is working. What if she decides to move things along and force us to take on Aidan?"

Fallon laughed. "She doesn't know where Feray and the boys are!"

"There are plenty of ears listening out there for word of Prince Kemal's family. She just has to whisper the wrong word in the right noble's ear and everything turns to shit."

Fallon shook his head. "We have nowhere else to take them. Aidan's men might have left our ship now but that is too exposed and I can't see us keeping them a secret in here, can you?"

"Find another house. Do something! We are close to finally getting everyone back. We can't risk that."

"And nor will I. If I can work on Feray, get her to persuade Kemal to make a new deal with the Duchess, then Dina will be content."

"I hope you are right," Padraig said.

"You know I am! Now, come with me and let's talk to Feray. Her boys love your magic and she seems to like you as well."

Padraig picked his nose, inspected the result and wiped it carefully on his robe. "It's my charm and manners," he explained.

CHAPTER 26

Training was moving apace, with the city becoming used to seeing the recruits running across rooftops or blocking the roads. As fast as barrels of crossbows rolled into the city, they were being splintered into targets by the crossbow company. The last of the spears was complete, as were the rooftop ladders, while Brendan and a dozen smiths were being kept busy altering mail shirts for the sword company.

The young men were all stronger, faster and far more skilled than they had when they started, while the people of Berry had embraced both him and the army, offering them extra food and drink, while there always seemed to be young women hanging around, especially in the evenings. That was getting so bad that he was thinking of posting guards over the recruits. Not that he begrudged them the female company, but they needed their sleep.

Cheers always seemed to follow him as he endlessly paced the streets, until the area from the docks to the castle was as familiar to him as the back of his hand. That also helped him avoid Duchess Dina. She had sent him several messages, requesting his presence. He knew what that really meant. She wanted his answer – and she wanted it to be that they would take the throne. As much as he wanted Aidan dead, he wanted his recruits alive. He had nightmares about an attack on the castle going wrong and hundreds of accusing eyes facing him as their owners lay dead on the cobbles. Why take the risk, when Bridgit and the others would be back in a half-moon? He had lost the families by acting rashly. He did not trust himself now.

He followed a group of crossbowmen over a pair of roofs, as they practiced loading out of sight and then leaning forwards to pretend to loose at enemies below.

"Are we getting better, sir?" one asked.

Fallon smiled back at him. It was hard not to think of some of them as his sons. If the first children he and Bridgit had lost had lived, they would be this age. "You're nearly as good as me," he told them.

They grinned at him.

"Maybe one day. Kerrin was telling us how you are the greatest ever with a crossbow, how you can shoot a bee's cock off at forty paces," the recruit said.

Fallon laughed – and then paused. "And did Kerrin tell you those exact words?" he asked suspiciously. If those were the words he was using, there was going to be trouble – for Fallon – when Bridgit returned.

"He might have," the recruit replied carefully.

Fallon shook his head. He needed to have a quiet word with his son and remind him that things would have to change again once Bridgit was back with them.

"Have you boys seen Kerrin today?" he asked.

"No, sir." They all shook their heads. "Do you want us to find him?"

Fallon waved them away. "Don't worry lads, keep training," he told them. "Let's try to make it across to that roof over there, quick as we can."

But as they quickly planned their route across there, trumpets sounded from below and Fallon peered over to see a handful of the King's guards, Regan at their head, hurrying down the street.

"Captain Fallon!" Regan shouted.

Fallon merely waved down to him.

"The King needs to see you! Now!"

Fallon sighed. Not another interminable session of the King saying how delighted he was with his new army. He waved again, to signal he had heard, then turned back to the recruits.

"Keep going," he said. "I'll be back as soon as I can."

He let them go and knocked on a window so the owner would let him in and he could head downstairs.

CHAPTER 27

Prince Kemal locked eyes confidently with Fallon. The cowardly Gaelish scum was frothing at the mouth, his eyes wild as he held a razor-sharp knife to Orhan's face.

"Tell me what I want to know or I will skin your son and wear him like a cloak!" he snarled.

Kemal imagined his mind was a steel spear and he drove it into Fallon's crazy eyes. "You will not. You will release my son and then release all of us. For that is the only way you will live and the only way your families will live. Harm a hair of his head and not one of your people will survive. They will die screaming and cursing your names."

Fallon glared at him but the Gaelishman's confidence broke apart on Kemal's rock-hard certainty. With a scream and a curse he threw his knife away.

"Now untie me. I shall give you the chance to get away before I come after you," Kemal said, his voice throbbing with power.

"You have to do it," Fallon's friend, the big Gaelishman, said.

Fallon cursed again but Kemal could see he was broken. He was no longer able to meet Kemal's eyes as he sawed his bonds apart and then stumbled from the room, head downcast.

Kemal stood to take the embrace of his relieved sons and then the passionate kiss of his wife.

"Aroaril, you are such a man," Feray whispered, her hand slipping down his body and cupping his groin.

He was just enjoying that when, over her shoulder, he saw Fallon walk back into the room. "High one! You are needed on the deck!" the man shouted in Kottermani.

Kemal jerked awake and flung himself out of bed, rubbing his eyes. He looked down and cursed himself. His body had betrayed him, and he buried his head in his hands. He groaned. The same dream again. When would he get some peace?

"I will be there," he called to the sailor outside his door.

He hurriedly washed and dressed and went up on deck to stare at the horizon with bloodshot eyes. The crew looked little better. He had been driving them hard and they stumbled around at their posts, struggling to complete even the most mundane of tasks. The wind had been with them and he had ordered the ship pushed as hard as it was able. His sailing master was exhausted, snatching a turn of the hourglass of sleep here and there.

To his men he seemed the same and outwardly he could project an image of calm and control. Inside, however, he was still weeping and begging for his son's life. He could not get away from that until he confronted Fallon again.

"What am I looking for?" he demanded. He blinked and rubbed at his eyes, feeling as if they were filled with sand.

"Land! Adana dead ahead!" The call came from the lookout at the masthead and he felt the relief wash over him. He could not stand the thought of Feray and the boys in the hands of that madman for one day longer than necessary. He would sleep for a day, while the ships were refitted and the army gathered, then start the return voyage. That one would be easier, for each day would be bringing him closer to his family, not taking him further away. And, of course, there was always the thought of revenge. Even though his foot was healed, it still seemed to throb with sudden agony at strange times, a reminder of what had been done to him. He owed Fallon twice as much pain.

*

"I don't think you should do this," Ely said.

Bridgit looked at her critically. The young translator had been growing more withdrawn and quiet as they prepared for their escape. Now it looked as if she had tears in her eyes.

"Don't be afraid," Bridgit said, reaching out to draw her in to an embrace.

"No!" Ely knocked her away. "This is madness and it will end in disaster. The children will be killed and we will all suffer a terrible end!"

Bridgit grabbed hold of her hands and forced the young woman to look at her. "Listen to me," she said harshly. "I spent most of my life living in fear. I let my worries rule me, and always thought about what could go wrong. I cannot continue. We have to have hope. Without it there is nothing, understand?"

Ely shook her head, big, fat tears gathered at the corners of her eyes. "You don't know what is waiting for you!"

Bridgit pulled her even closer. "But I do," she said. "I have gone out there. I know what risk we take – but do you know what happens if we do nothing?"

Ely shook her head, her eyes glistening.

"We betray everything and everyone. And we watch these children be sent away, one at a time, into slavery. That makes us as bad as Gokmen and his guards. And I will not be a part of that, no matter what it costs."

She was shocked to see Ely dissolve into tears then. She thought that little speech might have put some backbone into the girl, rather than make her feel worse. And she could understand Ely. If their places had been reversed, she would have been paralyzed by fear, imagining all the things that could go wrong. But she had not just the children but her baby to think about. For their sakes she had to concentrate on how to defeat these obstacles, not waste time and energy worrying about them.

"Sshh," she said, drawing Ely into her arms and rocking her gently, as she had done so many times with Kerrin. That thought brought a prickle of tears into her own eyes and a renewed determination to get out of there. She had to see him again. "We shall get out of here and we shall laugh about this once we are back in Gaelland."

Ely snuffled her tears to a stop and pulled away slightly. "Bridgit, there is something I have to tell you," she said softly.

"Of course, anything."

"You will hate me for it but I must tell you anyway."

"Whist! I know how you feel only too well," Bridgit said with feeling. "And with only a day to go, it is natural to feel fear."

Ely shook her head angrily. "No, you do not understand!"

"Then speak, tell me," Bridgit said. "Whatever it is, it is eating you up."

Ely nodded at that. She took a deep breath, let it out and looked unsure as to how to begin.

"Ship! Ship entering the harbor!" Riona called, racing into the room.

Bridgit turned around irritably. "There are always ships coming into the harbor!"

"Not ones flying the flag of Prince Kemal!" Riona snapped.

Bridgit felt a touch of fear then. Why was he back so quickly? And when would he want to speak to Gokmen, who would no doubt want to know if it was true that Bridgit was carrying his child. Their escape plans would come to an end on the instant.

"We shall be right there," she said, then helped Ely to her feet.

"What did you want to tell me?" she asked again.

Ely sighed. "It is foolish," she said. "I am scared of Gaelland and how they will accept me there."

Bridgit chuckled. "They will love you. Or I will want to know why not! Now come on."

They joined Nola and Riona on the terrace and watched the ship sail in, looking ragged and dirty.

"What does this mean?" Nola asked. "Should we delay?"

"There can be no delay," Bridgit said strongly. "Once the Prince is here, our people will be shipped out as slaves. And it can work in our favor. It means there are more ships down there ready to make the trip. We hold to the plan. Do not think of things that could go wrong. Think instead of what it will feel like to see our families again."

They looked at her and she smiled at them. "Tomorrow we shall be free, either way," she said.

CHAPTER 28

Fallon made his way through a series of groups of recruits being put through their paces by a mixture of villagers and guardsmen. With one trainer to no more than five recruits, progress had been swift, and each day the men were getting stronger, faster and more skilled. He still had no idea if they would be able to hold against a Kottermani army, but they could at least work together and that would give them a chance. He waved and smiled and wondered what the King would want this time. Surely there was nothing else that he could tell the man. The big decisions had all been made: now it was all about small increases in ability and stamina. He hoped Aidan was not going to call him the champion again in front of the nobles. He did not think he could take another one of those sessions.

"Quickly now," Regan said fussily, guiding him upwards towards the King's rooms.

At least this would mean their conversation would be without a huge audience, Fallon thought gratefully.

Quinn and a couple of guards were on duty outside the King's rooms. Quinn glowered at Fallon while the two guards snapped to attention, making the guard officer look even angrier.

"Leave all your weapons behind," Quinn said shortly.

Fallon was used to this by now, so unhooked the baldric that held his sword and shillelagh, took out a pair of Brendan's throwing knives and placed them all on the table.

"Is that everything?" Quinn growled.

"What do you think I am going to do?" Fallon snapped back at him.

"Search him." Quinn pointed to his guardsmen.

"What is this?" Fallon asked indignantly. "I have never been searched before!"

Regan was there a moment later. "It is a new set of orders, Captain. Nothing to do with you," he said swiftly.

Fallon glared back at Quinn. "Fine. But he has to do it," he said, jabbing his finger at Quinn.

Quinn bristled immediately but Regan nodded agreement. "Do it, Quinn," he said.

Grumbling, the young officer moved in and began to clumsily run his hands across Fallon's arms and legs, searching for a hidden weapon. Fallon smiled sarcastically at the officer as the man missed checking his boots, where he had another pair of throwing knives hidden. He was already looking forward to walking out of the office and dropping them into Quinn's lap.

"He is clean," Quinn said, stepping away.

"More than I can say for him. He pawed at me like a drunken sailor in a whorehouse," Fallon sneered.

Regan stepped between the two of them. "Just go right in. I shall see you later," he said, ushering Fallon into the room and shutting the door behind him.

Fallon looked around the room, expecting to see the King behind his desk, or in the armchair before the fire, but instead Aidan was advancing on him, arms wide and a broad smile on his face. Strangely, he wore a rust-red cloak inside, although the fire had the room nice and warm.

"My champion! Good to see you!" Aidan said warmly, enfolding Fallon in his arms and pounding him on the back. Fallon could not bring himself to touch Aidan, so he merely let his hands hang by his sides. Aidan did not seem to notice and changed position, moving Fallon into the middle of the room, with an arm around his shoulder.

"You really are a man after my own heart," he said with a wink. "People see you and they think there's a simple, straightforward man but really you are a thinker and planner."

"I try to be, sire," Fallon replied, wondering where this was all going. In conversations with Aidan it always felt as though only one of them knew what was going on.

Aidan chuckled. "When I first met you I did not know what to make of this country sergeant my poor Cavan had taken on. But you have proved yourself the equal of anyone I have met in this court. What you have done with those raw recruits is nothing short of magical. A rabble turned into an army in such a short time. And now this!"

"What's that, sire?" Fallon asked, a twinge of concern intruding into his confusion.

"You are too modest! And too clever! You had a little surprise for me, a special trick up the sleeve! The only thing I would say is you should have come to me first of all, but no harm done, eh?"

Fallon had no idea what Aidan was babbling on about. Previously he had found the best course of action was to nod and smile until things became clearer, so he merely did that.

"I admit, if there was one worry I had, it was I didn't think you were ruthless enough, but you proved me wrong. You are now ready to lead my army."

As he spoke, Aidan kept his arm around Fallon's shoulders and guided him across the room, past the pair of ever-present burly bodyguards. Both of them were also wearing cloaks in that not particularly pleasant color.

"I am willing to get the job done, sire," Fallon said.

"Oh, I can see that! So now, let me reveal everything to you."

Fallon could feel his heart begin to pound as the King guided him around the desk. Just in time he remembered he was not supposed to know about the secret door behind the hanging.

"Where are we going, sire?" he asked, putting some of his confusion into his voice.

"To prove you are the man Gaelland needs," Aidan said, giving him a wink. He let go of Fallon's shoulder to open the secret door and Fallon made himself look surprised.

"Where does that go, sire?" he asked, wondering why they were going down to the throne room this way, rather than in the normal manner.

"You'll see," Aidan said. "Come, all will be made clear!"

Fallon was mystified as to what the King was going on about. Aidan was smiling broadly and at his affable best, which was as usual more disturbing than when he was angry. One thing seemed obvious – the King was not going to stop talking in riddles until they got down to the throne room. So he stepped through the door. The last time he had been hiding in here, there had been no light and he had been terrified of falling. But this time it was well lit, a series of lanterns flickering away in recesses in the wall.

"Straight down, I'll tell you where to go," Aidan said cheerfully, the guards between him and Fallon.

Fallon walked down the steps, finding them much easier in the light than the dark. They finished in a landing and he saw the door to the throne room right ahead so naturally reached out for the handle.

"Not that one!" Aidan said. "Keep going down!"

Fallon turned and stepped out to the side, which revealed another staircase leading further down, one he had missed completely in the dark. He was already nervous but now he began to get a little frightened. That level merely held a series of storerooms – and the dungeons. He could not imagine the King wanting to take him down to show off his collection of rare Kottermani wines. Had the Duchess somehow been captured and blabbed about their talks, perhaps even blamed him for the plot to seize the throne and win over the nobles? That fitted into what the King had been saying but, if so, why was Aidan being so pleasant? He would have expected the greeting party to be Kelty and a squad of guards.

He walked down the next set of stairs feeling as though his heart was thumping loudly enough to be heard over the sound of his footsteps.

"This stairway was built to allow servants to bring valuables up to the King without being seen – and for the King to be able to slip down into certain parts of his castle in secret. There are things a King wants to do that his Queen does not need to know about," Aidan said.

Fallon could feel the hair on the back of his arms rising up now. After all, down here was where Swane and his Fearpriest had been holding their evil ceremonies. Padraig and Rosaleen's words about a huge evil came back to him and even the air felt colder down here. He was tempted to draw his hidden knives, try and put down the guards and demand answers from the King. But a glance over his shoulder showed him Aidan was several steps behind and the guards were both brandishing shillelaghs. By the time he had taken them out, Aidan would be long gone. Besides, if the worst was behind that door, it was a chance to destroy not just Aidan but Swane and, maybe, the Fearpriest too. He thought of Kerrin and Bridgit with a sharp shaft of pain, then the stairs ended in a thick wooden door.

"Here we are," Aidan said brightly. The guards stopped right behind Fallon. "I truly think you can lead my army to victory," he said sincerely. "Now I just need to see the final proof."

Fallon nodded nervously, not trusting himself to speak. Whatever waited on the other side of the door, he could have a knife at the King's throat in an instant.

A guard pushed open the door and gestured for Fallon to walk through. After a moment's pause, he strode through the door. It took his eyes a moment to adjust to the blaze of light – and then he was filled with terror and fury.

Time seemed to slow and every breath lasted an age as his eyes took in everything in less than three heartbeats. The first thing he saw standing before him was the Fearpriest, hood hiding his face, arms crossed over his chest. To his right stood Swane, his usual sneer on his face, his hands on his hips and no chains or ropes on either of them. Behind them were men wearing the robes of Guildsmen, as well as a scatter of nobles. Yet all of them wore the same rust-red cloak.

Before he drew his knives out of his boots, he caught sight of the second thing. Small figures, behind Swane and his Fearpriest, tied down onto a stone slab. Three of them. The room was well-lit, braziers at every column driving back the cold and dark, and he recognized them instantly. Feray, Asil and Orhan.

Then he saw the third thing, a small figure tied to a column, looking right at him. Kerrin. Beside him, Captain Kelty with a shillelagh in his hands.

Fallon saw all that and his mind raced through his choices, holding his rage in check only by the slimmest of threads.

"It looks like I should have ordered a new cloak," he said.

He heard Aidan laugh and had to hold back a shiver of hatred so intense it threatened to rip away his last vestige of control.

"My dear Fallon, you truly are a gem!" Aidan chuckled.

The guards escorted him into the middle of the room. Fallon still felt like his mind was racing almost out of control, going through what he needed to do, and he uttered a silent prayer that he would have the strength for what would come.

"So, this is where Prince Swane has been?" he asked, wanting to get Aidan in closer.

The King sniffed. "No, he and Brother Nahuatl have been locked up. I punished them because they disobeyed my orders by provoking Cavan and then failed to finish the job by killing him and, worse, got themselves captured. Their stupidity and incompetence was more than worthy of punishment but, ironically, without their failure I would never have seen your true value so, in a way, we have them to thank."

Fallon glanced at the Fearpriest, seeing glittering eyes and the tip of a dark-skinned nose beneath the hood, but nothing more. The Fearpriest stepped back, allowing Fallon to walk into the center of the room. He could see Kerrin, Feray, Asil and Orhan now and they could see him. All were gagged, all were crying and their eyes were desperately begging him to save them. He had to assume Devlin and the other villagers were dead, or as good as dead, for them to be here and the fury within him settled into his chest, a raging ball that threatened to burst out if he gave it even a hint of a chance.

Then he looked away to examine the other men.

He was in a large chamber, presumably some sort of storage room at some time, stone arches and columns supporting the roof above, and they stepped out from behind these, a score of them, nobles and leaders of guilds. He recognized the Count of Londegal and the Earl of Meinster, as well as others who had clapped him in the throne room.

"Sire, why a Fearpriest?" he asked, fighting for calm.

Aidan sighed. "I know what you must be thinking. Why not rely on the strength of the people? And I confess, if I had you by my side six moons ago, I might have tried that," Aidan said, his voice light. Then it grew darker. "But when the Kottermani Prince Kemal came to me, insulted and defied me in my own throne room, ordered me off the throne and declared we would be a part of the Kottermani Empire, I did not have that choice. What else was I to do? Give up my crown, that my family has worn for hundreds of years? Turn Gaelland into a farm for those filthy Kottermanis? Not be able to make a decision without asking that jumped-up camel-shagger for permission?" The King was working himself up into a fury and Fallon saw the guards and most of the others take an instinctive step back, away from him. Good. "Did he really think that I would just bend over, drop my trews and let him rut me over my own throne?"

"Gaelland should be free and you are its rightful King," Fallon said.

Aidan was pacing now, his eyes wild. "That is right! But how was I to stop them? We had no soldiers and they knew it. They mocked me and looked down on me! Well, there was no way I was having that. I made a bargain with them, pretended I needed time to hand over the crown and that I had to persuade my people to give up peacefully. So he handed me his three bodyguards, whom I altered with the help of the King's Wizard Finbar and used to take children off the streets, while Kemal was busy stealing peasants from the coast. He thought he was pushing us closer to becoming part of his Empire but he was working to my plan the whole time. The Kottermanis are always so pious, bowing and scraping to Aroaril, who gives them nothing. I knew my only hope was a power they could never have. And there was only one way to get it."

"Zorva," Fallon said flatly.

Aidan's eyes lost some of their wildness. "What else was I to do? Give in to the Kottermanis? I would rather die! So I sacrificed to Zorva and he gave me the power to bring Brother Nahuatl here, where he has been instructing my son Swane. I was ready to show Prince Kemal my power and tell him that unless he bowed to me, I would unleash our strength on him and destroy his people.

With the power of Zorva behind us, nothing can stop Gaelland from taking over the Kottermani Empire. And now we have an army to help enforce my will over those dirty camel-lovers, we shall be able to keep all we won. But, of course, Kemal ran off. I wondered what it was but now I see that you had your own plans to stop the Kottermanis!"

"So all those missing children?" Fallon asked, his throat almost closing off at the thought, but the men around him were relaxing as he did not react to the presence of the Fearpriest and he could sense the tension that had been there the moment he stepped through the door vanishing like the smoke from the braziers.

"Some were needed for power. Some were sacrifices," Aidan said carelessly. "Zorva requires a symbol of dedication before he grants his power to you. Every man here has had to sacrifice one of his children to be given this wondrous power. They pretended those children were missing, when we all knew where they were. Of course, my foolish son Cavan had to get involved, running around, trying to solve what he thought was a mystery. Every time I thought I had calmed him down and convinced him to keep quiet, he did something else!"

"And then I came along to help him," Fallon said, remembering again his horror as he turned over what he thought was Prince Swane, only to reveal Cavan's face.

"Indeed you did. I thought you might be a problem, then I discovered you could be an asset and now you are my champion," Aidan said with a smile on his face. "If only I had known how ruthless you could be! Kidnapping the wife and children of Prince Kemal and sending him scuttling back to Kotterman. I take it you intend to make him exchange your families for his?"

"That was the plan, yes," Fallon admitted.

Aidan nodded approvingly. "And a good plan as well. But when were you going to tell me?"

Fallon felt the tension level in the room rise again. "Sire, I was trying to keep you out of it. I had to threaten Prince Kemal that I would skin his sons alive in front of him before he agreed to my demands. He hates me with a passion now. But I am not Gaelland. If he thought *you* were holding his family, then he would not rest until Gaelland was a smoking ruin. Instead, his vengeance is focused on me."

Aidan clapped his hands together and pointed at Swane, then at Londegal and Meinster. "This is what I am talking about," he exclaimed. "So many of you do not think far enough ahead. But Fallon can see through to the end of things, just as I can."

Fallon saw the room ease further and he smiled as he planned their deaths.

"Still," Aidan continued. "Were you really going to hand them back over to Prince Kemal in exchange for your families?"

"Of course not, sire!" Fallon said with a snort of derision. "The moment I did that, Kemal would be after my head. I would use them to keep him here in Gaelland, a hostage to his father's good will."

Aidan clapped his hands together. "You see?" he said to the room at large. "I told you, this is a man we need to have on our side. He understands that you have to make sacrifices to succeed. He knows you have to get blood on your hands sometimes."

Fallon said nothing, but his eyes were watching the men around him. The Guildsmen and nobles were sheep, of no account, but the Fearpriest and Kelty were the real dangers. Take them both out, get his hands on Kelty's shillelagh and then take the other guards out. Once he had freed Kerrin and the others, he had to find a way out as well. He could see another door at the opposite end of the chamber and wondered if that led to the corridor he had stumbled upon with Padraig and Rosaleen. That took him back into the castle kitchen garden and maybe that was a better way than back up the stairs, although stairs were easy to defend ...

"Speaking of sacrifices, sire, what happened to the men who were guarding Prince Kemal's family?" he asked.

Aidan glanced over towards Kelty, who nodded.

"They are still alive of course," Aidan said. "A little bruised, I understand, but they should not have refused an order from a King's man. Consider that a just punishment."

"They were only obeying my orders," Fallon said.

Aidan waved a hand at him. "And I understand that. Loyalty to you is important. But loyalty to me is more important.

Anyway, as we are speaking of sacrifices, we come to the real reason why we are here."

"Sire?" Fallon asked innocently but the blood was pounding in his ears now and he itched to free his knives. "Surely you cannot mean Prince Kemal's family? If they are alive, they are a valuable weapon we can use against him. Dead, they will merely enrage him and bring an even bigger Kottermani army to our shores."

Aidan straightened up, arms clasped behind his back and all the warmth was gone from his voice. "We no longer need such things. There is no need to bargain with Prince Kemal. He will bow down before us or he will be destroyed. The blood of these Princes, as well as Kemal's Princess, will deliver us more power than any advantage we can wring from Kemal. Brother Nahuatl cannot wait to feel that power. I have had to prevent him from sacrificing anyone since he was captured by you and Prince Cavan, as a punishment, and he longs to feel power once more."

"But what of my wife and my men's families?" Fallon persisted, to cover the relief he felt at the Fearpriest not having his full power. The only thing worse than failing to wipe out these vermin would be failing and be forced to watch as Kerrin was killed. "Prince Kemal will take his revenge on them!"

Aidan shook his head. "He will give everything up when we see him again. You have not seen the true power of Zorva. Even the might of the Kottermani Empire cannot stand against it."

"What do you want of me?" Fallon asked. He had to hear it all, then he could unleash himself on these bastards.

"I am not so foolish as to hand over my army to an Unbeliever. After all, I know you have a priestess of Aroaril among your followers. I am delighted with what you have done with training the men but I need you to show your devotion to Zorva to go any further. Of course, once you are part of my inner circle, then the rewards will be great. Whatever you want, you get. And what do you owe Aroaril? All your prayers and going to church, what have they brought you? You and your wife have lost endless children. Zorva just wants one."

"My son Kerrin?" Fallon asked, his voice a husky whisper.

"It does not have to be him. Perhaps there is another you wish to sacrifice instead. Obviously I did not offer up one of my sons but instead a girl who was carrying my child. Do you have one like that? Kelty can fetch her for you while we watch Brother Nahuatl sacrifice the Kottermani Princess and her brats."

"Kerrin is all I have," Fallon said.

Aidan shrugged. "Then it must be him. But Zorva will grant you many sons, as many as you want. And they can be as strong as you like as well. Look at what has happened to my boy Swane!"

"What about Kemal's sons, the princelings? Can I not sacrifice one of them?" Fallon asked. He looked over to where the three of them were strapped down over stone tables, eyes wide and terrified, faces pleading with him.

Aidan shook his head. "They have no blood relation to you. That is the key for Zorva and for myself. Give up something you love and we will give you everything you need."

Fallon looked around as the Fearpriest Nahuatl drew a long knife with a curious blade with a strange sound. Instead of the expected steel blade, this knife had some sort of dark, jagged stone.

"You must use the obsidian blade," he said, his accent grating foully on the Gaelish words.

"Obsidian?" Fallon stumbled over the strange word.

"Some type of rock. Sharp enough to shave with," Aidan said conversationally. "It's the strangest thing. Where the Fearpriests come from, there is no metal, so they use that. Metal is the only thing they cannot affect with their magic. That is why you were searched before you came down here and why Kelty and my other guards just have shillelaghs. He hates metal weapons."

Fallon nodded, following Nahuatl over towards Kerrin, forcing Kelty to step back.

"You will speak the words after me, offering your soul to Zorva then, when I give you my blade, you will cut the boy's throat," Nahuatl said.

Fallon glanced at Kerrin, seeing his terror, the way he was trying to control his breathing, and he could take it no longer. He dropped to one knee in front of Nahuatl. The Fearpriest smelled like an old corpse and his rust-red robe was marked with bloodstains and worse.

"Rise, my friend," the Fearpriest said with a laugh. "Zorva is not like the foul Aroaril. He does not require you to bend the knee to him. He wants to raise you up."

Fallon kept his head bowed, then raised it and looked right into Kerrin's eyes, seeing the tears trickling down his face, the way he was trying desperately to say something behind his gag, while thrashing in vain at his bonds. He absorbed that, used it to feed his rage, then released it.

He rose to his feet, smoothly palming the throwing knives from his boots into his hands, as he had intended all along. But he did not want to throw it at this stinking Fearpriest. Instead he rammed it into the man's stomach, feeling it tear through the cloth and punch through the skin beneath. He twisted his wrist and ripped upwards and across, feeling the spray of hot blood spurting over his arm and the sudden release as the blade bounced off his ribs before tearing back out, followed by the horrible slithering sound as Nahuatl's guts slid out of the terrible wound and the hideous, high-pitched scream of the Fearpriest.

Fallon turned from the stricken Fearpriest, who collapsed on the floor, fighting to pick up his intestines, looking instead at Kelty. The captain of the King's guard raised his shillelagh up but Fallon's arm rose and fell and the throwing knife, covered in blood, spun lazily through the air to slam into Kelty's throat and send the burly captain crashing to the ground.

Fallon changed hands, moving the left-hand knife into his throwing arm as he turned, seeking the King. Aidan was staring at him in shock, eyes bulging and mouth opening to deliver a scream of fury. Fallon intended to stop that before it began and hurled the knife with all his hatred. But his bloody hand slipped a little on the hilt and his anger did not help his aim. Instead of driving home in the King's throat, it slipped up and sliced the King's cheek and ear.

Aidan howled in pain and outrage but Fallon was already moving.

The nearest brazier was but a pace away and he was there in an instant. It was a tall metal stand with a shallow dish at the top filled with red-hot coals and he grabbed it around the middle, grunted a little at the weight and swung it around as if it were a staff to his left. Red-hot coals sprayed out in a wide arc, driving back the nearest men there. A Guildsman bawled as a coal hit him in the face and then Fallon hurled the empty brazier to his right, stopping those advancing there and leaving the Count of Londegal crying out as his leg snapped from the impact.

Two more steps and Fallon picked up Kelty's shillelagh, grabbing it out of a growing pool of crimson as Kelty choked on his own blood. Fallon reached down and ripped out the throwing knife, hastening his end.

The two guards were charging forwards, shouting war cries, while several nobles were hovering, ready to dart in and grab him if he showed any hesitation. Swane was at the back, supporting his father, screaming at the men to close in and take Fallon out.

But his fury was too big to contain. He hurled the knife, the slender blade vanishing in the eye socket of the nearest guard, then he sprang to meet the other, shillelagh already whirling around his head. He blocked one blow then punched out with one end, breaking the guard's nose and snapping his head back, then brought the other end around in a huge blow that crushed the guard's throat and left him choking to death on the ground.

"Get him! Drag him down!" Aidan was bellowing and the other men pressed in, a little hesitantly because they were Guildsmen and merchants and nobles, not soldiers.

There should have been more than enough of them but Fallon was not looking at numbers. Did the wolf fear a flock of sheep or the shark a school of fish? He had thought he had felt fury while confronting Kemal but that was nothing to what he felt now.

He kicked over another brazier, driving back the men on his right, then charged into the others. His shillelagh spun in his hands, propelled by a massive anger, as he waded into them. He punched the ends out, almost too fast for the eye to follow and certainly too fast for the Zorva-worshippers to stop. He pulped an eye, broke a jaw, smashed a nose and crushed testicles, leaving a trail of groaning and screaming men behind him.

The others were hanging back now, hoping another would tackle him, but he was not having that. He sprang at a pair of Guildsmen, shillelagh whirring. He broke one's elbow, cracked the jaw of the other and then turned back to the first, driving the end of the staff deep into the plump man's ample stomach. The Guildsman folded over, whooping out a giant scream and Fallon brought up his knee, feeling the man's nose mash under it.

"Stop him!" Aidan roared but the men who were left were the older and more timid ones and they backed away as Fallon rampaged through the room.

A man turned to run but Fallon slammed his staff into his kidneys then, as he arched his back in agony, grabbed him by the back of the head and smashed his face into a stone pillar. Once, twice, then a third time, until his skull came apart.

The Earl of Meinster picked up a fallen shillelagh and took a swing at him but Fallon locked staves, used brute strength to spin them and flick the Earl's away, then struck with both ends, punching them out hard to send the Earl spinning away to crash into a column and collapse to the ground. Fallon grabbed the brazier beside the column and dropped its contents onto the stunned Earl, who began howling as red-hot coals burned his face and set his hair on fire. The Earl tried to get up but Fallon slammed the brazier down repeatedly, smashing knees and elbows then dropped the brazier on to him and left him there, pinned under their weight, screaming as the coals burned him slowly to death.

That was enough for the others and they turned and raced for the doorway to the stairs back to the King's rooms.

"Cowards! Stop him!" Aidan yelled at them but the room was filling with smoke from all the braziers Fallon had knocked over and Fallon was advancing through it, blood spattered over his face, lips drawn back from his teeth in a snarl of hatred, destroying any stragglers. There was no thought of mercy in his mind. Those trying to crawl away had the shillelagh smash into their heads and faces. The Count of Londegal tried to drag himself to safety but Fallon grabbed his head and ripped it up and back until his neck snapped.

A Guildsman staggered in front of him, disoriented, and Fallon knocked him to the ground with one blow, then lifted his knees high and jumped down onto the man's chest, hearing ribs crackle under the impact.

"Get him!" Aidan was trying to staunch the blood flowing from his cut cheek and Swane was supporting him but everybody else was running now.

Fallon picked up a fallen shillelagh, flicked blood off the end and pointed it at the King. This was for Cavan, for Bridgit and to pay back these bastards who had grabbed Kerrin and wanted him dead.

But that gesture was too much for Swane, who grabbed his father's arm and turned and ran, hauling the King back towards the door and safety.

"Guards! Get guards!" Swane howled.

Fallon began to chase after them but that shout cut through the red mist in his head. Kelty might be dead but there were still more than enough guards in this castle to kill him. Even his shillelagh was no match for a crossbow or two. And, once he was dead, there was nothing stopping Kerrin from going to sacrifice.

Instantly he spun and raced back to where Kerrin was tied up. His knives were lost among the chaos but beside the Fearpriest, who was lying on his back, trying in vain to hold himself together with ever-weakening fingers, was the obsidian blade.

The hilt was wrapped in some strange skin, which made Fallon's bloodstained fingers itch, but the strange stone blade was razor sharp and the ropes holding Kerrin back parted under it in moments.

"You're safe now," Fallon said as he ripped off the gag, even though that was not true, and hugged his son to him, feeling the boy's sobs. He wanted to hold him longer but there was no time to waste.

"We have to go. Are you ready to help me?" Fallon put his hands on Kerrin's shoulders.

He felt as though his chest might burst with pride as Kerrin wiped his eyes with grimy hands and nodded. "I told you I would be ready and I am," he said.

Behind him, he could hear the muffled screams of Feray and her boys and he and Kerrin swiftly cut their bonds, freeing them from the sacrifice tables.

The two boys fell into their shaking mother's arms, all three of them sobbing.

"We have to go! Get up!" Fallon told them harshly.

Feray turned away from him and he could only imagine what he must look like, covered in blood and soot.

"They will not get you while I live," he told them. "But unless we move now, that may not be long. You have to be strong, for your boys."

He saw the effort of will that it took to get her to stand and take her sons' hands.

"Come on!" he urged them and together they half-ran, half-stumbled towards the back of the chamber and the door there.

The chamber was now empty, except for the dead, the dying and the unconscious, and was filled with the smell of burning flesh as the Earl of Meinster slowly roasted under the weight of coals.

For a moment Fallon felt terror at the thought of what might be on the other side of the door, or that it would be locked. But he hauled on the door ring and pulled it open to reveal a simple passageway.

"Stay close to me," he ordered and crept through, the obsidian blade in his belt, shillelagh in his hands. He could feel Kerrin at his left, holding on to the cloth of his trews, while Feray was right behind him, so close he could feel her frightened gasps for breath on his back.

Yet the passageway was empty.

Fallon slammed the door shut behind them and slid the locking bar across. Hopefully that would buy them some time.

He hurried down the passage, the others at his back, turned the corner and came to a series of cells. Instinctively he glanced inside and gasped in horror to see small children there, huddled against the back wall. They wailed at the sight of him, then stared at Kerrin, Asil and Orhan stumbling along behind them.

"Aroaril, what are they doing here?" Feray hissed.

"Nothing for Aroaril," Fallon said grimly. "They were to be sacrificed by that Fearpriest."

"We have to free them!" Feray cried.

"We have to get ourselves out of here first," Fallon grunted, but he was already looking for a key.

There were six cells, all had at least two children inside, which must have been making the noise he had heard the last time he was here. He could not find a key and thought he could hear noises behind them from the chamber they had escaped.

"We have to come back for them," he told Feray. "We shall come back and free you," he told the children.

But that made them rush to the bars, holding out their hands, crying and begging to be taken along. Fallon could not bear to leave them but could not see how he could break into the cells either. He was wondering if the obsidian blade might work when something, or someone slammed against the chamber door they had locked.

"We must go. But we shall be back, I swear on my wife," Fallon said, grabbing Feray, who was crying as the children wailed at her. "Feray, think of your sons!"

That was enough for her to step away from the cell door and follow him as he raced down further. One more turn and they were at the place he remembered, with a second passage and an iron door. This was also unlocked and he ushered the others through and then swung it shut. This time there was no Padraig to lock it and speed was their only hope. The hammering against the other door was getting louder and he did not know how long it would hold.

"Run! Run as if your lives depend on it!" he told the boys.

They needed no further encouragement.

*

Feray was puffing and wheezing as she ran, each breath coming harder than the others. The boys had been used to running around and playing but she had not done anything more strenuous than walk up and down the stairs a few times since her capture and, before that, had been stuck on board a ship with little chance to exercise. She usually prided herself on her strength and fitness but the running on top of the stress and fear had left her short of breath, her legs aching. When the King's men had hauled her out of the makeshift prison she had actually been pleased, thinking that the King would have to release her now and that she could be on her way back to Kotterman with a merchant that very night.

But, instead of the honor due to her station, she and her sons had been dragged downstairs and tied to tables by terrifying men.

At first Feray had feared rape, then she understood her fate was something worse. She recognized the Fearpriest as something out of her nightmares. At least her sons did not know what the hooded man with the strange knife meant, even if she did. The short time lying there had been the worst of her life, outstripping even the time when Fallon had held a knife to Orhan's face.

When Fallon came in the room, she had been torn between hope and more fear. Yet she had not dared to hope, not until he produced knives and turned the room into a slaughterhouse. She could have embraced him when he freed them and she believed him when he swore he would protect them with his life. She glanced over at him as he helped Orhan along and marveled at the contrast to the first time she had met him.

But that thought was washed away by a simple desire to breathe. Her lungs felt full of liquid and she worried she would doom them all.

"Keep going. Just get my boys away," she wheezed.

He looked at her and she almost drew back from his blazing eyes. "I made a promise to keep you safe. I will not break that while I draw breath," he said shortly. "Now move!"

The two older boys were still running easily but Orhan stumbled so Fallon slung him over one shoulder, while also keeping tight hold of Feray's right wrist, dragging her along. She had just enough energy to reflect how strange it was that she was trusting their lives to the man who had threatened them.

"Not far now," Fallon told them, as they hurried down a set of stairs. "Stay strong!"

It was dark down there and stank of blood and decay. Then she slipped on something soft and tumbled over, coming face to face with a dead child. The boy's face was gray and something had eaten his eyes.

She screamed, unable to stop herself, then Fallon hauled her up.

"We are too late to save them. We have to save ourselves," he said roughly.

They stumbled and slipped through a pile of rotting bodies, hearing creatures race away into the darkness and trying not to imagine what else waited for them. There was a slim trace of light coming from ahead and they headed towards that. If she had been alone, she did not think she could have made it through that nightmare but Fallon took her arm and guided her onwards. They reached the light to discover it was sunlight coming in underneath a door. Fallon let go of her arm and she cried out, then he fumbled with a locking bar and rammed the door open with his shoulder.

Next moment they stumbled into the sunlight and her eyes adjusted to see they were in some of castle garden.

"My men are training just outside the gate. Once we are there, we are safe," Fallon said, his chest heaving. "Come on!"

But Feray was struggling to put one foot in front of the other and then they heard angry shouts coming from above.

*

Kerrin wished he had his crossbow. Or even a throwing knife. He had spent so much time training with them and now, when he really needed them, they were back in his room.

They had been playing with the ball when Kelty and a score of his men had raced into the Guild square, smashing down Devlin and the other villagers, then grabbing him, Asil, Orhan and their mother.

Now all they had to do was run away and Kerrin knew he could do that. He had been practicing, after all. The castle gate was no more than fifty paces away and he imagined he could see Dad's army out there, ready to come in and save them.

"There's no guards there!" he cried. He pointed, in case the adults had missed it, then tugged Asil towards it. "Hurry Dad!" he cried.

But Dad was not moving fast, with Orhan over one shoulder and a shillelagh in that hand and trying to pull along the Kottermani Princess with the other.

"Kerrin, run and find Brendan. Bring him back here," his dad said.

"What?" Kerrin turned.

"Go! They could be on us at any moment and then it will be too late. Only you can save us!" his dad ordered.

Kerrin straightened up. Time to make all that training pay off. He saluted and raced away.

His chest felt like it would burst but with pride instead of the usual pain from running. All those days of racing through the streets after his dad were for this and he tore through the grounds. He could see guards coming out of doorways but they did not give him a second glance and, even if they had, he was past them before they could do anything.

The gate was wide open and he flashed through it. A pair of guards saw him, too late. One made a grab for him but he ducked his head and was past them.

"Hey! Stop there, boy!" the guard shouted but he ignored them and they stayed at their posts.

The square was full of recruits going through exercises and he saw Brendan, towering head and shoulders above the young men and ran up to him, not even stopping, so he slammed into the big smith.

"What is it, Kerrin? What are you doing here?" Brendan asked, holding him at arm's length.

"Dad – Fearpriest – castle," Kerrin gasped.

"What is it?" His grandfather strode over and Kerrin grabbed his hand gratefully.

"Dad needs help! In the castle!" he said.

"What's happening? Start from the beginning, lad!" Brendan said.

The other leaders, Gallagher, Bran and Gannon, rushed over as well.

"We have to rescue Dad! Now!" Kerrin insisted.

"What's this? Some sort of training exercise?" Gannon asked.

"Or maybe a joke," Brendan said.

Kerrin did not have the time to explain. He sensed that time was running out for Dad and it was up to him to save him. He grabbed his grandfather's arm.

"Make my voice loud," he said.

Padraig's eyes widened but he gripped Kerrin's shoulder and Kerrin straightened up.

"Soldiers of Fallon!" he cried, his voice cracking a little but echoing across the square. All activity stopped and everyone turned in his direction. He had heard Dad make speeches often enough this past moon and the words came easily to him. "Your captain is fighting for his life, surrounded by Fearpriests and traitors! Will you let him die? I go to save him. Will I go alone?"

He grabbed the knife out of Brendan's belt then raced back towards the castle, not caring if anyone was following him.

The two guards on the gate, who had so nearly caught him, saw him coming this time and spread out, hands held low, ready. Kerrin gripped his borrowed knife tighter and prepared to cut and stab his way through, until they let him go. He would get to Dad if it was the last thing he did. He braced himself for the impact.

Then one guard grabbed the other by the shoulder. Their faces contorted in terror and they cried out, then turned and ran away.

Kerrin yelled out a challenge at them and brandished his knife. *Cowards! Scared of a boy!* he thought exultantly.

Next moment a rush of men came past him, on either side. Bran was there, sword in hand, Brendan was there too, hammer in his hands and Gallagher with his knives. With them were several, then dozens, then scores of the recruits, young men with swords and spears and crossbows, running like a stampeding herd.

Kerrin pointed his borrowed knife at the castle. "Get them!" he roared, as a stream of men poured in through the castle gate.

CHAPTER 29

Fallon watched Kerrin disappear through the gate and breathed a sigh of relief. At least he was safe. He put down Orhan.

"Can you run, lad?" he asked.

Orhan nodded convulsively and he patted him on the shoulder. "Hold your brother's hand and we shall get out of this," he said.

But he could see guards pouring out of the castle, like angry ants from a disturbed nest. Barely fifty heartbeats after Kerrin had made it out of the gate, the way ahead was blocked off and he grabbed Feray, dragging her back towards the stables, the frightened boys with them. Without Kelty the guards were obviously disorganized and Fallon hoped that they would remain so for just a little while longer, until Kerrin returned with help.

But that hope was swiftly dashed.

"There he is, get him!" someone shouted and a squad of guards clattered across the cobbles to surround them, all of them carrying sword and shield.

They were led by a familiar face and Fallon smiled humorlessly as he saw Quinn advance on him, although the officer stayed carefully behind a wall of shields. Fallon pushed Feray behind him and took a two-handed grip on his shillelagh.

"Give up, Fallon. You don't stand a chance," Quinn said.

"What would you know about fighting?" Fallon sneered, hoping to keep him talking for as long as possible.

"We only want the woman and the children. Give us them and we can forget all about this," Quinn said persuasively.

Fallon laughed at him. "Do you think the mad King will forgive and forget? He will want double the sacrifices to heal his face after what I did to him!"

Quinn's face whitened. "You dare insult the King?"

"He's a murderer, a Zorva-worshipper and a madman!" Fallon shouted back scornfully.

Quinn shook his head. "You have lost your mind. This is your last chance. Drop your weapon and give us the woman and children."

"So he can sacrifice them to Zorva? I think not. I have sworn to protect them, just as I have sworn to smash your ugly face into the cobbles, and I don't break my word," Fallon told him.

Quinn signaled to his men. "Take him," he said.

They eased into the advance as Fallon dropped into a crouch. Obviously they had heard about how good he was with the shillelagh, although that gave him no pleasure. He jumped forwards and punched out at a pair of guardsmen, forcing them back a step, but the others closed in and he prepared to sell his life dearly.

"I think you're about to break your word, Fallon," Quinn sneered.

Fallon glanced at him, then began to laugh.

"You think this is funny?" Quinn snarled.

For answer, Fallon pointed behind.

"If you think I am going to fall for that old trick—" Quinn began, then the screaming began, followed by the crash of metal on metal.

Quinn and his men all turned, to see what Fallon was enjoying. A flood of men, led by the massive Brendan, were smashing their way through any guards that tried to stop them, sweeping them away like pus from a wound.

"Form line!" Quinn cried, his voice cracking with fear.

His guards hesitated.

"Throw down your weapons if you want to live," Fallon advised as the rush of his men grew ever closer. The last few guards between them were demolished and his men were pounding towards him – Brendan, Gallagher, Bran, Gannon, Casey and scores of the young recruits he had trained. "Time is running out!"

"Don't listen to him! Follow me!" Quinn squeaked but his men threw down swords and shields and fell to their knees, hands over their heads. Quinn cursed, backed away and then turned to run. But he had got no more than a few paces when Brendan's hammer swung around in a vicious blow to crush his back and send him flying into his men.

A rush of recruits knocked the guards down to the cobbles and stood over them with reddened swords and spears.

Brendan flipped his dripping hammer up onto his shoulder. "Could someone please tell me what in Aroaril's name is going on?" he demanded.

"Where's Kerrin?" Fallon asked.

Next moment Kerrin squeezed through the lines of men and flung himself at him.

Fallon hugged him fiercely. "You did it! You saved us all!" he whispered.

"Why were they attacking you?" Bran asked.

Fallon kept an arm around Kerrin as he straightened. "King Aidan plans to convert us all to Zorva and then make us carve him out an empire, dedicated to evil. To stay as his captain, I had to sacrifice Kerrin to Zorva."

The growing circle of his recruits gasped and cried out in horror as they heard his words.

"And who are they?" Bran asked, pointing at Feray.

"The wife and children of the Kottermani Crown Prince. We had captured them and were going to use them to get our families back," Fallon said. "The King found out and sent Kelty and his men to grab them. Devlin and his men are beaten up but I think they are still alive. And we found the missing children. They are underneath the castle, being held by the King to be killed on Zorva's altar."

There were cries of anger, and horror at that.

"Where is the Fearpriest? And where is Kelty? Those guards were even more useless than usual," Gallagher said.

"I gutted the Fearpriest, put a knife into Kelty's throat and smashed up the King's filthy sacrifice room. You'll know anyone who was there – they will have the marks of my shillelagh on them."

Now there were growls of fury and cries for vengeance.

"What do we do now?" Brendan asked. "The ship?"

Fallon shook his head. This was a time for revenge. He had tried to avoid it and nearly brought disaster upon them again. Now he would embrace it.

"Gannon, take a squad and go and find the Duchess. We are going to need her before this day is out," Fallon ordered. *To answer some questions from Rosaleen, if nothing else,* he added silently.

The big sergeant saluted and ducked into the crowd, calling out for his men.

"Gallagher, stay here with three squads, Kerrin, Feray and her boys. Keep them safe and we shall find them proper quarters after this. Bran, take a squad and find Devlin and the others, bring them back here for treatment if they are alive, for burial if they are not."

"And what are we doing?" Brendan asked.

Fallon bent down and picked up a fallen sword. "The rest of you, follow me!"

The cheer that followed rattled the tiles along the castle roof.

*

They broke into the castle in several places, driving the remaining guards before them. Without any officers, the guards were confused and massively outnumbered. Some chose to fight and die but many threw down their swords and were sent to the throne room under guard. He sent fifty of the best recruits under Casey to watch them, as well as bar the door that led to the King's staircase, the one that led up to his rooms or down to the sacrifice room. Nobody would be getting out of there.

The corridors were quiet, except for the occasional ringing clash of steel and horrible scream, which revealed that another guard had tried to resist. The servants stayed hidden.

Fallon led them up to the King's rooms, sure he would have gone there. And there was perhaps a score of guards outside the room, the last loyal ones, led by Regan.

"Get back, traitor, before the King destroys you all!" the chamberlain spat at them, his usual air of calm torn away.

"Give up now, or you will all die," Fallon replied.

Regan gestured towards the cluster of guards, who were packed tight around the door. "You will never get past!" he said wildly.

Fallon snapped his fingers and a score of his recruits stepped forwards, crossbows in hands. Half went down on one knee, the others stood behind, and together they brought their weapons up.

"Last chance. If you have not converted to Zorva, there is still hope for you," Fallon offered.

A pair of guards dropped their swords and raised hands – only to be hacked down from behind by their former comrades.

"Loose!" Fallon snapped and the two lines released their crossbows.

A score of bolts converged on the huddle of guards and tore through them, then Fallon strode forwards, Brendan at his shoulder.

Regan was still alive, a bolt in his shoulder, and he lunged clumsily at Fallon with a knife. Fallon knocked it away and then rammed his borrowed blade into the chamberlain's open mouth and deep into his neck, so that it stuck out the back. Regan dropped his knife and was held there, eyes bulging as his lifeblood pulsed out through his mouth, then Fallon ripped the weapon out and let him collapse into death.

A few of the other guards still lived, but were quickly finished off by Fallon's recruits, then Brendan ran forwards and swung his huge hammer at the door, splintering the lock and sending it crashing open.

Fallon stepped over the writhing bodies of the dying guards and into the room.

The King stood there to meet him, as he had done not a turn of the hourglass ago, yet this time there was no smile on his face. Instead, dried blood from his cut cheek and wide eyes made him look like a madman. Behind him hovered Swane, no trace of a sneer on his face now.

"Run, Father!" he cried, and he vanished out the secret door, back down the stairs.

But Aidan did not run. "Fallon, you bastard, have you come to die?" he cried, a sword in his hand.

Fallon said nothing. His hate was too great to put into words. So he just advanced on Aidan. The King hacked at him furiously but it was easy enough to block the blows until Aidan stepped back, breathing harshly. Then Fallon advanced and, when the King swung his sword viciously but with little skill, he slipped sideways and lunged for the man's black heart. Aidan jumped backwards and cut out once more and Fallon parried and thrust again, this time at the throat. Aidan threw himself backwards, staggering, tripping and falling. His head slammed into the desk and he collapsed limply, sword rolling from nerveless fingers.

"Finish it," Brendan rumbled.

Fallon advanced and touched his reddened sword to the King's throat. From there it would be so easy to end it and gain some revenge for all the King's evil. But he could not make the final thrust. Not there; not like this. He wanted Aidan to know what was coming and, more than anything else, wanted the people to see what an evil bastard he had been.

"No," he said. "It's over. We'll have the church judge him. Maybe burn him the way he did those witches. Get some rope and tie this bastard up. We shall let the children out and leave Aidan in one of those cells, give him a taste of it." At the thought, Fallon sheathed his sword but gave the unconscious King a kick in the ribs.

"What about Swane?" Brendan asked.

"He can't get away," Fallon said confidently. Casey and fifty men waited in the throne room, while Gallagher and thirty men were watching the other way out in the kitchen garden. Then, with a shock of horror, he remembered the other passageway. The one they had not taken. He did not know where that went.

"Quick, follow me. And bring the King!"

CHAPTER 30

The children were having a great time but it was a different story for the adults. And as the sun began to sink and the time for their escape grew closer, even the little ones began to laugh less, picking up on the tension.

Bridgit had ordered everyone to eat and drink as much as they could manage but she had to force herself to swallow even the fruit, let alone the meat and bread and grains. Not that she had much time for eating. Everyone had to be organized, small groups of men assigned to watch larger groups of women and children. That way, if guards attacked any part of the column of Gaelish, there would be people ready to fight back. The men all had to be given at least some sort of weapon, even if most of them were sharpened chair legs. Still, as she had shown the first time she had crept out into the city, even those could take a life.

The men who had worked in the docks the day before quickly sketched out where the ships were and the most likely ones for them to take. Prince Kemal's ship had arrived the night before and the men reported all of the surrounding vessels had been cleaned and their water barrels refilled. And food had been stockpiled on the docks, as if they were planning to feed an army.

"It is almost as if they want to head out to sea again immediately," Ahearn said.

"Who cares what they want to do? It works in our favor," Bridgit said. She had been trying not to think about Prince Kemal demanding to see her that day but had reassured herself that surely she was low on his list of priorities after arriving back in the country.

Every so often she glanced up at the sky, scared that she had lost track of time and they had missed their chance. Escaping was going to take perfect timing. They had to act just before evening prayers, so they had that opportunity to get as far away as possible. Too early and the city was still busy, too late and they would run into all the guards arriving to take the slaves away. To everyone else she had to be the calm center, reassuring the worriers and pretending to be completely confident. Inside she was as bad as any of them but she just couldn't show it. It felt like being back with Kerrin, which just made her more determined to get home.

The women had been offering drugged drinks to the guards outside all day and now the soldiers were all sitting down and looking as though they were ready for sleep.

For the past few days, they had been using a stick propped upright in the courtyard to mark when prayers would be called. It cast a shadow that moved along with the sun. A line had been drawn on the ground to show when the call went out around the city and, just before the shadow touched that, they needed to act.

"Now is the time," she told Riona. "Give the younger children those drinks. Once they start to take effect, we shall strike."

"Get ready," she told Carrick and Blaine, the two foolish cousins from Killarney. She did not like them and certainly did not trust them but they were the biggest men she had and they were a vital part of the plan. She just hoped that the lure of escape – and the fear of punishment – would keep them from doing anything stupid.

The younger children gratefully accepted the fresh fruit juice, with the rest going out to the guards in the hands of the prettiest of the wives.

"Invite them inside for something to eat, tell them we have all this extra food and it will all go to waste if they do not join us," she advised.

"But they don't speak the King's Gaelish," one of the women protested.

Bridgit sighed. Did she have to think of everything herself? "Find Ely and get her to translate," she said.

But a quick search failed to find her in the building.

"Where is she? Look again, she's probably hiding under a bed somewhere or with a pack of small children," Bridgit said urgently.

She joined in this time, going through each room, yet Ely was nowhere in sight.

"Who remembers seeing her?" Bridgit demanded.

A couple of the wives who had been serving drinks to the guards volunteered that Ely had been there for the last round of drugged juice.

"And is that the last anyone saw of her? It must be a turn of the hourglass ago at least!" Bridgit asked, appalled. She had told the girl everything and had been determined to watch her like a hawk – except she had lost track of Ely during the craziness of the afternoon's preparation for escape.

She took one look at the shadow creeping over the garden and came to a decision. Either Ely had run away, hoping to save herself in the event of them being captured or she had gone to Gokmen with news they planned to escape. She prayed that was not the case.

"Has she betrayed us?" Ahearn asked the question they were all wondering.

"If she wanted to betray us, she would have told the guards outside," Bridgit said briskly, hoping that was true. "They would have taken us away and we wouldn't be having this talk now. She was scared of being caught trying to escape. Unlike us, she doesn't have anything to go home for. She's probably just hidden herself somewhere in the city and will hope to lie her way out of trouble tomorrow."

"It is an awful risk," Nola said worriedly.

"No more than the risk we already faced. We go anyway. Give it a count of two hundred to let the drugged drinks work and then we make our move. Go when I strike one of the guards," Bridgit said. "To your places. You all know what must be done."

She watched them hurry away and prayed she was right.

*

Kemal rubbed sleep from his eyes. Once back in Adana he had slept for a night and most of a day, waking only at the insistence of his servants.

"There is a girl here to see you – she displays your token, high one," they said, bowing low.

"Send her in. And get me something fresh to eat. As much fruit as you can find," he said, his stomach growling. He had enjoyed the best of the food on board the ship but there was little fresh to be had in Gaelland, with spices needed to disguise the taste of their salted beef and lamb.

He was wiping juice off his beard when she came in, bowing low. "Ely," he greeted. "And what brings you here like this? I thought you were to report to me only when I gave the signal?"

"My apologies, high one. But I have urgent news," she said. "As you ordered me to, I have gained the confidence of their leader Bridgit and she has included me in her plans."

He snapped his fingers. "Then speak. I do not have much time."

She straightened up. "High one, they are planning an escape. They will try to steal a ship this night and sail back to their country."

Kemal leaned back, trying to get his tired mind to think. His first instinct was to call for the guards but perhaps that was a mistake. He needed to get them back to Gaelland anyway and maybe this was a way to get that past his father. Freeing the slaves would outrage the Emperor – as would a slave escape – but at least if they escaped, the blame would fall on the likes of Gokmen. He could protect the man and gain an ally who would be pathetically grateful to him, as well as have the perfect excuse to take a large force back to Gaelland. He congratulated himself on the foresight that had led him to make Ely the translator for the Gaelish while he was away. She had been tutor to Feray, Asil and Orhan, as well as to himself, teaching them all the Gaelish tongue so they would be ready to take up their duties in the new land.

He had made her duties plain to Ely. She was to win their confidence and report back to him. Do her job well and she, her mother and her sister would be freed. Anger him and she would pray for death. She had been shown her expected fate and he had known she would not dare to fail. She would be forced to watch her sister and mother die horribly before joining them. He grimaced at the thought. Just a moon ago, the thought of using someone's family as a threat to make them do what you wanted was perfectly normal. Now it did not seem such an easy thing to do.

Kemal quickly considered his options. Letting them escape could help but what if some of them were killed? A death or two would normally not mean too much but what if one of those killed were the wives or children of Fallon's lieutenants? What would that cost him? He swiftly came to a decision.

"You stay with me," he ordered Ely. "But first, get me the captain of my guards. We have much to do."

*

Bridgit cursed Ely. Just at the point when she needed someone with a good command of Kottermani to talk to the guards, the girl had run off in fear. She also cursed herself. She should have stayed with the girl, kept a close watch on her. Ely had been trying to tell her something before. If only she had listened better then, perhaps they would not be facing this problem now.

Half of the guards were inside, while half were still outside. She needed to get them in somehow. Trying to attack a dozen men in the streets was doomed to failure. In desperation she grabbed Ena and another of the younger, prettier wives and took them into a side room, where others could not see them. There she took a knife and crudely cut at their skirts, ripping the hem until it exposed half their thighs.

"What are you doing, Bridgit?" demanded Ena. She had wide eyes and pale skin, even with the time she had spent working in the sun. Bridgit had seen how the guards always watched her.

By way of an answer, Bridgit took the knife to the loose top she wore, ripping down around the neckline.

"Is this some kind of jest?" Ena continued. "Answer me, for Aroaril's sake!"

Bridgit stopped tearing at her loose shirt. "We have to get the others inside," she said. "I need the pair of you to dance like it was your marriage night."

"Like this?" Ena asked indignantly. "Murphy would be shocked!"

"Well, he's not going to get the chance unless we do something fast," Bridgit said, moving on to the other woman and cutting away her skirt. "If you can think of a surer way to get those guards in here and not watching what the rest of us are doing, say so now!"

As she had expected, neither had an answer.

"Look, I would do this myself but we all know that won't get the guards so eager for an eyeful that they leave their posts and get in here. You are our best hope."

"And if it doesn't work?" the other woman, Clare, asked. Bridgit did not know her as well, for she was from Killarney, but like Ena she had red hair and pale skin.

"Drop your clothes on the floor and keep dancing. If there's a man out there who can stay at his post while that's happening instead of rushing in to watch, then we will just have to kill him, because he would have to be made of stone," Bridgit said shortly. She inspected the two women critically and nodded.

"Good. Now let's get moving. They will call for prayers at any moment and our chance will be lost."

*

Bridgit led the way, clapping her hands, while around her others took up the rhythm and formed a circle in the front room. The guards who were already inside came along, swept up by the others, and they swiftly joined the Gaelish in cheering as the scantily clad women gyrated around the circle.

"Give them more! As if you were dancing for Murphy!" Bridgit told Ena as she danced closer. "Do it for the children!"

She could see neither woman was happy or comfortable with what she was doing but they danced on, spinning and stretching, and the guards in the circle began to call out to their comrades outside.

Bridgit glanced over her shoulder and saw heads appear around the door then, as she hoped, the guards outside began to hurry in. In a city where the women went covered from head to toe to protect themselves from the sun, the chance to see bare limbs flashing pale skin at every turn was enough to get any man away from his post.

They had been dulled by the drinks they had taken, but she could see their eyes locked onto the dancing women.

Bridgit signaled to Ahearn, and to Carrick and Blaine, and men eased through the crowd to stand near the guards.

"Now!" Bridgit cried, jumping into the circle herself.

The guards all looked at her – then they were overpowered a moment later, struck and stunned or dragged down and choked. Half-asleep thanks to all the drugged drinks, none even put up a fight. Pieces of the makeshift rope she had used to get in and out of the house were used to truss them up, while their weapons were swiftly taken. Ahearn handed Bridgit a long knife, its blade gently curved, and she hurriedly slipped it into her belted robe.

"Get the children and get ready," Bridgit said, quickly embracing a puffing Eva and Clare.

Nola and Riona handed them cloaks and they all quickly lined up, watched by battered, bruised and dazed guards, whose eyes promised murder even though their mouths were gagged and hands tied.

"What if one of them escapes and raises the alarm? Would we not be better off silencing them?" Carrick asked.

Bridgit had considered that herself but the thought of killing helpless men turned her stomach. Besides, the soldiers' bonds had been secured by Ahearn's crew of fishermen.

"They will not get free in a hurry. By the time they do, we shall be long gone," she said firmly.

The children were brought out, the babies and toddlers sleeping gently in the arms of their mothers or older siblings. A cry at the wrong moment could bring them undone so she had been careful to make sure only those who could be trusted – and were strong enough – would run with the adults. Each of these children had a pair and they were all to watch out for each other. The only ones who did not have a small child to carry or a younger to hold hands with were the dozen older boys and girls with slings.

"Good. All ready?" She smiled at them, tousling hair or brushing the cheek of one of her many favorites. "When we hear the call of prayers you start to run and you don't stop until we are on a ship."

She left them, feeling confident, and turned back to the front door to hear strange noises going on. "Keep quiet until we get the signal!" she snapped, then saw it was not her own people who were making noise.

Instead it was the surviving guards, as Carrick and Blaine used borrowed swords to kill them.

"What are you doing?" she raged. "I gave orders that they were not to be harmed!"

Carrick turned to her, bloodied to the elbows.

"And I said they were too much of a risk," he said threateningly, his dripping sword pointed at her.

Bridgit saw the obvious threat but she was not going to be cowed by it. "Put down that sword and clean yourself up or you will give us all away," she snapped. "I will deal with you later."

"No, you won't," Blaine added, standing by his brother's shoulder.

"Step away or by Aroaril I shall make sure that you never get back to Gaelland," she told them. Behind her, she could sense that Ahearn and his men were moving to stand by her and the air in the room suddenly seemed charged with something other than the stink of blood.

For a long moment nobody moved, then they all heard the unmistakable call to prayers.

"Clean yourselves now!" Bridgit pointed at them and then turned back to the door, ignoring the brothers. Every moment counted. "Let's move, just as we planned!"

A group of men led by Dermot, the farmer from near Baltimore, hurried out the door and down towards the docks, followed by the lines of women and children.

Bridgit paused for one last look around the house, seeing only the blood-spattered brothers trying to wipe the blood off their arms and faces on the remnants of the cloth rope.

"You two bring up the rear and for Aroaril's sake keep up," Bridgit ordered.

She saw them sneer at her words but she did not have time to waste on them. Without a backward glance she hurried out the door and caught up with the long column of Gaelish. She shuddered at the thought of guards getting among the straggling groups and urged the ones at the back to hurry. The sounds of evening prayer were still booming out across the city but that could not last long and they would stick out like a fire at night. While there may not be many guards close, they only needed a little notice and any escape would be almost impossible.

She urged them on, until the older children were trotting along to keep up, then she rushed along to the front of the group, to where Dermot led the way.

"See any guards?" she asked.

"There is nobody around," the farmer said shortly.

That was not quite true. They had passed a score of people but they were praying, their eyes closed. One or two had looked up as so many hurried by, looking outraged, but had not said anything. Yet Bridgit knew that had to end. She had heard the evening prayers so many times, she knew time was running out.

"Push it along faster," she said. "We have to get off these streets before the prayers end."

The men looked at each other and then began to run, making the others behind them increase their speed as well. Bridgit stayed where she was, urging the others on.

"Take the children's hands. Pull them along," she instructed the adults. At the rear of the column, as she had requested, Carrick and Blaine thumped along, swords in hands. She disliked them intensely but had to admit they looked reassuring large and dangerous there. It was a hard job, perhaps the hardest of any to bring up the rear and slow down any pursuit long enough to let them get away and she promised herself she would think of them differently if they got everyone away safely.

Even though they were all running now, the adults carrying younger children and helping others along, it was still too slow for Bridgit's liking. She could hear the prayers coming to an end and they were still a street away from the docks.

"Hurry!" she urged them on, racing to catch up with the men at the front again.

Her worst fears were realized when the prayers stopped just as they reached the docks. All was quiet but a pair of guards stood up, brushing dirt off the front of their robes where they had been kneeling down, to suddenly block the way. The guards' eyes bulged at the rush of Gaelish slaves coming right for them and surprise held them for long enough for the Gaelish to swamp them and club them down, Dermot and another man taking their swords.

The men in and around the docks were also stirring after prayers, most of them thinking about returning home after a long day's work. The flood of Gaelish changed all that. Chained gangs of slaves backed away, cowering in fear, while Kottermanis tried to block the way. But they were isolated and disorganized. Bridgit guessed the shouts were for them to surrender and return but it was far too late for that. The Gaelish column flowed over them, spitting them out the other side, making for the left side of the docks, where the largest ships waited and where the main harbor wall stretched out from the wharves.

A handful of Kottermani sailors tried to move towards the children but the ones Bridgit had trained were ready with their slings and unleashed a hail of stones on the Kottermanis. The men dived for cover, crying out as they were hit, and others stayed low behind piles of goods rather than try to stop them.

"We're going to make it! Keep going!" Bridgit encouraged the others on. She was both relieved and disturbed by their progress. It almost seemed a little too easy. More than a hundred men were in sight around the docks but most just watched them go past, seemingly dumbfounded.

Then she caught sight of a dozen Kottermanis, a mixture of guards and sailors, advancing to their right. If they got in among the women and children ... she shuddered at the thought and grabbed Dermot's arm, pointing them out to him. "Hold them off!" she called.

As they had planned, Dermot and a score of men, armed with everything from captured swords to chair legs with sharpened ends, formed a fighting line, allowing the Gaelish women and children to continue in safety even though the Kottermanis slowly advanced.

Bridgit watched over her shoulder anxiously as her people rushed past, looking for Blaine and Carrick. The two big men were still bringing up the rear, threatening anyone who dared to come close. Neither had cleaned all the blood off themselves and Bridgit saw that was also deterring Kottermanis from coming close.

"Start to back away," she told Dermot.

But, before he could lead the men back to join the rear of the column, the Kottermanis attacked. The Gaelish hesitated for a moment until Bridgit shouted at them, breaking the spell they were under.

"Fight for your children!" she shouted.

They sprang forwards to meet the Kottermanis then, although a trio of Kottermani guards were a tight-knit group that drove through the Gaelish line, leaving a pair of men down and screaming in their wake. The rest of them swung makeshift clubs at each other and snarled insults that the other side could not understand.

Bridgit backed away from the three guards, drawing her knife. Time seemed to slow down and she recalled the endless lessons that Fallon had tried to give her, the talks about attacking in a straight line being so much better than wild slashes. She had been bored to tears listening then but it seemed some of it had stuck in her mind because, as one of them drew back his arm to cut her down, she jumped forwards and held out her knife. He ran onto the end, the sharpened steel sliding into his chest. Instinctively she pulled the blade back and he dropped his sword and staggered backwards, falling to the ground. His two companions spat hatred at her and closed in for revenge but then Blaine and Carrick pushed past, swinging their bloodied swords furiously. One of the guards was caught a glancing blow along the arm and dropped his sword, screaming as blood spurted from his ruined forearm. The other backed into a pile of barrels and fell backwards, losing his weapon. Even as he cried for mercy, Carrick slashed down viciously and blood sprayed high.

That was enough for the rest of the Kottermanis and they backed away, leaving four more of their number lying on the ground.

But it had been an expensive victory, for five Gaelish were also down.

"Bring them! We shall bind their wounds later," Bridgit ordered, smiling her thanks at Blaine and Carrick.

But they brushed past her, while Dermot and his surviving men dragged along their wounded, a mixture of broken bones, battered heads and, in two cases, of sword wounds.

"Quickly now." Bridgit ran with them. One man was dripping blood from a torn arm but still ran, while the other four were supported by men on either side of them. Only one was unconscious and being dragged along. The others at least could get their feet under them and be helped along.

The resistance of the Kottermanis seemed to have been broken and Bridgit could see nobody else threatening them as they raced along the wharves. She lengthened her stride, feeling herself beginning to struggle for breath but still determined to lead them out of here.

She caught up with Ahearn, whose head was turning constantly as he watched for a Kottermani ambush as well as a likely way out of here.

"I think this one," he pointed to a ship that sat by itself at the end of a long jetty, one lined with a variety of sacks and barrels.

"Then we take it," Bridgit said. She did not go down the jetty, instead encouraging the others as they ran past.

"Grab a sack, take it on board," she advised those going past. "Let the children walk now but if you see food, take it with us."

Some ignored her, just seeking to get on board the ship as fast as possible, while others stopped to lift up some of the sacks. Bridgit hoped there was food inside them. Getting out of the harbor only to starve to death at sea seemed like a horrible finish to their hopes.

There was no sound of alarm, no warning horns or anything but surely that had to end soon. She could barely believe they were this disorganized. Surely the relief guards had to have arrived at the house by now and discovered their slaughtered comrades.

But there was no sign of angry pursuit and she stopped Dermot and his remaining healthy men.

"I need you to come with me to take out those bows, or they will slaughter our people," she announced.

Blaine and Carrick had vanished onto the ship and she waved at them up on the deck.

"Help here!" she shouted but they ignored her.

She swore under her breath but there was no time to do more than that.

"Seven of you with me. The rest of you, carry everything you can on board that ship and help Ahearn get it under way," she ordered.

Dermot and six others followed her as she left the jetty and ran around the dock wall, towards where the giant bows waited ominously. There did not seem to be anyone near them but she shuddered to think of the havoc they could inflict.

The ship was going to take some time to get away from the jetty. The sails had to be raised and it needed to be pushed away from the jetty, perhaps even towed out by a rowboat or two. Hopefully they could get back by then. If not, it would be a case of jumping into the harbor and trying to get into one of those rowboats – or clamber up a rope onto the ship itself. Neither prospect appealed.

There were no Kottermanis on the harbor wall, for which she was hugely grateful, and they raced around to where the first bow waited, like a barbed bird of prey. She glanced across at the ship and could see the frantic activity on the deck. Women and the older children were dragging sacks up onto the deck, while others seemed to be wrestling a handful of goats on board. The men, meanwhile, were launching a pair of rowboats at the front, or clambering up the masts and slowly unfurling sails.

Then they were at the first bow and Bridgit pointed to two of the men.

"Cut the cord!" she ordered. "The rest of you, with me!"

The men began hacking away at the thick, twisted cord, with what looked like little success. She did not bother to watch them, instead rushing around to the next one, 10 paces away.

"Two more on that one," she told them.

She left another two on the third one and then she and Dermot raced around to the fourth and last one. From here they could see a hive of activity in the docks. Men who had been timid in small groups were coming together into a mob, picking up whatever weapons they could find and advancing on the ship. They looked leaderless but surely they could still cause all sorts of problems.

Dermot drew his sword, ready to start hacking at the giant bow's huge string but she stopped him.

"Load it first," she said, pointing to where the mob was moving across the wharves, perhaps a hundred paces away.

Dermot looked at her blankly for a moment then helped her winch back the huge string. It had two winders set into either side and she had to use all her strength to turn her one as Dermot worked on the other and drag the string back to the point where it clicked into place. The bow had a rack of long spear-like missiles, each one the height of a man and the width of her arm and she and Dermot laid one into the central trough.

"Have you any idea how to aim this?" Dermot asked.

"Let's find out," Bridgit replied shortly. It was set onto a base that could turn all the way around and must have been counterweighted, because it was easy enough for the two of them to turn it to face the docks. Another wheel halfway down could be turned to lower or raise the tip of the bow and Dermot adjusted it to her satisfaction, clicking the ratchet into place.

"Stand clear," she warned and slammed down the lever that held the string in place. It did not move. She heaved on it, exerting all her strength and it still did not move. Then she saw a large wooden mallet resting beside the weapon's base and snatched that up and belted the lever with that.

The giant bow bucked on its base and the missile streaked out to smash into a stack of barrels at the edge of the wharf, sending several flying into the air and knocking down a pair of men.

"We missed!" she said disappointedly.

But Dermot was laughing as the mob scattered in all directions, ducking for cover rather than moving on the ship.

"Now we just have to break this one," the farmer said jubilantly.

"Not so fast," Bridgit said.

He turned around and she nodded down towards the end of the harbor wall. The bow shot had woken up the guards at the end of the wall and they were now running towards them.

Let's go!" Dermot cried.

"Time for one last shot," Bridgit countered.

He glared at her but, as she grabbed hold of one side and began to wind the huge string back, he cursed and rushed to help her. The first time they had done it, it had strained every muscle of her arms and shoulders. But with angry guards bearing down on them, it seemed to go much easier this time as fear lent strength to their arms.

The guards were but twenty paces away when they dragged the bow around to face them and she smashed the lever with the mallet once again. The bow was pointing downwards after their attempt at the mob on the docks but there was no time to raise it. And no need, either. The guards were so close the missile barely had time to drop. It took out the legs of the first two guards, bounced off the stone and knocked down another three of them, bringing the whole pile of them down in a heap. Most were unwounded but the two who had their legs ripped off were doing enough screaming for all of them. Bridgit smashed at the lever again, this time from the side, splintering the wood.

"Come on, before they get up!" she cried.

Dermot needed no further encouragement and followed her back along the wall, to where the other men were still fruitlessly trying to cut their way through the thick bowstrings.

"Smash the lever! We just need a little time to get away!" Bridgit shouted at them. She had no breath for any more and every muscle seemed to be aching after her exertions. But she willed herself to go on. They had come so far: she would not fail now.

A few blows with the mallets and the loosing lever was broken on the other three bows. No doubt they could fix that in a few turns of the hourglass but that was all they needed.

"Back to the ship," she puffed but, as they turned to run back around, saw that the mob had reformed down on the docks. Worse, there appeared to be guards rushing to join them.

Bridgit was pleased to see the older children were clustered by the stern of the ship, sending slingshots whistling down at anyone who came close. But she was less pleased to see their way to the ship was now blocked.

"Down there. We need to swim for it," she said firmly. She did not like that idea, for it had been several summers since she had swum more than a few strokes. She did not like Kerrin going in the cold water and maybe catching a chill, so had only ventured to the beach on the hottest summer days – of which there were few in Gaelland.

On the ship, sails hung limply from masts, but men were packed into a pair of rowboats and beginning to tow the ship away from the jetty. She judged their progress, not wanting to spend any more time in the filthy harbor water than necessary, when Dermot grabbed her arm.

"We need to go – those guards are back on their feet," he warned.

Perhaps only half a dozen guards were sufficiently unharmed to want to tackle them but they were trained, armed and angry and her men, when all was said and done, were powered by fear and desperation rather than skill.

"Down the ladders. The ship will see us and pick us up," she said, more in hope than certainty.

She pulled off the robe she was wearing and kicked off her shoes as well, until she was wearing just a short cotton shift that came down to her mid-thighs.

"Do you think you'll be able to swim in heavy cloth?" she demanded of the men, when they stared at her. "Drop your swords and hurry!"

Wooden ladders were attached to the edge of the harbor wall and she led the way down, trying not to slip on the lower rungs, which had weed growing from them. She glanced over her shoulder to see the rowboats were moving closer, the ship picking up a little speed behind them. But it was so big that, even with men straining at the oars, it did not move any faster than a gentle walking pace.

She let go and clumsily splashed out, shuddering at the rancid smell of the water. Behind her, the other men jumped in, Dermot the last one down the ladder. He dived out from the ladder as the Kottermani guards arrived, shouting curses after them.

Bridgit floated on her back, watching them argue furiously with each other. After a few moments one of them pulled the others away and they raced back along the harbor wall. Bridgit watched them go with relief. If they hoped to turn the giant bows on their stolen ship they would discover an unpleasant surprise, she thought with satisfaction.

She swam slowly out to meet the rowboats, which did indeed alter course to pick them up. Her arms felt like they were about to fall off, while her legs had almost no strength as she kicked towards them. Every breath was a shuddering gasp and she had to fight not to suck in a mouthful of harbor water each time. For an instant she felt like closing her eyes and slipping below the surface, forgetting about all the pain and the struggle, but she saw Fallon and Kerrin in her mind's eye and she struck out with renewed strength and energy.

Strong hands reached for her and dragged her over into the rowboat. She did not care that her soaked cotton shift clung to her or that most of her legs were showing. Five of the men who had broken the bows with her were also pulled into her boat, while Dermot and one other were pulled into the second boat. It made the rowboats crowded but it meant there were more hands on the oars as they hauled the huge ship along.

Bridgit felt herself shiver, despite the late afternoon sun, and wiped her face dry, looking around. Over on the wharves, angry Kottermanis were shouting and waving angrily at them but they could do nothing. Despite the effort it was taking, the rowboats were making progress and the mob on the docks seemed to have no idea how to stop them.

The men were hauling away at the oars but they were out of time and she began to call the stroke for them. After a few moments they were together and moving better through the water, the rope tight between them and the ship they were towing.

"Keep going – we're nearly away!" Bridgit encouraged.

And it was true. It was almost hard to believe but no ships were stirring to cut them off. She watched the handful of Kottermani guards up on the harbor wall attempt to hurl one of the giant crossbow bolts at the rowboats but its size and weight defeated them and it barely made it over the wall before splashing into the water.

Now there was a tantalizing glimpse of open water and the sea ahead and the men in the boats responded, pulling with the last of their strength to bring the big ship around the edge of the harbor wall and give it a chance to spread its sails.

Then Bridgit saw the surviving Kottermani guards at the end of the wall, where they could look down onto the ship as it went past. And they all had bows in their hands. There were only six of them but at the speed the ship and rowboats were moving, the guards would have plenty of time to bombard the rowboats, with the men packed tight in.

Before she could yell out a warning the guards loosed, aiming at the other boat. Arrows splashed into the water, sunk into the wooden sides – and into flesh. A pair of men were shouting in pain but, with the extras they had taken on, there were still enough for the oars. Bridgit was torn between horror at her people being forced to sit there and relief that it was not her boat.

She glared at the guards, wishing she had thought to loose more of the giant bows at them. They were drawing back their bows, taking their time about it, no doubt hoping to cause more damage this time around. Next moment they were ducking for cover and dropping their bows, holding their hands over their heads.

For a moment she could not understand it but then glanced back at the ship and saw her slingers lining the rail, hurling stones at the bowmen. They were too far away for the stones to do more than sting but it was certainly enough to disrupt them. Bridgit wanted to cheer them, then saw the angry bowmen select new arrows and change their aim.

"Get down!" she shouted at the ship as the bowmen loosed at them.

From this angle she could not see if any were hit but the bowmen were ignoring the rowboats to pepper the ship's deck with arrows.

She turned back to the rowers. "Pull! Give it everything you have! We are almost there!"

The waves began to crash against the front of the rowboats as they dragged the ship out past the harbor wall, where the sea breeze made its sails suddenly billow. Suddenly the tow-rope went slack as the big craft picked up speed, surging forwards to overtake the rowboats.

"Down oars! Get ready!" Bridgit warned them. "Swing by on the far side!"

Both rowboats pulled across to one side, giving the ship a straight path out to sea. Whoever was steering the ship – Bridgit assumed it was Ahearn – brought them close, so close that it almost brushed past the rowboats, and ropes were thrown down to them.

"You go first," Bridgit said.

"No, you get on board," she was told.

The ship was moving faster now and there was no time to argue, so she grabbed the rope in both hands and was hauled rapidly upwards until hands helped her over the side of the ship. Just like the times when she had slipped out of the house to explore the city in secret, lines of women and the older children were walking back across the deck to haul the rowers upwards. They had six ropes going and they were bringing them over the side in rapid succession.

Nola and Riona rushed over to help her up, Nola offering her a fresh robe. She embraced them both before she pulled it on.

"We have done it," she whispered. "All the plans we made in the darkness, they all worked!"

"You did it," Riona said. "This was you getting us here!"

As they pulled apart, the last of the men came on board and fresh sails were unfurled, so it picked up even more speed.

Bridgit was the first to break their embrace. "Were many of the children hit by those archers?" she asked worriedly.

Nola smiled and shook her head. "We got them down below the rail as soon as we saw those archers aiming at us. But it worked – they left you alone!"

"But we still have wounded," Bridgit said, looking at a line of men, those injured in the little fight by the docks, as well as the two new ones nursing arrow wounds.

"Get the children together. We need them to find as many cobwebs in this ship as they can. We have wounded men and nothing packs out a wound better than cobwebs. Ship this size, there has to be plenty of webs," she told Riona. "Wash the wounds with saltwater, then seal them with cobwebs and honey. We'll have to hope they can last until we get back to Gaelland and a priest who can help them. And Nola, get a few of the other women we know and start making a tally of supplies. We have at least half a moon at sea. We need to ration out the food so it lasts."

She had barely finished speaking when there was a huge cheer from the massed people on the deck. Those who had families embraced their husbands and wives and children, those without just hugged each other and cheered their freedom, some of them even performing a little dance on the deck. Bridgit found herself the center of attention and had people bowing to her, patting her on the back and even kissing her hand.

"Three cheers for Bridgit, our leader and savior!" someone shouted and then they were all cheering her. That was more than uncomfortable and she smiled and nodded and waved but made her way up towards the stern. She could see Ahearn was at the wheel there and she wanted to thank him as well. After all, he was the one who had got the ship out of harbor and who would be guiding them home.

She made her way up to the steering platform, thinking that the last time she had done this was to speak to Prince Kemal. What would he be thinking now? She smiled to herself at that and waved to Ahearn.

He did not acknowledge her and she frowned. There was nothing in front of them and surely he could spare a moment. Then she was hurrying to his side as he slumped down from the wheel.

"Help here! I need help!" Bridgit bellowed as she tried to lift Ahearn.

He was too heavy but she was able to lay him on his side – and reveal the arrow that was sunk deep into his back.

He looked up at her but his skin was pale and his grip weak as he reached up to grab her arm.

"Sail north and east," he whispered, then his eyes rolled up and closed.

"Help! Now!" Bridgit roared, fear racing through her. Without Ahearn, how were they going to get home?

CHAPTER 31

Kemal looked out across the sea as the stolen ship began to slip over the horizon and smiled to himself in satisfaction.

"High one, why did you let them escape?" the girl Ely asked.

He did not bother to reply. He had done more than let them escape. He had helped them escape. By his orders the ship that patrolled the entrance to the harbor had been sent down the coast, while almost all the guards had been removed from the way to the harbor and from the harbor itself. He was disappointed to see the guards set to watch the house had been killed, almost to a man, but it would merely add to the reports of an escape, make them more believable when read back in the capital, Kankara.

He ignored Ely and turned to Erdogan. "How many soldiers have been gathered at my orders?" he asked.

"A little over two thousand, high one," Erdogan replied. "We have eight ships ready to load them now."

"Then do so. I want to sail within two turns of the hourglass. I want to catch them by dawn," he said. All would think he planned to catch and destroy them. Instead he would keep watch over them, make sure they were going in the right direction and that nothing went wrong. And, when they arrived back in Gaelland, he and Fallon would face each other once more, each holding the other's family. And he would take his revenge.

"What of the slave master Gokmen? Should he be sent to your father?" Erdogan continued.

Kemal broke away from his thoughts of making Fallon grovel. "No, bring him along, as well as any of the surviving guards who tried to stop the Gaelish, along with all the officers I spoke to earlier," he said. Bringing them along would give him some extra men, men who would depend on him to protect them from the fury of the Emperor. And, of course, with them on board they could not spread any tales of how the Crown Prince had sent guards in all different directions, anywhere but the one place where they could have stopped the attempted escape.

"And make sure there is more than enough food on board for both the trip there and back. Who knows what the future will bring?" he said.

CHAPTER 32

Fallon cursed himself as he led the way back down the stairs to the King's secret Fearpriest lair. How could he have forgotten the third way out of there? He had sent men around to Swane's rooms, with orders to smash down the doors and block the way out. Surely they would arrive in time to stop the foul Prince from escaping? Unless there was another way out along the way ...

Behind him came more men, as well as Brendan dragging the semi-conscious King. He would go into a cell until they decided what to do with him.

That was a question right there. After all their discussions and plans and plots, this had happened out of the blue. All he had wanted to do was get Kerrin, Feray and her boys out of there safely. From there it had spiraled out of control and now he had the King in his hands. But what was the next step? The Kottermanis were coming back and Prince Kemal, just like Aidan, was not going to be in a forgiving mood. Yes, he had just saved Feray and the boys from a Fearpriest but he was sure Kemal was not going to be overcome with gratitude. He had no ideas for what was to come, beyond hoping Duchess Dina might have some answers once she had replied honestly to all his questions. He certainly didn't trust himself to find the right path from here. Chasing after Prince Swane was almost a relief, a chance to put aside these worries.

The smell in the chamber was enough to make everyone choke and gasp. The stench of open bowels and blood was overtaken by the smell of roasted flesh, from where the Earl of Meinster was still cooking.

"Aroaril, look at that," Brendan gasped, pointing out the Fearpriest, lying spread-eagled on the floor, his guts tangled over his legs.

"No time for him," Fallon said grimly. Through the wafting smoke, he could see the door at the far end was open now. Whether his pursuers had battered it down or Swane had got it open did not matter. What counted was Swane had a way out. He prayed it would only take him as far as the men he had sent there. He had to get Swane, for poor dead Prince Cavan. It would finish things as well, although there was little to fear from Swane. After all, he had been his father's puppet and his arrogance and stupidity had nearly brought Aidan's plot undone. He was not the brains behind this.

The children in the cells shrank back against the walls as they came through, crying out in fear.

"Brendan, get those doors open," Fallon ordered.

The big smith needed no second invitation and dropped the limp King Aidan onto the floor to use his hammer to smash the locks and open the doors. The children still cowered at the back, clutching each other. Fallon dropped down to one knee.

"You are free now," he said gently. "We are here to take you back to your parents. You are safe now."

"That's what they say when they come for us," a small voice said accusingly.

"Well, we are going to leave the doors open. Your parents are on their way here and you can stay here until they arrive or you can come with us and see the sun once more," Fallon offered.

When none of them moved, he turned back to King Aidan.

"Your new room is ready, sire," he said harshly.

Brendan used his hammer to open the filthiest cell he could see, then the King was unceremoniously dumped inside. Fallon picked Craddock and four more of his villagers to stand guard there. After what they had seen in the chamber, and the terrified children in the cells, Fallon knew they would not listen to the King demanding to be let out. Just to be on the safe side Aidan was bound and gagged before the door was wedged shut.

"Now for Swane," Fallon said grimly.

He led the way back through the passageways, this time taking the second turning. It felt strange walking this way with armed men at his back, after stumbling through there with the children, just trying to get out.

He had never been down the second passageway and led the way cautiously but there was nothing until it ended in a solid wooden door, banded with iron.

Brendan stepped forwards without being asked and battered it until it sprang open. Fallon jumped through, shillelagh at the ready, to find he was in a richly appointed sitting room.

"These must be Swane's," he hissed. "So much for Kelty's search that time."

"He probably had a drink with Swane and laughed about us waiting outside," Brendan agreed.

Fallon nodded. The guard captain had paid the penalty for that back in the chamber. He advanced through the rooms cautiously. It looked as though somebody had been through here recently, for clothes were strewn over the floor. Chests had also been opened and tipped out.

"Looks like someone was packing for a long trip," Brendan said, obviously having noticed the same thing.

But there was nobody in the rooms. Fallon finally made his way to the door into Swane's rooms, unlocked it and hauled it open – to see the angry faces of the men he had sent there.

"Nobody has been through here, have they?" he asked, already knowing the answer.

"Well, where is he?" Brendan asked.

"We'll look everywhere," Fallon said. "He cannot get far."

*

Yet nobody had seen anyone leaving by any of the other exits. It was a mystery and Fallon's disquiet was growing. He did not like the idea of Swane emerging from a hiding place under the castle at some time and wreaking his mischief. But he was running out of time to worry about it, because there were a hundred other things to deal with.

He had to send men off to secure the city gates and remove the guards on duty there. Most of his villagers had to do that, because he needed men he could trust there, although he also sent along groups of his best recruits with them, because he could not risk any trouble at the gates.

"People can come in but nobody is to leave," he told them. "Not until we discover who else has sold their soul to Zorva. We know the Guilds are in this, as are some of the nobles. We must find the others."

While they had found some of the men who had got out of the chamber bearing the marks of Fallon's shillelagh, others had scattered. Then there were Archbishop Kynan and the King's Wizard Finbar. Search parties had not found either of them at their homes.

The good news was that Devlin and the others had been found alive and brought back to the castle, battered and bruised.

"I'm sorry, Fallon. They were onto us before we realized they were there. They took out our men at the entrance and then rushed in," Devlin said sadly, his left eye almost swollen shut and his lips split from a shillelagh blow.

Fallon gripped his friend's shoulder. "It is my fault," he said. "I must have led them to you. You have had no other visitors. At least you know that Kelty and the others who did that are burning in Zorva's pits now."

"I'd still have liked to throw them in there myself," Devlin said.

"Rest, my friend. I am going to make you a busy man very soon."

Duchess Dina had sent a message that she was staying in her townhouse until she could be sure it was safe to travel the streets. Fallon cursed at that. The streets were quiet, with people knowing that something had happened at the castle but unsure what. For now, Fallon did not want to tell them anything. He hoped the sight of his recruits would reassure them, for the city had become used to seeing them every day. More had to be sent to help bring Dina to the castle. He could see that she would be concerned for her safety. Now that the worship of Zorva had been revealed, Aidan's supporters had nothing to lose. He needed her advice but, more importantly, he needed to know she could be trusted. After all, he had just been forced to do what she wanted – depose Aidan and turn to her. Rosaleen needed to be sent, with a company of men, with very careful instructions.

All of the King's surviving guards were being brought back to the castle, where Bran and Casey were talking with Devlin and deciding what to do with them. The ones who were known to be cronies of Kelty were locked in store rooms, while those who were simply doing their job were asked to hand over their weapons and armor and sent home, if Rosaleen ruled they had not sold themselves to Zorva.

The parents of the missing children had been found and brought to the castle, where they were reunited with the surviving children. That had been hard. Each couple had not known whether their child was alive or not and while there were many tearful reunions as terrified children fell back into their parents' arms, nearly half of the rejoicing adults had to be given the devastating news their child had been sacrificed to Zorva.

A group of Kelty's guards was made to bring up the rotting bodies from where the Fearpriest had dumped them and over which Fallon and Feray had scrambled to safety. It was not just children but men and women as well. Worst of all, Prince Cavan's body was among them. The bodies were lain carefully out in the square and weeping friends and family came to collect them. All had the same jagged wound just under their ribs, where they had been ripped open and their hearts torn out. Rosaleen tried to comfort the horrified people but there was nothing anyone could say to take away the anguish.

"But why Cavan? He was already dead," Fallon asked.

Rosaleen shrugged in despair. "Maybe there was still power in his heart, for he was related to both Aidan and Swane. Still, at least we can give him a proper burial."

Fallon nodded, not trusting himself to speak. Seeing his dead prince only brought home yet again his part in all this. But there was no time to brood over it. Rosaleen had to be sent out to test the Duchess, and he had a hundred tasks to complete.

When the parents learned Aidan was not only behind it but in one of the cells, only the looming presence of Brendan stopped them dragging the King out and killing him right then and there. Fallon did entertain the thought things might be easier if he let them but, despite all Aidan had done, he hesitated. At the very least, it had to be done in the open. All Berry had to see and know what Aidan had done before he received the punishment he so justly deserved.

Yet what could they do to the King? Under Gaelish law, the King's word was automatically truth – and in any case every magistrate had been appointed by the King. They could hardly make a ruling on the man. He was pondering what to do with Aidan when Brendan tapped him on the shoulder.

"You need to come and look at this," the smith said ominously.

Fallon followed his friend immediately but, instead of heading upstairs, Brendan led the way into the Fearpriest's chamber. A group of recruits was dragging the bodies of the men Fallon had killed out of there so they would not rot and, more importantly, so all could see the Fearpriest was dead.

"What did you do to the Fearpriest?" Brendan asked.

"Gutted him," Fallon replied, mystified.

"Then it wasn't you that did this then?" Brendan pointed out the body.

Fallon had last seen the Fearpriest trying to hold his intestines inside him. Now it looked as though they had all been pulled out.

"We found the rest of him over here." Brendan walked across the chamber, to the darkest corner, where a pile of guts was strewn around.

"Weren't there a couple of bodies there?" Fallon asked, trying to remember what the chamber had looked like when they had gone through it earlier. His memory of that brutal fight was hazy but he did not think he had not killed anyone this far over.

"Aye. So either the dead are walking again or maybe Swane and his man lay here, draped their mate's guts over themselves until we had gone out the other way and then ran off in a different direction."

Fallon cursed. "They would have to have balls of iron to try something like that!"

Brendan shrugged. "Or just be very cunning. It seems to have worked for them."

Fallon rubbed his face. "Right. Follow me. Let's see what we can find."

The throne room still had two score of Aidan's erstwhile guards being checked and watched by his men, so he did not bother going through there. Instead he climbed the stairs to the King's rooms. With Brendan at his shoulder he sprang through the door – but the room was empty. Yet it was not without evidence.

"Look at this." He saw the blood-spattered and dirty clothes instantly, left beside the fire, as was an empty sack.

"They changed in here and walked out," Brendan said.

"How much of a lead would they have?" Fallon growled as they raced out of the rooms.

But the men watching the gate only had bad news for them.

"There's been plenty of guards and servants leaving here and going home," they admitted.

"Did one of them look like the prince?" Fallon demanded.

"Sir, what does the prince look like?"

Fallon forced a smile to his face. "Don't let anyone else in or out and if they complain, send for me."

"Where will you be, sir?"

"I have no idea," Fallon admitted. "Just keep searching until you find me."

*

"Highness, we need to get out of Berry. Fallon will have men looking for us. He will try to turn the whole city against you," Ryan said smoothly.

Swane scowled at the thought. How could it all have gone so wrong? His father had been annoying at the best of times but he was no fool. He had been watching Fallon carefully, letting the man think he was safe but always ready to act. Once the recruits were trained to the point where they could fight and Fallon was no longer vital, he had moved, grabbing Fallon's son and the Kottermanis and giving Fallon a simple choice, join or die. And once you had pledged your soul to Zorva there was no return. If he had refused, or hesitated, he should have died. The man should have had no weapons and there had been more than twenty initiates in that room – more than enough to handle him. And yet somehow he had got a knife in there and turned the place into a charnel house. Now Father was dead, or at least in Fallon's hands, and he was on the run. It was ridiculous! He shivered at the memory of lying still in the chamber while Fallon and his foul friends had dragged Father through there. He had wanted to run right away but Ryan had insisted this was the best way. Of course he went along with the plan, although it had taken all his control to lie still and pretend to be dead, Brother Nahuatl's blood and guts plastered all over him. He could still smell it now, even though he had cleaned off and changed.

"We have supporters in the city, highness. We shall meet up with Kynan and Finbar. They will get you out and keep you safe," Ryan added soothingly.

"Why can't we join them and march back on the castle? We should have Fallon strung up and executed in front of the whole city!" Swane snarled.

But Ryan merely laid a gentle hand on his shoulder. "Highness, our allies in the Guilds are without men. Remember, your father thought it was better to remove them and chose Fallon to see that done," he said soothingly.

"And look how it turned out," Swane growled.

"Highness, all is not lost. We just have to get you out of the city. Every noble in the country will rush to your father's defense. Between them we can quickly put together an army to take back Berry."

"How can anyone obey Fallon before me? I am the Crown Prince!" Swane raged.

"Indeed, highness. They will be punished for their insolence. But first we must contact our friends. We cannot have our revenge immediately but it will be all the sweeter for the delay."

Swane smiled. "We shall let all the traitors come together. Then when we take back Berry, it will be easier to destroy them all in one. They do not know what they have done."

"As always, you are right, highness," Ryan agreed.

Swane liked that. Father had always told him what to do, then Ryan told him what to do and Brother Nahuatl told him what to do.

He had always obeyed. Now they were gone, he had the chance to do things for himself. After all, he was the King now. And his first order was to revenge himself on Fallon.

CHAPTER 33

Fallon hugged Kerrin to him, while Caley gamboled around them.

"Thank you for our lives," Feray said solemnly.

Fallon kept an arm around Kerrin as he turned to face her. "I swore an oath to keep you safe and I am not a man who breaks his word," he said. "If your husband is the same, we shall both receive our loved ones back."

Feray nodded and gave him a little smile. "I think it was more than that," she said.

Fallon shrugged. "I was not going to let them sacrifice anyone to Zorva, let alone a child."

"And yet now you have more problems than before," Feray stated.

"Do you have the answer to some of these?" he asked. "I have much to do and little time to do it in. Just speak plainly. After what we have been through today, you owe me that much."

She inclined her head to him. "If you set yourself up as the leader of this land, or you help one of the nobles to take the throne, you will run headlong into my husband. He will arrive back here with not a full army but more than enough men to take the city. By leading this country, you will doom it."

Fallon sighed. "What would you have me do then?"

"Let me rule. Let the people know that Kotterman is here to save them from the evils of King Aidan. We shall rule here anyway but if my husband arrives here to find me already on the throne in his name and the country agreeing to become part of the Empire, he will be distracted by that and you will have the chance to go away, as you once told me."

Fallon thought about it. It was certainly tempting. "But what will the price for these people be? Slavery?"

Feray looked him in the eye. "And would that be worse than what some of them go through now? Half this city are servants for your nobility, or work from dawn to dusk to pay their taxes. What is so different? And it would only be a handful each year, just the criminals. See it as a punishment. Is it not a small price to pay for peace and safety?"

"It is too high a price," he said. What she said sounded promising but he knew what began nobly enough could soon be corrupted. Instead of merely criminals being sent into slavery it would become anyone who angered a noble. No system run by those bastards would ever be fair to ordinary people.

"Then what is your answer? Will you attempt to use this rabble of recruits to fight my husband's men? Because, I warn you, they have been fighting around the Empire all their lives, rather than running around a city and playing at soldiers for less than a moon."

"I don't know yet," Fallon admitted. "But it will not be to hand my people into slavery in Kotterman."

Feray reached out and touched his hand. "Please, listen to me. You will inflict far more misery on them this way than if you let me take over. After what you did to us, I never imagined feeling anything but hatred for you but you saved me and my boys. Let me rule and I shall protect you."

Fallon smiled. "I thank you for your offer but I cannot make any decisions now. I do not even have the power to rule. I am just a commoner. You need to speak to the Duchess Dina."

Feray shook her head, her frustration obvious. "However you were born, you are the power in this land now. Don't throw away this chance."

Before he could say anything else, a young recruit raced over.

"Captain, the Duchess Dina is approaching the castle," he announced.

Fallon nodded acknowledgement and the young man raced away.

"He has been using the sword for less than a moon. How will he fare against men who have been fighting for ten summers or more?" Feray asked softly.

"Devlin, find rooms for Feray and her boys. Somewhere nice, and find some servants to bring them whatever they want. I want at least ten men guarding them at all times as well."

"Prisoners, again?" Feray asked bitterly.

"No, guests. But guests who must be kept safe. You may go where you wish in the castle but we cannot be sure all of the King's men have been found and removed. Until the castle is ours, you must be protected," he said. "Our families' lives depend on it."

She smiled then. "At least let me talk to this Duchess Dina. Explain things to her."

"We will speak again," Fallon promised. He did not like the idea of Feray trying to cut a deal with the Duchess behind his back. The only important thing was to get their families back. Everything else came second.

*

Duchess Dina walked into the castle as if she owned it.

"Captain Fallon, I do believe you have saved our country!" she exclaimed, striding over to him.

"Your grace." Fallon bowed and she reached out and touched the top of his head, in what felt like a blessing.

"Now come, let us go inside. We have much to talk about."

Fallon lingered to wait for Rosaleen. The priestess looked exhausted but raised a wan smile for him.

"She answered every question, swore she had not breathed a word to anyone. And I could only find truth in her words. She wants to help, wants to wipe away Aidan's foul rule and bring Cavan's dream to life," she whispered.

Fallon breathed a sigh of relief and grasped her shoulder. He was reluctant to trust a noble, particularly Dina, but he needed help here. If Rosaleen said Dina was speaking the truth, that was all he needed.

"I have to go. There are many who need my help," Rosaleen warned.

He nodded agreement and hurried to catch up with Dina, getting caught up in her entourage. A score of servants in the Duke's livery, as well as carts filled with furniture and clothing. They were not just being escorted by his recruits but, in some cases, the men were helping pull them along.

"What is all this?" he hissed at Gannon.

"The Duchess is moving out of her house and into the castle. She said she needed everything," the big sergeant said with a grimace.

Fallon shook his head and hurried to catch up with her.

Dina led the way up to the King's rooms, where the bodies of Aidan's guards had been removed but the bloodstains still remained outside.

"Gannon, I want these rooms cleaned, my furniture inside and a fire lit. Drag anything of Aidan's out into the courtyard and we shall either burn it or give it away to the poor," she ordered.

"Wait, Padraig is in there, going through the King's papers," Fallon protested.

"He can continue that task elsewhere. Gannon, get the papers all bundled up and send them along to Prince Cavan's old rooms," she said crisply. "But first of all, we need the King's seal."

Fallon coughed. "That was taken, Duchess. Prince Swane escaped us and took it with him, by pretending to be dead."

She closed her eyes briefly. "That makes things even more difficult. Right then. Gannon, begin working. Fallon, follow me. We have little time."

With that she swept away again.

Fallon hesitated for a moment then hurried after her.

She led the way down to the throne room, where the last of Kelty's guards sat in a corner, watched by nervous recruits.

"Out of here. All of you," Dina said crisply. "Take them to the stables and finish the job there. We need to begin the work of ruling."

The recruits glanced at Fallon, who nodded.

While they prodded the guards and escorted them out, Dina walked around the other side of the room, looking at the tapestries and snapping orders to a pair of servants in her wake. Fallon felt like a bewildered sheepdog, trailing after a strange sheep.

"Those can go. The King had no taste," she said over her shoulder, pointing at a pair of tall tapestries. "We shall find new ones."

She glanced over to see the last of the recruits heading out of the throne room door and gestured to a table and chairs by the wall, the set that King Aidan used to eat in between audiences and where he had tested Fallon with the shillelagh and crossbow.

"Get every servant in the castle up here, ready for when we have finished, and then get me scribes and parchment," she ordered, then pointed at the chairs for Fallon.

He sat down awkwardly while she waited until the servants had hurried away before joining him.

"You did it!" she exclaimed, an enormous smile on her face. "But why did you not tell me first?"

"It was not deliberate. I just did what I had to," Fallon said stiffly.

"Well, we are going to have to work fast to hold on to what we have won. Swane escaping, with the King's seal, is a setback. We have Berry but the nobles control the rest of the country. So the first thing we need to do is execute Aidan publicly at dawn tomorrow. He must die. Not just for what he has done, which is beyond evil. But because the nobles will never declare for me while he lives. They are too afraid of him. And him being alive also gives Swane power, because he is the agent of his father, with his father's seal. Anything he signs and says can be made law by the King. But with Aidan dead, Swane is merely the second son and a contender for the throne. All the nobles hate him and news that Cavan is murdered will horrify them. The only other noble who might challenge me for the throne is the Earl of Meinster—"

"He is dead. Burned to death," Fallon interrupted.

She smiled briefly. "Good. Then I clearly have rank. Next we need to appoint people we trust to powerful positions. Your wife's father Padraig must become the Royal Wizard, while that priestess of yours should be the new Archbishop. Gannon will be captain of my guard and you, obviously, will be the head of our army."

Fallon felt his mouth drop open and shut it with a snap. "But who will pass judgment on the King? No magistrate can convict him."

"That does not matter. Drag the body of the Fearpriest out and hang it from the castle walls, for all to see. Then get the parents of the children he sacrificed to Zorva out here and let the people of Berry hear what he has done. Show them he had Cavan killed and then execute him."

Dina grabbed his sleeve and jerked on it, so he looked up and into her burning eyes. He shrank back from the intensity there.

"You must understand, until he is dead, everything we have won here today is at risk," she hissed.

He pulled his arm free and she seemed to subside a little.

"Fallon, we have a chance now. A chance to let Prince Cavan's dream come true. A fairer Gaelland, ruled not for the benefit of a few but for all. No more heavy taxes, no more strange parties where servants are beaten and killed, no more children starving to death in streets while nobles dine from gold plates and the church has its hand out for what little the people have. Think about a church that helps the people, without demanding favors in return, nobles who must care for their county rather than themselves and a ruler who obeys the laws the way the people are supposed to. Don't you want to see that?"

He could see the new country as she spun the vision for him. It was exactly what he and Cavan had talked about. It sounded almost too good to be true and he hesitated, until he remembered that Rosaleen had only heard truth from Dina. "You know that is what I long to see for Gaelland," he said.

"Then let us make it happen! We can do it. You have the only army in Gaelland."

"The nobles still have all their guards. They could match us, maybe outnumber us if they all come together," Fallon warned. "And then there is the fyrd. Each noble can summon every man between sixteen and fifty summers to fight for them. We could see ten, twenty thousand men outside the gates of Berry in a moon's time."

Dina chuckled. "The nobles all sent their stocks of arms and armor here, remember? They took the money Aidan stole from everyone with his selkie tax and there is no way their blacksmiths have replaced that much in such a short time. And they will not summon the fyrd, because they will fear it will turn on them. The ordinary people will not fight for Zorva."

"They might be forced to, if the nobles still call the fyrd," Fallon argued.

"They might," she said, "if you leave the King here. Every noble will know that Aidan will be demanding why they did nothing to free him. While he is alive, they will do everything they can to defeat us and save him, for fear they will be killed by him later. But remove the head of the snake and the others will not know what to do. Once he is dead they might follow Swane but all that will come with them will be their guards. And you know how to defeat them."

"Aye, I do," Fallon admitted.

"So why do you hesitate? He tricked you into killing your Prince, sold your families into slavery and tried to kill your son. What else does he need to do?"

"Nothing," Fallon said harshly. Any one of those reasons was good enough to kill Aidan. But he was still the King. Down in the chamber he had been happy to kill Aidan and had even tried to. If his hand had not been so bloody he would have ended the King's life and not thought twice about it. But that rage was gone and he worried about being the man who judged and executed the King. He remembered what he liked about being a sergeant. Other people made the big decisions and you just carried them out.

"Why do you hold back? I would have thought you eager to finish him off," she asked.

"I wanted the church, the magistrates, to pass judgment on him. He was happy for the church to burn innocent women for being witches. Why can't the church do it? That way it is Aroaril passing judgment on Zorva. I will be happy to enforce the death penalty on him for them," he said.

"No, we need to do this. If the church kills the King then that makes the Archbishop more powerful than the throne. And the nobles will never allow that. I can never allow that," Dina said with a shake of her head. "It is too dangerous a precedent. We might as well crown the Archbishop. No, everyone will understand what had to be done. And, by killing him, we clearly take power for ourselves. None can doubt who the new rulers are."

"But this way I am just the man who murdered the King," he said. "I know what people are like. They cheer for me now but they can turn on me just as quickly. Aidan was the one who told the people to love me." Although he did not say it, it also meant he must turn his back on the plan to escape to Cavan's island. Once he killed the King, he tied himself to Gaelland forever, and made himself responsible for the people. And that was a responsibility he did not want. He did not trust himself to live up to it.

She smiled at him. "If you give them a better country, they will love you more. They will remember you destroyed an evil King who wanted them to sacrifice their children to Zorva and who starved their families but asked for more and more of the pittance they had. If they have food in their bellies and coin in their purses, they will love you."

"And Kotterman? They still want us as part of their Empire."

"Indeed. And that is why the King must die. The agreement dies with him. They can push pieces of paper at us all they like but the man who signed it will be dead."

"Then they will try to make new demands on us."

"But we have their Crown Prince's family," she said triumphantly. "They can do nothing while we hold them."

"I gave my word they were to be returned once our families were back," Fallon protested.

"And so you did. But, if I am the ruler, then I can hold them and you have not broken your word," she reminded him.

"But I still break my word—"

"Fallon, do you want Kottermanis ruling this country and sending our people off as slaves?"

"No," he admitted.

"Then leave it to me. Listen now, much has happened in the past few turns of the hourglass and your head must be whirling. I have much to do to begin to establish our control. Can you grant me one favor?"

"What is that, your grace?"

"Go down and talk to King Aidan. Speak to him and then come back and give me your decision as to his future. If you still decide you cannot kill him, then we can leave him imprisoned. Or perhaps give him to the Kottermanis!"

"That is one thing we cannot do," Fallon said. "If they got hold of him, they would use him as a puppet to justify their claim on the country."

"Please, speak to him and then talk to me. I have the noble birth but you are the man who put me on the throne and I shall never forget that," she said gently.

Fallon nodded. "I shall speak to him, although I do not know what good it will do."

"Perhaps nothing. But do it anyway."

*

The smell had not improved much in the chamber, even though the bodies had been cleared away. His men were clustered down one end of the cells, keeping away from the one that held the King.

"Has he been making much noise?" Fallon asked.

"Nothing with his mouth gagged. But he looks like he wants to murder us all," Craddock replied.

Fallon patted him on the shoulder and walked on down to the cell. The door was wedged shut and he eased that away before stepping inside.

King Aidan had rolled over until he was sitting with his back against the far wall, although his hands and feet were tied. His mouth was blocked with rags but his eyes blazed. Fallon stepped around to the side, where Aidan could not kick or bite at him, and jerked the gag down, allowing the King to speak.

"What are you doing here, Fallon? Come to beg forgiveness?" Aidan snarled.

"Forgiveness?" Fallon laughed. "For stopping you killing my son? For refusing to sell my soul to Zorva?"

"You fool," Aidan said. "I thought I saw greatness within you but I was mistaken. I offered you the world and you threw it away. How could you not understand that? Unlimited power. The chance to lead armies across all of Kotterman and even beyond, to other lands. Everything you ever wanted!"

"You know nothing of what I want. And I would have had to kill my own son to get it!" Fallon cried.

"Nothing comes without sacrifice. I should know. I had to have my first-born killed," Aidan said.

Fallon dropped to one knee beside him, grabbing Aidan's tunic. "You made me do that. He was my friend, he was my Prince and killing him nearly destroyed me!" he cried.

"I would do it again in a heartbeat. Nothing good comes without blood. That was the secret I learned from Zorva."

"You are mad," Fallon told him, standing up and turning away.

"Don't turn your back on me!" Aidan raged, an insane fury in his voice. Fallon turned to see him raving, almost frothing at the mouth. "You are a little man and even Zorva will be disappointed when I tear out your heart and give it to him!"

"You sit in a cell, with your hands tied, and you still threaten me?" Fallon asked.

"You struck your King – cut my flesh even! Your death will be long and terrible and I will make sure that every one of your friends and family dies first. I will rip apart your wife and son and let them die slowly for days. You will see your friends die screaming and, at last, when you are begging me to end your torment, I will give your heart to Zorva," Aidan screamed.

Fallon's fury ignited. Dina was right. This was not a man but a creature. Every moment he drew breath was an affront to Aroaril. He touched the knife at his belt but left it in its sheath, contenting himself with replacing the gag. Aidan tried to bite his fingers and Fallon was forced to kick him in the side, winding him, to get the fabric back in.

"The next time I see you, it will be to kill you," he told Aidan.

The King was still raving at him from behind the gag but he could not understand the words. Nor did he care.

"Are you all right?" a shaken Craddock asked as Fallon wedged the door shut again.

"I will be tomorrow, when I kill that bastard," Fallon said. "Give him nothing."

He could feel their eyes on him as he walked away but did not care.

CHAPTER 34

Bridgit gathered all the men together. The ones who were still healthy anyway. The children had found handfuls of cobwebs but of the seven men who had been wounded, only two looked like they would recover. Ahearn had died before they could do anything for him. Bridgit had the women all busy, going through the sacks of supplies they had thrown on board in the final rush to get out of Adana. Night was falling and there was no sign of pursuit. The wind was blowing briskly and she had made sure there would be no lights showing on the ship. By the time the Kottermanis sailed after them, she hoped to be over the horizon and out of sight. Granted, the slavers would know they planned to sail back to Gaelland and would know the route. But they would not catch them. She would not let them. For the first few moments after Ahearn's death she had felt panic but she had crushed it ruthlessly. He had been her main hope but he was not her only hope. They were free. Getting home was not the hard part.

"Who knows the stars? Who can look at the night sky and see where we are?" she demanded. "You are fishermen and farmers, used to moving at night. We need to travel north and east to hit Gaelland again."

She looked expectantly at them but they merely shuffled their feet and looked at each other, waiting for someone else to take the lead.

"Look, Ahearn gave me the directions to sail home before he died. We just need someone to make sure we are sailing in the right direction each time. We do not have to sail into Baltimore, or Killarney. We just need to find Gaelland and then we can sail around it from there," she said briskly, injecting confidence she did not feel into her voice.

But, once again, they said nothing. Finally Dermot cleared his throat. "I worked all the hours of the day, never into the night," he said reluctantly.

That broke the dam and Bridgit listened with mounting frustration to a series of excuses from the men. Even Ahearn's crew were reluctant to step forwards.

"He was the one who steered us true. He never liked anyone else taking the tiller," one of them said.

"My grandpa said you just need to look for the north star at night. It's the brightest star up there and we just sail towards it," someone else said.

"The north star isn't the brightest star. It's the one above the brightest star," another objected.

Instantly six more of them began arguing, all offering their old hints and tips for directions.

Bridgit held back her anger. She remembered Fallon telling her once that most men liked to be led: only a few wanted to be leaders. But, if they were not given direction, they fell to fighting with each other.

"Enough!" she roared and they fell silent.

She took a deep breath, thinking fast. The last shadows from the setting sun were falling across the ship and would be gone very soon. She walked through the men and held out her hand to Dermot.

"Your knife," she ordered.

Mystified, he handed it over and she took it and walked across the deck, until she was level with the mast. Raising it high in her hands, she rammed it deep into the ship's rail.

The men watched as she walked briskly back and took another knife from another man. She made sure she was level with the mainmast, then rammed that knife home in the other rail.

"Get some rope and stretch it across the deck. Quickly now!" she barked.

For a moment they did nothing, then a handful of men raced off, coming back with rope so they could form a line across the deck.

"Now we need to turn the ship. Dermot, you and another man to the ship's tiller!"

Quicker to obey now, they raced up to the tiller.

"Make the shadow of the mast line up with the rope!" she called.

The sun was slipping below the horizon and she could feel hope slipping away with it but she refused to panic. The ship altered course until the shadow from the mast slowly eased around until it lay across the rope line she had stretched across the deck.

"We know that now we are heading north, with west to our left," she said. "So we just need to hold that course until the morning. We shall check it again then, with the first light of dawn, so we get due east, so we can turn more towards that direction during the day, before heading north at night. We check it twice a day and we shall be sailing in the right direction."

She was not entirely sure this would work but the men seemed far happier and she began to breathe again as the last shadows slipped off the deck.

"Find your families and hold them. We shall determine who will work through the day and who needs to be there at night, in case of storms or high winds to bring in the sails," she called.

They walked away, all except the two largest, and she groaned to herself.

"When do we eat?" Blaine demanded.

"When we have worked out how much food there is and how many people we have. Be patient. I told you all to eat well today. We shall eat tonight but we have to be sure we have enough to last for the trip."

"We did the most to get us here. We need feeding now!" Carrick demanded.

"You can either have cold scraps now or a proper hot meal later. What would you prefer?" Bridgit asked, quietly furious that these two were already causing problems.

"A hot meal. But you had better hurry, woman," Blaine announced.

"It will be ready when I say it is and not before," she retorted. "And woman is not my name. So, when you have eaten you can stand watch through the night."

"What?" Blaine cried.

"There is only one captain of this ship and that is me. You would do well to remember it."

Blaine looked ready to keep arguing but Carrick grabbed his arm. "Agreed," he said, leading his brother away, where they sat down on coils of rope, leaning up against the rail and muttering to each other. She glared at them. That had seemed a little too easy. Then she chided herself for such a thought. They always backed down when pushed. And they had saved her back at the docks. She would just have to keep a close eye on them.

She did not spare them another look as she hurried down the ladder below, where Riona and Nola were organizing a score of women to count the supplies. It felt strange to be going below on one of these ships, where they had traveled as prisoners from Gaelland and she had first learned to lead.

Here it was darker and several lanterns showed piles of sacks spread across the lower deck.

"Do we know where we are going?" Nola asked softly.

"I used the setting sun to find east and west and we are sailing north, as we need to," Bridgit announced loudly. "We shall check that twice a day and that should bring us to Gaelland at least. Once we find our home country, we can sail around to Lunster once more."

The light was dim but it was still easily light enough to see the obvious relief on faces.

"What have we got?" she asked, before they could ask any more about the way they were sailing. The ship was so different from anything they were used to. The men had worked out how to get out the sails, and could bring them in again, but she was sure they were not sailing it properly. It felt different from the way they had sailed there. Slower, somehow. She pushed that out of her thoughts. An extra night or two at sea was not going to kill them.

"Well, we should have enough for a half-moon voyage. But we are going to have to tighten our belts," Riona said. "There's plenty of dried dates and oranges and even sacks of those strange, hard fruit they like. Those, at least, have water inside, which can be drunk. There is flour, which we can use to make a flat bread on their stove, and some salted mutton. But little of that. There will be complaints at the lack of meat within a day or two. We have four goats as well, so we can get a little milk and maybe some meat if the milk dries up."

"We'll keep them as long as we can," Bridgit said, although she was already wondering how much the goats might eat. "Can we make it last for at least half a moon?"

"The children will be complaining but yes, we can get there. But we will be chewing on the last few dates when we finally see Gaelland," Nola warned.

"And water?"

"There are plenty of casks aboard and we should drink from those. Once we get closer to Gaelland it is bound to rain and we can replenish them. And there is always those coconuts to drink, which can make things last longer," Riona added.

Bridgit chewed on her lip. There were several wounded men who were unlikely to last the trip. If she banned them from eating and drinking then it would mean more for the others – but their families would be outraged and horrified with the thought that hunger and thirst would kill them quicker than their wounds. That was a question for another day. She would see how they did over the next day or so and decide then. Meanwhile there were other hard decisions to make.

"We need to lock the food and water away. None can come in and take any of it. If any do, then we shall punish them by not allowing them food for the following day," she said.

"There's many who are not going to like it. Not to mention the children who are used to getting more food and who won't understand why there is so much of it and they are receiving so little," Nola warned.

"That does not matter," Bridgit said firmly. "We did not risk so much, and lose brave men like Ahearn, so that greed starved us to death within sight of our home. We shall give them a hot meal of mutton and bread tonight and tell them what we face. They will understand."

She saw Nola and Riona exchange glances and knew what they were thinking. Blaine and Carrick were not going to understand anything. But with the whole ship against them, they could do nothing. "I know I swore to get them home but I'll throw the pair of them overboard rather than have them kill the rest of us," she said and Riona and Nola nodded agreement.

CHAPTER 35

The word had spread across the city like wildfire. Few people had actually seen King Aidan but stories of his fury and revenge had been told and retold across the city a thousand times. All had felt the lash of his anger, if not from him then from his guards. Before dawn, the square was packed with people, with more trying to squeeze in all the time. Every window that overlooked the square was full of people and there were hundreds clustered on the roofs of the houses that lined it. The only space the crowd could not fill was in front of the castle, where a makeshift platform had been by built by Brendan and a score of helpers. It was a simple affair, barely enough room for a dozen men to stand on, and it was only half the height of a man off the ground. But it was enough for it to be seen. A triple ring of Fallon's men surrounded it. None of them were wearing surcoats now, for none wanted to wear the badge of the King, while there were not enough surcoats of either Prince Cavan or the Duchess of Lunster to dress so many. They all carried shields but kept their swords in the scabbards. The idea was to keep people away, not hurt them.

"Are you sure about this?" Padraig asked as he and Fallon looked over the huge crowd.

"He has to die. And nobody else has the courage to do it," Fallon said. Dina had been right. Talking to Aidan had cleared his mind. Aidan's evil had to be snuffed out. With Archbishop Kynan and almost all the bishops having conveniently disappeared from the city, the church was left without leadership. And they had no way of knowing how far the corruption went. Rosaleen had been made the new Archbishop, which would outrage more than it would please, but there was none other he trusted. Even if there had been an older Archbishop beloved of Aroaril, the church could not depose a King. With a village priestess newly put into the role, there was no question of it.

"While he is alive, Kerrin, you, everyone I care about is in great danger. And Dina is right: he is a rallying point for the nobles. With him gone, they will not want to fight for Swane. The ones who he had won over to Zorva are already dead and the others will be happy enough as long as they can still live like kings," Fallon said.

"But how long will you let that go on?" Padraig asked shrewdly.

"Just long enough to have the country in our hands. And then they will learn that there is a new way of life in Gaelland," Fallon said fiercely.

Padraig looked over the crowd again. "This won't bring back the people he killed. Cavan is not going to live again," he warned.

"I know," Fallon said bleakly. "But it will send a message to future rulers. These people are not your playthings. Protect them or you will pay the price."

Padraig reached out and patted his shoulder. "I hope you feel the same way afterwards. Do you want someone else to do it? Brendan has said he cannot wait to use his hammer on the man who sold Nola and his children into slavery."

Fallon shook his head. "I cannot ask any of them to do it. I must take the responsibility."

Padraig tightened his grip on Fallon's shoulder. "Well, you had better go and get started, because the people are getting restless. I take it you have sent Kerrin well away from this. He does not need to see this."

"Aye, he is with Feray and her sons, at the other end of the castle."

"Good. I shall be up here. Just raise your left hand when you want me to make you heard by the crowd. Raise your right hand if you want the King to be heard."

"Why should he get the chance to speak to the people?"

Padraig chuckled. "I was thinking they should maybe hear him threatening death and Zorva on all of them."

Fallon gave the old wizard a wink. "Good idea," he said.

"Aye, well I do have them now and again. Just don't expect them too often!"

Fallon strode up the stairs and onto the platform, to a huge cheer from the crowd, and raised his left hand, partly to calm them, partly as a signal to Padraig.

"Today, we finally clean the evil from our city!" he shouted, which brought a thunderous roar. He pointed down at Gallagher and it began.

First came the Guildsmen, nobles and guards taken in the castle and in the King's evil chamber, many of them still bruised from Fallon's whirling attack. Rosaleen, resplendent in ill-fitting robes, blessed a cup of water and then poured it over their heads. Each one of them shrieked as the holy water burned their skins, showing they had sold their souls to Zorva, then they were dragged over to a makeshift block where Brendan wielded his huge hammer, crushing their skulls with one blow.

The crowd cried and screamed and shouted as each was dispatched and the body dragged away to be flung onto an unlit pyre. Fallon was surprised none of them begged for mercy but just went to their deaths spitting hatred.

Finally the last was dragged away and a sweating, blood-spattered Brendan stepped back.

Fallon signaled again to Gallagher and stepped down off the stage as Rosaleen offered up a final prayer, leading the crowd in an impassioned plea to turn from darkness and back to the light. Once she had finished, she would leave. Fallon guessed she would be more than happy about that. He slipped his hand into his pouch and felt the bloody quarrel there, the one that had killed Cavan. He drew strength from it for what was about to come.

Cavan's body, cleaned as best it could be and dressed again in fine clothes, was carried gently onto the stage. Even though he was decaying, he was still recognizable as their beloved Crown Prince, and the crowd sobbed and cried at the sight.

"He was killed at his father's orders and his heart offered to Zorva," Fallon shouted. "Now I shall bring up King Aidan to face judgment for his crimes!"

They howled their approval and he turned away, wondering what they would say if they knew it was he who had loosed the fatal quarrel.

*

King Aidan proved difficult to get out of the cell. Firstly the ropes had cut off his circulation and he was barely able to walk and had to be dragged along by Gallagher and Craddock. When his gag was removed he immediately demanded to be let go and for breakfast to be brought to him. They kept his hands tied and hauled him up the stairs and out through the throne room. Duchess Dina was there waiting, looking pale but composed, although the King was glaring daggers at her.

"It has to be done," she said, falling into step behind them.

The corridors were lined with many of the men Fallon had won over from Kelty's guards. Aidan seemed to recognize some of them and ranted and raged at them until Fallon was forced to replace the gag. The King tried to break free but against the grim villagers he did not have a hope. They hurried the King along towards the front gate of the castle.

The platform almost hid them from sight as they went out the castle gate but the closest people could see, and instantly a huge roar went up, which was taken up by the rest.

Aidan began to struggle in earnest then, especially when they reached the platform steps – it was impossible to get him up them until Fallon thumped him in the stomach. They dragged him up and dropped him on the raw wood, stained with the blood and brains of his cronies.

Fallon looked at Dina, who nodded to him. "You know what must be done," she said.

He raised his left hand and then pointed down at Aidan. "This is King Aidan, who is here to be judged and punished for his crimes against you all!"

His voice echoed across the square and silenced the crowd, who leaned forwards to hear his next words.

"He has sold his soul to Zorva!" Fallon called.

Half of the crowd screamed in horror, the other half in outrage.

"He planned to convert you all to Zorva and make you sacrifice your children to that foul god of death, so he would grow in power."

The crowd howled back at that and Fallon had to wave for calm before they quieted down.

"There were no witches. Instead it was the King's men, stealing children for him to sacrifice on an altar to Zorva! All the women he burned were innocent!"

That also caused a shockwave through the crowd but this reaction was more mixed. Fallon feared that was because some of them had helped with the burnings.

"There were no selkies. Instead he sold our people to the Kottermanis as slaves, to make himself even richer!"

This accusation brought a far stronger roar of anger.

"He will make us part of the Kottermani Empire and drag us into evil. He even had his own son killed! Prince Cavan is dead because he would not convert to Zorva, while Swane has run because he did!"

Now there were cries of horror, for the people had loved Cavan. Fallon felt the mood of the crowd and waved to the side of the platform.

Bran helped a line of parents forward, men and women broken by their grief, led by Conor, the man Fallon had rescued from the snatchers.

"They took my daughter Becca," he cried, Padraig making sure his voice carried right across the square. "Stole her from our home, then cut out her heart for Zorva and left her body to rot in a cellar in the castle. We cannot even be sure whether she rests with Aroaril after death or is doomed to serve Zorva for ever more."

The crowd was silenced by horror at this, parents dragging their children closer.

Fallon nodded to the grief-stricken Conor and the man, tears streaming down his face, walked off the platform to allow others to come forwards and explain their stories. All were the same.

A weeping woman haltingly told how her son had been snatched from the street itself and Prince Cavan had tried to save the boy, only to lose the snatchers across the rooftops. He had lingered at the marketplace because he wanted a new cloak, not one handed down to him by his brothers. The next time she had seen him, rats had been at him and there was a hole in his chest where his heart had been.

On and on it went, until half the crowd was weeping as well, the others baying for blood.

Fallon let the last woman step off the platform then nodded to Brendan, signaling for him to drag Aidan to his feet.

"For years he has stolen your money and punished you for no reason. Now he wants you to worship Zorva and give your blood as well as your silver to make him rich and powerful. What say you? Will you give him your children to be killed?"

"No!" they screamed back at him.

"He killed his own cousin, the Duke of Lunster, when he too rejected Zorva!"

That provoked a smaller response from the crowd but an enormous one from Aidan. Dina, meanwhile, covered her face with her hands and staggered back off the stage.

Fallon glanced down at Aidan and the King's eyes were bulging madly. He pulled the gag clear of Aidan's mouth.

"I never touched Kinnard!" the King snarled.

"Why should I believe a liar?" Fallon asked.

"You have no right to do this. I will make you suffer!"

Fallon had seen Aidan at his most reasonable and that King might have cast enough doubt among the crowd to make things difficult. After all, they had known nothing else and many would still feel an allegiance to the King. The only person who could break that was Aidan himself and the King had worked himself up into one of his furies. Perfect. Fallon raised his right arm. Instantly the King's voice boomed out over the square. At first he raged at Fallon then, when he realized all were hearing him, turned to address the crowd.

"You think you have the right to judge me? I am appointed by the gods! Aroaril gave me the right to rule and Zorva has given me the strength to do so! What are you against that? You are ants, worth nothing! Your lives are mine to take, for you belong to me! The only way you can save yourselves is if you bring me the heads of Fallon and all who support him. Then throw yourselves down at my feet and beg forgiveness and I might not kill you all!"

The crowd drew back in the face of his anger.

"I own you, all of you and I will do with you as you wish. Now I command you to rise up and free me and any that do not will beg for death by the time I finish with you! How dare you oppose me?"

The angry mutterings started then.

"I am your King and I am ordering you to free me or so help me, I will see every one of your heads decorate the walls of this city! I will make you watch me rip out the hearts of your children and you will learn your folly then! I am your King, given to you by the gods! You are nothing! Free me now or the country will shudder to hear what I have done to you!"

Fallon dropped his right arm. He had heard enough and he could see the crowd had too. Mothers were covering their children's ears, while fathers were shouting back at Aidan. He reached into his pouch and brought out the bloody quarrel, the one that had taken Cavan's life.

Aidan stopped ranting at the crowd, his voice now washed away in the anger that was coming back from the people.

"What are you doing?" he snarled at Fallon, his voice harsh and hoarse.

For answer Fallon grabbed the King by his shoulder and rammed the rusting point of the bloody quarrel deep into the King's side, punching the heavy point through skin and muscle and into the organs beyond. Blood sprayed over his hand and the King gave out a terrible, high scream that silenced the crowd.

Fallon felt the quarrel sink in until his fist was pressing against the King's side. He twisted the bolt viciously, sawing it back and forth, making blood splash out, while Aidan shook and shrieked. Fallon ripped the quarrel out and the King's legs seemed to lose strength and he sagged against Fallon.

But Fallon pushed Aidan away, hatred for the King washing away any disgust he felt for what he was doing.

The King, screeching in pain, staggered around the platform, head thrown back against the agony.

The crowd was silent, watching him with a mixture of horror and delight and satisfaction.

He almost made it to the edge of the platform but his legs gave way and he fell to the ground, shaking and scrabbling.

Brendan started forwards but Fallon held out a bloodstained hand.

"Let him die hard. He has made the rest of us suffer for long enough," he said harshly.

Seeing Aidan's twitches and moans growing weaker did not diminish his anger and hatred. The King had infected the whole land with his evil and while killing him was long overdue, it was not the end of things.

The King's back arched and he screamed once more, then fell still. Fallon walked to his side, dropping to one knee. Aidan's eyes snapped open and he focused on Fallon.

"You will never rule this land. Your choices will fail and fall and doom my kingdom," he said, clearly and distinctly, his words just carrying to Fallon's ears. Then a huge pulse of blood spilled out of his mouth and he choked for a moment, then was truly still.

"Did he say something?" Brendan asked.

Fallon shook his head, feeling shaken by the King's words. He had heard that dying men had the strength to see the future and just enough power to share it with others. But whether that was another tale, like stories of selkies, or the truth, was another matter. He knew Aidan was full of hate to the last and maybe that was all his words were. But he still felt a shiver up his spine.

"What do we do with him now?" Brendan asked.

"We string him up here, so all can see him and know he is dead. That way word can spread to the other nobles. I am sure they have people watching us within this crowd. Then we throw him on the pyre with the others. Cavan will be buried with honor, in the castle."

*

Fallon washed the King's blood off his hands and ripped off his bloodied tunic as well. The King's execution had taken the crowd's anger but they had all wanted to press in and see the body. Fallon thought he would feel better after Aidan's death but the King's words stayed with him. Not just the last one but also the comment about the Duke's death. Why deny it, when he had been entirely shameless about everything else?

He decided it was worth asking a few more questions about. He had never been happy with the idea of Hagen as a traitor. Dina had satisfied Rosaleen she was telling the truth but maybe they were asking the wrong questions. She was doing and saying all the right things but he could not shake a nagging suspicion about her. He went straight to Gallagher.

"Gall, I want you to take a few men and Rosaleen and head down to Lunster. Dig around Hagen's home, find his neighbors and see what you can turn up."

"Isn't that going to be a waste of time?" Gallagher asked. "I know he was your friend but Hagen's been dead for moons. And many of the people living around there now will be ones who arrived from Berry. They won't even know who he is."

"No," Fallon said. "This is where it all started. In Lunster. I am sure there is something of import down there. The King admitted to worshipping Zorva but not killing the Duke. Why?"

"But why do I go down there with Rosaleen? Isn't she the Archbishop now and needed here?" Gallagher objected.

"I thought you would like to spend some time alone with her," Fallon said with a wink.

Gallagher flushed a little. "That wasn't what I meant!" he said heatedly.

Fallon patted him on the shoulder. "I know. But you will need her, for she can discern the truth. And Aroaril knows it's been bloody hard to get at that since the day the Duke's ship sailed into our lives. And I need you to help me persuade her to do this."

Gallagher nodded. "Then I will do it."

"Good. We'll say that you are helping her investigate the church and speak to the priests still loyal to Aroaril. I'll give you the Crown Prince's seal. In Lunster it would command even more weight.

And the Prince had a sack of gold in his room for some reason. There should be more than enough to buy a fishing boat big enough to get you down there and give you enough gold to get a few tongues flapping."

"When you say it like that, it almost sounds as though it could work," Gallagher said lightly.

*

"Is it done?" Feray asked softly as he visited them. He had installed her and her boys in Prince Cavan's old rooms. They were both comfortable and safe and he could think of nowhere else he could call that.

Fallon nodded. "I thought I would feel happier but I just want a long bath."

"You might have done better to hand him over to us. We could have made his life a misery," Feray said bitterly. "If Kemal knew he wanted to sacrifice us to Zorva, he would make Aidan suffer. Why did you have to be the one who killed him?"

"Who else would do it? One of the parents of the children he murdered might have agreed, or Brendan or Gallagher or Devlin. But then I would have been a coward for walking away and letting others do what I feared to."

"You have no courts to do that?"

"And do you have courts that would go after your Emperor?" Fallon retorted.

She smiled. "Of course not. That was a foolish statement. Anyway, it is a relief to know he is gone. What is your plan now? Will you seek to use us hostages against my husband?"

"I swore on Kerrin's life I would return you in exchange for my family," he said.

"So why are you here?"

"To ask if Kerrin can wait with you until this afternoon. We have much to discuss about holding on to the parts of Gaelland we control, let alone the areas still under control of the nobles."

She glanced over her shoulder to where the three boys were playing a dice game together and laughing. "Of course. But do not trust the nobility. They will say one thing to your face and another behind your back. Remember, they have been playing this game against Aidan for years. You will need to be ruthless with them."

*

Fallon thought about her words as he joined Duchess Dina, along with Brendan, Devlin, Padraig and Gannon and a host of scribes in the King's old rooms. He decided to keep Gallagher and Rosaleen's mission a secret for now. Dina was doing everything she could to help but he didn't know how she would react to news he was investigating Hagen's death. He would watch her carefully.

The King's old room was completely different. All the furniture was gone, replaced with the Duchess's, and the wall hangings and the rugs had changed too. The hidden door at the back of the room was in plain sight, although obviously barred shut from the inside. It even smelled differently. The Duchess Dina looked completely at home there. In fact, had Fallon not known its history, he would have sworn these were her rooms from the start.

"It was a brave thing you did, Fallon. But it was the right thing. Now, thank Aroaril, we are free and the people are out of the nightmare. The crowd shows no signs of reducing at the gates. As some people leave for their homes or work, others are arriving. It is achieving all we hoped for. Soon all of Berry will know the King is dead, killed for his crimes, and that better rulers are in his place."

"What next?" Fallon asked the moment she paused for breath.

She nodded significantly towards a group of servants, who bustled in bringing trays of drinks and food, which they set down on the table. They were all looking much happier than the servants Fallon used to see around the castle.

"We have checked out most of them now," she explained when she saw him examining the attendants. "Any who had missing children or other family members have been sent away with a payment, just in case. The rest have all sworn in church to serve us faithfully. Thank you." She smiled at them and they left the room.

"Still," she continued, "we should be careful what we eat and certainly should not talk about important matters in front of them. It would not do for the wrong word to reach the wrong ear."

"What now?" Fallon persisted.

"At least four of the minor nobles have sent me discreet offers to help, in exchange for keeping their positions and their lands. I think we need to make the same offer to all of them."

"Help? How would they help?" Fallon asked.

"Food," Dina said simply. "That is the thing we shall need most, with winter approaching. Berry depends on its tithe from the counties. If all that food stops arriving by wagon and ship, we shall have a hungry city before long. And, with winter on the way, that is not a good place to be. We can control the surrounding countryside but there are too few farms to sustain a city of this size, with so many people inside. Of course we shall always have food sent from Lunster but the farms and fishing boats are producing far less there because so many of our people were stolen by the Kottermanis. So we need all the help we can get."

"But how do we know which ones helped Aidan turn to Zorva? I killed two of the main ones, Meinster and Londegal, but there will be others," Fallon warned.

"Of course. But we have to be realistic. We need to keep the nobles on our side for a little while, at least, until we are strong enough to bring them to heel."

"Cavan would not have done this," Fallon objected.

"Cavan would have done the same. He told me his plans, as he did you. He would have played the Guilds off against the nobles, reducing the power of each as he went along. We need to do something similar."

"The Guilds as well?" Fallon cried. "But they have been helping Aidan from the start. They used their thugs to try and kill us and then there were enough of them down in that foul chamber as well!"

"Yet they have money. Money we need to buy food, fuel, weapons and armor, and to keep this city running. Men need to be paid. Without money, we have nothing."

"What about the King's gold?"

"We can use that, true, but a great deal of it has been sent out to the counties to pay for the arms and armor that was used to equip your army," she said. "What is left will not last us long. But the Guilds have more than enough gold to keep us warm through the winter."

"And what will they want in return?"

"Just the right to keep trading. We can break our agreements with them once spring is here. But we need them until then."

Fallon glanced over at Padraig. The old wizard hated the Guilds more than he despised washing his robe, which was saying something, so when he reluctantly nodded, Fallon turned back to the Duchess.

"So what do we offer them?" he asked. "And how do we get them in here? I doubt that many of them will be willing to put themselves in my hands, especially after what we did to some of their friends this morning."

"True," she admitted. "But we have other means. We can send messengers to each of the nobles, offering them the chance of everything going on as before."

"They will not trust us," Fallon said.

Again she smiled but this time there was warmth there. "They will believe me. After all, I am one of them. And I can be most convincing. They will want to hear that you will be removed once the danger of Kotterman is past and Gaelland will return to normal rule. Not only will I leave them thinking that, but also plant the idea in each of their minds that they should be the next King. They are small men, with large dreams. They will all be thinking about that."

"And the ones who do not agree to your offers?"

"They are the ones who are already sworn to Zorva," she replied evenly. "We do not need them all. We just need to win over perhaps half of them, in order to keep the city running. Once we hear back, we will need you to take some of your army out in the countryside. Nobles who think they can defy us in safety will get a nasty shock when we arrive at their home with a thousand spears. They can either fight and die or hand over all we need from their storerooms. Either way we win."

"And the Guilds?" Fallon asked.

"We merely ask them to bring all their new leaders to meet with me in Aroaril's cathedral. And then I shall make them pay a fine to the crown. Or, to us anyway. Nothing too much but enough to keep us going, along with what they must pay in taxes and what we have already in the treasury."

"You are being harsher on the Guilds than on the nobles, yet the Guilds are inside the city," Padraig observed.

She chuckled. "They will expect it. In fact they will suspect a trap if we are too fair to them. The King has bled them white all these years and they expect the Crown to have its hand out for gold. Asking them to pay us money will reassure them, rather than alarm them."

Fallon shook his head. He wanted to cleanse the land of the filth of the Guilds and the nobles, scourge them away and start again. He still remembered what the nobles had done at those banquets with the King.

"Fallon, this is only until the Kottermani danger is past. They will pay for their crimes," Dina said, breaking his thoughts.

"I know, Duchess," he said, a little surprised by her concerned tone.

"Good. Gaelland will not forget the debt it owes you for ridding us of Aidan. We will have a new land, a happier land. No more will the people live at the whims of a vain and ignorant noble. We shall end the nobility. Without the need for local lords and their greed, we can reduce taxes dramatically. Of course we need to split the country into regions to organize it but all will be simpler and better. Look, I have drawn up some ideas but you are free to add your own, or change these as you see fit. I was inspired by the way you ran Baltimore and see that as a way to run the country."

She pushed a sheet of parchment across the table and he looked over it quickly, Padraig at his shoulder. As he read, his excitement grew. Each village would vote for one of its own to be the headman, while each town would have a small council of three, five or seven, depending on the size. Each region would then gather together its headmen and they would elect one of their number to represent them in Berry, where they could bring problems right to the heart of power. As well, traveling magistrates would roam the land, with the power to make judgments on disputes and to check on what the local headmen were doing, to keep them honest.

As for taxes, one part in ten would be sent to Berry, where it could be distributed to the poor, as well as used to improve the country. Improved how would be decided by the men sent to Berry by their regions. And, to ensure none of them could become nobles in all but name, every three years there would be a new vote.

Fallon looked up happily. "This is exactly what Cavan would have wanted," he said, his voice thick.

"I had hoped so." She smiled. "Eventually all noble titles will be removed. Your birth will no longer matter; it will all come down to ability. Men like you will rise, while men like Aidan will fall."

"As long as we defeat the Kottermanis," Gannon said, his words puncturing the bright vision of Gaelland the others were enjoying.

"As usual, Gannon is right," Dina said. "Fallon, we need you back out there training your men. Can you trust me to keep the country running while you protect it? And then, in the spring, we can make Cavan's dream come true."

Fallon did not hesitate. His relationship with Dina had been unusual, to say the least, and there had been times when he doubted where her loyalties lay. But he could find no fault with her plans now. Besides, having her make the decisions meant he did not have to, and the King's words could not come back to haunt him.

"Of course, your grace," he said.

*

"There is something missing," Padraig said in frustration.

"What?" Fallon asked.

"There are gaps here. It looks as though the most important papers have been taken out of here."

Fallon looked around the room. There were scrolls piled up in all sorts of areas, while the old wizard's eyes were red-rimmed and glazed.

"You need to take a break," Fallon said.

"I need to find the answers!" Padraig growled. "I have been through piles of the most boring, useless, pointless scrolls just to find the few that mean anything to us. Whenever money is moved in this country, there is a piece of paper for it. Follow the money and you find the truth. But the money trail keeps vanishing."

"Maybe you haven't found the right scrolls yet."

"Or maybe they were never given to me," Padraig said ominously.

Fallon paused. "That suggests that an ally of the King's took them. Are you saying Gannon or one of his men had something to do with it? If they did, we know whose orders it was on."

Padraig rubbed at red eyes. "I don't know," he admitted. "Perhaps it was never there. Perhaps that bastard of a chamberlain hid it somewhere else."

"I'll ask Gannon to look again. If he acts strangely then I'll ask a little harder," Fallon said.

Padraig reached out and grabbed his arm. "Be careful," he said. "We may have cut the head off the snake but there would be many others in Berry who were inside the King's plots. It doesn't have to be Gannon. An ordinary guard would do just as well. We heard much about the King's agents hidden in the city, but I have found nothing to identify them yet."

Fallon sighed. "Maybe I shouldn't have sent Rosaleen down to Lunster. Meanwhile I'll keep an eye on Gannon."

CHAPTER 36

"How soon can we march on Berry?" Swane demanded.

He ground his teeth in anger as he saw Ryan's face blanch and the horror on the face of the new Earl of Meinster, a weak-chinned man even younger than Swane.

"Highness, we need to wait a little first," Ryan said in that soothing tone of voice that annoyed Swane even further.

"Why? We have wasted days traveling here and every turn of the hourglass that bastard Fallon sits in Berry makes him that more secure and insults the shade of my father. You know what they did? Dragged him up in front of a baying crowd, let him bleed to death and then burned his body! Fallon needs to die and his death needs to be a warning to every man, woman and child who was there. We have to strike and we have to strike soon. The peasants are getting ideas that they can do what they want, not what they are told! Where will it end? No, we have to gather your guards and march on Berry, calling up the fyrd as we go and rallying other loyal troops to us. By the time we arrive at Berry, the people will hand Fallon over to us or they will share his penalty."

"Highness, we cannot do that," the Earl said firmly.

Swane glared at him. Despite his lack of chin, the Earl's mouth was set in a strong line.

"I only have two hundred guards. With luck, we might be able to have one thousand gathered to us by Berry. But that will not be enough to take back the city."

"We have the fyrd!" Swane howled.

"Who cannot be trusted. My county, as well as every other county, had to send young men to Berry to be trained. They are now this Fallon's army. The fyrd will be made up of their fathers and uncles and cousins and friends. If we call out the fyrd, they could turn on us and we will be destroyed. Even if they are loyal, they will have no weapons. We sent all of them to Berry too, to outfit your father's new army, which is in Fallon's hands. And we might not even reach Berry. Fallon could hear word that we are marching on him. There are many places where we could be ambushed on the march."

"Then we march with what we have. The other lords will rally to my banner."

"That may not happen, highness," Ryan warned.

"And why not? They are sworn to my father's service and now he is dead I am the rightful King of Gaelland!"

"Duchess Dina of Lunster has sent messages out to every noble in the land, promising they can keep their lands if they refuse to follow you," Ryan said gently.

Swane forced himself to breathe slowly through his nose. He had seen how his father had made people jump with his temper – but that was when he was seated in his throne room, with guards lining the wall all waiting to do his bidding. He had no guards, nothing other than Ryan and his birthright. Until now, he always had people to tell him what to do. Thinking of things himself was proving harder than it looked.

"How was this done?" he asked stiffly.

"She must have paid the Wizards' Guild in Berry, for it arrived personally to me, brought by a fast-flying bird," Meinster said. "Naturally I showed it to your man Ryan and have it here for you to inspect, highness."

Swane took it with what he knew was ill-disguised politeness and read swiftly, his anger mounting again. It was full of gentle promises and veiled threats. Do nothing but send the regular tithe to Berry and you will retain all your lands and titles. Or be visited by Captain Fallon and his army as they seek to take what is due. King Aidan had turned to worship of Zorva and had to die but, come the spring, there would be a new king chosen, from among the nobles who had stood by Gaelland in this time of crisis. The Duchess, as the widow of the King's cousin, would step in as regent until then but would stand aside in the spring.

"Now word will spread that my father was worshipping Zorva!" he growled. "We need to get Archbishop Kynan into every church in every county, telling them that is a lie and it is every man's duty to rise up against the traitors who hold my capital."

"That is impossible I am afraid, highness. After the rites that Kynan has performed, he is unable to enter a church of Aroaril. It would burn him."

Swane shook his head in disbelief. "Well, how many nobles will listen to this filth?"

"For the lords close to Berry, it is a potent threat. Many of the smaller counties would only have a small company of personal guards," Ryan said. "And then there are the ones who have their own ambitions for the throne. As Meinster rises, they were set to fall. But this gives them the hope that they will be the next King. We can count on Meinster here, and Londegal's heir too, but who knows about the others?"

"That traitorous bitch! I'll see her eyes pulled out and then rip out her heart myself!" Swane growled, crumpling the parchment, taking out his anger on that, for he could not release it on anyone else.

Ryan and Meinster said nothing.

"So what can we do?" he asked finally. "You have told me I cannot bring an army together to take back my throne and avenge my father, nor count on the nobles who swore oaths of loyalty. What have I got?"

"We still have Finbar, Highness. We should send our own message to the nobles, reminding them of their oaths and telling them that those who show loyalty now will be rewarded later. Once we have mustered together more men, then we can issue threats of our own. Join us or die."

"Now that is more like it," Swane said approvingly. "I cannot wait for spring. I need to have Berry back and Fallon's body hanging behind my throne."

CHAPTER 37

Kemal looked out across the sea, chewing on his lip nervously. He had eight ships, each carrying two hundred and fifty soldiers, almost all of the men who had been brought together in Adana. In another half-moon he would have ten times that number in Adana but there was no time to wait for them. The weather would have turned by then and he had no wish to see his fleet wrecked by a Gaelish storm. His ships were the best the Empire had but on an unfamiliar coast, with weather that could change in an instant, that was not good enough.

Besides, the thought of waiting all that time while Feray and the boys were in Gaelland was impossible.

He felt he had enough men to seize Berry and hold it for the winter. Once he had two thousand veteran soldiers in King Aidan's castle, the Gaelish would need five times that number to get them out – and they had nothing that could match the Kottermani bow. Once the winter was over, a full Kottermani fleet could follow and relieve them.

That was not the concern. Instead, he was worried he had not sighted the ship Bridgit and her people had used to escape. He knew many of them came from fishing villages and could handle a small boat, but surely they could not sail a Kottermani ship at the same pace his trained men could. He had no intention of boarding the ship, but he did want to keep it in sight, so he could keep it safe and tow it in to Berry, ready for the two sets of families to be exchanged. He had expected to see Bridgit's ship at dawn on the first day of the pursuit but they had been sailing for three days now and, although his fleet was spread out so that each ship could only see the mast of the other, none had sighted the one they were chasing. He hoped it did not mean they were lost. If necessary, he would spread his fleet and search for them but that would take time and he could feel the sailing season slipping away. He decided to keep going for the rest of the day. If they had not been sighted by nightfall, he would have to search a wider area.

"What are you doing, Bridgit?" he muttered.

*

Bridgit patted the hand of Taidgh, a young man who lived along the coast of Lunster with his two brothers. All three and their families had been taken by the Kottermanis. Now they were all clustered around him as he lay on the deck. He had taken an ugly slash from a Kottermani sword across the chest and, although they had tried to close it up, he was still losing blood. It smelled bad and his skin was a waxy color.

"I am sorry but he is not going to make it back to Gaelland. And we cannot afford to feed him or give him water," she told the families evenly, hating the words but meeting their eyes strongly. She liked Taidgh's two children and had spent many a turn of the hourglass playing with them over the past moon. It was for them, as well as for the other children that she spoke. The food was going down too fast. The goats' milk had dried up after just two days and the beasts had been slaughtered and eaten, for there was no salt to preserve them. Nothing was going as she had planned. This was the last of the families of the dying men and none of these conversations had been easy. Others had wailed and protested and sobbed and begged but she had stood firm. As she would here. If these poor people had to suffer through losing a loved one, the least she could do was face them with courage.

Taidgh's wife dissolved into tears, as did his children, while his two brothers scowled.

"If he gets no food or water then he will never last," one of them muttered.

"He will never last anyway. And the food and water we are giving him could go to your children," she said. "I am sorry but I have to think of them."

"So we just sit here and watch him slowly die?"

"That is happening anyway," she said gently. "But, if you wish, you can help him on his way. That way he will not suffer any more."

Taidgh's wife burst into fresh storms of tears at this.

"I am sorry. I had vowed to get everyone home and I am breaking my word. But I cannot let us starve to death within sight of Gaelland. Men must have strength to sail the ship."

"What about those fat bastards from Killarney, Blaine and Carrick? They still look as though they are eating enough for three men apiece," one of Taidgh's brothers said.

"Don't worry. I will deal with them," Bridgit said grimly.

*

The ship was all quiet as it sailed through the night, its tiller hanging loose and alone. Two large shadows appeared from below decks and walked slowly towards the tiller, their arms full.

"What did you get?" Blaine asked softly.

"Nice bit of meat. Buggered if I know what it is though. Could be that camel," Carrick said. "Tastes like shit."

"Well, I'll have it if you don't want it," Blaine offered.

Next moment, lanterns were unhooded and the two of them stood in the center of a blaze of light.

"No, we'll have it," Bridgit said sternly.

"What's the problem, woman?" Blaine asked.

"You are," she said coldly. "For sending us on the wrong course and stealing the food from the mouths of our children."

"What are you talking about? We just stepped away for a moment to keep our strength up so we could spend all night looking after this ship," Carrick mumbled.

"You have let us drift off course while you broke into our food store and stuffed your stupid faces!" Bridgit snarled at them.

The pair of them strode over towards her, their obvious guilt now fading away into anger.

"You lie! We have been taking care of this ship while everyone else sleeps! We took that shift when you told us to and nobody else wanted it. Who dares say we have not done our job?" Carrick demanded.

Beside him, Blaine glared around at the crowd, daring them to stand with Bridgit.

"I do," Bridgit said evenly. "The truth is, you threatened anyone else who offered to watch the ship at night, until you had it to yourself. Our food supplies have been going down far faster than they should. So tonight we watched you. As soon as you thought the ship was asleep, you left the tiller and disappeared below. Meanwhile while we sail in Aroaril-knows-what direction. Obviously you have been doing that every night."

"That is a lie!" Blaine bellowed, raising a huge, hairy fist, his warning obvious.

"You might have got away with it for longer if you had the sense to at least lash the tiller and keep us on course for the night, and stole only a little food, instead of eating like greedy animals," Bridgit told them coldly. "I have had to tell the families of our wounded men we can no longer feed them because you have eaten the food reserve we had. Men will die because of your greed. If we are to make it to Gaelland, this cannot happen again."

The two men glanced around the deck and she could see them adding up how many men stood around them. The families of the dying men in particular looked furious, with Taidgh's two brothers pushing their way to the front.

"It won't happen again," Blaine said. "You have our word."

She glared at them. Even now they thought a weak apology would be enough to see them escape the consequences of their actions. She had given them chances, time and again, more than they deserved, in memory of their cousins. She would not make the same mistake again.

"Your word? I wouldn't trust that further than I could spit," she told them. "You have robbed those men of any chance for life. And you have endangered the rest of us. We have less food and a longer journey because of you."

"Who made you in charge anyway? You're just a fishwife, good for cooking and cleaning and that's it. Certainly too old for anything else," Blaine said with a leer.

"You don't know what you are doing or where you are going. You can't sail a ship or plot a course. People, why are you listening to her? She doesn't know what she is doing! We should be in charge. At least we are the strongest!" Carrick cried.

Bridgit stared at them. A few moons ago, she would have agreed with them or, at the very least, run away from their challenge. But not now. "I am in charge because I will get us home. You will get us lost and killed. Now you will do what I say," she told them.

"Are you going to make us?" Blaine challenged.

"And what are you going to do about it if we say we won't listen to you?" Carrick asked nastily.

Bridgit took a pace forwards herself, her voice conversational. "Make you pay for your crimes," she said, then pivoted on her left foot, bringing her right fist upwards in a vicious uppercut with all her bodyweight behind it. If she had struck just about anywhere on Carrick, he would have shrugged it off. But Fallon had taught her that to fight fair was being foolish. She drove her punch into his groin, and then danced away as he folded over, squealing in pain, and thumped down to the deck.

Blaine turned to see his brother writhing on the floor and cried out in mingled anger and fear. He took a step towards Bridgit but she brought out a knife from behind her back.

"You are fat and slow and I will make you bleed if you take another step," she hissed at him.

He was twice her size but hesitated, as she had thought he would. He was used to people stepping around him and plainly was surprised by her defiance. She knew that would not last. He was a bully but just standing up to a bully was not enough. Yet she only needed a few moments. Blaine was dragged down from behind by half a dozen men, Taidgh's brothers leading the way.

She used her foot to roll over the gasping, moaning Carrick, who was still clutching where she had punched him.

"The pair of you will be taken below and locked up. You will receive no more food than the smallest child until we reach Gaelland. And there you will answer for your crimes," she told them. "Now take them away."

The pair of them protested, although Carrick was more screeching with pain than saying anything, as they were hauled away.

Bridgit turned back to the silent crowd. "We only have a little of the goat meat left. If you are a fisherman, tomorrow is the time to use your skills. We have to catch something, anything. We need a few men to watch the tiller and everyone else should get some rest."

They rushed off then and she slid her borrowed knife back into the sheath in the small of her back and leaned up against the side rail, so she could cover the sudden shaking in her legs.

"Are you all right?" Nola said softly, joining her.

"I will be. And I shall be much happier now those two fools are locked up below," she said.

"You did well taking care of them. All saw it and will remember," Riona added, hearing the last as she walked over.

Bridgit shook her head. "I was a fool. Nearly as big as they were. I should have been on to them earlier. I have let them gorge themselves for three nights and sail us around in circles. We have lost time and, worse, food. If I had seen it on the first night, perhaps we could have saved one or two of those wounded men."

"You can't blame yourself. They were cunning enough to hide much of what they were doing. It wasn't until they turned their attention to the goat meat that it became obvious," Nola said.

"Who else can I blame?" Bridgit demanded. "It is my responsibility."

Riona reached out and held her hand. "We all believe in you. You will get us home. Apart from those two, there is not a man or woman aboard who would not give their lives for you."

Bridgit looked at her askance, sure her friend was making some sort of jest, but she appeared serious and Nola nodded her agreement.

"We trust you. And you confronting those two idiots has only impressed everyone more."

"A fat load of good that will do, unless we can make it home," Bridgit said.

"We will. You will get us there," Riona said.

Despite their words, Bridgit could not shake the feeling that she was failing. She looked out across the sea, wishing she could spot a landmark, or somehow find an easier way home. Blaine and Carrick had been right about one thing. She did not know how to get them home. And she was worried that others would come to that same conclusion. It was all very well sailing north and east during the day and north at night but those two fools had let them go in any direction. For all she knew, they had turned back towards Adana. As soon as dawn came they could carefully measure their direction and get back on course but who knew how much they had lost. There would be muttering soon, as the rations grew smaller and there was still no sign of Gaelland. She did not know what to do then, except press on and hope.

She placed her hand on her stomach and offered up a swift prayer to Aroaril. That was the one bright spot. For the last two pregnancies she had basically stayed seated or in bed the whole time, trying to give the babe a chance to grow. Yet both had ended in blood and tears. This time she had been running, swimming and fighting – and nothing had gone wrong yet. Of course, lack of food was a worry, but there was nothing she could do about that.

*

"High one, our lookouts still cannot see a ship anywhere around us," Gokmen announced.

Kemal looked at the slave master. Out of his normal life, he was clearly uncomfortable. But he knew his life depended on Kemal's happiness, so he was a useful man to have around.

"Signal the other ships in line and see if someone else has seen something," he ordered.

To keep in touch across wide distances, the Kottermanis used a series of flags. Kemal's ship was in the center of the line and could only see the ships to either side, but so could every ship. By displaying a bright flag at the top of their mast, they could send messages up and down the line in moments. By the time Kemal had taken up his usual position on the stern deck, under a covering, the answer had come back. Nothing was in sight.

Kemal ran his fingers through his beard while he thought. It was a habit Feray had warned him about but he could not break. They should have caught up to the Gaelish by now. He had the best sailors and they had been pushing the ships to the end of their abilities. There was no way a pack of Gaelish slaves could get the same performance out of a Kottermani ship.

"High one, maybe they are trying to be clever and sail a different route, rather than the direct one," Gokmen suggested. "Or they are sailing as fast as us."

"Impossible," Kemal said instantly, but the idea nagged at him. What if they turned now and Bridgit was just over the horizon? She would get back to Gaelland and he would be left with nothing and no way to face down Fallon again. He came to an abrupt decision.

"We keep sailing fast for Gaelland. Maybe they are better sailors than we thought. But if we have not caught up with them in another quarter moon, we shall turn back and search for them. We have to find that ship!"

CHAPTER 38

Rosaleen worried that she should not have sailed down to Lunster. There was so much to do in Berry, with the church in disarray. If Fallon had asked her to go, she would have refused. But Gallagher was harder to say no to. She told herself it was about finding out the truth and ensuring that Duchess Dina could indeed be trusted. Yet the attraction of time alone with Gallagher was the real lure. Their cover story was he was escorting her around the counties, so she could see how far the evil infection had spread through the church.

Priests and priestesses of Aroaril were encouraged to marry and have children, to tie them closer into their communities. That was always easier for the priests than the priestesses. Rosaleen could still remember the crusty old Bishop at her training house warning her not to get too close to young men while encouraging the male novices to hurry up and marry.

The young men of the village, mostly boastful and foolish, had not appealed to her at all. But Gallagher, although he was nearly ten summers older, did. Perhaps because of the sadness and tragedy that he carried around inside him, perhaps because of his politeness and dignity – perhaps because he alone of the village did not love Aroaril. After all, she had been raised on tales of how Aroaril welcomed the conversion of one disbeliever more than the prayers of a score of uninterested worshippers. Of course, his lack of belief also meant he was seeing her as a woman, not as a priestess.

It was not something they had spoken about much but she could see the struggle within him and he had openly admitted he could not think about the future while the families of his friends were trapped in Kotterman. She had been happy to go along with that, for being happy among the misery of the people they knew would be cruel and probably poison anything they did have. But she watched him surreptitiously as he guided their boat into the harbor. Maybe he could help her heal the church …

"What are you looking at?" he asked softly, his eyes on the way ahead but obviously not missing her gaze.

"Just looking around, seeing things of interest," she replied casually.

He turned his head and winked at her. "The sights around here are beautiful," he said.

Rosaleen turned her head to hide her laugh. The hull bumped as it nudged through rubbish, while overhead a huge flock of seabirds fought and screamed over the stinking piles along the shore. The smell was incredible and not in a good way.

"Here comes the harbormaster," Gallagher said, straightening up and pointing towards an approaching boat, propelled by a dozen oarsmen. "I wonder if he will remember us from the last time."

"He'd be more likely to remember Fallon and Brendan, after what they did to him," Rosaleen said.

One of the villagers had also seen the rowboat. "What should we do?" he called, hurrying back to where Rosaleen and Gallagher stood.

Subtly she moved away as Gallagher waved the man off. "Don't worry. We have the Crown Prince's seal."

"Maybe he knows where Hagen lived," she suggested.

Gallagher snorted. "Unless Hagen was his drinking mate, I doubt it."

Rosaleen sighed. "We would have had an easier time of it if we could have brought along Gannon, or one of his men, or even had directions from the Duchess herself. Are we supposed to wander the streets, asking for people who might remember the old captain of the guard?"

"Too risky to bring them in," Gallagher said. "Fallon is right. There are answers hidden here. If the Kottermanis did not take the Duke, then who did? And we never found out how we were betrayed so well."

"The Duchess was speaking the truth. I would have felt it otherwise," Rosaleen said.

"But that does not mean she was giving us all the truth. Just because you do not say lies does not mean you tell all the truth," Gallagher said, signaling for the mainsail to be lowered.

"Then what is the truth?"

"Maybe we can find out," he said, then reached out and touched her arm. "Better show the seal to the harbormaster. He's going to be less inclined to ask questions of a priestess than of an old sea dog like myself."

"Not so old," she said softly, her arm thrilling to his touch.

*

The walk through Lunster was even better, for the crowds meant there were many times when he had to take her arm to help get through a press of people.

The harbormaster was useless when it came to information about Hagen but eager to please when he saw the seal of the Crown Prince. Their boat had been tucked away in a prime berth and Gallagher left three of the men on board to deter any thieves while he, Rosaleen and the other three set off to search for answers.

"If Fallon was such good friends with the man, why does he not know where he lives? A two-story house with a white door somewhere near the harbor is hardly helpful," Gallagher grumbled as they trudged up yet another street, looking for something that compared with Fallon's description.

"Maybe I need to use this robe to help," Rosaleen suggested.

"What, it's magical and can find directions?" Gallagher asked with a wink that only she could see.

"In a manner of speaking," she said and stopped an older couple with a smile and a slight bow of her head. "Peace be upon you, brother and sister," she said gently. "I wonder if you might help us?"

"If we can, Sister," the man said immediately, while his wife reached out and took Rosaleen's hand, kissing it and raising it to her forehead to ask for a blessing.

Rosaleen glanced quickly over at Gallagher, who raised his hands in a gesture of surrender.

The couple did not know where Hagen lived but the middle-aged mother they directed her to was more helpful. Her small house was filled with piles of washing, in between which ran laughing children. The woman, who reminded Rosaleen a little of Bridgit, wiped a damp forehead with a reddened hand and stretched her back, seemingly glad of the chance to stop from her work.

"I do the washing for many around here, merchants and the like," she said, her forearms impressively muscled from her skillful use of her scrubbing board. "I used to look after Captain Hagen, Aroaril bless his soul."

Rosaleen and Gallagher exchanged smiles. "So where does he live?" she asked. "Can you show us?"

The woman gestured to the piles of washing around her. "Does it look like I have the time to do that?" she sighed.

Gallagher pulled a gold coin out of his pouch and laid it on the top of her scrubbing board.

"Does that help your memory?" he asked.

The woman's eyes bulged at the sight of the gold. Without saying anything she reached out a hand and plucked a running child from the ground with the ease of long practice. She held it up to see who it was.

"Eamonn. Take these people to where Captain Hagen lived. Do it and there's an extra chop in it for you tonight. Go now!"

The child, a lad of no more than ten summers, nodded vigorously and grabbed Rosaleen's hand in his own grubby paw and tugged, his legs churning.

*

Hagen's house was exactly as Fallon had described it, two stories, white door and close to the harbor, although in a side street they would have missed had they not had a little guide. The neat little door was locked but Gallagher and two of the other men drove their shoulders at it until it finally splintered away from the lock. Unsurprisingly, this drew quite a crowd.

"We are here on royal business," Rosaleen announced loudly, holding up Prince Cavan's seal. The combination of that and her distinctive robe kept them back and they showed no signs of running for the town guards, at least. This was a respectable part of town, with houses owned by shopkeepers and tradesmen. She glanced around quickly to see if any of them knew anything about Hagen's disappearance but there was only curiosity on the faces there. Except for one man, who was hanging around at the back, looking nervous.

She whispered her suspicions to Gallagher and he indicated to two of the villagers, who pounced into the crowd and fished out a small man wearing a flour-covered apron. He was dragged over to the broken front door, where Gallagher grabbed his apron in his fist.

"What do you know about Captain Hagen?" Rosaleen demanded. "Tell us and there is gold in it for you."

"Play us false and you will regret it," Gallagher added, his hand resting on the hilt of one of his fearsome knives.

"They took him," the man whispered. "I am a baker and awake long before dawn. I saw a pair of men carry him from the house and taken him down towards the harbor."

"Did you know the men?" Rosaleen demanded.

The baker turned haunted eyes on her. "They were covered in his blood. He was a good man. I hid and covered my eyes. I did not want to know who could kill the captain of the guard and laugh," he whispered.

"But you do know, don't you?" Rosaleen said, feeling the truth behind his words.

Tears began to flow from his eyes in a silent stream. "Please, I have a wife, a family, friends ... They would be in danger!"

"Tell us," Gallagher insisted, his hand tightening on the man's tunic.

"You have to tell. Or it will haunt you for the rest of your life," Rosaleen said, far gentler.

The baker nodded and let out a little sob. "They wore the Duke's tunic!" he whispered.

Rosaleen and Gallagher exchanged horrified looks, then she nodded at the baker. Gallagher pressed a pair of gold coins into the man's tunic and let him go. Instantly the man raced away, losing himself in the crowd.

"If Hagen's own guards killed him, then that means Hagen could not have been the traitor," Gallagher said. "Let's look inside his home."

They all slipped inside to find the house had been gone through by someone already, judging by the mess. There was no evidence a woman had lived there, but it had still been a better house than most of the town enjoyed, until it had been turned upside down.

"They never found what they were looking for," Gallagher said, stepping over piles of clothes. "Because everything has been searched. So either they found it in the very last place they looked, or not at all."

She stood very still and looked around the room carefully. She had never known Hagen but she could imagine how he would think. He was a warrior who would want some sort of victory, even in defeat. And he was Fallon's friend. She allowed her gaze to sweep over the house. Then her heart leaped as she spotted what she was looking for and jumped over the remains of a chair to reach it.

"Here!" she exclaimed proudly, holding up a shillelagh. "Fallon was the expert, not Hagen."

"Many people have them," Gallagher said.

But she ignored him and pulled and twisted at the staff – and smiled as one of the metal ends came away. She fished out a small piece of parchment, unfolding it to reveal tight, cramped writing. She read it and nearly dropped it.

"We need to get back to Berry and show this to Fallon," she said, her voice hoarse.

Gallagher did not ask questions, he merely reached out a hand and helped her across the piles of possessions and out of the door.

They both froze then.

"I was wondering when you would be coming out," a strange voice said.

And they discovered the crowd was gone, replaced by men with swords instead.

CHAPTER 39

"And where are the rest of the Guildsmen?" Dina asked sharply, her voice echoing.

Rather than meet with the new leaders of the Guilds in the throne room, they had ordered the men to meet them in the main church in Berry. This was a drafty old stone building, with little light and even less comfort. But it had the decided advantage of showing up instantly anyone who had given their souls to Zorva.

"I do not know, your grace. Your instructions were most clear," the new leader of the Bankers Guild said, sweating profusely even in the cool of the church.

"We will need their names and where they live," Fallon said flatly.

"What will you do to them? Kill them as you killed the King?" the Banker sneered at him.

Fallon took three quick steps forward, until he was right in front of the Banker. The man had nowhere to go and could only wilt back against his hard wooden seat.

"I will not harm them. I will bring them here and allow them to wash their faces in water blessed by Aroaril himself," Fallon said. "What happens to them after that is up to Aroaril. Do you think that is unfair? Would you care for a cup yourself?"

"No, I think that is fair and reasonable," the Banker said, his eyes darting around, looking for a way out.

Fallon glared at him a moment longer before walking backwards. Dina gave him a sideways glance and he knew she was silently imploring him not to upset the Guildsmen. That was going to be hard. He had faced them too many times in nasty little fight, and seen too many of them praying to Zorva to trust them.

"We know that you are as horrified as we are that the King forced some of your number to join him in the worship of Zorva," Dina said, her voice pouring oil on the troubled waters.

Fallon could see the Guildsmen relax as she moved among them, and contented himself with crossing his arms and glowering at them.

"All we require is that the men who have been converted to Zorva are brought forwards, for their own good as much as for anyone else. Here, they will be given the chance to save their souls. At the very least, they will be unable to do more harm. And once we can all be sure all is safe, then we can continue as before."

"Captain Fallon is known to hate the Guilds. How do we know he will not destroy us, no matter what we do here?" the head of the Silversmiths asked cautiously.

"Everything will continue as before," Dina said immediately. "There are no plans to take away any license for trade. We know that Berry and indeed Gaelland runs on the Guilds. King Aidan attempted to use you for his own ends but he has been amply punished for his deeds. We want Gaelland to be stronger than ever and that prosperity will be built on the Guilds. Look at how we have worked with the Guild of Magic. Let that be an example to you all."

"It is true, we have both benefited," the head of that Guild agreed, making them all nod.

"And the nobles?" another asked.

"As I said, the only change is that a mad King who had turned to evil has been removed. In the spring, we shall choose a new King and I don't doubt he will have his own way of doing things. I cannot speak for him. But, until then, we continue as before."

Fallon could see the relief on their faces and wished he had the power to go into every Guild and use his shillelagh to get some answers out of them.

But while he gripped and re-gripped his shillelagh, aching for the chance to use it, he merely sat and listened as Dina took them through the new tax arrangements and elicited their pledges of coin.

Bags and bags of coin, which could be used to keep the city running while the nobles were slowly brought back under control.

They bowed deeply to Dina as they left, promising that the first payments would arrive the next day.

Some of them even looked like they would try to shake Fallon's hand, but he glared at them and they quickly moved on. The only one he reckoned could be trusted was Lorrissa, the new head of the Guild of Engravers. But there were many more that looked suspicious.

"Fear and greed will keep them in line," Dina said contemptuously as the last of them disappeared out the door. "Fear that we will make them pay for the evil they have done and greed that they can continue as before."

"For how long do we have to put up with them?" Fallon asked. "They may not have known everything Aidan was doing but they were happy to go along with it nonetheless."

"Only until we have the country secure," she said soothingly. "One summer, no more. Then there can be a proper reckoning."

Fallon knew he had to see the bigger picture. She had told him that often enough. But Aroaril it was hard.

"So that is the Guilds in hand. Tomorrow we need to start on the nearest nobles, make sure the ones who have promised to stand with us live up to their word and those who ignored us will be brought over to our side by fear or force," she said. "You see, we make the perfect team. I provide the carrot and you provide the stick."

Fallon patted his shillelagh. "You're right about that!"

*

"Finally, we are getting somewhere," Swane said with satisfaction.

"Highness, I would still caution against moving too soon. We do not have enough men or weapons," Ryan said carefully.

"Nonsense. I am the rightful King. Once they see me, all will rally to my banner. Finbar's messages to my nobles in the west of the country have worked. They have all agreed to help destroy the traitor Fallon. Besides, we need to move now, or we shall never get through the passes across the Spine."

Ryan bowed his head. "Indeed you are right, highness. As it is, our men shall need to rest and recover on the other side. We will be vulnerable if Fallon decides to attack—"

"He is peasant scum and I am the rightful King! We shall do what I say!"

"Yes, highness."

*

The incessant training had toughened the young recruits up but Fallon still took most of them on the march through the countryside. Part of it was to get them stronger and more confident, part of it was protection in case some noble decided to raise his fyrd, but most of it was intimidation. Fail to live up to your promises and we will be back.

The sight of so many armed men marching through the countryside was enough to send the people into a panic but when they marched around and past villages and towns without touching anything or, even better, used good silver to buy food and drink, people began to bring out their goods for sale, or just stood and watched and cheered as they marched past.

"We should tell them we are here to free them from the nobles and give them a chance at a better life," Fallon said.

"Too dangerous," Dina said immediately. "Not until we are through this winter. We have to let the nobles think they are in no danger, right up until the moment we drag them before a crowd and behead them for their crimes. They have to trust us and believe us."

Fallon did not like the idea but he did not have nearly enough men to hold Berry and take over this many counties as well. Stretching his forces too thin would just be an invitation for the nobles to unite and strike back. Besides, he was beginning to trust her. She had been invaluable so far.

Their first stop was the town of Kenkilly, the home of the local Baron. As the closest noble, he had promised help to Dina in a letter but, aside from a few wagons of potatoes, nothing had arrived from his county. The rich, fertile dark soil of Kenkilly was perfect for potatoes and they had marched for two days through endless fields, with men and women working furiously to bring in the crop. Enough to keep Berry bellies full for winter, if they could but get their hands on them.

Baron Kenkilly had no castle, merely a stately manor that would never hold out against the force they brought, while his small company of guards vanished like mist in the sun at the sight of Fallon's force. Just in case the noble thought to run, Fallon had sent Bran and a hundred men on horses to watch the eastern road out of Kenkilly. But they were not needed.

The Baron was a plump man, resembling one of the vegetables his county was famous for. He looked friendly enough but Fallon had seen him stabbing a helpless servant with a fork at the King's feast and listened to him wheel and deal at the council.

"My dear Duchess, to what do we owe the pleasure?" he asked, perspiring even though the day was overcast and chill.

"Potatoes, my dear Baron," Dina said. "I have a longing for potatoes. You may remember you promised to send us some in Berry but they seem to have been misplaced."

The Baron glanced over at Fallon, who glared back at him, then the nobleman looked at the mass of soldiers behind them and pasted a smile onto his face. "We have been hard at work harvesting them for you. Let us discuss how we can get them there," he suggested.

*

Fallon led his men out of Kenkilly that day, all but a company under Casey, who would escort more than a hundred wagons piled high with potatoes back to Berry. The Baron had listened to Dina's flattery and promises both about the upcoming council to decide a new King and payment for extra supplies. By the time they had all sat down to dinner with the Baron, he was complaining about how Aidan had behaved and exclaiming in horror at the thought of Zorva worship going on in the capital.

"You are used to sending half to the King anyway. If you sent more, for which we will pay, and then purchased supplies from other counties for your people, then everyone wins. Those who are frightened of being seen to support us in Berry can hold their hand on their heart and pledge that they merely sold food to a fellow noble," she explained.

Baron Kenkilly nodded wisely but also grasped the unspoken threat of the army waiting outside his home and agreed to send everything he had, in exchange for Guild silver that he could use to buy food from elsewhere in Gaelland.

"There'll be cheers when that lot arrives in the markets of the city," Dina said.

"It's a good start," Fallon agreed. "Now the real fun begins."

*

The Count of Rork had not replied to Dina's messages but his fields were full of fat lambs, just ready to be killed and salted for winter, so they marched there next. Rork did not border Kenkilly but Fallon did not want to give them any warning. He had marched his men slowly through Kenkilly but now he led them on a fast march, pushing them swiftly and pounding along the roads, moving at night and then hiding them in the day, using woodlands to disguise them. He guessed that the Count of Rork would have heard about their slow march through Kenkilly and be watching for something similar through his own county. He did not intend to give him the time to prepare. If Rork tried to raise its fyrd, they would discover it was too late. The recruits were left gasping and staggering by the end of each night but they were still cheerful enough. They all trusted Fallon – and he had made sure none of the ones he brought along were from these counties. That way they would not have to feel any guilt about what they were going to do.

Like Kenkilly, Rork did not have a defendable castle. The Count's home had towers at each corner but they were for decoration rather than practical use. Fallon had no idea what Rork looked like, of course, because he had never been there. But he solved that by sending Bran and a handful of other men to ride ahead and scout the town. Dressed in ordinary clothes, they shopped in the market and looked at how the Count defended his town.

It allowed him to rest the recruits in a large wood about ten miles out of Rork during one last day, then lead them on a brisk march through the night to surprise the town.

*

Rossmore, the Fourteenth Count of Rork, usually woke late. After all, being up before the dawn was only for those who needed to work for their living. Since he had fled the uprising in the capital and therefore all the city's luxuries, he had tried to sleep as much as possible, because the entertainment in his ancestral home was sadly lacking compared to what Berry offered. But now he was unsure when he would be able to return. Like just about everyone he had feared King Aidan and mourned his death not at all, but that was not to say he liked the idea of some commoner wielding power. Bowing to a peasant? Even the presence of Duchess Dina was not enough to make that appealing. So when messages from Prince Swane arrived, brought to him by magic, he had agreed to act as a base for Swane's gathering army. His flocks, which would normally have gone to Berry, would be used to feed the men Swane and Meinster were bringing down. From Rork, it was possible to march hard and fast for Berry, especially with plenty of fat lamb inside. He had been promised extra lands in exchange for such help and was looking forwards to picking those out. It meant he had to keep out of Duchess Dina's way but that should be easy enough. The men from Berry were marching slowly across the countryside and he would have plenty of warning of their approach, with men out watching every road. Without that to worry about, he could relax and enjoy the few diversions that Rork presented.

But this morning was different. Instead of waking some time around noon for a leisurely breakfast, he was disturbed by shouting. No matter how many times he rang the bell beside his bed, nobody came to his bedroom, and he was finally forced to wrap a robe around his shoulders and go and see what was happening, swearing that someone was going to be flogged to within an inch of their lives for this.

To his shock, he found not his usual servants downstairs but instead a pack of dirty soldiers, led by a grim-faced captain and accompanied by Duchess Dina of Lunster.

"What is the meaning of this?" he squawked, clutching his robe to his chest.

"It means, my dear Rossmore, that you have decided to do what is right and send what you owe to the capital," the Duchess said cheerfully.

Rossmore looked over at where half a dozen of his guards sat on the floor, their hands on their heads, surrounded by young men pointing loaded crossbows at their faces. He had thought his men were tough but they seemed small and helpless now.

"But I want no part of what is happening—" he began, only for the grim-faced captain to stride forward and lay a heavy hand on his shoulder.

"I am Captain Fallon. You may have heard of me. I was the man who gutted King Aidan in front of a cheering crowd," the captain said.

Rossmore felt faint and held onto his bladder only with the greatest of difficulty. "I have heard of you," he whispered.

"Either you help us or people will stop whispering about how I killed that foul King and start talking about what I did to an unfortunate Count."

Rossmore looked into the implacable eyes and had to clear a dry throat before he could speak. "What do you need?" he whimpered.

Fallon dragged him along towards his study. "To find out what you have been up to."

*

Unlike in the King's rooms, Fallon had quickly found what he was looking for in the Count's study. He shoved a handful of parchments into the Count's face. "When is Swane coming? What foul plans have you made with him? Have you sold your soul to Zorva? Talk, or so help me I will tear your guts out with my own hands."

The terrified noble seemed unable to speak, his teeth were chattering so much.

"Obviously Rossmore was forced to do this, out of fear of his own life – isn't that right?" Dina said soothingly.

The Count nodded so hard his head looked like it was about to come off. "I will happily to swear to Aroaril!" he gabbled.

"And you will write to Swane, tell him you no longer have any supplies, or men, and Rork has a huge garrison of Captain Fallon's men just waiting for the chance to hang him up from the nearest tree," Dina continued.

"I will?" Rossmore said weakly.

"Or we can just send him your head. Your choice," Fallon snarled.

"Give me the quill. You can rely on me. Swane will not want to come anywhere near Rork by the time I have finished," the Count promised, sweat pouring off his face.

*

"You didn't have to be that harsh on poor Rossmore," Dina said, the smile on her face robbing her words of any sting.

"The bastard was plotting with Swane! If we hadn't paid him a visit, he would have joined that evil bogger in marching on Berry," Fallon growled. "Fear and force is the only thing these nobles understand."

"We are going to need him, and others like him," Dina said in mild reproach. "Have you not heard the expression you catch more flies with honey than vinegar?"

"I prefer to squash my flies," Fallon stated. "But at least we can stop Swane's plots before they start. A few more messages like that and he will stay in Meinster until we can go and put an end to his evil."

"True enough," she said. "This trip is proving to be very useful." She pointed to where another company of recruits was herding a seemingly never-ending flock of sheep down the road towards Berry. "Between confiscating food, every weapon and piece of armor we could find and even the Count's wizard, we have removed any danger to us from Rork. Swane will soon discover the west of the country is ours and that he is pinned behind the mountains in Meinster. Thanks to the Guild of Magic, they will not be able to see what we are doing. So, you see, the Guilds are proving useful."

Fallon snorted at that. "So, who is next?"

Dina looked across the countryside.

"I think south to Eastmeath and then across to Rexford. That will bring us grain and cattle," she said.

"And the chance to terrify more fat nobles and sow a little fear in Swane's dreams," Fallon added.

"I like the way you think, Captain," she said with a laugh.

*

"What is your excuse for delaying now?" Swane demanded.

"Highness, we were ready to leave but marching now would be pointless," Meinster said fiercely.

Swane closed his eyes and counted to ten before opening them again. He needed this man but, Zorva knew, it was getting close to the point where he was going to have to make an example of someone.

"And what is that?" he asked, his voice dangerously calm.

But Meinster did not seem worried. "Highness, look here," he said, gesturing towards a map.

Swane clenched his fist but a touch on his shoulder from Ryan steadied him.

"Highness, you need to see this," he said gently.

With ill-disguised bad grace, Swane allowed himself to be seated at a table to see a large map of Gaelland.

"We had messages from many of the nobles, pledging support and men to your cause. We were planning to march through the land, gathering men to us as we went, before arriving at Berry to demand the people fulfill their oaths, rise and deliver the traitor Fallon and his accomplices to us," Ryan said.

"But, in the past few days, we have received messages from Kenkilly, Rork, Eastmeath, Rexford and others, warning us that Fallon is already there. He has stripped those counties of men, weapons and food, sending them to Berry, then left strong garrisons behind in a swathe of county towns. If we march, we would march to our doom. Our men would arrive tired and hungry and, instead of collecting food and reinforcements, they would instantly be attacked by a bigger force."

"How is this possible?" Swane growled. "He does not have so many men!"

"It seems that Fallon has been busy," Ryan said. "Some of this may be lies, designed to trick us. But we cannot know for sure. The Guild of magic is blocking all of Finbar's attempts to discover the true picture of what is happening on the other side of the mountains and sadly, we have not been able to make contact with your father's network of informants in Berry. After Regan's death, it seems they have gone into hiding."

Swane thumped the table, biting back curses. "So what do we do?" he demanded.

"We must wait for better weather and redouble our efforts to find out what is really happening in the west of the country. If we march blindly into a trap, then Fallon will have us all dragged before a jeering crowd to our deaths."

Swane hit the table again. But he could think of no way out of this. It ate at his insides but he was helpless. That could not continue. "How much of what we did with Brother Nahuatl do you remember?" he asked Ryan.

CHAPTER 40

Rosaleen cursed herself for not leaving a couple of the villagers outside on guard. Hagen's house was at the end of a tight street, so escape would have been difficult, but at least she would not have blundered out into this trap. The men did not look like soldiers, more like thieves, but that was hardly a comforting thought, especially as they had three times as many and Gallagher and his men only had knives, not swords.

"Did you think you could just walk through our streets, asking questions and flashing gold and not have anyone hear about it?" the leader of the swordsmen asked.

"Let's back into the house and let them come get us," Gallagher whispered.

"Not yet, we need to find out where they are from," she murmured back. Turning away from him, she looked around at the rough group. "If you want gold, then we have plenty," she offered loudly. "More than you have seen. Walk away and it is yours."

She held her breath for a moment but even though she watched them carefully, not one set of eyes betrayed interest.

"We are already being paid well," the leader boasted.

"Who by?" Rosaleen asked.

He laughed at that. "I could tell you, since you will not leave here alive. But even to speak the name aloud is worth more than my life."

"And I suppose the fact that I am a priestess of Aroaril means nothing to you?" she challenged.

"Only makes this more fun," he assured her.

Rosaleen took a half-step backwards. "Into the house then," she whispered. "But we have to take that one alive."

Gallagher snapped his fingers and the villagers raced back into Hagen's house.

"Get them!"

The swordsmen ran after them, swords held high and bloodlust in their faces.

"As they come through the door, I will hold them: take them then," she called quickly, seeing the fear on the villagers' faces.

There was no time to say anything more, because the swordsmen were about to burst through the open door. She took a deep breath to calm herself and waved Gallagher forwards.

The other villagers were backing away from the door but he stepped in, his wickedly long knives in each hand. She offered up a quick prayer of thanks that he trusted her and then one to Aroaril for the strength to handle this task.

The first swordsman burst into the room with a bellowed war cry. He was tall and heavily muscled, with long, straggly brown hair that billowed around his face, and a thick beard that covered all but his eyes. She brought down her power and froze him, locking his muscles so he could not move, leaving him with his arm held high and his eyes bulging with shock.

Next moment Gallagher swung one of his gutting knives and the razor-sharp edge ripped across the man's bearded throat, tearing through hair, skin, muscle, cartilage and blood vessels. A crimson spray painted the next man through the door, who blinked in shock firstly at being covered in hot blood and secondly at also being frozen in place, his every limb locked.

He had no chance for escape, because Gallagher stepped around the collapsing body of the first man and ripped his second knife up in a vicious blow that tore into the swordsman's heart.

"Help Gall!" Rosaleen ordered, waving the other villagers forwards.

The thieves pressed in, jumping over the bodies of their fallen friends, only to be frozen in turn and lose their lives to ferocious stabs. The villagers picked up fallen swords and rammed them into guts and chests and necks, covering themselves in red.

Rosaleen hardened her heart to the screams and pleas for mercy, knowing that she and her companions would not have received any and that it was too dangerous to leave their assailants alive.

But the swordsmen were not fools and after five of them had been slaughtered like pigs, the others hesitated outside the door, unwilling to go inside.

"After them!" Rosaleen pointed at the two closest and held them in place. Gallagher had not bothered with a sword but still had his knives, each more than a foot of evilly curved steel, and he raced through the open door to thrust one into each neck and then rip them clear in a blinding gout of blood.

That was enough for the rest of the swordsmen, who broke and ran.

"Stop that one!" Rosaleen stepped over the corpses, slipping on the blood and entrails, and spotted the leader, who had stayed at the back while his men had raced in and died. Once more she reached out and held him as he tried to flee. He stood frozen on one leg, terror-filled eyes looking over his shoulder.

"Drag him back here and let's find out what he knows before he joins the rest of his men," Gallagher said, his face and arms covered in blood.

Rosaleen nodded, thinking he had never looked better to her.

*

A battered chair had been found in the wreckage of Hagen's house and a space cleared by dragging a pair of bodies over towards the window, where they left a thick smear of blood on the wooden floor.

The dazed leader of the swordsmen was slammed into the chair and held there by two of the villagers while the rest of them changed their bloody tunics for cleaner ones from Hagen's floor. None fit too well but at least they could walk the streets without exciting comment.

Rosaleen stepped over a body and approached the leader. The smell in Hagen's house was revolting: shit and blood mingling to make a stench that bit at the back of her throat and made her eyes water. But she did not intend to be here long.

"Who are you?" she asked him.

He glared up at her and spat, forcing her to skip aside or have his phlegm hit her robe.

"Answer the sister!" Gallagher barked, back-handing the man across the face and making his nose and lips bleed. "You saw what we did to your men. Do you want to have your guts decorating this floor?"

The man spat blood from his torn lip, this time aiming for the floor. "Do what you will. I can say nothing," he said dully. "I am a dead man either way but at least this way my family might live."

Gallagher drew his knife slowly. "We'll see if you tell the same story while I'm slicing your balls off a piece at a time," he growled.

Rosaleen grabbed his arm, keeping him back. "There is another way to discover what he knows," she said.

The man looked up at her suspiciously as she stepped around the chair and placed her hands on the man's temples.

"What are you doing?" he demanded.

"I'm using Aroaril's power to draw out your thoughts. Try to resist me and it could leave you a drooling idiot. I had to be careful not to use this power on a Kottermani Prince and the Duchess of Lunster. But we don't care what happens to you," she told him coldly. Partly that was to disguise her nervousness. The last time she had done this to a man, his mind had been guarded by a Fearpriest and she had ended up covered in his brains and skull.

"Gall, ask him questions. As he thinks about them, the answers will come to me," she said.

"They will not!" the man cried.

"Your mind will be like an open book to me," she told him, then nodded to Gallagher.

Offering a prayer to Aroaril, she reached out with her power and delved into his mind. Images spun at her, almost too fast to see, and she forced them to slow down.

Beneath her hands, the man twisted and wriggled, his temples slick with sweat, his breath coming in short, sharp gasps. But the villagers held him down and there was no escape for either his body or his mind.

"Fight me and you will end your days with the mind of a newborn babe," she warned again, and he whimpered and slumped down.

"What do you see?" Gallagher asked, his voice sounding as though it were coming from a long way away.

"His name is Mika. He is a king of thieves in Lunster, employed by several of the big guilds to make sure anyone who does not hand over their fees pays a penalty," she said, seeing images of him beating helpless traders and even burning out shops.

"Who set him to watch here?"

As the man wriggled, those images swam up to the surface of his mind.

"He was handed a bag of gold and told to watch this house. If anyone came asking questions about Hagen, they were to be killed and the house sealed up."

"Who gave him the money?"

Rosaleen gasped and the man's head nearly slipped from her grasp. "It is a man in the uniform of the Duke. He is wearing the tunic of an officer!"

"Who killed Hagen? Was it him?"

This time the images were more murky.

"He thinks so but he is not sure," she said, interpreting what she was seeing in her mind's eye. "Read out the message Hagen left."

Gallagher paused as he took the parchment from her belt pouch. "What is important about the Duke's summerhouse?" he asked.

The images were much sharper now.

"The man who paid him is there. And it was there he met the Kottermanis and told them where to attack!" Rosaleen cried. She let go of Mika's head. "We need to go there."

CHAPTER 41

The days crawled past on the ship, while the food supplies seemed to go down far faster. They were catching fish and each one was a joy but, shared out among so many people, it was nothing. Bridgit was forced to give priority to the men working the sails, the nursing mothers and to the younger children. The women and the older ones had to go hungry. The men needed strength to work the ship, while she was afraid the younger children might get sick without a little extra.

Yet that was not her greatest worry. They were still checking their direction at dawn and dusk and thought they were going north-east, although that was more hope than certainty.

On the days they could see the sun, this was easy enough. But there were days when the sun hid behind thick clouds and they could never be sure which way they were going.

And then there were the storms – nothing like the winter tempests that lashed Gaelland but foretastes of what was to come.

The sky turned black and the waves pounded at the ship, tossing everyone around and making the children scream in fear. They took in the sails and the men worked on the pumps instead, forcing a steady stream of water up out of the ship's bowels to be washed into the waves that scoured across the deck.

The ship groaned and grumbled and Bridgit watched lightning light up the sky and joined the others in praying to Aroaril that it pass, and they would get home safely.

On such days there was no chance of fishing, while the men on the pumps needed even more generous rations, for the exertion of forcing the heavy wooden paddles around left them exhausted otherwise.

Luckily no storm had so far lasted for more than a couple of days, and then they could emerge from below to dry themselves out, try to fish – and try to find their course again.

"It would be nice to see Fallon and the others coming to get us now," Bridgit said. The three of them were basking in the sun after two days of being cramped below decks as the wind howled and the water lashed the ship. The sea had been so bad they could not even refill the water barrels, for fear the rain would be tainted by the saltwater breaking across the deck, and many had been unable to eat even their meager rations.

"Well, they are certainly not coming to rescue us," Riona said. "When I see Devlin again I won't know whether to kiss him or hit him over the head for leaving it all for us to do. He always was lazy when I wanted him to do something."

"This is not like him refusing to hang the washing out!" Nola said with a laugh, flapping her wet sleeves.

"Exactly. Where are they? And why did they not come for us? I would have sworn they would do anything to get us back," Riona grumbled.

"Aye. Thank Aroaril for Bridgit or we would still be waiting back there," Nola said.

Bridgit did not say anything but it had been filling her thoughts as well. What was Fallon doing? She had been so sure he would come for her. Had something happened to him? She felt like imagining a series of horrible deaths for him and, a couple of moons ago, she would have. But now she pushed that aside. There were bigger worries, real worries. She would get them back to Gaelland and then find Fallon. All questions could wait until then.

"What is the word below decks? Are people grumbling too much?" she asked instead.

"Well, everyone is hungry. But they are in good spirits, because they think we are going in the right direction and should be home soon. Besides, after what you did to Blaine and Carrick, they know you are protecting them. And they can see you are eating no more than they are, so they have no cause for complaint there," Nola said.

"Well, I'd like to complain about it. Devlin won't even recognize me when I get back," Riona said. "And Nola should be really unhappy. When your husband is the size of Brendan, you need more than a little padding or you end up black and blue!"

"Well, if you can make jokes like that, then you can't be too bad," Nola said with a shake of her head.

"Come on, Bridge, cheer up. We have done so much. Everything is under control now," Riona said.

Bridgit sighed. "I wish you hadn't said that. There is always something that could go wrong."

"Well, there it is over there," Nola said, pointing.

Bridgit followed her and saw three men lurking by the mast. They were well known. Keegan, Arron and Fitz, a trio of useless lumps who were always the first to complain and the last to do any work. Their stories of how they had been caught by the Kottermanis did not ring true and, after what happened with Blaine and Carrick, she was not prepared to give anyone the benefit of the doubt.

"You three! Get below and ask to be given some work!" she snapped.

The trio looked at her with a mixture of guilt and bitterness, but they sloped off anyway.

"There you go, nothing to be worried about. Problem solved," Riona said.

*

"Get us out of here," Blaine growled. "We're bogging well starving!"

"And you think we are all lying around shoving bread and honey down our throats?" Keegan snapped back. "I've spent the past day on the pumps until I couldn't feel my arms!"

Carrick laid a hand on his brother's shoulder. "Then let us out and we'll make sure there's food for the right people. Like you and us."

"There's not much left," Keegan warned.

"So? We'll throw some of the brats overboard, more for the rest of us. And we'll feed that bitch Bridgit and her friends to the fishes. Use them as bait maybe," Blaine said harshly.

"We can keep some of the younger women. But that's all," Carrick agreed. "We'll even let you have first pick. All you have to do is get us out of here!"

"Easier said than done," Keegan grumbled.

The two brothers had been shut into a sail locker deep inside the ship. There was space for the two of them to lie down and little more than that. Once a day they were brought a little of the fluffy grain couscous, dates and water and the rest of the time they were left alone. Keegan was not sure how he had come to be given the responsibility of feeding them but he and his cronies Fitz and Arron knew nothing about sailing or fishing and that bitch Bridgit kept making them do all the dirty and smelly tasks. He hated being treated like this but there was no denying Bridgit. Whatever she said, you had to do. Fitz and Arron were back sweating on the pumps, keeping water out of the guts of the ship, but he had been told to bring the food down there before he joined them. He had been surprised but perhaps they had all forgotten he and his mates had once sided with Blaine, Carrick and their two cousins, who had died writhing under the brutal sun, their eyeballs burned to a crisp. After all, they had been careful to stay away from them since then.

"Just give us a knife. One knife and we can be out of here in a night," Blaine pleaded.

"Are you mad? What if you can't and they catch you? We'd join you in there!" Keegan protested.

Carrick pushed forwards. "If you don't help us, we'll tell them that you were stealing the food too. We know how you got caught back home, stealing the tribute people had left out for the selkies."

"They won't believe you," Keegan said.

"Bridgit will. She will remember you from before, that you were with us and Sean and Seamus. And if there's as little food as you say, she will jump at the chance to throw you in here with us and starve you slowly to death," Blaine said.

Keegan cursed them but they just stared back at him.

"What have we got to lose?" Carrick asked. "But give us what we want and you will have the pick of the women and the food, not have to lift another finger until we are back home."

"Or walk away now and join us later," Blaine added.

Keegan looked over his shoulder but there was nobody down there. "You promise to help me?" he hissed.

"You have our word," Blaine said.

Keegan drew his knife, a chunky, curved dagger that he had taken from a Kottermani guard. He passed it between the thick wooden bars in the top of the door, designed to air out the old sails and prevent mold from setting in – but which also made the locker look like a prison.

"Keep your word," he said, then turned and hurried away.

CHAPTER 42

The leader of the thieves in Lunster who had tried to kill them was less than impressed at being dragged along but Rosaleen wanted to be sure she could look again into his memory whenever she needed. They kept his hands tied and two men were always by his side, knives ready.

His memories led them down the coast to a beautiful little home by a secluded bay, where he remembered being taken, given wine and gold and his orders. Gallagher's sharp eyes spotted men moving around so they sailed past, anchoring in another cove for the day.

"We shall go in at night. There is almost no moon, so they will not see us," Gallagher said.

"But there are so few of us and we don't know how many they have," Rosaleen pointed out.

"They will be asleep and unaware. And we have you," Gallagher said.

That was all very flattering but it did not stop the nerves in her stomach as they crept forwards that night.

Gallagher had sailed their little ship into the bay with his customary skill, bringing it alongside a wide jetty. Obviously none of them had been to the Duke's summerhouse, but they had heard of it, a cool escape from the stench of Lunster in the height of summer. But what was happening there now was a bigger mystery.

The jetty was big enough to allow the biggest of ships to berth in safety. But, apart from their own vessel, the only other boat tied up was a rickety old fishing sloop.

There were no sentries and all eight of them slipped up to the house silently. Mika had been left tied securely to the mast – Gallagher had been more than thorough because the thief looked like he was covered in rope. Yet there was still enough left for each man to be wearing a coil around their waists.

The heavy wooden door was locked and barred and the time it would take to batter it down would give those inside more than enough notice to grab weapons and give them a rude welcome. But with Rosaleen guiding them they were able to move around the side to where a window had been left unlocked. It was not visible from the front, being hidden by a screen of bushes, but she led them right to it.

"This will bring us into the kitchen. From there seem to be six men sleeping in a large room and a seventh in a smaller room," she said.

"Me first, the Sister second-last. Edan, you're the smallest, so you come last," Gallagher ordered in a whisper. "You six take the ones in the room, we'll take the man alone."

Three of them lifted Gallagher up and helped him ease through the window. Rosaleen could feel her heart hammering as he vanished inside and she had to remind herself to trust in the knowledge that Aroaril was giving her. The men inside were asleep and, until they awoke, Gallagher would be safe.

With men on the outside and inside, it was much easier to get through the window. When it was her turn, she clambered onto the back of Edan and strong hands lifted her up. She got one knee onto the windowsill and then overbalanced. But Gallagher was there and rather than falling heavily, she landed in his arms.

For a moment she enjoyed the sensation as they were locked together. Then he released her and, after an extra heartbeat or two, she stepped away. Behind them, Edan was dragged in through the window and they could all look around the kitchen, lit by the embers of the dying fire. It was huge, with enough room for an army of cooks.

Rosaleen led the way forward. Each man had a hand on another's shoulder so they formed one long chain. One turn of the corridor away from the kitchen and the place was in darkness, only a hint of moonlight. But Rosaleen, guided by a higher power, led them through a series of large rooms to the barrack room, where they could all hear the snores of sleeping men. A fire was dying down to embers, one last log glowing to show the carved wooden beds.

"Knock them out and tie them up. If any wake and give you trouble, use your knives. No hesitation," Gallagher ordered.

They looked nervous but determined and Rosaleen left them to it as she and Gallagher hurried down the corridor to a much larger room, where one man snored under heavy blankets in a huge four-poster bed.

"Do you think this is the Duke? Maybe he faked his own death," Gallagher murmured into her ear.

Rosaleen enjoyed the sensation of his lips brushing her ear and his warm breath on her neck for a moment before replying. It seemed almost perverse that she could think of such things at a time like this but every nerve was on edge, every breath was crisp and clear and her senses were heightened, both by the danger and the magical help she was getting. She had never felt more alive. "This is not the Duke. It is the man in Mika's memory. And he has all the answers."

The man snuffled in his sleep and turned over. Instantly Gallagher pounced on him.

"What—?" the man gasped as the covers were dragged back but he said nothing else as he felt the prick of Gallagher's knife.

"Follow us," Gallagher ordered.

Rosaleen hung back as Gallagher marched the man back down the corridor and into the guard room, where the villagers were lashing up the last of the other men. All six were alive but only two were conscious, the others sporting blossoming bruises on their heads.

"Poke up the fire and let's see what is going on," Gallagher ordered.

Their prisoner was made to sit on the bed nearest to the fire, revealing him to be a young, fit man with an arrogant face and a bandaged arm. Gallagher stepped back a pace, taking the knife away from his throat.

"Start talking," he ordered.

"You don't know what you have done. You have doomed yourselves," the man told them angrily. "Do you know who owns this house?"

"The Duke of Lunster," Rosaleen said, stepping into the light so he could see she was wearing the robes of Aroaril. "But you are not him, so why are you sleeping in his bed? Who are you? What do you know of Hagen's death? Why did you have a watch on his house – a watch that tried to kill us when we came asking questions."

The man clamped his mouth shut so Rosaleen stepped forward and reached out for his head.

"Leave me alone!" the man cried, raising his hands.

Next moment Gallagher was there and the knife was back at the man's throat.

"Go on, kill me. I will never talk," the man said defiantly.

Rosaleen stepped around to the side of him and grasped his head. "You don't have to," she told him.

She closed her eyes and plunged into his memories. Unlike Mika, this man tried to fight her but his mind was weak and malleable and easy to read.

Rosaleen's eyes snapped open. "We have to get him back to Berry and Fallon. Now!" she said, urgency making her voice crack.

"Why? What is it?" Gallagher asked.

"I know what happened to the Duke of Lunster and why that ship sailed into Baltimore. Our friends are in terrible danger. We have to tell them before it is too late."

CHAPTER 43

"What are we going to do when we get home?" Bridgit asked.

Nola looked at her quizzically. "Well, I want a big plate of stew for starters. Maybe some kippers as well."

"Lamb chops and mash for me. Three plates of it," Riona said. "I can almost taste it now."

Bridgit shook her head. The last of the wounded men had slipped away, his body carefully sent overboard accompanied by the tears of his friends and family. She needed something to take her mind off that, and whether she could have done more to save him, and the others. "Well, obviously we are going to eat until our stomachs burst after this voyage is over but what happens after that?"

"Well, I can guess what Brendan has in mind but I'll want a nice rest first," Nola said with a smile.

Bridgit sighed. "But how do we stop the Kottermanis? They will be right behind us with an army."

"Whist, woman!" Riona snorted. "That will be none of our business. That's up to the King and the nobles. We have done more than enough."

"But we know more about the Kottermanis than anyone and we have a duty to keep protecting these people, especially the children."

"You are thinking too much," Nola advised. "We are still in the middle of the ocean, with dwindling food and a pack of fishermen who seem unable to land more than one fish a day."

Bridgit smiled dutifully but it seemed that, as they ate less, she thought more. It was as if the last of the old Bridgit was being emptied out and new ideas were coming in to replace that. She had never wanted the responsibility for these people but since it had been forced on her, she could not walk away from it.

"Let's get home first and then worry about it," Riona said, as if reading her thoughts.

*

Fallon held the knife to Orhan's face, his eyes wild.

"You won't touch my son," Kemal said confidently.

"I'll make him bleed!" Fallon screamed.

"Look over there," Kemal said persuasively.

The Gaelishman glanced behind him and Kemal acted. Since they had crushed his toes, they had not bothered to tie up his leg and now, ignoring the pain, he raised his foot and smashed his heel into Fallon's face. His nose broke and he fell backwards, losing his grip on both Orhan and the knife. Kemal lifted his chair and bounced forwards, slamming it down across Fallon's throat, pinning the Gaelishman there.

"Back, or I crush his throat!" he snarled, making the other foul Gaelish stop their advance.

Orhan seized the knife and quickly cut the ropes holding Kemal to the chair, so he could rise. With one last heave of the chair, he finished off Fallon and then advanced on the other Gaelish.

"Let my wife and son go, or I shall send your souls to Zorva," he promised them.

The Gaelish looked at the dead Fallon and then turned and ran.

Kemal embraced his family, as Feray kissed him passionately.

"You are the greatest man I know," she said, her hand slipping down his body.

Then the dead Fallon coughed and spoke in Kottermani: "High one, we have sighted Gaelland."

Kemal opened his eyes and groaned. Each night he defeated Fallon in some other way. And each morning he woke to the realization it was only a dream and he had lost. His family despised him for not saving them and he still could not find the missing slaves.

He looked down. At least his body had not disgraced him this time. "Time is ticking away," Kemal muttered to himself. They could not have beaten his finest sailors to Gaelland. They must be lost.

"High one?" Gokmen asked from outside the door.

"Signal the fleet. We turn back and search the ocean. Anyone who finds them is to bring them here. If necessary they can be subdued but I will have the skin of any man who kills one of them. Is that clear?"

Gokmen paused. "It is clear, high one. Although the captains will wonder why we do not seek to punish runaway slaves."

"They can wonder all they like. But they will obey me or the last sight they will see is their own entrails being slowly pulled out of their bodies. We shall meet back here again in a quarter moon."

"Your will, high one."

Kemal heard Gokmen stride away and laid back on his bed, rubbing his face. He could not bear falling asleep again. Where were they? He had to find them.

*

Blaine had given up, the knife's blade long since blunted on the old, hard wood. But Carrick worked on, chipping away small splinters away to expose the locking bar. His fingers were torn and bloody but he sustained himself with visions of the revenge he would exact on Bridgit and her friends once he was out of there and controlling this ship.

"Give me a hand here," he told his brother.

"It's useless," Blaine complained.

Carrick stepped across and kicked his brother's leg. "Get on your fat feet and help me! We are nearly through!"

Grumbling, Blaine rose and Carrick showed where he had opened the edge of the wall to reveal where the locking bar slid into it from the door.

"If we work together, use our weight," Carrick suggested.

They hauled at the door, trying to bring it inwards and force the locking bar through what was left of the wall. Once, twice, three times and then on the fourth impact, the locking bar tore free of the wall and the door swung open.

The brothers looked at each other and froze guiltily, expecting someone to come and investigate the noise. But nothing happened. There was always noise on the ship of course, everything from the usual sounds of sailing to screaming children. This morning the ship was crashing through the waves and the noise of that was enough to disguise the screech of tortured wood they'd just created.

"What should we do first?" Carrick asked, picking up the blunted and dented knife. It was not much of a weapon now but better than nothing.

"Food," Blaine said instantly, his mouth caressing the word.

*

Almost everyone was asleep and the only ones awake were up on deck, so they found it easy enough to slip along the corridors. Neither was normally quiet and graceful but after a quarter moon of eating almost nothing, they found the thought of food was a powerful motivator. They knew where the food store was, having visited it several times in the night before that bitch Bridgit had stopped them.

The store was locked but they merely slipped the tip of the knife between the ill-fitting door and the frame and forced the locking bar up with brute strength, powered by the knowledge of what was inside. Carrick shut the door as Blaine fell onto a pair of fish, cramming the flesh into his mouth.

"Don't take too long. We have to find Keegan and then take the ship back," Carrick said.

Blaine turned to him, mouth full of fish and shook his head. "Not until I have had my fill," he mumbled.

*

Bridgit was dreaming of home when the scream woke her. Woke all of them.

"What is it?"

"What's happening?"

Children were wailing and adults were either trying to soothe them or get themselves to their feet as the screams continued to echo through the ship before being cut off suddenly. Bridgit was awake and running while most of the others were still rubbing eyes and trying to find their children.

The noise was coming from the direction of the food store and fear gave her extra speed. She rushed up, men and women beginning to follow her, to see one of the women lying sprawled on the floor, blood on the part of her face she could see.

Bridgit shouted in shock and anger – and shouted again when the familiar flabby figure of Blaine emerged from the food store, hand cocked into a fist. She drew her knife and did not even bother about thinking of a warning. She slashed it at his stomach, which looked suspiciously full for someone who had spent the last few days locked in a sail locker eating hardly anything.

But Blaine was not alone. Even as he staggered back down the corridor, trying to avoid her attack, his brother Carrick emerged from the doorway and swung wildly at her arm. His hand connected with hers and the knife was knocked away, to bounce off the wall and land at Blaine's feet. She turned to try and hit him, only for Carrick to raise a knife to her throat.

"Nobody move or I cut her bogging throat!" he shouted.

Men and women, who had been converging from both directions, stopped, glaring hate at the brothers.

"Now, things are going to change around here," Blaine said with satisfaction, picking up Bridgit's knife.

CHAPTER 44

Fallon led the march back into Berry at the head of a wagon train filled with sacks of grain. Their trip around the western counties had proved fruitful indeed and they were cheered loudly as they marched back into the capital. The slaughterhouses were busy again and the markets full, while the millers would also soon be hard at work.

Best of all, any chance of Swane marching towards the capital before winter gripped the country was gone. Many of the nobles had been talking to the disgraced Prince but that was all finished now. Without men, food or anyone capable of sending messages by magic, they could do nothing to help Swane. And, as far as Swane knew, a massive army waited for him. No, they were safe until spring now. Or, rather, he was trapped until spring, when they could go hunting for him.

Fallon walked with his recruits, Dina was riding beside him, graciously acknowledging the grateful crowds. It was slow going through the streets and even worse when they reached the square outside the castle. There they pushed gently through the people, many of whom were waving fresh bread or other food.

"Now all we have to worry about is the Kottermanis. And we have Prince Kemal's family," she said. "So there is little to worry about there."

Fallon shook his head. "I gave my word," he said softly. "I swore on Kerrin's life."

She reached down and tapped him on the shoulder. "Fallon, trust me. We make a good team," she said. "Let me take the responsibility for this decision, to protect Gaelland and keep us free and strong. Sometimes you have to make sacrifices to get what you want."

He had been growing increasingly comfortable with her but this reminded him unpleasantly of Aidan. He was saved from replying by the roar of the crowd and he let the crush of people naturally carry them apart, until she was a good ten yards behind him and occupied with waving.

Then he saw the crowd parting ahead of him, making way for his friends, not just Brendan but a whole pack of Baltimore villagers, including Gallagher.

Fallon rushed forward to meet them, shoving people aside carelessly in his sudden fear. Had something happened to Kerrin?

"What's happening?" he demanded.

Brendan jerked his head towards Gallagher. "They got back not six turns of the hourglass ago. And they have big news."

"What is it? What did you find out?" Fallon demanded.

Gallagher did not reply straight away, while the rest of the villagers kept walking, until they had formed a circle around the front of the column.

"What is going on? Will you stop being so bloody mysterious and talk to me!" Fallon growled.

Gallagher sighed. "I am sorry my friend but we have to be careful. We know what happened to the Duke of Lunster, to your friend Hagen and why the ship ended up in Baltimore."

"Well, what?"

Gallagher nodded towards the Duchess. "She was behind it."

Fallon kept from turning around only through an immense effort of will. Instead, he swore furiously. "Just when I was beginning to trust her!" he said. "Aroaril save us. You know she just helped us get enough food to last the city through the winter?"

"Aye. She has been helpful. But she has also been playing her own game. We cannot trust her," Gallagher said. "Her men tried to kill us in Lunster and we are only alive because of Rosaleen. We have witnesses back in the castle."

Fallon patted his friend on the shoulder. "Good. We shall get her back quietly and do this without alarming anyone. Whatever else she has done, she is a reassuring presence for the people after we killed Aidan."

He saw Gallagher's eyes widen in warning and turned to see Dina rein in her horse beside them.

"What is going on?" she asked.

"Vital news," Fallon said. "We need to go back to the castle to discuss it."

"What is it?" she demanded.

"It is not for the open street. We would do better to wait until we are back in the castle," Fallon suggested.

Her face did not change but she began to turn her horse, so Fallon reached out and grabbed the bridle.

"You need to follow us," he said.

"What are you doing?" she demanded. "Let go this instant!"

Behind her, the squad of Lunster guards that accompanied her everywhere began to hurry forwards – only to stop when Fallon's villagers formed a wall in front of them.

"It would be better to come with us," Fallon said stolidly.

Dina glared down at him. "Do not be a fool, Fallon. We are a good team. Don't make the mistake of breaking this."

"I have been foolish many times already. One more won't make any difference," he said. "Now smile for the crowd and let's get going."

"I will not!" she exclaimed loudly. "I am a Duchess of this realm and I demand that you let go of my horse this instant."

Instead of answering, Fallon tugged on the horse's bridle to get it walking. "Let's get inside the castle. And make sure all her guards come with us," he ordered.

"Already done," Brendan promised, signaling to the men he had brought with him.

"Help! Someone help me!" Dina cried out.

The crowd stopped cheering and watched uncertainly.

"Set me free and you will be rewarded!" she shouted. "Remember your oaths you swore by the royal seal!"

"All right, that's enough!" Fallon growled, dragging her horse along by its bridle.

A few men stepped forwards, a little cautiously, to try and bar the way, only for Brendan and the others to shoulder them aside. But the others merely watched, confused, as Fallon and the others hurried the Duchess inside the castle gate.

"Make sure nobody gets in," Fallon ordered. "I want all of the Lunster guards disarmed and watched."

"All the rest have been done already," Brendan said.

"What about Gannon? Him too?" Fallon asked.

"He's a Lunster man, isn't he?"

Fallon nodded agreement. Something was telling him that Gannon was on their side but perhaps that was because the man had been there almost from the start. And, besides, he could hardly trust his own judgment any more. Just a turn of the hourglass ago he'd have sworn Dina was on their side.

"Fallon, have you gone mad? Berry will fall to pieces without me," Dina said angrily.

He reached out and grabbed her arm, tugging until she was forced to dismount or be pulled from the saddle. "Let's see how mad I am," he said. "Let's get to the bottom of this, once and for all."

*

Rosaleen was waiting for them in the throne room, along with a line of men tied to chairs. One looked strangely familiar.

Fallon heard Dina's sudden intake of breath at seeing the men waiting for them. He let go of her arm and she turned away – but Brendan was right behind them and there was nowhere for her to go.

"This way, Duchess," the big smith said harshly.

Fallon ignored Dina's protests to look at the seated men. Most of them could not meet his gaze but the one at the end, the familiar-looking one, glared at him defiantly.

"Lieutenant Keverne," he said slowly. "Hagen's old deputy. The man who supposedly vanished with the Duke of Lunster in a mysterious attack. Are you going to tell me why you are here and not at the bottom of the sea in the embrace of a selkie – or slaving in some Kotterman field?"

"I will say nothing to you, dog," Keverne snarled. "I am loyal to the Duchess. I answer to her and nobody else!"

Fallon turned to see Dina shrinking backwards – but Brendan had his big hands on her arms and she was not able to move an inch.

"Sister, can you shed some light on this?" he asked, his voice rising to a shout. "I for one am heartily sick of not knowing what in the bogging hell is going on!"

"Give me your hand. He will not say a word but he does not have to. I can show you what happened," Rosaleen promised.

Fallon took her hand and she pressed it to the top of Keverne's head.

"No! Stop it!" the man yammered but she closed her eyes and her fingers tightened in Keverne's hair.

Next moment Fallon gasped. The throne room had melted away and instead he was somewhere else. It felt like some sort of dream. Some aspects were clear as day and over the rest there seemed to be a fog.

Yet things began to make sense now. He saw Keverne meeting with Dina, watched her flirt outrageously with the guard officer. In exchange for promises of being not just her trusted captain but, later, her companion as well, he would do what she wanted. Using gold and a combination of promises and threats, he won over six of the Duke's guards and organized them to be on the ship. Then, while the sailors slept, they were tied up and thrown overboard. The Duke was surprised in his cabin while he ate dinner. There was almost no bloodshed – except for when the Duke produced a small Kottermani crossbow and loosed a bolt that creased Keverne's arm before disappearing behind a storage chest.

The Duke was also overpowered and thrown overboard, his feet weighted with chain, while the guards scrubbed away any traces of blood in the cabin.

But they were rushing because the tide was turning, and they missed the little bolt, hidden behind the chest. The sails were raised and the tiller locked in place and the ship aimed at the cliffs near Baltimore, where tide and wind would cause it to crash and founder, while Keverne and his gang of traitors made their escape in a fishing boat. Except they had spent too long in the Duke's cabin searching for the missing bolt and trying to clean up the blood and instead of taking the Duke's ship into a watery death at the cliffs, the rushing current took it two miles to the west, to Baltimore. A furious Duchess had sent Keverne and his men to wait out the resultant storm in the Duke's summer retreat down the coast. There they had made contact with a Kottermani ship and helped guide the Kottermanis in their attacks on the Lunster coast, with messages carried down from Lunster by another man, a man Fallon recognized but did not know. Worse, Fallon saw Keverne travel back to Lunster in the dead of night and lure Hagen out with false promises of answers to the mystery that had engulfed Lunster. There Hagen was killed, his body dragged away and dumped at sea as Keverne returned to the Duke's beachside cottage.

Then the visions lifted as Rosaleen removed her hands.

"This is the other man," she said, guiding Fallon down the line to the man from Keverne's thoughts, a vicious-looking scarred man who was tied up even tighter than the others. "His name is Mika and he is a leading light among the scum of Lunster. He tried to kill us and, as you saw, killed Hagen."

"What do you want to know?" Mika asked fearfully. "I don't want the Sister to rip my thoughts out of my head and leave me a bogging fool. I did what I did for gold, not love."

"Then talk. And it had better be the truth," Fallon growled.

"How can you believe a man like that? He would lie to save his own skin!" Dina cried.

"Duchess, not another word, or I will see you gagged. You will get your chance to talk soon enough. For now I want to hear what this man has to say," Fallon snapped.

Dina opened her mouth again but Gallagher silently produced a filthy rag and gestured with it towards her face and she shut it swiftly, pressing her lips together.

So Mika explained how a servant from Castle Lunster had brought him information and gold and he, in turn, had ridden down to the Duke's summer home where it could be passed on to the Kottermanis. He had also set men to watch Hagen's house, in case anyone came calling.

"I didn't ask why; I was paid well," he said.

Fallon wanted to drag him out and hang him high for what he had done to Hagen, to Lunster and to Baltimore. He controlled his anger and turned back to the Duchess.

"Time for you to talk now," he said. "Why?"

"Let go of me!" she demanded, struggling against Brendan's powerful grip and Fallon nodded to his friend.

She stepped away, rubbing at her arms and glaring at them. "How can you believe anything these traitors and liars say?" she asked coldly.

"So what is the truth then? And don't tell me that they are making this up, because I saw the memories and it all fits now."

Dina's shoulders sagged a little and she wiped her eyes with her hand. "I was tricked into it by King Aidan, forced to do his bidding," she said in a small voice.

"What? How?" Fallon demanded.

"You know what he is like," she said fiercely. "He did it to you as well. He says one thing and makes it seem as if you are helping yourself, then, once the deed it done, he has you. He told Kinnard what was happening with the Kottermanis and how the only way to stop them was to become what they feared. The Kottermanis are obsessed with Aroaril, even though their priests gain no power from him. Aidan had seen the power of the Fearpriests before, when he was a boy. He was a man possessed. He thought it was the key to saving Gaelland. He wanted Kinnard to help him but the Duke refused, said he was going to take it to the next council and have the nobles remove Aidan if he did not change his mind. So Aidan came to me and promised me the world. He was going to have Kinnard killed, one way or the other. I could either join my husband in death or I could save my county and my future. He promised that if I got rid of Kinnard then he would protect Lunster from the coming Kottermani attacks and then, after the danger was past, make me his Queen."

"No!" Keverne cried in horror from his seat.

Fallon took two quick steps across to the traitor and backhanded him brutally across the face, rocking the tied man on his chair. "Another word and I will cut out your tongue," he said. "We don't need you to talk to read your mind."

He turned back to see Dina wiping away tears.

"I made a terrible mistake. I thought I could save my people," she said. "What else could I do?"

"You could stand by your husband, the Duke, and stop the King's evil!" Fallon cried. "How could you think otherwise?"

"Because we would have both been dead! You have to make sacrifices sometimes and I knew that Kinnard would die for his people."

"And you would rise at the same time," Fallon said sardonically.

She dashed away her tears. "How can you judge me? You were also lured by the King's promises. He made you kill Prince Cavan, for Aroaril's sake! You killed the Crown Prince and landed us all in this mess!"

"That was different!" Fallon shouted.

"It was the same," she screamed at him. "You told me yourself. He promised you anything you wanted, as long as you did one thing for him. And then it all changed. Just like with me."

"No, because you knew you were allying yourself with Zorva," Fallon said.

"You were going to lead his army! You were going to be the General of Zorva's armies! You cannot stand there and judge me, when you made all the same mistakes!"

"You are wrong!" Fallon howled. "I refused all of that! I never betrayed my people! You sat with us and sympathized with Cavan in my own home and all the time, you knew what was happening!"

Dina crossed her arms. "Once Kinnard was dead, he could force me to do whatever he wanted. I had to help the Kottermanis or he would arrest me and do it anyway. And, all the time, I was trying to work against him. I helped Prince Cavan and then I helped you. I helped feed this city and keep it from falling into chaos after Aidan's death."

Fallon walked over to face her, fighting to keep a lid on his fury. "You betrayed us. You sold our families into slavery with the Kottermanis," he hissed.

"I am sorry. I was trapped. I have been trying to make up for it ever since," she said, her voice throbbing with sincerity. "The Sister there showed you I was speaking the truth when I offered my help."

Fallon shook his head. "You have always done what is best for you. No more, no less. As far as I am concerned, you are no better than the whores on the street, willing to do anything for money. Only your coin of choice was power."

Her hand whipped out and he only just dodged the slap, feeling the wind of it across his face.

"How dare you?" she snarled. "You were a wreck after killing Prince Cavan. I saved you from yourself and then from Aidan's men. Then I held this city together for you. You need me! Without me, the nobles will all turn back to Swane and the Guilds will stab you in the back. We are a good team, don't break it up now."

Fallon did not whether to laugh or bellow at her. "You have to pay for your crimes," he said remorselessly.

"And your crimes? You killed the Crown Prince, killed the King and tortured Prince Kemal. You deserve death for one of those alone. And yet you walk around as if you saved the city."

Fallon shook his head. "It is pointless arguing with you, because you do not see the world as we do," he said. "You have lied and betrayed and brought misery to this country. You could have stopped all this before it began."

"You tell yourself that," she snapped. "Tell yourself you are better than me. But the truth is you are just like me."

"What are we going to do with her?" Brendan rumbled. "She was the one who betrayed Baltimore and made our families suffer. You said you would skin the bastard that did that to us."

Fallon looked at Dina and saw the fear in her eyes. But she drew herself up.

"Kill me and this city will fall into chaos," she said. "I am the one thing they are holding on to. Without me, you are finished. Think of me what you will. But you are lost without me. You will make the wrong choices and doom this land."

Fallon tried to shut out those words but they had an uncanny echo of what Aidan said with his dying breath. He tried not to let his discomfort show and pointed at the line of men tied to chairs. "Take these bastards down to the cells. There is no punishment too painful for them."

"And what of the Duchess?" Brendan asked.

Fallon glared at her.

"Give her a cell to herself. She deserves that much but no more."

Before she could do more than offer a token protest, Brendan had hustled her away, while her men were untied from the chairs, leaving their hands and feet bound, and dragged off to follow her.

"Don't listen to her words about Cavan. She cannot compare what happened to you and what she did," Gallagher said.

"And yet Prince Cavan is dead and life would be much easier if he was still alive," Fallon said. "And you know what Dina's treachery means?"

"That we finally have all the answers to the mystery that has plagued us?"

Fallon paused. "Well, yes. But we are also now running the country – or the west." And he felt the weight of those words come crashing down onto his shoulders. *You will never rule this land. Your choices will fail and doom all.*

CHAPTER 45

"This is an outrage and if this is the way you intend to run the city, you can forget about the support of the Guilds," the new head of the Bankers Guild declared.

Fallon glowered at him but a sheaf of requests for money had arrived just that morning from the nobles of the neighboring counties. With money he could purchase, through them, food and goods from counties further away. The food situation was better but it seemed there were many other things the city needed for winter, from firewood to wool for clothing, while the animals stabled within the city to be slaughtered and eaten later needed fodder for the next moon or two. He might get enough gold if he raided the Bankers Guildhouse or he might not. And he could not take the risk.

"What are you talking about?" he asked innocently.

"Duchess Dina. Arrested in the square outside this castle! The Guilds are all happy to deal with her but if she is imprisoned or executed then we shall have to rethink our support," the Banker said loftily.

"And what if I decided to come calling and look into your affairs, see whether you are secretly worshipping Zorva?" Fallon challenged.

The Banker sat up straighter. "We have all sworn loyalty to Aroaril," he said. "And if you destroy the Guilds you will throw this city into chaos. No merchant will deal with you and none of the nobles sending food and goods in from the counties will trust you.

Duchess Dina was someone we could all deal with. You, on the other hand, are the man who gutted the King in front of a cheering crowd. They are too afraid to work with you."

Fallon leaned back in his chair, his mind racing. *Was this part of Dina's plans? Had she made the Guilds secret promises in exchange for their support if anything should happen to her? Do we even need the Guilds? Why not just march into every Guildhouse, arrest their leaders and take their money, share it out among the people?* It was tempting but they were clever men. They would have planned for this possibility, while he had not. By the time he had men mustered and marching, the Guildsmen would be scattering like rats in torchlight. Unless he got their leaders and their money then he was creating more trouble. He had to get ready for a fight with the Kottermanis and make sure Bridgit got back safely. Fighting his own people in Berry, even if they were Guildsmen, was foolish.

"Well, I am afraid you are mistaken," he said. "Duchess Dina was not arrested. She is merely resting in her townhouse. We have had a strenuous few days of fast marches and hard camps. Not something she was really used to. She will be available for meetings tomorrow, where she can tell you herself."

He smiled at the Banker, thinking that he could take a page from Aidan's schemes.

The Banker looked uncertainly at him. "She was not arrested? Not taken screaming and crying into the castle?"

Fallon made himself laugh lightly. "A foolish jest between friends. She will tell you herself when you see her tomorrow. Shall we say noon, so she does not have to rise early? Bring as many Guild leaders as you feel necessary."

He could see the confusion on the Banker's face and enjoyed it. If nothing else, this would buy him enough time to be ready to search every Guildhouse at a moment's notice.

"We understand the Duchess might be tired after the success of your march through the counties. We shall make it brief."

"Excellent," Fallon said. "Well, if there is nothing else that concerns you?"

"No, that was my reason for visiting."

"Good. Well, I am glad I could clear that up. And after you have met with the Duchess, we can perhaps discuss terms for a short-term loan to keep the city operating?"

He saw the man out to the door, where Gallagher was ready to take him back out of the castle.

"What are we going to do? That traitorous bitch is not going to help us," Devlin said. "What in Aroaril's name were you thinking of when you said that?"

"She will help us. She has spent a night in the cells. We offer her the chance to live in her townhouse and, if she behaves, the chance to go and live quietly in the country somewhere after all this is over."

"Why not keep her here, right under our thumb, in her rooms?" Gallagher asked.

"Partly because we need to use them but mainly because I don't want her hearing or knowing what is going on around here. Who knows what servants she has in her pay?"

Brendan thumped the table. "I will not see her get away with it!" he growled.

"And nor will she. We will lie to her, pure and simple. And at all times she will have two dozen guards around her. Men we trust. If she tries anything then she will suffer a tragic accident. And we shall be ready to raid the Guildhouses at a moment's notice, if they kick up a fuss."

Brendan grimaced. "I don't trust her any further than I can throw her."

"Well, that could be quite a way," Padraig said with a wink. "She's pretty small, you know."

"This is not a laughing matter," Devlin said.

"No, it's not. But we need to use everything we can to get this city ready for the Kottermanis. If that means tricking and lying to Dina, then so be it. We have just forced the nobles around here to help us. If they smell weakness then they will all stop the food coming and then we will have even more trouble," Fallon said forcefully. "And what about the Guild of Magic? With their help, we have blinded Swane. If they turn against us then we would have more problems than a lack of flour. I would not like Swane to see how weak we really are here."

He looked around the table and they all nodded, even Brendan.

"We had better keep a close eye on her though," he added. "We'll pick at least a score of our best recruits and put Casey in charge."

"Not one of us?" Brendan suggested.

Fallon shook his head. "We're too well known. The Guilds will smell a rat if we are there. They don't know Casey."

"Aroaril, I hope you are right about this," Devlin said. "It might be safer to keep her here."

"Would you invite a snake into your house? I fear she will be up to mischief here. In her townhouse she will be all alone, watched by a score of our best men at all times and only those we allow can enter. I don't like keeping her around any more than you do but you heard that bloody Guildsman. People are talking and we don't have the time or the energy to waste on fighting inside Berry. We have to get ready for the Kottermanis. Besides, there is a kind of justice to it. She used us to help her plans. So we use her now."

*

Fallon had been prepared to argue and threaten but Dina jumped at the opportunity to leave the cells and seemed delighted to be able to bathe and eat and dress in silks again at her ducal townhouse. That aroused his suspicions a little but her servants were all sent away and replaced with two dozen of his best recruits, led by Casey, who had proved himself time and again since his fearful moment at Killarney.

When three Guild leaders – the heads of the Bankers, the Potters and Tanners – arrived, she charmed them, and not only sent them away happy but having also signed notes of credit that Fallon could send off to the nobles in exchange for firewood and bales of both wool and hay. That allayed some of his suspicions but he was not about to let his guard down.

"Do not let her out of your sight and send word to me the moment anything strange happens," he told Casey.

"You can rely on me, Captain," the young man said with a smile and a salute.

He was barely older than most of the recruits but he had developed an air of authority. Fallon patted him on the shoulder and walked away, mind already busy on other problems.

*

"Dad, when can we go down to the range and use our crossbows again?" Kerrin asked.

Fallon laid down the parchment he was reading and was about to send his son away when he caught sight of the huge pile of other requests waiting for him. He had never thought ruling a country would need so many scribes and pieces of paper. Aidan seemed to do it without going to any effort but perhaps he was not the best example. Every time he turned around it seemed like people wanted something. He shoved the paper away.

"Let's go down now," he suggested.

It was a relief to forget his worries, wash them away in the familiar action of loosing a crossbow, although he soon forgot about his own practicing to watch Kerrin. He was good with both the small Kottermani crossbow and the larger Gaelish one, picking out targets with cool precision.

"Dad, I need to help you when the Kottermanis come," he said, after one particularly fine shot with the full-size crossbow.

Fallon looked down at his son and saw he was deadly serious. "Son, you should never want to fight. Sometimes you have to fight but it is not something you go looking for. How would you go loosing one of those bolts, real bolts, at a man who was running at you, trying to kill you? Or trying to kill me?"

Kerrin was silent for a few moments but when he looked up, his jaw was set. "I don't want to hide away again. I want to stand up if they come for me. Like you will and just like Mam did."

Fallon felt a lump in his throat and he had to swallow several times before he could speak again.

"Let's hope it does not come to that," he said gruffly. What would Bridgit say when she saw Kerrin now? There was no spare flesh on his frame and his shoulders were firm with muscle after all the work he had been doing with crossbows. The worried look had left his eyes and face and he never coughed now. She was going to be pleased about some of that – but not all. He could not wait to be scolded for the rest of it. For that would mean she was actually there with him.

Then his thoughts were interrupted by Devlin hurrying over.

"Fallon, we have a problem."

*

"I shouldn't be down here. And at least half of these men should be out there as well. We can help you – we have been helping you. You need us," Gannon said. "I didn't know what the Duchess was doing – most of us had no idea. Why else do you think she was using gutter scum to do her bidding? She knew we would never stand for it. We were Hagen's men, as you were."

Fallon looked at the big sergeant skeptically. Keverne and the men captured with him were in one cell, Gannon and the others spread out across the rest. These were not the cells Aidan had been using to keep children; these were the castle's real cells, dark and forbidding. Fallon liked it like that. It reminded these bastards why they were in there.

"Let me guess, you want to guard the Duchess? Or maybe be given responsibility for one of the city gates? And then I turn my back and the Duchess is gone and Swane is back in here with an army."

"I wouldn't want to be near her ever again," Gannon said. "I want to stop the Kottermanis. We both know they are coming and you will need every man you can get. Hagen trained us, which means we are worth three of your recruits. Come on, man, I was on board your ship the night they hit Baltimore! Hagen was my captain: he picked me out of the gutter and gave me a uniform. I owe him. And we helped you get away from Lunster, don't you remember?"

"You didn't stop us, which is a different thing," Fallon corrected him. "Look at it from my point of view. I have been tricked and betrayed by just about everybody. How can I take the chance on you?"

"The priestess! Bring her down here and she will show we do not lie."

Fallon shook his head. "Dina showed me how it is possible to fool Sister Rosaleen. You just have to avoid speaking a lie, while not telling all the truth."

"I can help you," Gannon insisted. "I didn't know what the Duchess was doing but I did see some strange things."

"Like what?"

"When we went through the papers in Aidan's office, I had orders to clear them out and bring them to the old wizard. I was doing that, but I noticed some go missing."

"How did you see things go missing?" Fallon asked suspiciously.

"Well, there was one pile of scrolls that got smaller much quicker than the others. And then there were scraps of parchment in the fire the next morning."

Fallon sighed. "Well, even if this is true, that is no use to us if they are all burned. And if she destroyed some papers, they were probably evidence of her dealings with King Aidan. Is that all you have?"

Gannon thrust his hand through the bars. "Please, give me a chance. Just give me a sword and let me fight the Kottermanis when they come. Promise me that, at least."

"I'll think about it," Fallon said, then turned on his heel.

"Should we lock them all up and consider them all traitors?" Rosaleen asked.

"Yes, we bloody well should!" Brendan growled.

"Gannon was right in one way. We need trained men," Fallon said.

"We cannot trust anyone, ever again, except for us," Devlin said. "Every bastard we have gone to has stabbed us in the back or sold us out."

"But we also need all the help we can get. Sister, can you speak to them and see what is in their hearts?"

Rosaleen looked down at the table. "Once I would have said yes," she confessed. "Now I cannot trust myself. I still find it hard to accept that I could sit next to the Duchess, hold her hand and tell you she spoke the truth, when she hid such a terrible lie from us."

"It was not your fault," Gallagher said immediately.

Fallon felt he could understand her fears only too well. The words of both Aidan and Dina hung over him. He had made so many bad choices and no longer trusted his gut. He could not make a mistake that doomed all of Gaelland. "If it is any consolation, it did not hurt us. The damage had already been done and since then she has worked to help us," he said. "And, even now, she seems to be keeping her bargain. Casey reports that she never goes out, just requests to see a dressmaker and spends half the day designing new outfits."

"And who is paying for that?" Brendan asked indignantly.

"You are," Padraig said. "But at least you'll get to wear a few of them afterwards!"

Fallon let them laugh before tapping the table. "So what are we going to do with Gannon and his men?"

"Either try them or let them rot," Devlin said.

"We can't put them on trial," Rosaleen said. "The memory of the witch trials is too fresh, as is the execution of King Aidan. People trust us but that won't last if we keep killing people. They'll start asking if we are like Aidan."

"What about these missing scrolls that got burned? Maybe that was something important. Maybe even the details about Regan's informers in the city," Padraig said.

"If Gannon wasn't lying to us," Fallon sighed. "I don't trust anyone or anything. We keep them locked up and have Casey watch the Duchess like a hawk. She can do nothing with our guards around her."

CHAPTER 46

With the knife pressed into her throat, Bridgit was forced to accompany them up onto the deck, where a crowd gathered. Blaine was threatening the others with Bridgit's knife, but it was Carrick's blade at her neck that was keeping the others back.

"Where's Keegan, Fitz and Arron? Come forward now and take your reward!" Blaine called out.

Nobody came forward but the crowd parted to show the three of them standing sheepishly at the back.

"So they helped you escape?" Bridgit asked coolly.

"That's enough from you! I have heard the last of your stinking orders! Telling us to obey you as if you dropped out of Aroaril's chamber pot. You're a stupid bloody woman and if you say anything again I will cut your tits off!" Carrick screamed at her then moved the knife down until it was resting on her breastbone, emphasizing his threat.

Bridgit looked down at the knife, seeing how dented and blunted it was, and how the hand that held it was scratched and bloodied, and something Fallon had once told her came back to her then.

"Keegan, Arron, Fitz, get up here. We are going to be running the ship now and things will be done right," Blaine announced.

The trio did not move at first but, with everyone staring at them, they finally shuffled forwards to stand with Blaine.

"We five are going to eat, and you are going to work for us. We were the ones who got you away from Kotterman and we are the ones who will protect you if the Kottermanis come back. We have your precious Bridgit and if you want her to keep breathing, you are going to do what we say. So it's time for some tough decisions. Some of those little kids are just useless mouths to feed—"

A cry of horror and outrage rose out of the crowd and Carrick turned away from Bridgit to glare at them, keeping his knife pressed into her chest.

Instantly Bridgit surged forwards. The tip of the knife dug into the skin over her breastbone but hit the bone and went no further. Instead, the blunted knife twisted in Carrick's grasp and dropped to the deck from his wounded fingers.

He turned back but she was already swinging her right arm, her hand in a fist but with the thumb cocked out. It drove into his eye and she felt it give beneath her sharp nail, spattering her hand with warm ooze as the eyeball burst.

Carrick squealed in pain and shock and jerked his head back. She lashed out with her foot, driving it into his groin. He staggered away, one hand clasped over his ruined eye, the other to his breeches.

His brother spun around and shouted in anger but before he could take more than two steps towards Bridgit he was swamped under a wave of angry parents, knife plucked from his hand, quickly beaten unconscious by a score of fists.

The other three, Keegan, Fitz and Arron, held out their hands in surrender but nobody was in the mood to be merciful and they were also beaten to the deck.

"Bring them all over here," Bridgit said coldly.

The five of them were dragged over to the rail and there, battered and bruised, they were lashed tight with rope and propped upright, unable to move.

Carrick was weeping, tears of pain from one eye, tears of blood from the other, while Blaine snuffled to breathe through a broken nose and smashed lips. The other three were pleading their case, claiming they knew nothing about it, but she was not interested in hearing what they had to say. She checked on Caron, the woman whose scream had woken everyone and discovered she had a bruised face and a nasty cut on her cheekbone from where Blaine had punched her but nothing worse.

"Are you all right?" Riona asked, examining the gash on Bridgit's chest. Luckily the days of rationing had meant there was little flesh between the knife and her breastbone, and while she had an angry-looking cut, it was easy enough to staunch with a torn scrap of cloth that she kept pressed there.

"What were you thinking?" Nola gasped. "Throwing yourself on a knife?"

Bridgit smiled. "He had it pressed against my breastbone and you would need one of Brendan's hammers to knock a knife through there. Fallon told me once he had stabbed someone in the middle of the chest and had the knife just bounce off. A sharper knife would have done more damage but I was not going to let them hurt a child, no matter what it cost."

"Even so—"

"I did what I had to. Now I must again," she told her friends quietly and then waved for silence. "I am sorry," she told the crowd. "I was trying to do the right thing and get these men home, especially after the way their cousins were killed."

"That's right, you killed them!" Carrick cried in a voice cracked by pain.

She pointed at him. "They broke into our food store, gorged themselves, risking the lives of everyone aboard, then threatened the children. Even if we wanted to return them for judgment for their crimes, we cannot. They have to go, if we are to live."

Instantly the five of them, even the dazed Blaine, sent up a howl of protest, begging for mercy, promising to be good, promising anything for another chance.

The pain from the wound on her chest stopped any pity from reaching Bridgit's heart. "Too late," she told them.

She walked over to Carrick, who still had his eyes screwed shut against the pain of the missing one. He was leaning against the rail and she bent, waited for the ship to tilt with the waves, then grabbed his tied legs and lifted. He screamed and tried to thrash around but was held too tight by the ropes. For a moment she thought she could not do it, that she was too weak from lack of food, but then he reached the tipping point and vanished over the side.

The other four looked at her with sheer terror on their faces as Carrick's wail was cut off by the splash as he hit the water. She looked at Blaine's size and took a deep breath.

"Give me a hand here," she said.

For a long moment nobody moved, then there was a rush to grab the wailing Blaine and flip him up and over the rail.

Beside them, the youngest of the other three, Fitz, had wet himself and was shaking with fear, tears running down his face.

"Please, we didn't do anything! We didn't even know!" he begged, as hands reached for him.

"Then why did they ask for you? And how did they get a knife?" Bridgit demanded.

"It was Keegan! It was all his idea, to steal from the selkie tribute, to give them a knife, everything!"

"You just went along with it," Bridgit said coldly.

"Please. We will do anything! Just don't kill us!" Fitz wept.

Beside him, the other two, Arron and Keegan, were also white with fear and pleading for their lives.

Bridgit looked at them carefully. If she had seen any of them in Baltimore before this, she would have instantly called for Fallon to run them out of the village. They looked like they would rather thieve and lie than work and nothing they had done since then, especially on the ship, had changed her mind about them.

"Keegan, did you give them the knife?" she asked.

All eyes turned to the tall, skinny thief and he twisted in his bonds, looking for a way out. "They threatened me," he said finally. "But I didn't do it. It was Fitz what gave them the knife!"

Bridgit strode over to him, bent down, grabbed his knees and flipped him up and over the rail.

The other two were now openly sobbing and Fitz's bowels opened, to add to the stink of his piss running down his legs and puddling on the deck. She was tempted to hurl them both overboard and be done with it but she wanted to believe something could be saved from this and, besides, the tears on the face of the youngest one were reminding her of Kerrin.

"Aroaril, please, have mercy, I don't want to die!" Fitz begged, while Arron just begged for his life, praying to Aroaril over and over and over again.

"Listen to me," she told them and they stopped their whimpers and looked at her, terror and hope warring on their faces.

"If you stay on this ship, you will be tied to the mast and you will work from dawn to dusk, for less food than a small child, and if you try anything, you will go over the side. What say you to this?"

They gabbled their agreement, almost breaking their necks they nodded their heads so fast and hard.

"Release them but keep a rope tied around their ankle to the mainmast. Their first task will be to clean up themselves and the deck and then they will do anything else anyone can think of," Bridgit ordered.

People moved to obey and she stepped back, exhausted. She leaned against the ship's rail and looked back but could see nothing in their wake, not even a bobbing head. She looked inside herself and could not find any regret for what she had done. Three men were dead at her orders, two of them at her hand. It had been a choice between them and the children on board.

"You need to rest," Riona told her softly.

"I need to find out how much food went into their useless guts," she replied and pushed herself upright. All the people on board were her children and what mother rested when her children needed her?

*

A huge cheer startled Bridgit and she walked over briskly, to see a grinning Fitz bring a fish on board. A few days ago she would have run over there to get a closer look but she had little energy and none to waste on running. At least Fitz and Arron were bringing in a few fish each day. With little useful they could do, it was a good use of their time. And, without the fish they were catching, things would be even worse. As it was, they were all down to one meal a day. The nursing mothers, the men and the younger children always got some fish with it, to give them some nourishment but, for the rest of them, it was a small handful of grains and a few dates. The oranges and coconuts were long gone. That diet had given many of them stomach upsets as well and now she was also worrying about the water. They had to be getting close to Gaelland but, while the weather was definitely colder and the sky often clouded, it stayed stubbornly dry. She did not wish for storms to return but they needed rain. They had few barrels left and the water tasted foul.

"Well done, Fitz. See if you can catch a few more. As big as you like!" she told the young man gently.

He nodded nervously. He was always hesitant around her now, which was only understandable considering she had been a heartbeat away from killing him, but he was eager to please and she felt he might even be worth saving. Away from the poisonous influence of Keegan, he was a different man. Even his friend Arron was trying hard to help.

Yet, as she walked away, she reflected that she might have saved them from a quick death for a slow one instead. If they did not find Gaelland soon, they would starve to death. The old and young would go first, despite the way she was giving the children extra. The weight was melting off all of them.

She found a quiet space of rail and looked out to sea, straining to see something that resembled land. She reached down and rubbed her stomach, feeling her ribs more than she had in the past ten years at least. How was the baby doing? There had been no pain and no blood, which was at least something. But she had deliberately given herself the same small rations as the others, not the more generous amount offered to the nursing mothers. How long could she live on that before her body had enough and decided it had to get rid of its little passenger? Once that would have terrified her, sent her screaming into the darkness below decks, where she could sob her fears out in secret.

But she could not afford that now. Besides, there were other lives to worry about. Several of the older women and men were talking about refusing food, or even throwing themselves overboard, to give the others a better chance. She had crushed such talk so far and the few fish that came on board gave everyone just enough hope to keep going. After all, the next day might be the last they spent at sea.

She sighed. It was hard not to wonder what might have happened had she done things differently. If they had stayed a little longer to throw just a few more sacks of flour onto the ship. If she had caught Blaine and Carrick earlier, thrown them overboard the first time, or even left them back in Kotterman. Yet there was no use crying over spilt milk. They just had to press on and hope.

CHAPTER 47

"What is it now? I thought you told me we could do nothing until spring, just sit and watch that bastard Fallon grow more confident and secure on my throne as my father's shade cries out for vengeance," Swane grumbled.

Ryan cleared his throat and brought out a small scroll.

"Sire, this has arrived from Berry. You remember your father's chamberlain, Regan?"

"Aye. Cut down by the murdering traitor outside my father's rooms," Swane grunted.

"He had a network of men through Berry who kept their eyes and ears open for the crown. Of course nobody knew who they were except for Regan, who fed the information they supplied to your father. But it seems this net of ears is still working and it has heard things."

"Tell me more," Swane demanded.

"The Duchess Dina has been arrested by Fallon and is being used as a puppet to keep the Guilds and neighboring nobles happy."

"She will pay for that!" Swane spat.

"But it seems that she now has Regan's network working for her and promises support to you, sire."

"What can that do?"

"She seeks your promise of pardon and reward before she will give us any more. But, as a token, she sends us Fallon's plan for using the streets to defy and destroy any attacking army.

She swears she can give us Berry and, for a reward, will tell you how it can be done."

Swane held out his hand for the scroll. "I like the sound of that."

CHAPTER 48

"What have Fallon and the others been up to?" Bridgit asked. "Now would be the time to see them come sailing for us. I could almost forgive them leaving us to find our own way home if they appeared over the horizon with food."

"As long as it's not dates. I would be happy if I never had to eat another date again," Nola said grimly.

"You might get your wish. After tomorrow, there are no more dates and we are down to the last bag of grains," Riona said, trying for a smile but not quite making it.

Bridgit closed her eyes. The previous night, an elderly couple had stepped off the side of the ship. Dermot had seen it and reported that they had even waved as they jumped. The truly sad thing was, it would make no difference. Maybe if they had done so at the start of this cursed voyage then there would be more food but an extra two handfuls of dates was not going to keep everyone alive longer.

The taste of failure was even more bitter than the water they were drinking.

"Tell me I'm dreaming, or is this the answer to our prayers? A ship is coming this way! Maybe it is them, or even a noble! I wouldn't care which, as long as they have something to eat and drink!" Nola exclaimed.

Bridgit's eyes snapped open and she pushed herself upright. If everyone had not been so tired and listless, someone would have noticed it before, because it was more than just a mast on the horizon. She could see the sails and the hull. From the bow wave, it was heading straight for them. She watched it for a long moment, relief flooding through her, before she realized it was not a Gaelish ship.

"Get up," she ordered her friends. "Go below and – quietly mind you – tell every man and woman to come up on deck, with whatever weapons they can find. The children are to stay below and not come up for any reason."

"What, is it really a ship? I thought I was dreaming," Nola gasped.

"It is Kottermani. They have found us. We have to get ready. Hurry," Bridgit said.

They scurried off and she walked up to the tiller, where the brothers Barry and Alroy were holding on wearily, conscious only of the need to keep it in line with the knife they had stuck into the deck that dawn to indicate where north-east was.

"Wake up!" she snapped. "There is a Kottermani ship sailing right for us!"

They came fully awake and began to haul at the tiller, to turn and run away.

"Don't," Bridgit said. "They will catch us. Our only chance is to sail right at them, force them to turn aside and then try to get past them. Turn at them and then do not turn away, no matter what happens. Can you do that for me?"

"But we shall both be sunk, and all will die," Barry whispered.

"Only if they strike us. But they will turn away, for they want to live. We have nothing to lose. And, if we go, they come with us," Bridgit said fiercely. "I ask again, can I trust you?"

The brothers looked at each other and then nodded. "Aye. You have got us this far. We will follow you to the end," Alroy said.

She left them and walked back down the deck, to where dazed and frightened men and women were spilling out onto the deck.

"Listen to me!" she shouted, using the last of her strength to push away the tiredness and the gnawing hunger inside. "We must be close to home. That's how they found us. We shall sail right at them, make them turn aside, then we shall run up every sail and stay ahead of them long enough to make it home. I want us at the ship's rail first. As they go past, some of them might try to jump aboard. We cannot let them live. They might even throw ropes or the like to stop us. We must cut them."

"And if they hit us?" Dermot asked.

"Then we shall sink, and will have nothing else to worry about. They will expect us to surrender. They will look down on us. One last effort and we can give them the slip. I know you are tired. Aroaril, I know you are hungry. But stand with me this last time."

She glared around at them but they looked listless, defeated.

"I am with you!" Fitz called, from his usual position near the mast. "If I can save us, I will."

A moment later Arron also agreed, and that seemed to spur the others on. They were not enthusiastic, they were obviously scared, but it was all she could hope for. It was a harsh blow, to have come so far, suffered so much and now to face the Kottermanis at this time. But perhaps it was better this way, she decided. They could face their enemy and make a brave finish, if nothing else.

*

The gap between the two vessels narrowed rapidly, the Kottermani vessel thumping through the waves.

"If we don't make it through this, I want to tell you both how much your friendship has meant to me. I could not have done it without you," she told Nola and Riona.

"We will not die here," Riona said determinedly. "We have come too far to fail now. We shall escape – and we look forward to you annoying us for years to come."

Nola merely reached out and gave her a hug and Bridgit felt her iron control crack a little at the contact. But the Kottermani ship was too close for anything else and she drew her knife, drawing strength with it.

She remembered how she had taken on the Kottermanis and told herself she could do that again.

They were aiming right for its bows and she pointed the knife at them.

"Don't stop! Right through them!" she cried and the others took up the shout, hurling their defiance out at the approaching Kottermanis.

"If I don't see Devlin until the day we both stand before Aroaril, I am going to make his eternity a misery for not coming to get us," Riona said, with the ghost of a smile.

Bridgit smiled dutifully. What had happened to Fallon? Then she pushed that thought away. As long as Kerrin was safe, that was enough. It was the bargain she had made that night back at Baltimore and she had no regrets about it.

For a few moments, it looked as if the Kottermanis were going to take up the challenge and smash their own bow into theirs, but then their ship swung violently to the right, sails fluttering as the wind spilled away from them. The two ships passed so close that Bridgit felt as though she could reach out and touch the other.

"Let none on board!" she roared and led a rush to the ship's rail, where they brandished what weapons they had and shouted threats at the Kottermanis.

But, instead of the expected rush of warriors swinging across, there was nothing. Instead she saw massed ranks of Kottermanis, bows in hand.

"Down!" she screamed, fearing a devastating volley that would cut her people to pieces. But still nothing came. She peeked over the rail to see them staring at the ship, no arrows on their bowstrings or in their hands.

"What in Aroaril's name are they up to?" Nola asked.

"Who cares?" Bridgit replied, then cupped her free hand around her mouth. "The sails! Get everything up!"

But while the men rushed to obey, the lack of food meant they were slow and clumsy, moving in slow motion as the sails were unfurled.

Meanwhile the Kottermani ship kept turning, swinging back around into the breeze. Its sails billowed with new wind and more dropped into place, and it took off after them, eating up the distance as if they were standing still. This time it moved across to the left side.

"Stand firm!" Bridgit shouted, feeling her voice crack even as she did so. "Show them what it means to be Gaelish!"

The cheer that followed her words was thin, even to her ears.

"Get down! Stand ready!" Bridgit shouted up at the men trying to fix sails in place. It was painfully obvious they could not outsail the Kottermanis and she needed the men to join the fight to hold the deck. Getting warriors across the sea was going to be difficult and dangerous and she thought they could well make the Kottermanis pay dearly. But the bowmen worried her. They could sail around and pick her people off and there was not a damned thing she could do about it.

The Kottermani ship came alongside, slowing smoothly to match their speed, its rail lined with silent bowmen. Again, they held no arrows in hand, nor were there any on their bowstring.

"What are you waiting for? Come on then, you bastards!" Bridgit roared at them.

"Bridgit, we are not here to attack you!" a voice called from the stern of the Kottermani ship and she looked wildly down there to see Prince Kemal standing by the rail.

"Then what are you doing?" she demanded.

"I think you have seen that, if we wanted to do you harm, we would have done so. Please, come and talk to me, as we did before, and I can explain everything."

Bridgit glared at him. "Why don't you come on board here?"

Kemal smiled, his teeth showing white, yet there appeared little humor there. "I am here to help you. But I am not an idiot. Come aboard, or I shall have to come and get you!"

He raised his hand and his bowmen produced arrows as one, placing them on the string and drawing back.

"Stop!" Bridgit called. "I will speak to you!"

"Don't do it: it has to be a trap," Riona said urgently.

"What choice do I have?" Bridgit asked, as the Kottermani bowmen returned arrows to quivers at a gesture from Kemal. "We are dead either way. If nothing else, I'll get to him and make him set us free."

Ropes were thrown across and tied tight, bringing the two ships close together.

"As soon as I am on board, let go and move away," Bridgit ordered. "I'll talk to Kemal and if this is another game of his I'll come back with his head."

Dermot, Nola, Riona, Fitz and a few others nodded but she could see the fight was draining out of the others, taken by their hunger and exhaustion. It was all down to her. For a moment she wilted. She was tired and starving and there was a child growing inside her. Maybe it would be better to give up? Then she crushed that thought. They would not beat her. And if there were a chance to get a knife to Kemal's throat, these Kottermanis would fall over to save their Prince's life. Weakness was her one weapon and she planned to use it. Again, the slaving bastards thought they held all the power. She would prove them wrong.

Nola and Riona helped her to stand on the rail and then she stepped across the narrow gap between the two ships, determined not to glance down at the rushing water beneath. One slip and she would be crushed between the two hulls. She ignored that and looked at the Kottermanis waiting for her on the other side. With a shock of surprise, she recognized one of them as the slave master Gokmen. He held out a meaty paw for her and she nearly jumped backwards. But it was too late for second thoughts and she stepped decisively across, taking his hand so he could help her down to their deck.

The Kottermanis gave her space and she drew herself up.

"Take me to Prince Kemal," she ordered.

Gokmen's eyes glittered angrily but he merely nodded and led the way up to the stern of the ship.

The Kottermanis looked well fed to her eyes and it was only seeing them that made her realize how thin her own people were.

Kemal was pacing the deck when she arrived and he turned swiftly at her approach, snapping out orders in Kottermani. "Weapons?" he then asked her.

Bridgit shook her head wearily, making her shoulders slump as if she had not even the energy to answer. The knife was back on board with Nola.

But Kemal clicked his fingers and Gokmen grabbed her arm, patting her down to make sure there was nothing hidden. She was aware that her clothes were hanging loose on her now.

"She has nothing," Gokmen said, then gave her a push.

She turned that into a tired stumble and Kemal snapped out new orders she could not understand.

Gokmen said something back in Kottermani but Kemal was insistent and Bridgit could see, out of the corner of her eye, Gokmen and the other guards all leaving, so she was alone with the Prince. For a moment she thought it was a trap, then she rejoiced anyway. They thought her weak and helpless. Perfect. She would let him get close and then go for the jeweled dagger in his belt. Once that was at his throat, they were hers.

"Bridgit, I am here to help you get home to Gaelland, not to bring you back to Kotterman," Kemal said softly, urgently.

She glanced up in surprise, her plan of attack vanishing in her shock. She stared at his face and saw the lines of worry, the bags under his eyes that had not been there the last time they spoke.

"What?" she gasped.

"You obviously need food, and you have become lost as well. We shall send food over and then guide you to Berry," he said.

Bridgit looked at him. Was the hunger making her imagine things? "I am sorry, but I thought you said you were going to help us get home, and feed us?" she said. "Did you mean to say something different in our language?"

"No!" he hissed. "I am here to help you. I helped you escape from Adana, sent away the guards so you could escape. Now I will help you get the rest of the way home."

Bridgit blinked twice, then pinched herself. When nothing had changed, she decided it could not be a dream. "Why?"

Kemal glanced over her shoulder but everyone else was obviously sufficiently far away that he felt he could talk.

"I have met your husband Fallon," he said flatly. "He has my wife and children. We shall exchange you and your people for my family. You have to reach Berry safely or my wife and boys will die."

Bridgit felt a surge of triumph, so strong it made her head feel light. Then, instinctively, she questioned it. "How do I know this is not some strange trap?" she demanded. "Fallon would not hurt a woman or child."

Kemal's eyes widened and his calm demeanor cracked. "He captured me first and tortured me, then he grabbed my wife and boys and held a blade at my youngest son's eyes," he snarled at her.

"The thought of what he might have done to them haunts me every night. And as for a trap, why would I need that? You are half-starved and at my mercy. If I so chose, I could shoot you down like dogs or simply sink your vessel and all aboard."

Bridgit had to admit he had a point and the ragged emotion in his voice gave it the ring of truth. She also enjoyed the thought that Kemal had been in fear for his family held in a strange country. Perhaps he would have a better understanding of what he had put them through. And, if not, well, that served him right anyway.

"Well then, we need medical help. Many of my people have wounds and sores that are not healing. And we need food. Plenty of it," she instructed.

"You shall get it. We shall also escort you into Berry. You are heading in the wrong direction, not by much but enough to make you miss your homeland."

"Why not give us a map and directions?" she challenged and saw a shadow pass across his face.

"I have risked much to find you, and have other ships out searching. If one of them was to find you without me there, a mistake could be made that could not be undone. And I cannot risk you not arriving."

She nodded thoughtfully but her mind was racing ahead. "And what happens when you get your family back?" she asked.

"We are both happy," he said quickly, a shade too quickly for her liking. "I shall stay on in Gaelland for winter and to discuss a new deal with your King."

Bridgit smiled. "That will be a day we are both looking forward to," she said. "How was Fallon?"

Again she saw a shadow flash behind his eyes. "Well enough to lead me into a trap and then torture me and my family."

Bridgit smiled sympathetically but she could see problems ahead. Kemal was not the sort of man to forget a grudge and it was plain as day that he wanted revenge on Fallon. She wanted to know why Fallon had not chosen to sail after her but instead done this. She would have preferred him to have arrived about a quarter moon ago, with plenty of food, but this was better than nothing. It was also interesting to hear that Kemal had aided their escape from Adana. Not enough to save the life of poor Ahearn, and the others who had been wounded and died on the way. But, as the old Gaelish saying went, better late than never.

"I will have to tell my people what is going on, otherwise they might do something foolish," she warned.

"Agreed. My people do not need to know, nor will they ask. They just obey."

Bridgit nodded again, having already seen that first-hand and used it to her advantage. Then something struck her. "How did you know we were going to escape?" she demanded.

Kemal smiled thinly. "Ely came and told me, as I told her to. You should be glad I did so, for without my help you would have failed, and died."

Bridgit was torn between fury at the betrayal and relief that they had been able to get away at all. "Why?" she asked through gritted teeth.

Kemal shrugged. "I have her mother and younger sister. She knew that she had to obey my orders or they would be handed over to my guards."

Bridgit felt a pang for what Ely had been put through, as well as a renewed pulse of satisfaction that Kemal had been made to suffer. "Well, lucky for both of us then," she said coolly.

He inclined his head. "When we have transferred the food, we shall fasten ropes from our stern to your bow, so there is no possibility of you being lost. I would hate to see you disappear in a storm."

Bridgit pasted a smile on her face. She did not trust Kemal but he just had to get her back to Berry, and Fallon and Kerrin. Anything else could be worried about then. But, she reflected, this was bloody typical. Even when Fallon was trying to help her, he left a mess for her to clean up.

*

The Gaelish did not worry about listening to explanations. They were just delighted to see the sacks of flour and barrels of salted meat and fish come across. With them came more barrels of water and small casks of honey, as well as sacks of oranges. They were even happy to see their ship loosely tied to the Kottermani flagship and to follow it towards Berry, altering their course so it was more east than north.

Bridgit made sure all were drinking honey in water and not devouring the oranges too fast, but she could not help wonder why there was so much food on board the Kottermani ship. After all, there was a large company of soldiers on board and still days of sailing before they reached Berry. But her aching stomach consumed her thoughts even faster than her people consumed the food. The oranges tasted like heaven and she also ate a piece of salted fish, luxuriating in the feeling of something solid in her stomach.

"Why are they doing this?" Nola asked.

"It is Fallon and the others," Bridgit said loudly.

The others stopped eating to listen.

"They captured Kemal and are holding his family. They will only give them back when we are home safe," Bridgit said, then stopped as her people from Baltimore cheered and clapped.

The others knew of her history and her promises, of course, but they looked more curious than delighted.

"He reckons he helped us escape, ordered some of the guards away to give us a chance. And it means they will escort us into Berry. We are safe. We will be home in another few days," she added.

Now they all cheered, friends and families embracing. Some children even stopped eating to join in.

"No, this is your doing, Bridgit," Dermot told her, stepping out of the crowd to grab her hand and kiss it. "You have kept your word to us and got us out of there."

She smiled but inside she was thinking of the vows she had broken, the wounded men who had died, the elderly couple who had jumped overboard and Blaine, Carrick and Keegan, thrown overboard.

"We are going home. At last!" Riona said softly, breaking her thoughts.

"Aye. But maybe we won't be going home right away. If Fallon is in Berry, working for Cavan, then we will be going there."

"Well, you will be," Nola said.

"The others are with him. He would not have left them behind, nor would they have stayed," Bridgit said. "But we are going to have problems with Prince Kemal. He told me Fallon tortured him and threatened his son with a knife to make him give us back."

"I'm begorrah glad Fallon did! That bogger deserves everything he gets!" Riona said indignantly.

"But torture? Threaten a child? Would Fallon do that? And Brendan would never stand by and let that happen!" Nola cried.

"Who knows what has happened since we were taken? It may be that things have changed without us."

"But that much?"

Bridgit smiled. "Well, look at us. We have changed as well. I would say for the better, but are we surprised that our men have done something stupid without us to keep an eye on them?"

"Well, put it like that and it makes sense," Nola admitted. "But hurting a child? Whist! What has been going on there?"

"Until we find out, we cannot judge them. Yet we have to assume Kemal is telling the truth, and that we could be sailing into more trouble," Bridgit sighed. "Fallon will exchange Kemal's family for us and then what will happen? The Kottermani will want revenge. Can Prince Cavan protect him? And does Fallon have any plan for after we get back?"

"Surely he has," Nola said.

"I wouldn't bet our lives on it. Because that is what we are doing. Our adventures may not be over yet," Bridgit said grimly. "But that is just between us three, understand?"

"Aye. How did Kemal know we were escaping?" Riona asked.

"Ely," Bridgit replied.

"That little traitor! If I ever see her again ..." Nola said with a shake of her head.

"You will, if I have anything to do with it. Kemal had her mother and sister and threatened to hand them over to his guards unless she did what he ordered, the ruthless bastard. Who of us would have done things differently to save loved ones? And I think she was trying to tell me. She was definitely fond of the kids," Bridgit said.

"Still, she betrayed us. We could all have died!" Nola said indignantly.

"But, if he was right, she actually helped us. And I reckon her mother is Gaelish, even if her father was not. So that makes her one of us and I swore not to leave one of us in slavery over there."

"How are you going to get her back?" Riona asked.

"I have no idea. But that won't stop me trying, once we are safely home," Bridgit vowed.

*

Bridgit was amazed how quickly her people recovered from their enforced starvation. A few days of careful rationing but full meals three times a day saw them regain weight, color and energy. But the sight of the Gaelish coast did the most good and the Kottermanis on the other ship flocked to their stern rail to watch the Gaelish sing and dance with joy.

Bridgit did not join in the dancing. She had spent the last four days trying to think of a way out of the mess Fallon had probably put them in. The only way around this that she could see was somehow slipping Kemal's leash and sailing into Berry by themselves. That way, they could also keep Kemal's family. Only with them in their keeping could they hold back the Kottermani's vengeance.

She waved Fitz over and the young man instantly stopped dancing and hurried to her side. Since she had spared his life he had been acting as if she had saved it, following her around and always eager to help, like some sort of puppy.

"Bring them over, quietly," she ordered and he nodded and raced to obey.

After the first two days, when the people had recovered enough to take more of an interest in what was going on around them, she had the men watch the Kottermanis and how they handled the sails, to see where they were going wrong.

"Can you sail this ship as fast as they can now?" she asked.

They looked doubtful. "We can go faster than before. But they still know more than we do and will catch us," one said.

She nodded. "Then we can only slip away at the last moment. By the time they realize it, we have to be safely inside Berry, where they can't touch us. So practice at night, for they cannot see us trying anything. They have to think we are docile and helpless. Then, when they take in sails to enter the harbor, we put up all the canvas we have, cut the ropes and go past them."

They nodded agreement and she shooed them away. "Now dance around as if you have not a care in the world."

"What if the King's men are not ready for us to do this? What if the Kottermanis catch us?" Nola asked softly.

"Fallon had better bloody well be ready, or else," Bridgit said.

CHAPTER 49

Fallon was trying to stay awake, Caley snoozing at his feet, while a succession of Guild masters droned on with their litany of complaints. He had a couple of scribes taking notes but if parchment had not been so valuable, he would have burned them afterwards. This was the part he hated the most. Pretending to like Guild bastards was even harder than having to make decisions that could doom everyone. Then Gallagher burst into the room, his eyes wild.

"Fallon! Kottermani sails sighted on the horizon, sailing right for Berry!" he cried breathlessly.

Fallon came awake instantly and surged to his feet, Caley jumping up with him and giving a bark of warning.

"This meeting is over," he announced, striding out of the room past the outraged Guildsmen without a second glance.

"Do you think it is Kemal, back with the families?" he asked the moment the door shut behind him.

"Who else could it be?"

"We all head down to the harbor. And make sure we have plenty of men there."

"What about Feray and the boys?" Gallagher asked.

"I'll go and get them. We need to bring them too but make sure we have a full company around them. Kemal will want to see them before we get anyone back. But if he tries anything, we have to be ready. This could be a trap, a plan to rescue them."

"He's waited a bloody long time for it in that case," Gallagher said.

"Even so. We don't take chances. Tell them to be ready. If all goes to plan, they will be reunited with Kemal by day's end."

"You are really going to give them back?"

"I gave my word. More than that, I swore on Kerrin's life. Aroaril knows what will happen if I go back on that. Besides, we are the ones ruling Gaelland now. We can use them to make a deal with Kemal."

Gallagher looked skeptical but did not press it. "And the Guildsmen?" he asked.

"Send two men to escort them out. They were boring me to sleep anyway," Fallon said dismissively. "They love to complain but what are they going to do? Their wealth is all tied up in Berry, and they will never do anything that loses them money."

Gallagher looked, if anything, even less happy but Fallon ignored him. Bridgit could be on the ship, could be just a turn or two of the hourglass away!

*

Kerrin took the pass from Asil and kicked the ball at Orhan, who caught it spectacularly and made them all stop and clap, including Feray.

"Did you see that, Ana?" Orhan asked.

"Let's go again," Kerrin invited. His new friends could speak Gaelish well but often threw in strange Kottermani words. Their word for mother was "ana". How silly was that? "Mam" was so much better sounding. "Come on!" He did not know whether it was the exercises he had been doing with dad and the recruits, all the crossbow practice or the running and playing with the two Kottermani boys but he felt like he could run all day. In fact, he often did.

He waved impatiently at Orhan, who was standing there with the ball in his hands.

"What are you waiting for?" Kerrin asked.

By way of answer, Orhan pointed. Kerrin turned to see his dad racing towards them, a big grin on his face and a joyful Caley capering at his heels.

"What is it?" Feray stood and walked over to join the boys.

"Kottermani sails sighted coming into the harbor. I hope, and pray, that it is our families and we shall all be reunited soon with our loved ones," dad said.

Kerrin felt his heart leap and then began to pound. "Mam's back?" he managed to say.

"I think so. I hope so and I pray so," Dad said, his voice also cracking a little. "Who else could it be?"

Kerrin ran over and grabbed Dad around the waist, burying his face in his chest until he got control of himself and his friends did not see his tears. Dad's arms tightened around him and he felt Caley's nose at his side as well. But, when he had calmed down and turned around, it was to see Feray embracing her own sons.

"Come, get your things and we'll escort you down to the docks, where we can meet them," Dad invited.

"I don't have a gift or anything for Mam's return," Kerrin said, feeling a touch of panic at the thought.

"I think seeing you will be all the gift she needs," Dad said with a smile, and Kerrin had to hold down the joy that leaped up inside him.

"Come on then, what are we waiting for?" he cried.

"We'll all go down together," Dad said, looking over towards Feray, Asil and Orhan.

"Do they have to leave us?" Kerrin asked wistfully. Not seeing his two friends, maybe ever again, took the edge off his excitement at seeing Mam again.

"They want to go home. Just like Mam. And, once she is home, you probably won't want to spend all day running around with Asil and Orhan."

Kerrin thought about what life would be like. "Will we go home now? Leave Berry? Will it all go back to the way it was before?" he asked.

He saw his dad's face twist at that. "I don't think things will ever be the same," he said sadly. "And we can't really leave the people here now. But, we get Mam back! And that makes it all worthwhile."

Kerrin laughed aloud at the thought. He had so much to tell her! "I have to get my crossbow!" he cried.

But dad's hand tightened on his shoulder. "We might leave that for tomorrow, eh?" he said. "Take it easy for the first time we see her."

Kerrin grinned at that. "Don't worry, Dad. I won't say anything bad!"

Dad laughed too. "Well, if you are going to say it, make sure it is on the first day, when she'll be so happy to see us, she won't care!"

*

Every man from Baltimore, except for the handful, like Murphy, who had been killed fighting the Fearpriest, was there. Fallon felt a pang for Ena and the other widows who would return only to discover their husbands had died trying to get them back. He also planned to ask a few hard questions of Sean and Seamus, the two lazy bastards he had left to watch the harbor that fateful night, as to why the Kottermanis had been able to surround Baltimore and capture everybody without any warning.

But with the Baltimoreans came another four companies of his best recruits, just in case. With Feray, Asil and Orhan at his mercy he did not think Kemal would try anything foolish, but he was not about to take the risk.

And with all of them came hundreds of townsfolk, wondering what all the fuss was about and eager to see what was happening. Fallon tried to discourage them but it was hopeless. It gave the march down to the harbor even more of a feel of a triumphant procession.

Kerrin was almost skipping along beside him, chattering away to Asil and Orhan, all three of them excited.

"You must be looking forward to seeing your husband again," Fallon said to Feray, who was but a yard away from him.

But she did not seem nearly as excited as the boys.

"What is it?" he asked, moving across so he did not have to speak loudly.

Feray smiled briefly. "I long to see my husband again. But I worry about what will happen between our countries now. I have seen you take on a roomful of dreadful men to save me and my sons, then watch you overthrow an evil King and try to give your country new hope. My husband has seen none of that and, as far as he knows, Aidan still rules, and defies him. Kemal's father, the Emperor Yonetici, wants Gaelland in his Empire, and Kemal is sworn to do his father's bidding."

Fallon felt a pulse of anger at the thought. "Things have changed. Prince Kemal will have to see that," he said. "I have an army now and by the time spring is here and it is safe for him to sail his soldiers towards us, I will have even more men trained and the whole country behind me."

"It is not that simple," Feray warned. "You would do better to negotiate a deal with my husband to give you some freedom and accept your fate."

Fallon ran his fingers through his hair. None of these choices looked good. How was he supposed to pick the one that saved Gaelland, when all appeared to doom it?

"Please, Fallon, think about it," Feray urged.

"I do little else," he growled. This was spoiling his happiness, taking away his thoughts from Bridgit's return. "Gallagher, watch them," he ordered and signaled to both Kerrin and Caley. "Come, let us see where these ships are."

By the time they reached the docks, the ships were only a couple of miles out from the harbor and obviously Kottermani.

Please, let Bridgit be on one of them, he prayed.

CHAPTER 50

"Is everything ready?" Bridgit demanded.

Dermot and his small group of men, which included Fitz, brandished sharpened axes and swords and nodded. They would cut the ropes that tied their ship to Kemal's.

The other men and boys also gestured their agreement. They had studied how the Kottermanis tied down their sails to get the most out of the wind and Bridgit was confident they could, if not match Kemal's ship, certainly get far more speed up than they had previously.

"Will our friends in Berry be ready for us?" Dermot asked the question that had haunted Bridgit since she thought of this idea.

"I pray so. Anyway, we cannot be led in there like a dog. We shall sail in under our own power. Once we are in the harbor, they cannot touch us," she said, with far more conviction than she felt. "One more effort and we shall be safe, back with our families."

The sight of Gaelland had lifted them all and they were more than ready to listen to her.

"Listen for my call and then give it everything," she said and they hurried off to their positions.

"What do you think the Kottermanis will do?" Nola asked worriedly.

"Who cares? They cannot hurt us, for fear of losing Prince Kemal's family. And once we are safe in a Gaelish harbor, we can use the Prince's family to get rid of the Kottermanis once and for all."

"He did save us. We were dying out there. Do we not owe it to him to see his family returned?" Riona asked softly.

Bridgit snorted. "He was the one who took us in the first place. We owe him nothing. Our first duty is to our people, and I know he will want his slaves back. The only thing that can stop him is a threat to his family."

"But will King Aidan listen to you? The stories we've heard about him do not make it sound good," Nola said.

Bridgit smiled. "But he will listen to his son, Prince Cavan. And we know that Cavan will listen to Fallon. All I have to do is make Fallon listen to me. Once I convince Fallon, the rest will be easy."

"He didn't exactly listen to you about not hunting the Kottermanis," Riona said.

"All the more reason for him to listen now," Bridgit said briskly. "He made one mistake; he won't make another. Now, no more nonsense. We need to judge this right to give Kemal the slip."

Berry eased agonizingly closer but she knew distances were deceptive at sea. Things moved much more slowly than on land. She had watched enough boats and ships sail around the hook of Baltimore to know that you could not make your move too soon.

She could feel the tension coming from the others, people willing her to give the order. But she ignored them and tried to judge the speed of both ships, while the entrance to Berry harbor loomed ever larger. The temptation was there to go but she quelled it ruthlessly. They would have one chance at this and she would not fail.

Men were glancing at her now, looking around from the bow like so many anxious squirrels, but she kept her eyes on Berry. They were muttering now, their noises getting louder as they fretted, but still she waited.

"Bridgit!" Nola whispered and she held up a warning hand. As her friend drew breath to make more of a complaint, Bridgit waved up to the men already up the masts, who were watching intently, and the first new sails were dropped and tied into place, where they billowed with the afternoon wind – this all achieved with a speed that revealed the men's long-suppressed tension. But she was not watching that, instead signaling to Dermot at the stern, who swung the tiller over so that the ship hooked out to the right. Even more sails were unfurled, so the ship picked up more speed. The ropes at the bow, which had been tight with pressure, now hung slack. She watched them carefully as they came out of the water and began to tighten again, holding her ship back.

"Cut it!" She slashed her hand downwards.

The men at the bow fell on the ropes with a fury and the tough fibers parted swiftly under their attack.

"Give it everything!" Bridgit shouted. "Then get under cover!"

The sails were tied down and white water frothed at their bow as they swiftly overtook Kemal's ship.

She held her breath as they surged past. The Kottermanis were reacting, sailors scrambling up the masts to raise their own sails. But they were almost inside the harbor and she could see they would be too late to catch them. Yet the deck was still packed with bowmen who could do fearful damage.

"Get down! And stay close to me!" she ordered. She knew Kemal had to keep her alive but men up the mastheads might be seen as fair game if the Prince was in a vindictive mood. It was his move now.

*

Kemal stared at the entrance to Berry harbor with a mixture of fear and relief. Those three days sailing back towards Kotterman, his fleet going in all directions, had been terrible. He had reproached himself again and again for losing Bridgit and the rest of the Gaelish. He had even found himself desperately praying to Aroaril that he found them. Coming across them had been both a stroke of luck and a huge relief. He suspected they might have sailed more north than east, taken that way by the current, and so it had proved. Getting them safely under his control had felt like a huge victory. He hoped with all his heart that he would soon see Feray and his boys again and yet he was consumed with the thought that bastard Fallon had hurt them or, worse, had handed them over to King Aidan. At least with Fallon he had the leverage of the Baltimore families. Aidan was completely unpredictable. If anything had happened to them ... He promised himself he would have his revenge. True, his fleet was scattered across the sea looking for Bridgit's ship but in less than a quarter moon they would all be there and he could make the Gaelish pay for what they had done. The transfer was going to be difficult. He wanted to get Feray back safe and then somehow snatch back Bridgit before she was away. That way he could get his revenge on Fallon while he waited for the rest of his fleet to arrive. He longed for a final reckoning with the Gaelishman almost more than he longed to see his family.

He was occupied with these thoughts as they slowed down to enter the harbor. Next moment, there was shouting all across the deck and he spun to see sails bloom on Bridgit's ship as it overtook them, the tethering ropes falling into the sea.

"What are they doing?" Gokmen cried.

Kemal did not bother to reply. It was obvious. Bridgit wanted to escape him, to give all the power to Fallon. "Full sails! Stop them!" he bellowed.

Footsteps thundered as the crew raced up the masts, while soldiers poured up from below to form ranks on the deck.

Kemal saw Bridgit's ship move smoothly past them and into the harbor mouth, sails tied correctly and full of wind. There was not enough time to catch them. Although his sailors were some of the best the Empire had to offer, the trap had been sprung perfectly. For one horrible moment, Kemal admired Bridgit's courage for waiting until the last possible moment to strike. She had some nerve. Then he was consumed with fury at the thought of Fallon having his families back and still holding Feray.

"High one, do I give the order?" Gokmen asked, pointing down to where the bowmen were poised to deliver a withering volley onto Bridgit's ship. It was still close enough that each of his highly trained men could land six arrows apiece on the deck before it was past. He was dangerously tempted. If he could not have his family, then nobody would get theirs back.

He was about to give the order when he heard Feray's voice in the back of his head, urging him to think before he acted in anger.

She was right. He only had three companies of men aboard, not nearly enough to punish the Gaelish. He would give them a chance to do the right thing. If they failed, then he would leave the entire country a smoking wreck. They would regret harming his family for the rest of their miserable lives.

"Stand down! But hit the docks right after them! Prepare to either attack or take us out of there at a moment's notice," he ordered.

Bridgit had outwitted him this time. But it was but the first move in a larger game.

*

Bridgit cringed: the Kottermani bowmen looked ready to begin loosing at her ship. But no arrows came down and she sighed with relief as they slipped into the harbor and charged towards the docks.

"Do we slow down?" Dermot shouted.

She glanced backwards and saw Kemal's ship still hard on their heels. "Just get us into the docks! I don't care if this ship never sails again!" she cried back.

He looked startled but waved acknowledgement.

"Get all the children up. If we're holed, I don't want anyone below," Bridgit ordered.

Nola and Riona rushed to obey and she looked for a likely spot on the docks. There were many spaces on the jetties, for few merchant ships sailed as the weather turned, but she wanted to be as close as possible to the city. Then she saw a familiar sight – the Duke of Lunster's ship – and an empty space on the main dock near it.

"Over there!" She pointed. It was a feeling, rather than a considered choice, but she stuck with it. "Stand by to drop all sails!"

Now, where was Fallon?

Then she caught sight of a crowd surging forwards on the dock and her eyes misted with tears and it took her three attempts to speak. "Let go the anchors and furl all sails!"

The ship slowed dramatically as the men frantically hauled in the sails and the anchors bit into the soft harbor bottom. Dermot and two others threw their weight against the tiller and the ship swung around sharply, robbing it of more speed. But it was still dashing too quickly towards the stone dock; the crowd at the docks, who had been rushing closer, surged backwards in fear. All except a handful. Bridgit knew she should be looking for Kemal and seeing what he was doing but all she could look at was the two figures on the dock, one tall, one short – and the dog jumping around their feet. All the strength that had filled her since she had hidden Kerrin and gone out to face the Kottermanis seemed to be draining out of her. All she wanted to do was hold them again and the fact the ship looked as though it would slam into the dock did not concern her.

*

Fallon's first thought was a horrible reminder of the Duke of Lunster's ship and how it had crashed into Baltimore. As before, the crowd was backing away but, unlike last time, they could see men hauling in the sails and – best of all – they recognized the faces along the ship's rail.

Fallon did not even think of backing away once he caught sight of Bridgit. Devlin and Brendan stepped forward to be right there beside him, just as Nola and Riona were beside Bridgit.

"There she is!" Kerrin shouted excitedly, jumping up and down beside him. "It's mam!"

Fallon grabbed his son's arm and made sure he was safely behind the bulk of Brendan. Who knew what would happen when the ship hit the docks? Brendan was heedless of that, sobbing helplessly as his daughters waved frantically at him while Devlin just stood silently, tears trickling slowly down into his beard. Fallon could feel the tightness in his own throat and his eyes burned as he fought to keep control. Sometimes it had seemed as if this moment would never arrive and he had to pinch himself to make sure it was not a dream.

"Gangplanks! As many as you can find!" he shouted over his shoulder. The thought of having to wait to get them off the ship was too much to bear.

Behind Bridgit's ship, another Kottermani vessel was coming in under full sail, which made him wonder how many Gaelish had been taken. And where was Prince Kemal?

Next moment the ship scraped along the side of the dock with a hideous screech and crunch, the impact making everyone on board stagger, and he forgot all about the second ship.

Ropes were thrown down and Baltimore men on the docks raced to make them fast and bring the ship to a complete stop, while others hauled over the gangplanks and sets of steps on wheels, thumping them into the side of the ship and racing up to find their families, heedless of anything else.

Fallon and Kerrin hurried down, Brendan and Devlin at their shoulders, to where their wives and children stood nearer the stern of the ship. The gangplanks only reached to where the ship's side was lower at its belly and there a dozen joyful reunions were happening, with more every moment as men clambered on board and women and children ran or jumped down to the dockside.

"Jump!" Brendan shouted to his daughters, his voice ragged.

They flung themselves on their father, who caught them easily, then held them as if he would never let them go.

Bridgit and Riona were helping Riona's smaller children step and jump down; Will, the youngest boy, clambered over the rail and jumped to the dockside, stumbling as he landed but racing to his father at the same time, so that he tackled Devlin around the legs and brought him down as well.

Devlin lay on the ground, Will on top of him, with his older boys leaping on top of the pile.

"Sorry, Dad!" Will cried. But the farmer just laughed, the noise booming out, sounding as if he could not stop.

*

Bridgit helped Riona over the side and then swung over herself. It was a drop to the dockside, easily six feet and she knew she would never have tried it a few moons ago, never mind the last time she'd been pregnant. She would have imagined herself falling and breaking something or, worse, landing on Kerrin and hurting him. But now she bent her legs and jumped, landing lightly.

Next moment Kerrin was there, hitting her with the force of a missile, his arms around her and squeezing with a strength she did not remember. She leaned down and took a deep breath of his hair, just smelling him and kissing the top of his head hard, just as she had done the last time. That was enough and she let the tears come. She lifted his head up, seeing his own tears, and cupped his face in her hands, not wanting to break contact with him, drinking him in, feeling him nourish her as if she had been starving all these moons without him. Wordlessly he clung to her and she hugged him back, feeling solid muscle in his shoulders and back where before there had been none. At least he smelled and looked clean, and he seemed to have grown incredibly since that terrible night in Baltimore. She wanted to tell him how proud she was and how he must have done as she planned that night but her throat simply wouldn't form the right shape for talking. She kissed his face, his cheeks and his head, making up for all those days without him.

In turn he reached up and touched her face, as if to reassure himself it was really her. "What happened to you, Mam?" he asked hoarsely.

She paused. Where to even begin to answer that question?

"Look at your skin, it's a different color; and you're all skinny as well," he said, running his hand down her face.

Ah, that was easier. "The sun in Kotterman is much brighter than here. And we did not take enough food on the ship," she said. "And what about you? You've grown – you look like you could wrestle a wolf now!"

"I had to be ready to save you next time," he told her seriously.

Bridgit patted his face one more time, thinking they would need to talk some more about that later, and then finally looked up, to see Fallon standing there, his eyes shining.

"There are times I thought I would never see you again," he said thickly.

"I never doubted I would see you all again," she said, then took a quick step towards him and flung her arms around him.

"I am sorry," he said softly, his voice breaking. "If only I had listened—"

"No, I am sorry. If only I had—" she said, then could not stand to say any more and just kissed him instead. There was so much she wanted to say but this was not the time. It was a time to luxuriate in his arms around her and the feel of him in her own arms.

*

Fallon had been content just to watch her with Kerrin, letting his eyes get used to seeing her again. Her skin was burned darker and she looked like she had lost weight but, even more, there was something different about the way she stood and the way she looked, all fierce and bright, even though tears were pouring out of her eyes as she embraced Kerrin.

There was so much he wanted to say but the words would not come out and, anyway, they would be wrong if they did. Nothing could say what he felt.

Then she was in his arms and he could feel her and smell her, kiss her and taste her and he never wanted to let go. She was thin, yes, but her breasts were full, pressed into his chest, and her lips were like silk on his. His body reacted so swiftly, almost painfully, to her being there so close to him that he almost wished it were just the two of them, with nothing and nobody to disturb them – although in another way it did seem like everyone had melted away and it was just them. And it was not just everyone else that was gone. Everything else, all the worries, all the plans, that was also gone. With her in his arms all he cared about was leaving this place and going home, just the three of them. Maybe Cavan's secret island was the place for them after all. "I will never let you go again," he whispered.

*

Bridgit had to reluctantly break their kiss, because she was struggling for air. She stroked his face and his back and looked into his eyes with a smile – she could feel how he was reacting to holding her.

"Some things never change," she whispered.

He grinned at her and she took a deep breath. There was so much she needed to tell him about what she had been through. Most importantly of all she had to tell him that she was pregnant again. But that had to wait. There was an even bigger problem about to sail into their lives.

"Fallon, listen to me," she said, pulling his face away from hers. "There's a reason we raced into the harbor. Prince Kemal is right behind us."

"I expected that," he said, pushing his face down to kiss her again.

"No, we don't have time for that," she said, pulling away.

"You are back. I don't care about anything else," he said thickly.

"Will you just listen to me for a moment?" she said sharply. "We have to act quickly!"

"There is plenty of time for that," he said dismissively.

She stopped his next kiss with her hand, angry now. "You are wrong. We are running out of time."

He looked at her with a hurt expression on his face and she shook her head. All his brains had obviously sunk down to his trews. Next moment her worst fears were confirmed.

"Captain Fallon!" a voice roared in accented Gaelish. "Time to live up to your word!"

She cursed as Fallon looked up and she turned to see Kemal's ship swoop in like a bird of prey, scraping along the other side of her ship, a solid line of grim-faced bowmen facing them.

She slapped him on the chest, trying to get him to think again, to focus on what had to be done.

"Prince Kemal's family? Are they safe?" she asked urgently.

"Yes, they are over there. But how did you know about them—?" His face flushed and she knew that Prince Kemal's words were true – her Fallon, kind, honorable Fallon, had tortured the man and threatened the child. Again she pushed that thought away for later.

"Never mind that. You must not give them back," she said quickly.

His attention was interrupted by shouts of delight from further back on the dock and Bridgit saw a woman and two young boys rush forwards. She recognized them as the ones she had seen in Kemal's house but, even if she had not already seen them, as the only Kottermanis on the dock they would still have stood out.

"They cannot be given back," she repeated, then turned back to her ship.

"Get everyone off! Now! Move it!" she roared at them.

Although the deck was still a mob of reuniting families and friends, the women and children at least were used to obeying her instantly and hurried towards the gangplanks. Their menfolk were a little bewildered by the call to action but were tugged along by children and wives, so that the ship emptied rapidly.

"Archers, crossbowmen – what have you got? We need them ready now," Bridgit snapped, hitting Fallon on the arm.

"What? Why?"

"Where is Prince Cavan, or King Aidan? Who is in charge?"

Fallon's face tightened up and she grabbed his tunic.

"Where are they?"

"Dead. Both of them," he said, reluctantly.

She felt the ground tilt beneath her feet and she was pretty sure that was not just due to being back on solid land for the first time in half a moon. "How?" she croaked.

Again his face darkened and his eyes closed. "I killed them both."

Bridgit felt her mouth drop open and closed it only with an effort of will. A crunching sound behind her revealed that Kemal's ship had come to a stop alongside hers and time was slipping away.

"What in Aroaril's name has been going on here? I go away for a few moons and look what happens!" she gasped, then shook her head at the expression on his face. "That can wait for later. We are going to have to have a long talk tonight. But first, take me to Kemal's family, and for Aroaril's sake get some of these soldiers ready to fight!"

*

Fallon let Bridgit pull him along for a few steps, his mind a whirl. This was a very different Bridgit from the one he had last seen.

Apart from the physical changes, she was shouting orders and people were leaping to obey her.

Worse, she was obviously horrified by what he had done while she was away. Kemal must have told her how he had threatened Orhan.

As for the rest of it, he could not understand what she was going on about. Kemal had returned with the families, as he had promised, and now they needed to hand back Feray and the boys. Yet Bridgit was acting as though it was a life and death situation. He got his feet under him and stopped her.

"What is going on?" he demanded.

Her face twisted into an expression of frustration, one he did remember well.

"Listen. Whatever deal you had, or think you had with Prince Kemal, it doesn't exist," she said, spitting the words out. "We escaped by ourselves and stole a ship. Kemal just met up with us in the last few days, by pure chance, and was going to bring us in on a rope. We gave him the slip to get in here first. If you give back his family, he will kill us all. I know him. He made me leader of these people. He hates you with a passion and will do anything for revenge. He has a fleet out there somewhere. The only thing keeping him at bay is the knowledge you have his family. We cannot give them back."

He felt awareness slowly return as her words hit home. He looked over at Feray and the boys, seeing the tears coming down their faces, and it was like a blow to the stomach. He did not want add breaking his word to torturing Kemal and Orhan. What might that mean for Kerrin's life? A promise to Aroaril could not be easily thrown away. Aidan's words about his choices dooming Gaelland came back to him and he groaned. He wanted to spend time with Bridgit, not make this decision! "Have you seen the fleet?" he demanded.

"No," she admitted. "But he would not have sailed with just one. I have looked into his eyes and he is not a man used to being crossed."

"I too have looked into his eyes," Fallon said softly, remembering that night when he had beaten and tortured the man.

"Captain Fallon! Come and speak to me!" Kemal bellowed.

"Do not give him anything," Bridgit said warningly.

Fallon waved to Bran.

"Shieldwall along the docks. Get all the families behind it and crossbows to the sides. Keep Feray and her sons close," he ordered.

Bran saluted and Fallon left him to it.

"I'll go and talk to the man," Fallon said.

"Then I am coming too," Bridgit said instantly.

He looked at her, seeing new determination in her face. Losing weight had made her jaw stand out stronger or maybe something else had done that. The doubt and hesitation he had seen so often on her face were gone.

But he was not going to lose her again.

"You are not going into any danger," he said. "If he hates me as badly as you say, then I cannot risk it."

"I have been risking my life for the past moon or more!" she said indignantly. "I am with you, now and forever. And I know this man better than you do."

He shook his head. "I saw him break. I was the one who broke him. I have all the power between us. But, if he wants revenge, the best way to hurt me will be to harm you. I cannot allow that. And I failed to protect you once. I will not make that mistake again."

"You don't understand!" she protested but he waved at Brendan, who put down Nola and rushed over.

"I go to talk with Prince Kemal. Keep Bridgit safe, no matter what happens. Swear on your daughters," he ordered.

"Fallon, don't be a bloody fool!" she snapped but he and Brendan ignored her.

"Come on, Bridge. We'll watch in safety," Brendan rumbled.

She shouted in protest but he pointed to Kerrin. "Think of him. He cannot lose you again. Stay with him, please," he begged. "Kerrin, keep your mam safe."

Kerrin snapped to attention and immediately grabbed her arm. That, more than anything, took the fight out of her, but she still yelled at him.

"Do not give Kemal's family back! Keep them, whatever you do: they are the only thing stopping a Kottermani invasion!"

Fallon nodded, then turned away to run lightly up the gangplank and onto Bridgit's ship.

Prince Kemal was standing alone in the middle of the deck, although the rail of his ship was packed with grim-looking bowmen. But he was smiling gently.

"Welcome, Captain," he said. "I was wondering just what you were doing down there. Of course you would be enjoying a reunion with your wife, but I was sure you would not remember your promise and our deal together."

"I have not forgotten," Fallon said. There was none of the anger or hatred he had expected, and of which Bridgit had warned. If anything, Kemal seemed warm and pleasant.

"Good. Because I have lived up to my end of the bargain. I helped your families escape, while making it look like a simple slave revolt, then I followed them at a distance and, when they were starving to death and sailing in the wrong direction, fed them and led them here. They were overcome with eagerness to see you and raced ahead, but they would not be here without me. So now I need my family back, as agreed."

Fallon looked at him critically. Bridgit's words were still ringing in his ears. "What will you do when your family is returned? Do I have your word that you will leave me and my family alone?"

He looked carefully at Kemal as he spoke but the Prince's face merely tightened a little in anger.

"Does that mean you are thinking of keeping my family from me? When you gave your word? When I upheld my end of the bargain?" he snarled. "What will your King Aidan say about this when I inform him? For whether you return my family or not, my next visit will be to the King's court, for the business I began but could not finish because you attacked, kidnapped and tortured me."

Fallon crossed his arms. "You won't be speaking to King Aidan because he no longer rules here. I do."

Kemal smiled and shook his head. "Very amusing. But I think we need to be serious now. I will be seeing your King—"

"He is dead. He was worshipping Zorva and tried to sacrifice your wife and children to the Dark God. I saved them and overthrew him, then publicly executed him," Fallon said harshly. "Your wife will tell you if you don't believe me."

Kemal said nothing for a long moment, merely studying Fallon carefully. "I would like to hear that," he said finally.

Fallon stepped backwards. "Gallagher! Bring Feray up here. But she is not to step on board this ship, and keep the boys with Kerrin!" he shouted.

"If this is true, you have taken much upon yourself for a simple village sergeant," Kemal said.

"I am no longer a simple anything," Fallon retorted.

They waited, neither of them saying anything, then Gallagher appeared at the head of one of the gangplanks, Feray at his side, and half a dozen of Fallon's biggest recruits with them, all holding shields. The fisherman held Feray's arm, not cruelly, but enough so it was clear she was not going anywhere.

"I see you, my husband," she said calmly.

"I see you, my wife," Kemal replied, his voice catching a little. "Are you well?"

"I am well," she confirmed. "We have been treated with care, even kindness."

"And is what Fallon said true? That King Aidan is dead and Fallon rules Gaelland?"

Fallon heard the quickening in Kemal's voice with the last question but did not even bother turning around. He suspected the first few questions had been some sort of code, so Kemal could know whether Feray was being made to say anything.

"It is mostly true," she said evenly. "Aidan captured the three of us and wanted to sacrifice us to Zorva. That was his plan to stop you. He was going to summon the power of the Dark God to rule not just Gaelland but the whole of the Empire as well. Fallon stopped him and killed him. Yet he does not rule Gaelland. He controls Berry and the surrounding countryside but Aidan's son Swane is still out there."

Fallon saw her words hit home with Kemal, although he said nothing, merely looking thoughtful. He nodded to Gallagher who instantly hustled Feray away and back over the side.

Only then did Kemal react. "Wait!" he cried. "Not yet!"

But Gallagher ignored him and Feray did not fight the fisherman, so they vanished back to the docks.

Kemal took three quick paces forwards as if to pursue them, and Fallon moved to cut him off, only for the massed Kottermani soldiers to react angrily, drawing arrows from their quivers.

Kemal seemed to come to his senses then and wave the soldiers down. He also stepped back a pace, breathing heavily. "It seems we have much to talk about then," he said. "Firstly, I thank you for stopping that madman from harming my family. I know that few indeed of my men would have done the same, were the positions reversed. But it seems you have some equally big decisions to make now. There may be no King but it is obvious that whoever rules Berry rules Gaelland. And, from what I know of what has been happening in your country, I cannot imagine your people will have any love for Swane, even before they hear about his father worshipping Zorva. So you will rule Gaelland, which means we need to discuss how this country of yours becomes part of the Kotterman Empire."

"That is not going to happen," Fallon said instantly. "I will have no more of my people become your slaves."

"Fallon, you cannot stop it happening. But you can spare your people much bloodshed," Kemal said gently. "You stand here at a fork in the road. Down one path, Gaelland will grow strong and safe, nurtured within the Empire. Yes, there will be slaves, but we shall only take the criminals. Thieves, rapists and murderers – the ones you would normally execute or banish anyway. And instead of paying half of everything to the crown, you will pay but one part in ten to the Empire. You will all grow richer and—"

"Have Kottermani soldiers in every village? We are a free people. What price would you put on that freedom?" Fallon interrupted.

"The price for not listening to me will be too much for you to pay," Kemal warned. "For I will return with a fleet and an army in the spring and I shall bring Gaelland into the Empire by fire and sword. You cannot stand against us, for we are too many. It is already decided. You cannot stop it: you can only make the best possible deal for your people."

Fallon swallowed awkwardly. Was this Aidan's prophecy coming true? "And what if we keep your wife and children? Could you attack us knowing we shall kill them? What then?" he asked.

Kemal met Fallon's gaze steadily. "That would be the worst choice of all," he said softly. "I would not attack you under those circumstances, but my father the Emperor would. And he would no longer be interested in having a few of your people as slaves. He would kill most of you and enslave the rest. Gaelland would be a ghost country, with nothing but a few wild animals. Peasants from around the Empire would be shipped here to work it but not a single Gaelish person would be left."

Fallon wanted to snarl defiance at him, but Kemal's words were spoken simply, not as a threat but sounding like the truth. None of the choices sounded good and he frantically searched for a way to preserve Gaelland.

"Listen to me, Fallon. I respect what you have done and what your wife Bridgit did. You are brave, resourceful people and you could be good friends to the Empire. Give me back Feray and my boys and I swear to you that Gaelland will have a friend at the highest level of the Empire. I will be appointed the first Governor of Gaelland but I shall need a trustworthy local adviser – or two. You and your wife, for example. You would effectively rule the country, albeit in the name of my father. You could make sure that your people still feel free and that none are harmed. As I said, the only slaves we would take are the criminals you have spent a lifetime catching, and the tithe we will take is far lower than King Aidan and the nobles demanded. You say your people need to be free but how free are they, having to devote their lives to making the nobles and the Guilds rich? You want to get rid of the nobles, the Guilds, let the people enjoy some freedom? Then join with me and rule this country. I will finish off Aidan's filthy son Swane and make sure there is no more Zorva worship going on. A new country, and you will be at its head. All you have to do is return my family to me. Or you can make the biggest mistake of your life and doom your people to death."

Fallon hated that he was agreeing with it, but Kemal seemed so reasonable and his words made so much sense. A glance at the other ship and the ranks of bowmen there told him holding off a huge army of them was going to be almost impossible. He barely controlled Berry, and the bloody nobles, not to mention Swane, would probably side with the Kottermanis rather than fight them. He could not let Aidan's prophecy come to pass!

"And what is to stop you taking your family and then destroying Gaelland anyway?" he asked, mustering his defiance.

"Burning the country and enslaving the survivors would not deliver much in the way of gold or honor to my father," Kemal said simply. "I am my father's servant in this. He has sworn to be the first Emperor in a hundred years to bring a major new province into the Empire. He will have Gaelland, one way or another. A smoking ruin is not much of a boast. Far better to tell the court of a beautiful new province, with a happy people who will sing his praises for delivering them from an evil King."

Fallon shook his head, trying to blot out the words. Yet they sank deep into his mind. Did he really want to keep arguing with the Guilds and dealing with the treacherous Duchess Dina and the rest of the slippery, corrupt nobles in an attempt to keep the firewood and food flowing into Berry? Would it not be easier to give it all up and slip away to Cavan's island? Then he thought of all the recruits he had trained, as well as the people who had cheered him as he marched through the city streets. He could not let them down.

"You know it makes sense. I can land ten thousand men anywhere on your coast and then march them through Gaelland like a plague of locusts," Kemal said.

"A plague of what?"

Kemal smiled. "Something from my homeland that you should be happy you know nothing about. They strip everything away and leave only barren land behind."

Fallon nodded as he desperately tried to think of how he could get his country out of this. Kemal would not want to admit to his father that he had been captured, his family held by the Gaelish and the Prince forced to help the new batch of slaves escape and return home. For all his confidence and apparent lack of care, Kemal wanted to come out of this looking good. Maybe there was a way to give him back his family in exchange for a better deal for Gaelland.

"Can I trust you?" he asked bluntly.

He saw Kemal's eyes flicker in surprise, then the Prince let out a short bark of laughter. "You ask me that? After you lied to me, led me into a trap, tortured me, threatened my son and now are delaying returning my family to me? Whereas I have lived up to my end of the bargain. Your families are home, thanks to me. The word of a Kottermani Prince is better than gold. Once we say a thing, it is, how do you say it here? As solid as rock."

"That is the problem. Because I worry that you want to take revenge on me. My wife told me you are consumed by hatred for us."

Kemal laughed again; this time it sounded more natural. "Your wife is a cunning woman. She has been saying whatever comes into her mind if it gets her what she wants. You see that giant of a man back there?"

He pointed back at his ship and Fallon followed the gesture warily, seeing a large man with a huge scowl and an even bigger moustache.

"That is my slave master Gokmen. Your wife told him she was pregnant and that the child was mine in order to make him do what she wanted. She hates me for attacking your village, for making her the leader of your people and taking the children away from their parents."

Fallon stopped, thunderstruck. Bridgit was pregnant again? He flashed back to her breasts – never far from his thoughts anyway – full despite her terrible thinness and to the fierce light inside her. And, Aroaril, if she could lie about pregnancy, of all things, she had indeed changed as much as he had. He glared at Kemal. What had the Kottermanis done to them while they were away?

It appeared Kemal was following his line of reasoning, because he held up his hands.

"Of course the child is not mine; nor is it Kottermani. I merely told you that to show you there are two sides to every story. And that you can trust me. If I give my word and sign my name, then that is unbreakable."

Fallon walked closer, until they were no further apart than they had been the night when he had tortured Kemal. That knowledge lay between them, unspoken but lurking like a hungry pike in a river. He stared into Kemal's eyes, sure that he could tell when the man was lying. The slightest flinch and he would know Kemal was trying to deceive him. The Prince looked tired but that was only to be expected. It was the eyes that would seal the deal.

"Then let us make a new treaty for Gaelland, you and I. One where we both get what we want," he said. "You get a piece of parchment that says Gaelland is now part of the Kotterman Empire. Your Emperor gets to sail here in the summer and be cheered by adoring crowds. Your tithe of gold, as well as a ship full of criminals, will arrive back in your country each year, to do with as you wish. But the only Kottermanis here will be merchants, albeit merchants who are paying less tax. We rule ourselves. Our duties to you consist of paying you each year and giving you honor every time you or your Emperor want to travel here." This way he could avoid an invasion, while buying the time and space needed to build a proper army. Train them in the mountains, away from prying Kottermani eyes. Let them bring their fleet then! Aidan's dying prophecy would never come to pass.

"And how can I trust that you will keep to such an agreement? You could say that to get me to sail away, then break it," Kemal asked sharply.

Fallon liked the sound of that. If Kemal had been too eager, he would have mistrusted it. And the man's eyes were rock steady.

"You still have your army and fleet. If we do not pay up, you arrive and take what you want, as you threatened," he said. "And we will need some soldiers based here, for the first few moons anyway."

"Really? You would let Kottermani soldiers stay here?" Kemal's voice betrayed his disbelief.

"I need them to break Swane and the nobles who are still allied to his cause, the ones who had pledged themselves to Zorva. They are the ones who tried to sacrifice your wife and sons, so I would have thought you would be pleased to help destroy them."

He watched Kemal stroke his beard.

"So, I return with a small army, which we use to crush Swane and his nest of Zorva-worshipping vipers, then my father has a triumphant parade through your cities and we all go home, leaving you to rule Gaelland in our name, sending tribute each year?" the Prince asked.

"You sign that treaty and, in exchange, you sail away with your family this very day," Fallon offered. "That is what we give you. Anything else, you will have to take. And you will lose your family and your position as well."

"My position? How will I lose that?" Kemal asked, a half-smile on his face.

"Because if I or any of my men are taken before your Emperor, we shall tell him the truth of this. That you helped slaves escape to cover up your family being captured," Fallon said fiercely.

Kemal sighed. "So there is the stick to go with the carrot. A threat to end me as Crown Prince and heir to the Elephant Throne. A threat that, in your death throes, you will reach out and sting me."

Fallon shrugged. "It seems that we can both come out of this looking good, or we can both suffer. It is your choice."

He stared evenly at Kemal, who matched his gaze. Neither of them said anything for a long time, then Kemal nodded.

"Draw up the treaty. If it promises what you said, then I shall sign it, take my family and sail away, to return in the spring with two thousand men to destroy Swane and then, in the summer, bring my father back so he can be cheered from one end of Gaelland to the other."

"Agreed. I shall have scribes write it up now," Fallon said, letting a little smile slip onto his face. He had the measure of the man. Kemal would hold to his word.

"And food. I shall need more food for the return trip. I gave much of my supply to your families when they were starving," Kemal added.

"That will not be a problem," Fallon promised.

*

Bridgit had waited on the dock, barely able to disguise her impatience as Fallon talked with Kemal on board her ship. She tried to break out of his grip but Brendan held her back easily.

"Brendan, you know I am going to make you pay for this later. I need to be up there. Look what trouble Fallon got into without me. Who knows what is happening now?" she threatened, but the smith was implacable.

"Fallon has been going crazy without you. He is right. If Kemal is planning a trap, then he will try to seize you and then where will we be? Having to hand back Kemal's family to get you both," he said. "Besides, seeing you and Fallon together again will only infuriate the Prince. He might do something foolish."

Bridgit shook her head. Brendan might think he was making sense but she knew she had to be up there. Fallon was too trusting.

She tugged again at his arm and he tightened his grip, only for Kerrin to rush over and poke the big smith in the chest.

"Brendan, you need to let Mam go," he declared.

"I can't do that. Your dad told me to keep her safe," the smith replied.

"I will keep her safe," Kerrin said aggressively. "Let her go or you will have me to deal with!"

Brendan looked more amused than angry but Bridgit reached out to grip her son's shoulder and pull him back. Except he did not move back but withstood her grip to still face Brendan.

"When did you turn into such a little lion?" she asked.

"I won't let you be hurt ever again," Kerrin said, eyes boring into Brendan.

"It has been quite the journey for all of us," Brendan said, without a smile. "But I can't risk letting her go."

Padraig pushed his way through the crowd and into the middle of them.

"Well, would you look at you?" he exclaimed, embracing her.

She smiled, not just to see her father again but because he looked so different. His face and body had filled out and his clothes were clean, but the biggest change was in his eyes, which sparkled with life again.

"It has been amazing," he said, seeing her surprise. "You stop cooking and I put on weight and you lose it! Maybe we should get Fallon to move into the kitchen from now on!"

Everyone smiled at his flood of nonsense, but he reached out to both Kerrin and Brendan.

"Nobody is going to hurt your mam, lad," he said. "And Brendan, you can let her go. Because she is going to wait with me, isn't that right?"

Bridgit hesitated, then nodded. Brendan released her arm and Padraig hugged her again.

"By Aroaril it is good to see you," he said hoarsely. "You have been through the fires – literally, for you look like bread sat too long on the toasting fork."

"It is good to see you too, Father," she said. "And see the real you, not a shell."

"Well, to be sure I am the fine figure of a man now. Getting on for two men, even!" He released her and sighed. "We have much to tell you, but I have kept an eye on both Kerrin and Fallon, and kept them mostly safe for you. But what about you? What have you been doing?"

She did not know where to start, and was worried about saying too much in front of Kerrin, so merely patted him on the arm. "Maybe later. Now I want to know what Fallon is up to."

Waiting there was not the hardest thing she had had to do in these past moons but it was still frustrating. And when Fallon finally returned, to tell everyone he was ready to make a new treaty with Kotterman, that bubbled over and she was unable to hold back her words.

"Are you an idiot?" Bridgit demanded. "You cannot trust a word he says!"

Fallon rubbed his face. "Can you keep your voice down a little? These people think that I am a wise and careful man, worthy of their trust, so they will accept this treaty when I tell them about it. Having my wife announce I am an idiot at the top of her voice is not helping!"

"Well, if you are going to be an idiot, then the people need to know! Keep the family but send him packing. He is bluffing. He would never risk his family," she insisted.

Fallon turned away, ordering men to find scribes in the nearby warehouses, then waved to Gallagher for Feray to be brought over.

"Why are you asking her?" Bridgit demanded. Was the man going out of his way to annoy her?

"Because she is his wife and she knows him better than we ever could."

"And you think she is going to help us?"

"I think she owes me something after I saved her life, and that of her sons," he said, an edge to his voice.

But Feray appeared less than happy when she was escorted over. "What is going on?" she demanded.

Fallon swiftly explained. "I know I have no right to ask this but can you tell me if Prince Kemal will hold to a signed treaty?" he finished.

Bridgit looked at Feray closely. She was a graceful woman, with an intelligent face. It seemed open enough. Kemal might be used to disguising what he was thinking but she reckoned she might be able to see if Feray was trying to lie.

"If he signs a treaty then he will hold to it," she said with a shrug. "He has always been an honorable man. And the Kotterman way is not to get something through trickery. They have never needed to resort to that, when threat and force are always more than enough."

Bridgit could see nothing there to tell her the woman was lying. But that was not enough to risk the whole country on!

Fallon nodded his thanks but Bridgit grabbed his arm and pulled him away.

"You have listened to his wife; now you need to listen to your wife. Kemal wants you dead and probably thinks the same way about Kerrin and me. We cannot trust him. His family is the only leverage we have—"

"His family will give us nothing. The Emperor wants Gaelland for his empire and nothing is going to stop that," Fallon interrupted. "If we threaten Kemal's family then they will come and get them and turn our country into a smoking wreck. Our only chance is to make a new treaty with the Kottermanis, one where they do not rule here but we run the country. It will be like Baltimore, where we send a duty off to our Lord and they leave us to run things as we see fit."

"Except they want slaves as well," Bridgit said flatly.

"One shipload of criminals a year. The ones we would be sentencing to death anyway," Fallon replied.

She shook her head at him. "You need to speak to me before making these decisions."

He laughed. "This is not about whether we get a new chair carved! This is the future of these people. Aidan warned me with his dying breath that my choices could doom Gaelland. I can't risk that. You don't understand what it is like, having so many depending on you—"

"Are you mad?" she demanded. "What do you think I have been doing? I risked everything to bring these people home, and I will not risk any of them being sent back! You have to tell me what is going on, so we can decide together."

"What you went through was terrible. But you can't compare it to what I am doing—"

"Oh, really?" she growled. She hadn't been back for a turn of the hourglass and already he was driving her mad. She took a deep breath. "Put that aside. Listen to me. Nothing Kemal says is true."

He looked at her strangely. "So are you pregnant or not, like he told me? And was he right in saying the baby is not his, nor any of his men's?"

She staggered back, feeling as if she had taken a blow to the head. That was her special news, the thing she wanted to tell him quietly tonight, when everyone had gone away and definitely when Kerrin was asleep. Now Kemal had dared to tell Fallon? He had ruined what was an intensely intimate moment between her and Fallon. What they had gone through, what she had endured over the past twenty years had nearly broken her. It had created something between them, something nobody else could understand. It had nearly destroyed her this time. That was her news!

Some of that must have shown on her face because Fallon reached out for her. She knocked his hand away. This was too much.

"Yes, I am pregnant." She managed to force the words out. "Maybe two moons in. Aroaril willing, we will have another child. I wanted to tell you tonight, when it was just us—"

She could say no more and he jumped in, ignoring her outthrust arm, and gathered her up.

"We will keep this one," he said fiercely. "I know it."

These thoughts were too painful, coming on top of everything else that she had endured. She could not answer him. It was all she could do not to lose all control.

"How dare he say that? How dare he take that from me?" she hissed.

"I am sorry. I cannot imagine what you have been going through, having that on top of everything else," Fallon said gently. "And of course I trust you. But I have made so many mistakes, been so scared that I will make a decision that will destroy the country. I fear holding on to Feray might protect me but doom Gaelland. And I swore on Kerrin's life to return them."

"You vowed for Aroaril to take Kerrin if you break your word?" She clenched her fists at the thought. "How could you do such a thing?"

"I am sorry," he said helplessly.

She closed eyes that burned with tears of many types. This was not a time to be making these sorts of decisions! "He has a fleet out there," she said. "If we give him his family, he will return with them and seek revenge. You have to make him wait, make him reveal them. Once he has sent them back to Kotterman then you can give him his family and his treaty."

He kissed her head and she felt the strength of that kiss travel all the way through her. "I shall look him in the eyes. I have broken him before and I will know when he is lying. Stay strong."

*

Kemal watched impatiently as his agent, Abbas, rowed a small boat across the harbor to the far side of his vessel, then scrambled up a rope to get to the deck.

"I set off as soon as I saw your ship, high one," Abbas puffed as he bowed.

"There is no time for that," Kemal said irritably. "Tell me quickly, who rules here and what has been happening in my absence?"

He listened impatiently, one eye on the other ship, wondering when he would see Fallon reappear, while Abbas described the death of King Aidan, how the Duchess had first taken control but had now been restricted to a townhouse while Fallon ran the capital.

"He has been creating an army, high one. It is a rare day they do not train through the streets. They use the rooftops and plan to entangle any force in the tight streets," Abbas explained.

"Interesting," Kemal tugged on his beard. He remembered the streets of the capital and how tight and twisting they were. Even a small force could hold up a much larger one there.

"The Princess Feray has been staying at the former King's castle and is never without a large guard. But my men have seen her out walking in the courtyard most days, while your sons play a game with Fallon's son."

Kemal found all this very useful. "So will Gaelland respect a treaty he makes?"

"He is honored and respected, high one. King Aidan had him kill your father's three bodyguards, the ones Aidan wanted in the first place, and he revealed that their doings were part of the King's plan. The people think him a hero."

"And can he hold on to Berry? Or will Swane try to take it back?"

"I am sure the Prince will want to. But the people will stand with Fallon."

Kemal dismissed the man with a nod. He had used a code with Feray to discover some of Fallon's story was true but it was always good to have that confirmed. It was very interesting. The man was a peasant, yet he had risen to control the country. That was something his father would never let happen. Fallon and Bridgit were dangerous, for having overthrown one ruler, they would be naturally thinking of overthrowing any others. Although Fallon's idea for a new treaty could work, he could not trust them to hold to any bargain.

But he had to get his family back.

Gokmen interrupted his thoughts politely. "High one, Fallon approaches again."

Kemal saw the Gaelish leader standing defiantly on the other ship's deck, arms crossed and no sign of a new treaty or, worse, his family.

"Watch him carefully," Kemal ordered. He did not think this was a trap but, after what happened last time, did not plan to meet with Fallon without at least a company of archers to watch for treachery. He took a deep breath and crossed back onto the other ship. The last moon of worry and fear had been exhausting. Now to know his wife and sons were almost close enough to touch and yet out of reach was excruciating. Part of him wanted to order his soldiers forward, to take his family back by force. But the rest of him wanted to defeat Fallon himself, the way he did every night. Only then could he have peace. Kemal could never forget this was the man who had used a blacksmith's hammer on his toes and then held a knife to Orhan's eye. His foot gave a sympathetic twinge at the memory. "Have you drawn up the treaty yet?"

Fallon shook his head. "What about this fleet that you have waiting beyond the horizon? You need to send them home before we can sign anything."

Kemal let nothing show on his face. "I have no fleet," he said calmly. "I have two other ships, which were searching for your wife and the rest of your families, because I knew they had not taken enough food to last them the trip and nor did they have any maps showing them the way home. They know to meet up with me at a point a hundred miles away in the next quarter moon. If I do not appear by then, they will come here to see if something has happened to me. But what good are two ships to me? Do you really think I am so arrogant that I can take your entire country with so few? And we cannot wait for them to arrive here. Your winter is almost upon us. If we linger, we could all be lost. If that happens, then Gaelland will be utterly destroyed in the spring when my father comes to take revenge for my death. Your only chance is to get me back to Kotterman, healthy and happy, with your new treaty. Otherwise you will see the full fury of the Kotterman Empire."

Fallon unfolded his arms but still made no move to produce either a treaty or Feray. "But that's what you would say, if you had a fleet out there ready to take your revenge now."

Kemal stepped closer and let some of his frustration and anger leak into his voice. "I am not playing games here," he said. "I want my family back. I am willing to make a new treaty with you but do not make the mistake of thinking I will give you anything you want.

You tricked me, tortured me and held my wife and children, remember? If you break the deal we made before, then I know I cannot trust you and any treaty you sign will be just to give you enough time to build a new army to defy us. So I am giving you a choice. Give me a treaty and my family and I will sail away and help preserve Gaelland. Or break our deal and I will sail back to my father and unleash a vengeance on you in the spring that will make every other province in our Empire shudder in fear. Choose now."

He crossed his arms and stared at Fallon, letting some of his bitterness leak out of his eyes.

"And your family? What of them then?" Fallon asked.

"I shall mourn them on the way home, for I know that you will never let them go. And then I shall avenge them."

He glared at Fallon, locking eyes with the man, just as he had done that fateful night when Fallon had held a knife to Orhan's face. That night, Kemal had blinked and it was a memory that burned his soul. He would never do that again, no matter what it cost. But now, just as he feared he was going to have to sail away and mourn his family, the Gaelish leader was the one to blink.

"Wait here. I have scribes preparing the treaty documents now. I shall have refreshments sent to you and we shall exchange treaties and then, if all is agreed, we will bring you your family," he said.

Kemal almost staggered from the weight of relief that dropped into his chest. But he would rather burn in the pits of Zorva before showing any of that to Fallon. "I am pleased you have seen sense. Both our peoples will be grateful for this day. Let it be so," he said.

He watched Fallon walk away and turned his back before he closed his eyes and offered up a small prayer. Aroaril willing, everything would work out now. It was not the same as taking back that fateful night when Fallon had broken him but it was a first step.

*

"Have we got the scribes? Get the treaty drawn up, then get drinks and food for the signing, as well as supplies for their trip home," Fallon announced as he walked back down the gangplank.

Bridgit broke away from Brendan and hurried to his side. "What are you saying? Does this mean you have agreed to give his family back?"

Fallon sighed. "It was either have a treaty now or he would walk away and return in spring to burn Gaelland. I looked into his eyes when he gave in before and agreed to bring you back. But there was no give in his eyes this time. You were both right and wrong. He was prepared to let his family die in exchange for his revenge. The revenge meant more to him than they did."

Her shoulders sagged for a moment, then her eyes blazed. "It is not too late," she said. "We can—"

"Bridge, it is done," he interrupted. "The die is cast and we must hope that Feray can bring him to his senses. She could be our best weapon against a Kottermani attack. Staying here just means there *will* be an attack, one we cannot hold back. We have no choice but to trust he will uphold the treaty we will sign."

"I hope you do not regret this moment," she warned.

He let out a bark of humorless laughter. "You are not the only one," he said. "But at least it gives our people a chance. And I need you to support me. If we are to make it through this, then we need to work together."

"As long as you listen to me, there will be no problems," she assured him.

CHAPTER 51

Kemal watched the harbor of Berry slip past on either side before nodding to Gokmen. "I shall be going below to my cabin. Sail to our meeting point and tell me when we reach it," he ordered.

"Your will, high one," Gokmen bowed.

Kemal walked past his men without a backward glance. They had watched him sign the new treaty and drink a glass of wine with Fallon without emotion. He was also proud he had welcomed his family back without any fuss. The men had been told his family had stayed behind in Gaelland as proof the new land was safe. He did not know how many believed it, nor did he care. Their lives were forfeit if they even whispered of it. But now there were no cursed Gaelish watching, so he hurried below.

He flung open the door and Asil and Orhan flung themselves into his arms. He fell to his knees and held them close, kissing them both on the head and feeling them sob into his shoulders.

"You are safe now. Nobody will ever hurt you again," he promised. He held them tight. Finally they stopped crying and he stopped needing just to smell their hair and feel them in his arms and he stood, releasing them gently.

"Go and wash and change," he told them. "There are fresh clothes for you – you no longer need to wear those Gaelish items."

Accustomed to obeying him, the boys began to move off, then rushed back and hugged him again. He patted their backs until Asil took Orhan's hand, leading him to their adjoining cabin space.

Kemal watched them go and then turned to see Feray standing at the window. Wordlessly he strode across and held her.

"I died a little each night without you," she said softly.

"I am sorry. It was my fault you were taken and put into Fallon's hands," he said, drawing back a little from her. "Did he treat you with respect?"

"He did. He showed he is not the monster of that night when he hurt us. And he also saved the boys and me when the mad King Aidan took us and wanted to offer our hearts to Zorva. He risked his life for us. He, alone and barely armed, took on a King, a Prince, a Fearpriest and a whole roomful of Zorva-worshippers to save us. His son, Kerrin, even became friends with Asil and Orhan. When we return, I am sure they would like to—"

"That will not happen," Kemal said harshly.

"What do you mean? I thought we had a new treaty with the Gaelish?"

Kemal produced his sealed copy of the treaty, ripped the wax open, tore the parchment into pieces, then threw it into the sea. He turned back to her. "There is no treaty. There never could be a treaty with one like him."

"But I do not understand," Feray said. "You agreed, gave your word. And Fallon is the leader of the Gaelish, we need to deal with him—"

"I will never deal with that bastard!" Kemal spat. "I have spent the last moon dreaming of my revenge on him for what he did. Every night I relive that night when he threatened Orhan and made me do his bidding. Every fiber of my spirit cries out for vengeance. I have to humiliate him to restore my pride. That will always be between us and I must wipe out that stain."

She reached out and grabbed his hand. "There is no stain," she insisted. "You did what you had to, to protect your family. He was driven to it by the need to get his family back."

He snatched his hand back. "I never thought you would defend him, after he held a knife to our son's face!"

Feray reached out again, this time with both hands. "He fought for us, faced down real monsters disguised as men. I have to respect that and I have talked with him, seen he is a man not unlike you—"

"He is nothing like me!" Kemal snarled, outraged at the thought. "And saving you means nothing. If it were not for him, you would never have been at risk."

She hung on to his hand. He was tempted to pull away but it had been so long since they had been together.

"What will you do?" she asked.

He let a smile creep across his face at the thought. It had taken a steady nerve and a quick tongue but he had finally turned the tables on Fallon. "I have seven other ships. They will meet us a day away from here. Then we shall return at night and take our revenge. I shall have a force of more than two thousand men. More than enough to strike at Berry and take the city. Without King Aidan, the country is ripe for the picking. I can secure Gaelland and return to Adana with Fallon and his family in chains to drag before my father and take a leisurely revenge."

She pulled her hands away from his. "So you sat there and lied to them? Signed a treaty you intended to break?"

He stared at her in surprise. He had expected her to be delighted with his cleverness and applauding his acting skills. "I did what I had to, to free you!"

"I told them you could be trusted," she said, her voice almost a wail.

"Good! Anything that helped fool that bastard. When next we see him, he will be in chains and groveling at my feet. And then the dreams will stop and I shall be a true man again," he said, the thought of it filling him with a delicious joy.

Next moment she was in his arms again and he kissed her lightly. This was more like it!

"My love, do not do this," she pleaded. "You do not need to prove your manhood and you lost nothing by agreeing to Fallon that night. You saved us and now we are all together again."

Her hand slipped down his body, just as it did in his dreams every night. But he did not react to it. He did not want to hear he had no need of proving his manhood. He wanted her to see him for a true man. He stepped back.

"My love, Fallon is a better ruler to deal with than the mad King Aidan and his Zorva-worshipping son. Think of what is best for the Empire—"

"This is best for me, which is best for the Empire," he said. "There will be no ruler in Gaelland but me and then, when the Gaelish are cowed, one of my brothers can take over so I am free to sit on the Elephant Throne. Now, no more about it. We shall wash and dress and eat together. We must make up for the time we have lost."

She opened her mouth again but he placed his finger across her lips. He could see in her eyes that she wanted to keep arguing but his mind was clear. Fallon must pay for his crimes. Give him a couple of days to relax and then the trap would snap around him and the dreams would stop, replaced by Fallon on his knees, weeping and pleading helplessly for the lives of his family.

CHAPTER 52

Duchess Dina watched the cheering crowds from her window, sourly, seeing the joy of families reunited. She should be at the head of the parade. She should be receiving the cheers. Without her, this would never have happened. But that bastard Fallon had been unable to see what she had done to help him. Ungrateful wretch. It wasn't as if she had ever set out to harm anyone. She was just trying to make the best of a bad world.

She had thought she would enjoy being the Duchess of Lunster, although that enjoyment swiftly palled. Rather than spend most of his time in Berry, her husband Kinnard stopped that life and instead stayed in Lunster, which was a foul pit, denying her the adulation and luxury she deserved as his wife.

Then he had to get on his high horse and defy his cousin the King, declaring he would not have any part of Aidan's plan to use Zorva to defeat the Kottermanis. What choice did she have? When your King tells you to silence someone or you will die too, naturally you make the choice to survive. The fact he promised the county would stay hers and dangled the possibility of marriage had almost nothing to do with it. It was a shame that guardsman she had prepared botched the job and sent the ship in to Baltimore rather than into the cliffs, but that was hardly her fault, now was it?

Yes, she had helped the Kottermanis take her people but that was inescapable. It was part of Aidan's plan and, once she had helped him by killing her husband, there was no refusing him. But she had not liked doing it and had tried to help Prince Cavan. Aidan was a madman and she would have happily seen Cavan take the throne – especially if she could be sitting beside him when he did so. But the Prince had not grasped the possibility and, when the King had talked about making her his Queen, what could she do but to help him with that? It wasn't her fault that men fell over themselves to fall for her.

Of course the mad bastard had then let Meinster drip honeyed words of poison into his ears, so he agreed to marry the Earl's daughter instead. That meant all deals were off and she could help Fallon, as she always wanted to do. That had worked well, for a time, until the fool of a guardsman blabbed his mouth off and Fallon was too stupid to grasp what she had done for him and turned on her.

She glared out of the window. It was not her fault! The men around her were the dimwits who had tricked her and forced her to do what she must to survive. She had never intended to hurt anybody, just to make her way in this wicked man's world. And then they looked down their nose at her and accused her of treachery! Well, if that was how they insisted on seeing things, then she must look elsewhere for advancement. And where else was there to go but to Prince Swane?

"Duchess?"

The man's deep voice disturbed her contemplation but she turned from the window with a smile. Munro was pretending to be an expert dressmaker at the moment but his real job was being head of the King's informers. The former chamberlain, Regan, had had quite the network spread throughout Berry, keeping an eye and an ear on what people were doing and saying. She had found all the details in the King's papers and taken over the running of the network. Yes, maybe she should have said something to Fallon about it, but he would not have grasped how important such a network could be. He might have even demanded it be destroyed. And, given the way things had turned out, she had been right to keep it from him.

Once Fallon had betrayed her and stuck her in this gilded prison, she had been able to get word out for Munro so at least she knew all that was going on in the city – even if she could do nothing much with that information.

"What is the latest news from Prince Swane?" she asked.

"He is locked in Meinster, as much a prisoner there as you are here, your grace," Munro replied. "He does not have the ships to sail to Berry, nor can he cross the mountain passes at this time of year, especially without a base on this side. Without any of the nobles here to help him, he is stuck in the country's east. So our message has intrigued him. He wants to know more."

"Was there any mention of my previously helping Fallon? Did he indicate I will have a place high in his favor if we can regain his kingdom?"

"Duchess, that I cannot say. I learned long ago not to try to predict the mood of the nobility," Munro said simply.

Dina chewed her lip. She was confident she could do much to bring down Fallon, but it was only worth risking if she knew Swane would reward her. An exchange of scrolls was not enough reassurance. She needed to look Swane in the eye.

"I need to get out of here," she said abruptly. "I know things about the Guild of Wizards that their ruling council would not want made public. They will have to help me. With magical help, I can make sure Swane gets over the mountains. And then the nobles around here will open their warehouses to the prince, if I speak to them first and remind them of the promises they made to Aidan, promises I found in his papers. Finally, with your help, we can open a gate into Berry for Swane's men. Yet I need to speak to these people myself, both to convince them and to make sure Swane knows it is me he has to thank for returning him to his throne."

"But your grace, we have discussed this before. There are too many guards on this house. I have some men who can sink a knife into a back but no one trained for this," Munro said carefully.

"We need a distraction. Something to summon most of the men away from here. Perhaps a fire."

"Your grace, we would need more than a distraction. We would need something big to happen to take away the attention of so many guards," Munro warned.

"Something will occur to me," she said confidently. "Get the men ready and have them nearby. I will get out of this and I will make Fallon rue the day he ever turned on me."

*

Fallon held Bridgit close.

"I should have been there. I should have listened to you when you warned me," he said softly.

An exhausted Kerrin had been finally put to bed, still protesting he was fine, and now had Caley snoring away with him in one room. Fallon had felt bound to offer the dog back to Dermot, her original owner, but Caley listened carefully and then stayed with Fallon. Dermot agreed it was the dog's choice.

Finally, Fallon and Bridgit began to tell each other what had been happening for the past moon.

He listened in horror to her tale, although the horror soon turned to pride at what she had done. "I always said you would surprise yourself with the strength you have inside."

"I would have been happier not to have to find it," she said wryly.

He grimaced at the deaths of Sean and Seamus, although a little regretful he couldn't try something similar on them himself, and shuddered as she told him of the escape and the fight to make it back across the sea, how they had nearly starved and then run into Kemal.

"You did something to him when you took his family, and he cannot forgive you," she finished.

Fallon was not listening to that, still overcome with the thought of all she had been through, how she had held the people together.

"Your father was right. I should have just sailed for Kotterman and tried to get you all back, so you did not go through that," he sighed.

"You probably would have died," she said flatly. "It would have been a slaughter and, even if you got most of us out, they would have chased us and sunk us all."

"But still—"

"I am back now, and safe. It has all worked out."

"But so much could have gone wrong! And you did it all while pregnant!"

She closed her eyes for a moment. "Not all of it. I did not realize at first."

"But—"

"Will you stop saying 'but'! I am here, you are here, we are safe and alive. We should give thanks to Aroaril for that."

He hugged her closer still. "This baby will be a symbol," he said. "It shows that our lives have changed and our luck with it. After all we have been through, surely we deserve this child."

"I thought we deserved all of them," Bridgit whispered.

"You know what I mean."

"When the child is born, then I can relax. Not before," she said. "Then I might believe that it is recompense for all we have been through."

"I will protect you. You, Kerrin and the new baby," he swore.

"Don't make promises you may not be able to keep. We might have to protect you," she said, poking him in the chest. "What have you been doing while I was away?"

Fallon hesitated. He had made so many bad decisions, what would she think of him? Then he began anyway. Talking about it with her might lift some of the guilt he had carried.

*

Bridgit too listened with a mixture of horror and sympathy as Fallon's tale grew: the escape from Lunster, saving Cavan, fighting the spawn of Zorva, being unable to help Kerrin, Fearpriests, killing Cavan, becoming a hero to the city and then killing Aidan.

"Now you are back with me, everything will be fine. We have Berry and the west and south now and in the spring we shall take the rest of the country. We can make Cavan's dream of a better Gaelland come true. With you by my side, what is to stop us?"

She stroked his cheek. "It may not be that easy," she warned. "Swane will not sit back and let us take his kingdom. And then there are the Kottermanis ..."

He stroked her face fondly. "In the daylight we have lookouts scouring the horizon. And at night we have the boom placed across the harbor each night, fishing boats tied together to make a barrier with men patrolling it. If Kemal tries to play us false, he will get a horrible surprise. I have trained the men to fight Kottermanis in the streets and we'll drive them into the sea and capture him and his family. The only Kottermanis left are a couple of merchants and we are keeping an eye on them."

She sighed. "I hope you are right. But I still feel uneasy about him."

"That is only to be expected, after what you went through. But you are safe now and I swear to Aroaril that I shall never let anything happen to you again."

She shivered a little at that.

"What would I do without you?" he asked.

"Well, Aroaril only knows, because you managed to get yourself into quite the pickle here," she said with a smile, trying to forget his earlier promise.

"I missed you so much. Like my heart had been cut out."

She kissed him then. "Enough talking," she said. "We can talk more later."

"There are so many more things—" he began, but she reached down.

He grabbed her hand. "But what about the baby?" he asked hoarsely.

"After all it has been through so far, I don't think this will worry it," she said.

CHAPTER 53

Kemal inspected the sky carefully. His fleet had been buffeted by a short, sharp storm the day before, giving them a taste of what it would be like in another moon or so. He could not wait any longer.

"High one, we are ready," Gokmen announced. "The attack ships only await you."

Three of the ships had been converted over the past two days, their masts taken down and the soldiers transferred there. Skeleton crews would sail three of the other ships, towing the attack ships into position, where they could row into the harbor after dark. The other two ships would stay out to sea overnight and then sail into Berry in the morning, when the harbor had been taken.

Kemal ignored the former slave master and turned instead to his agent. "Your men are ready, Abbas?" he asked.

"I shall return there now and then we will strike, two turns of the hourglass before dawn," Abbas promised. He had sailed out, hidden in the hold of a small fishing vessel, crewed by a pair of Gaelish that were being very well paid for their efforts. He had brought with him vital information about the harbor defenses.

"They will not trouble you?" Kemal asked.

"They think I carry important cargo and I have been careful not to say anything in their language they might understand. When we return, two of my men will dispose of them. By the time they are missed, it will be too late."

Kemal nodded in approval. He had left two score of his soldiers with Abbas when he left a moon before, in case a rescue of Feray and the boys could be arranged. Now those men would kill the guards on the floating boom made of boats and then open it up to Kemal's ships. Without their masts, the ships would be much harder to see and, once on the docks, would pour soldiers onto Gaelish soil. Abbas's men, who had spent the last moon learning Berry's streets, would then guide them through the darkened capital. If all went to plan, Fallon would wake to discover Kemal was inside his castle and he was at the mercy of the Kottermanis. Then he could make sure he had Gaelland firmly in his hand while he took his leisurely revenge. If something went wrong then he had a second plan, to turn Fallon's strategy against him.

"I shall see you at the docks, high one." Abbas bowed and hurried away.

Kemal looked up at the sky. It was mid-afternoon and all that remained to be done was ensure his men were fed and well rested for their night's work. He leaned on the ship's rail and imagined his nightmares over, with Fallon in his grasp.

A gentle hand touched his shoulder and he knew without looking it was Feray. Nobody else would have dared. "Are you sure about this, my husband?" she asked softly.

"Did that Gaelish bastard put some sort of spell on you?" he asked. "Why else would you take his side in this?"

"I am on nobody's side but yours," she said angrily, her eyes flashing. She looked beautiful that way and it only reminded him more sharply of what he had lost that night to Fallon. He had thought, after being without his wife for more than a moon, that they would sleep little that first night. Yet he had found himself unable to be a man for her. It had to be Fallon's fault. Until he brought Fallon down, he would not be able to rise. Her sympathy had only put even more of an edge on his temper.

"I think of what your father might say. Of how this will be explained," she continued.

"He will hear about Gaelland being brought into the Empire and that is all he will want to know. I shall tell him that Aidan and his sons fought back and were killed, removing that problem from our new rule," Kemal said icily.

"But what if you lose? What if they are ready for you?"

He laughed. "They are but peasants. We are warriors. And we have Abbas. He knows what they have been doing. They do not stand a chance against us."

She reached out and gripped his arm. "My love, you have not seen them fight. I told you: Fallon took on a roomful of men to save me and your sons. The fact I am standing here now shows what a fighter he is. And his troops took down the King's guards in less than a turn of the hourglass. I have been without you for a moon. I could not stand to lose you for longer."

He turned away slightly. "I am no good to you now," he said bitterly. "I am but half a man. Fallon robbed me of the other half. I have to take it back."

She pulled on his arm. "You are still the man I love. And as for that, do not worry. It means nothing to me and it will return to you soon. Maybe even now. Let me show you—"

"It means everything to me," he said coldly. "Manhood is not something that can be given. It can only be taken. I shall return to you as a real man once more."

He knew she wanted to say more but it was simple to him. Seize back his honor and return to her a man, the new ruler of Gaelland.

"Gokmen! I leave now! You will watch my family as if they were your own until I return!" he shouted.

*

He brooded on the slow trip into Berry. Abbas had said the Gaelish would use their cramped, twisting streets as a weapon, while springing ambushes from the rooftops. He planned to split his force into two, where each could come to the aid of the other if they became held up, while his archers had been told to look to the rooftops at all times. Despite Feray's words, he had no doubt his men were much better fighters. Against men who were half-asleep and disorganized, it would be easy.

They took care to stay out of sight until night fell, then the attack ships were towed to within a mile of the harbor, then the rowers bent their backs. The ships were not designed to be rowed but it was a short trip. Lanterns along the boom, thoughtfully provided by the Gaelish, showed them where to go. The signal that Abbas had the boom in control was to see the lanterns raised and lowered repeatedly. Kemal watched for that sign while, packed onto the deck of his ship, soldiers waited for their chance to bring a new province into the Empire.

*

Brasso was bored. Not just a little bored but hugely bored. Not to mention cold, wet, miserable and hungry. Back when ships had been disappearing, walking the boom at night must have been exciting, nerve-racking and fearful. Every noise could have been selkies. Keeping watch for Kottermani ships was just not the same. Walking up and down these stinking fishing boats for four turns of the hourglass was not his idea of fun. It wasn't why he had sweated and trained with Captain Fallon for so long. Tonight was cold, with a persistent drizzle that worked its way under his cloak and ran down his back. He trudged on, hunched against the weather, praying for the bell that announced each turn of the hourglass. Just two more and it would be dawn and he could go and have a hot breakfast – and go back to sleep. Maybe even find a woman who was impressed that one of Captain Fallon's recruits had kept the city safe through the night.

A splash made him turn out towards the sea. The sound of rain on the boat timbers and on the hood of his cloak had dulled his senses but he was sure that sounded like an oar. But who would be out in this weather, at this time of night?

He strained to see something though the gusting rain, then heard a muffled cry from the next boat over. He looked across to see figures struggling in the light cast by the lantern hanging from the boat's mast, a lantern that was now swinging wildly as men fought on the boat. Even as he watched in horror, a sword flashed in the dim light and someone went down. The other two men kneeled over the body, stabbing down again and again.

Brasso realized, with a spurt of fear that banished the cold, that the guard on the next boat was dead. And for attackers to have got that far, they had to have killed everyone else that side. He turned in the other direction and began to run, desperate to get away and sound the alarm. Except there were figures there too, looming out of the darkness. A sword swung at his neck and he jumped backwards, fumbling to get his blade out. But it was caught in his wet cloak and, as he struggled, another sword sliced at him. It cut along his chest and, worse, overbalanced him so he went backwards into the freezing water with barely a time for a shout.

*

Abbas tapped his bloodied knife on the mast of the center boat and received answering knocks in reply. He smiled in relief. The boom was theirs and no alarm had been raised. He snapped out orders and his men sawed at the wet ropes holding the boats together. One by one they parted, then the men took up oars and began to row the boats apart, opening a gap through the middle more than wide enough for the ships to come through.

Once he judged they were far enough apart, the lanterns hanging from the masts were raised and lowered, again and again, a signal for the Prince's ships that Berry lay defenseless before them.

*

Brasso hung on to a rope with one hand while he frantically kicked off his boots and untied his cloak with the other. He was a child of the water, having grown up on boats, and the distance to the docks was not far. Except he had never tried to swim in heavy wool clothes before, nor with his blood leaking into the water with every heartbeat. The wound on his chest hurt like the pits of Zorva but it told him he was still alive: something not one of his fellow boom guards could say. Part of him wanted to climb back on board the boat and get some revenge. But the rest of him said he had to raise the alarm. He kicked off his trews and shivered. Time was running out. The cold water would kill him as surely as a knife. He pushed away from the boat and began to swim towards the lights of the dock, trying not to think about what might be coming through the boom after him.

*

Kemal saw the faint lights moving up and down and clapped his hands with delight, feeling the excitement of the hunt course through him. He had waited in the dark just outside the harbor, pacing up and down the deck as he imagined things going wrong. The rain was both a blessing and a curse – it would help disguise their presence but the water would stretch the archers' bowstrings and reduce their range and power.

"Now!" he cried.

The sailors bent to their task, driving the ships through the water. Now was not the time to worry about noise, only speed, and they formed into single file, Kemal's ship at the front, driving for the widening gap between the lanterns. His men wanted his to be the third of the ships through but he would rather burn in Zorva's pits for an eternity than wait any longer. The ships tore through the gap in the boom and headed right for the marked place on the docks, where more of Abbas's men stood, waving more lanterns in the rain. Kemal clenched his fist. Everything was going to plan and the Gaelish did not even know he was loose in their city.

*

Brasso reached the nearest jetty and reached up with a half-frozen hand for a tarred rope that hung down from the wooden platform. His feet and hands felt like lumps of ice and, blessedly, he had long since lost feeling in his balls. Yet his chest still hurt. He hung on the rope, panting, knowing that his strength was slipping away with every heartbeat. It was dangerously tempting to give up and let the cold claim him. But Captain Fallon was relying on him. The Kottermanis were in the harbor and, unless he raised the alarm, would be in the city soon after. With a cry that was half defiant shout, half agonized groan, he hauled himself up and out of the water, lying on the rough wooden jetty. Again he wanted to just lie there but he could not let the bastards win. Not when they had killed his mates, cut him and left him to die in the freezing water. He rolled to his feet and pushed himself into a rough trot. He had come this far. They would not beat him.

*

Bran had his feet up on the harbormaster's table, enjoying the warmth from the fire and trying not to watch the sand trickle through the hourglass, which would mean he had to go out in the wind and the rain to check on the guards. It felt like a pointless guard duty but Fallon had ordered it, so there he was. The Kottermanis would not be out in this weather. They would be sailing for home. He did not want to go out in it, for Aroaril's sake! He was tempted to close his eyes but that would be setting a bad example to the rest of the guards, who sat around playing dice. A few moons back he would have gone to sleep anyway, but that was before he met Fallon. Being punched in the throat by the Captain had been a wake-up call for Bran. He had despised most of the officers, especially the coward Quinn and the brutal bastard Kelty, both dead now. But Fallon had shown him something different, and now he was an officer himself.

His memories were abruptly cut short by a thump at the entrance, sounding like a body hitting it. He jumped out of his chair and threw open the door, the rest of his men abandoning their dice game, to see one of his recruits hanging on to the lintel. He was soaking wet, without any trews on, and his shirt was torn and bloodstained. His face was white and he was shivering violently.

It took Bran a heartbeat to recognize him. "Brasso! What happened? Get him something warm to drink and a blanket," he snapped over his shoulder.

Brasso let go of the doorframe and lunged at him, frozen hands raking at his face and his breath coming in gasps. "Kottermanis.

In harbor. Everyone else dead," he gasped, then his eyes rolled up and he slumped towards the floor.

Bran lowered him to the floor but could not spare the time to take care of him.

"Get those lights out!" he ordered, darting out into the rain, blinking his eyes clear of the brightness and peering into the rain and the gloom. It took a few moments for his eyes to adjust and then he saw a small group of lanterns down by the Kottermani jetty, waving up and down. He looked out to the harbor and saw white water: big ships were moving through where the boom should be. Already they were closing in on the jetties and he realized, without Brasso, the first he would have known of it was when the rowers burst through his door. He cursed himself but did not take too long doing so, because time was running out. He was tempted to race down and kill the men with the lanterns but realized with a sick sense of horror that the harbor was lost. The only chance was to try and save the city.

"What do we do, sir?" one of his recruits asked.

"Drag Brasso over by the fire and cover him with a blanket. If he lasts until the end of this, and if any of us are still alive, we will come back for him. You four, race to Captain Fallon and tell him there are hundreds of Kottermanis in the harbor. I'll wake the guard company and block the main road to the castle, try and slow them down. Try to get back before we are all killed," Bran said. "Go now!"

His fastest men raced off towards the castle while he led the rest to where a company of men was sleeping in a nearby warehouse. The plan was to have them meet any advancing ship with a hail of crossbow bolts, but it was too late for that. He wiped rain out of his eyes and ran hard. Brasso had given them a chance. They owed it to him to use it.

*

Bridgit was nestled into Fallon when the horns sounded. They had just fallen asleep, having talked long into the night, trying to tell each other all that had happened since that terrible night in Baltimore. At first she thought it was a dream, then he sat bolt upright and she realized the alarm was for real.

"What's that?" she asked.

Fallon rolled out of bed, looking wide awake as he hauled on his trews. "That you were right and the Kottermanis are here," he said grimly. "I need you to stay here with Kerrin."

"I thought we weren't being apart again? I can lead men. I destroyed the Kottermani weapons during our escape," she said.

But he was not listening, instead running out of the room as he pulled a tunic over his head.

She cursed. Once she would have been happy to stay out of the way, but not now. Worse, it was obvious that Kerrin had spent far too much time with the recruits and even longer practicing his crossbow. He would be even more eager than she was to get into the battle. She cursed again and went looking for her son. On no account would he be allowed to join his father.

*

"Where are they?" Fallon demanded as he joined his friends and officers in the shadow of the gatehouse, where it was dry, even if still cold.

Gallagher pointed to four panting recruits, who leaned up against the wall.

"The harbor is lost. Kemal must have hidden men somewhere in the city. They opened up the boom and sailed in. Bran is slowing them down on the main road to the castle."

Fallon did not waste time kicking himself. "You know what to do. Your men have trained there often enough. They will be looking to strike through to the castle. Get to the rooftops, hit them from all sides, just as we planned."

"The roofs will be slippery. And the rain will slow down the bows," Devlin warned.

"The same for them. Get into the city as fast as you can. I'll take my company down and see if we can't save Bran and buy you some more time."

"Is that wise?" Gallagher asked.

"No, but I have to do it anyway. They want me more than anything. Once they see me, they will throw their main strength where I am. We can use that. And, besides, it will protect the rest of the city from them. See you down by the docks!"

*

Bran waited nervously. He had roused the guard company easily enough but the plan to block the main road out of the docks with burning wagons was doomed to failure in this rain. Instead the men had tipped the wagons onto their sides and then dragged barrels and boxes out to form a crude fighting step behind the shelter of the wooden vehicles. With most of his original squad and a hundred recruits, he had enough men to form a comfortingly thick barrier behind the wagons, but he had seen several ships breaking through the boom and Aroaril knew how many Kottermanis were coming.

The recruits were all nervous, while some were plainly terrified. They had been awoken abruptly and told they had to spend their lives holding this spot. He tried to encourage them but the rain was dampening spirits and strings on the dozen crossbows he had. Worse, they had woken some of the nearby people, who were watching from the shelter of doorways, despite his best efforts to get them away, or at least out of harm's way.

The thud of boots on cobbles told him something was coming, then the rain seemed to take on a different sound. It took him a moment to realize why.

"Arrows! Take cover!" he roared, ducking closer to the dripping wagons.

Next moment the wagons shook and rattled as arrows thumped home, or bounced off the cobbles with a sharp noise. Then the screaming started: a handful of men who had been too slow or had not heard his warning and been caught in the arrow storm.

The wounded were dragged into shelter as more arrows fell. The rest of them hunched into the shadow of the wagons, which splintered and groaned at the assault. Then it stopped as abruptly as it started and was replaced by cheering and the thud of many boots running.

Bran risked a glance over the top of the wagon to see a wave of Kottermanis flooding towards him.

"Up and at them lads!" he screamed, leaning down to haul up a recruit onto the barrel beside him.

Next second the Kottermanis struck the wagons, some of them trying to shove them over, others clambering up to slash and stab with swords.

But the wagons were too heavy to move and the Gaelish were higher up and most had spears, rather than swords. The recruit next to Bran lunged down, the leaf-shaped spearhead driving home into a Kottermani chest. The Kottermani shook and screamed and thrashed, nearly hauling the spear out of the recruit's hands and Bran had to grab hold of the haft to help, until the man fell off the other end. A Kottermani reached up to grab the shaft but Bran slashed downwards, opening the arm to the bone and breaking the elbow.

The recruit thrust again, his spear opening a throat and silencing a challenge and Bran risked a glance to the left and right. His young charges were standing firm, thrusting their spears and swords down to knock Kottermanis back. A handful of Kottermanis tried to push through the space between two wagons but a pair of Gaelish triggered their crossbows and sent Kottermanis flying, then both sides jabbed impotently at each other with swords that could not reach flesh. Bran leaned over and hacked down, feeling the shudder as his sword struck the back of a man's head, taking off part of his skull like a fresh-boiled egg.

To Bran's right a group of Kottermanis was forming a pyramid to get on top of a wagon, and he leaped down to race across to help the defenders there. He hurdled up onto a thick wooden box just as a Kottermani appeared above him and rammed his sword up into the astonished man's mouth. Hot blood poured onto hands made cold by the stinging rain and the Kottermani disappeared, only to be replaced by more. Bran hacked at knees, bringing one man tumbling down on their side of the wagons, where recruits rammed spears into his torso, despite his desperate cries.

One of the recruits rammed a spear into the groin of the Kottermani above him and the man's terrible scream cut through even the furious noise of fighting.

Bran wiped his face clear of blood and rain, the thick taste and smell making him want to vomit, and cheered on the recruits. They were suffering too – he saw one Gaelish spear grabbed and the recruit behind it hauled over the wagons and into the crowd of Kottermanis to be chopped to pieces. Kottermanis who made it over the wagons were slashing around themselves like men possessed and any who tried to match swords with them were cut down. But the spears proved a decisive advantage and the last of the Kottermanis on or over the wagons were brought down.

Bran shoved a wounded Kottermani off the top of the wagon but, instead of landing on the men below, he hit the cobbles with a wet thump. Bran peered out into the rain and saw the Kottermanis pulling back, dragging some of their wounded with them.

The ground in front of the wagons was a charnel house of severed limbs, blood and brains, with wounded men moving weakly and crying out in different languages, while on his side of the barricade, a dozen recruits were begging for help as their lifeblood leaked out onto the cobbles.

"We did it! Get the wounded moving back to the castle, then get ready for the next ones," Bran shouted.

The recruits cheered themselves, roaring out their delight at surviving and clapping each other on the back. Bran did not have the heart to tell them that worse would follow.

*

Kemal wanted his men off the ships as quickly as possible and, although they raced down the prepared planks to the empty docks, he still chafed at the delay. As soon as he had a company of about a hundred he sent them up the main road under the command of one of his boluk-bashi, leaders of a company, to scout the way.

He decided he would lead the main body up the road, while the second group was given over to his senior officer, or corbaci, a tough, seasoned veteran with an impressive moustache, called Nazim. Abbas and his men, fresh from their exploits in opening the boom, would lead them around the back, ready to come in at the castle from behind, or crush Fallon's forces as they tried to fight back. This regiment had further to go and so he let them get organized first: a thousand of his best men, almost all of them with bows. The rest of his force, about fifteen hundred soldiers and sailors, would crash their way through from the front.

He finally had them ready, as Nazim and Abbas led the other wing off into a dozen small alleys and a maze of warehouses. But before they could begin, the scout company came straggling back, dragging a score of wounded men with them.

The boluk-bashi, Mahir, a hulking man with a thick beard and a scarred face, bowed his head. "High one, they have barricaded the road and in such numbers that they turned us back."

"We cannot delay," Kemal snapped. "Forward!"

He set off at a run, knowing his men had to stay ahead of him. The wounded were left by the docks and Mahir overtook him swiftly, others forming a thick line between him and any Gaelish.

"What is the barricade?" Kemal asked as he slowed down to a jog.

"Wagons, high one. We tried to push them over but could not move them."

"They must be pulled down. One company to do that, one to keep the defenders occupied and the third to drop arrows down their throats," Kemal decided.

"What of our men attacking the barricade? Should the archers not hold off?" Mahir asked.

"We do not have time. Every moment gives the Gaelish a chance to fight back. We have to break that barricade."

"Your will, high one," Mahir said, and snapped out orders.

A few doors and windows opened as they went past, people looking out at what was happening. As soon as they saw the endless stream of soldiers, the doors were slammed shut again. Kemal ignored them – there was plenty of time to deal with them later.

The barricade was hard to see in the darkness and it was the smell of blood and opened bodies that first alerted him.

He slowed down as one company raced at the barricade with a roar, while another sent arrows hissing down through the air. In an instant there was fighting all along the barricade, as Gaelish thrust at his men with spears and swords and his soldiers fought back, both sides falling to the arrows that sprouted like magic across the top of the wagons.

But he was more interested in the other company, the one that jumped up and grabbed the wagon wheels on their side. More and more men hung on them and hauled them downwards. The defenders tried to shove them away with spears but they were almost out of reach, and those Gaelish who exposed themselves were easy meat for the swords below.

With a roar, one of the wagons began to tip, and Kemal watched in approval as his soldiers flung themselves at the top of it to haul it over. Men fell as it toppled and several had their hands crushed under the wheels, but the barricade was open and his men swarmed through.

The Gaelish fought back briefly, slashing and stabbing, but those on boxes and barrels were hauled down and hacked up, and the rest ran, sprinting down the road towards the castle, a company of Kottermanis in pursuit.

"Clear this away," Kemal ordered and his men hurried to obey.

"Their wounded, high one? Put them to the sword?" Mahir asked.

Kemal shook his head. "No. We will rule here. Killing their wounded might come back to haunt us later. Form up and press on. And have the archers watching the rooftops!" He remembered only too well what had happened when Fallon had trapped him before – the vicious hail of crossbow bolts that had slaughtered his guards.

He joined the middle of the march, acknowledging the men around him. The way to the castle was open and Fallon would not have time to stop him.

*

Bran looked over his shoulder, seeing the Kottermanis staying close. He had fought furiously to stop them pulling the wagon over but once it went, had bellowed for the Gaelish to run. Those too slow had been killed and he guessed he had barely sixty of his original number left. Most were spattered with blood and gasping for breath but all still held their weapons. Which meant they could fight. Time to really test the training, he decided.

"Hedgehog!" he roared and skidded to a stop, turning abruptly.

For a heartbeat he thought they were going to keep running and he would be torn apart by angry Kottermanis but then they stopped and turned too, clumping close together the way they had practiced endlessly, creating a thick spine of spears bristling with sharp points.

The Kottermanis barely had time to be astonished before they ran onto the blades, sharp spearheads ripping through armor and into ribs, stomachs, chests and throats. Men screamed as they were forced onto the points, then the Gaelish ripped out the spears and turned to run once more.

The Kottermanis gave a roar of fury and redoubled their efforts, closing faster.

Bran looked left and right and could see his men were struggling to keep going. The fighting had left them exhausted. Some were slipping on the rain-slicked cobbles and soon the stragglers would be dropping behind, where they would be slaughtered by the Kottermanis. He could not stand that, so there was nothing for it but to form line and fight.

"Again!" he shouted and he thought his heart would burst with pride when they obeyed him instantly, even though they had to know this meant their death.

This time the Kottermanis were prepared, and slowed down before running onto the blades. They waited, their numbers increasing by the moment.

"Give up or die!" one of them shouted in thickly accented Gaelish.

"Bog off!" someone cried back and Bran grinned in the darkness, panting for breath, as they all howled it at the Kottermanis. It was a fine gesture, even though the Kottermanis could not know what it meant.

"Show them how a Gaelishman can die!" he cried as the Kottermanis moved in.

And then the horns sounded.

CHAPTER 54

Fallon wanted to sprint down to where Bran had to be fighting desperately but exhausting his men was not going to help them fight, so he just had them march fast. The rain made that easier too, for everyone instinctively sped up and hunched together.

Doors and windows opened as they trotted past and while he shouted at the first few townsfolk to get back inside and lock themselves in, they ignored him and he saved his breath. Dawn was approaching but it promised to be a dull and dark day. If he knew they would all see the sunset he would have been happy to be rained on. There was no chance to try and sit back and see what was happening: he had to get in there and trust that all the training they had gone through was drummed into his men's heads and that they would fight as they had been taught. That just left him free to curse himself for not doing more to guard against a Kottermani attack. Kemal had fooled him and broken into the city. Thank Aroaril Bran had seen it and at least raised the alarm, but things were about to get desperate. The boom had been about giving him enough time to get his men positioned around the harbor so that when the Kottermanis landed, they walked into a trap. That chance was gone but the streets were still tight, tangled and in their favor. With luck he could still throw them back.

Shouts, screams and the clash of steel told him that Bran was close and he picked up the pace. "Sound the horns, let them know were coming!" he shouted. With no way to keep all the different groups in sight, they had instead worked on a series of horn calls to let all know what was happening.

Embattled shapes were materializing ahead out of the gloom, shadows cast across the cobbles by firelight from surrounding windows, obscured by fresh gusts of rain. He could see far fewer of his men than he had hoped, clustered together in a hedgehog. Drawing his sword he broke into a run, his favorite recruits tight at his shoulder.

Horn calls in the dark bellowed out their message and Bran's man parted in the middle, melting back and away so Fallon could lead the charge through the gap they created.

There was a thick pack of Kottermanis on the other side, although they were not in any formation, and he struck them before they could rectify that. A man loomed out of the darkness and he stabbed ferociously, feeling leather armor resist for a moment and then give beneath the razor-sharp steel, the blade driving deep into stomach before scraping against the backbone. He sawed the blade and the Kottermani shook like a hooked fish, his mouth open in a hoarse scream. Fallon ripped the blade loose, blood following in a stream, then stepped on the falling man and jumped at another, hacking down this time. The Kottermani blocked his blow but Fallon elbowed him in the face and then slashed the sword across the exposed neck as the soldier's head rocked back.

All around him, his men were tearing into the Kottermanis, the speed of their charge driving them deep into the enemy ranks. The surprise and ferocity made up for their lack of skill – this was not battlefield fighting but a cobbles brawl, where you were close enough to smell the spiced food on a Kottermani's breath as you fought him. Men stabbed, slashed, punched, kicked and clawed at each other. You could not teach this but it came naturally to the Gaelish, who had had to fight for each meal since they had been born.

Then the Kottermanis broke and streamed away and Fallon skidded to a halt. "Form up! Sound it!" he roared, looking around for his men with the horns.

A handful of his recruits, their blood up and maddened by the slaughter, raced after the Kottermanis, heedless of his calls, and he knew he would never see them again. But he had bigger problems. Like where were the rest of the invaders.

*

"I have to know what is going on out there," Bridgit said.

Padraig scratched his chin. "I will do what I can but it's dark and wet. I doubt even Fallon knows what is going on."

"Then find something. A bird perhaps, so we can watch what is happening," she insisted.

He looked doubtful. "It would have to be a bloody stupid bird to be out on a night like this." He sighed. "But of course I shall try."

*

"Bran? Where are you?"

The sound of clashing weapons and shouting men died away but the wounded still screamed and moaned as they thrashed and bled. A wounded Kottermani drew a knife and lunged at Fallon's leg but he saw the flash of steel in the firelight from a house opposite and stepped away, then kicked the man in the head, sending the knife flying.

The burly guardsman pushed through the ranks to his side. He was still heaving for breath and covered in blood, some of it his judging by the cuts on his arms and chest.

"They have more men coming. They had maybe three ships stuffed full," he said.

"We have more as well," Fallon said. "Can you fight?"

"Give me a few moments to catch my breath and I'll be beside you," Bran promised.

"Take your men to the back for now. Find some of the ones who have fought enough for now and have them drag our wounded back to the castle. We'll tighten up and find where Kemal's main force is. I have to let him know where I am so he comes for me."

"You want him to come for you?" Bran asked, his face invisible in the rain and dark but the incredulity in his voice easy to hear.

"I don't want him running off into the city. And besides, Gall, Dev and Brendan are nearby with their companies, ready to give Kemal a nasty surprise."

He patted Bran on the shoulder and then formed the recruits up into tight ranks, with shields in front, ranks of spears behind that. This time he stood in the third rank, where he could see what was happening, while keeping Bran and forty of his remaining men as a reserve behind.

"Advance!"

This was slower but they had less distance to go, because the Kottermanis soon appeared out of the rain. Unlike before, when they had been chasing a broken foe and had therefore split apart, now they were in tight ranks also. As soon as they saw the Gaelish, they stopped.

From behind their front ranks, bows snapped.

"Duck!" Fallon yelled, unnecessarily, as the men at the front raised shields and everyone else hunched down.

Most of the arrows bounced off shields but a dozen men went down, crying out as the arrows sank into their flesh. A recruit next to Fallon fell, gargling blood with a shaft in his chest, but all Fallon could do was take his spear as he collapsed.

"Get close to them!"

His men needed no second bidding and hurried forwards, struggling to keep their order as another volley of arrows arched towards them. The tight ranks of the Gaelish began to fray as they hurried forwards, and Fallon worried that they would break apart on the rigid block of Kottermanis.

"Tight! Stay tight!" he shouted but they did not listen.

He felt fear then, that his men would die – and then a new noise cut through the din in the street. With a surge of relief he recognized it was the snap of crossbows.

"Get them!" he screamed.

*

Gallagher peered over the dripping roof, using one hand to keep himself steady. The wooden shingles were unstable at the best of times but the rain had made them treacherous. There was no choice, though: they had to help Fallon.

"Loose!" he cried.

From both sides of the street, his groups aimed crossbows down and triggered them. The rain was affecting the strings, making them harder to wind back and robbing them of their power, but at this range it made no difference. The tight block of Kottermanis seemed to crumple at the edges as the quarrels found targets.

Below, the Kottermani archers immediately changed their aim from Fallon's men to the roofs above. Like the crossbows, their weapons were affected by rain and arrows pattered onto the roof with little of the brute force he had expected. Two of his men were hit, one in the arm, the other in the leg, but the Kottermanis were loosing blind into the dark, at men sheltering behind the crest of the roof. By contrast, Gallagher's men could just aim down at the street below and be sure of hitting something.

"Stay low! One more volley then we change to the next roof!" That was going to be a challenge, in the dark and the wet, but the shower of arrows landing around them said that staying there would be worse.

Then a cheer from the side streets told him the others were there.

*

Devlin held his men back, having them press tightly against the walls of the side street, so they could use the darkness. Men cursed as they stepped into unpleasant piles but he hissed at them and they kept their disgust silent. Ahead, he could see a solid block of Kottermanis. They were facing the other way and, although some were glancing down his street, there was almost no light to give him away.

When he judged they were as close as they could get without being seen he stepped into the center of the street and raised his sword. "Go!" he roared and led the charge.

They cheered as they followed him and, while the Kottermanis had the time to turn, they could not block him because he was striking at the right-hand side of the invaders' column – and they all held their shields in their left hands.

The Kottermani flank crumbled as his men struck home, their soldiers unable to turn and defend themselves because of the press of bodies. Devlin rammed his sword into a man's side and jerked it up and down before ripping it out in a gout of blood. The Kottermani next to his victim tried to stab him but a spear reached over Devlin's shoulder and tore open the attacker's throat. The Gaelish powered into the Kottermanis but Devlin could see the enemy soldiers were pressing forwards from either side of their alleyway, looking to cut off his men and then kill them.

"Back!" he shouted, his voice reaching over the screams, moans, ringing of steel on steel and butcher's sounds of metal in flesh.

Devlin grabbed one of his wounded men by the tunic and hauled him backwards. A Kottermani tried to stop him but he lashed out, his sword ripping across the man's face and tearing out his eyes. The agonized shriek gave his fellows pause and Devlin enough time to make it back into the side street. He almost threw the wounded man into the waiting men and backed away, calling his men into formation. As they had practiced so many times, the men with shields pushed to the front and spearmen stood behind. The street was narrow, only wide enough for a dozen men to stand side by side, and although the Kottermanis pushed after them, their greater numbers meant nothing in such close confines. The men with shields ducked down and covered up and let the spearmen do the damage, thrusting their long weapons into faces and bellies.

"Back it up, slowly now!" Devlin ordered, blinking rain out of his eyes. At least he hoped it was rain.

Then came what he was hoping for – one of Gallagher's groups had seen the fight and now crossbows snapped above, loosing quarrels into the tight street, where they thumped into heads and shoulders and rang loudly off the Kottermani steel helmets.

The Kottermanis drew back and Devlin pulled his men away, moving to his next position.

*

Brendan could see the Kottermanis marching past him had all their shields facing his men and knew he had drawn the harder task.

It would be a simple matter for them to form a shieldwall, but he was needed to break one apart. Getting back Nola and his girls had not stopped his lust for violence. He had seen the horror in his wife's eyes when he showed her his hammer, encrusted with the blood and brains of men he had killed and, worse, he had seen the pity there. It made him even angrier. He just had to think of the foul Kottermanis dragging away his family and all the hatred bubbled back to the surface. He did that now, summoning his fury, then led his men in a screaming charge down the street into the Kottermani left flank.

They instantly crouched into a shieldwall, just their shining mailed heads showing above the line of wood but he was not there to jab swords at them. He swung his hammer from left to right at head height, taking out three men. The first had his head pulped, the second got a crushed skull and the third was stunned senseless, all three of them falling and dragging down the men around them. Before they could recover, Brendan brought his hammer back around from right to left, this time at chest height. One Kottermani tried to block it with his shield but the force of the blow splintered his shield, smashed his arm and caved in his ribs, throwing him like a rag doll into his fellows.

The other Kottermanis drew back as Brendan brought his hammer up and slammed it down, crushing a Kottermani helmet down into its wearer's chest cavity. Now they really fell back and Brendan's men poured into the gap he had created, stabbing and jabbing at everything they could see. Brendan cursed at not being able to reach a new victim but none wanted to face him. He lengthened his grip and swung it down onto a Kottermani locked in combat with one of his Gaelish recruits. The man saw it and raised his shield, only to have his arm and shoulder crushed. As he reeled away his Gaelish opponent finished him with a thrust to the throat.

"Back! Back!" Brendan bellowed and his men obeyed, just as the Kottermanis tried to cut them off from the safety of the dark street behind. Brendan strode away, daring the Kottermanis to come and get him. None took up the challenge.

*

Fallon rejoiced: the tight block of Kottermanis stopped and seemed to fall apart as crossbow bolts fell on them from above and Devlin's and Brendan's companies struck them from either side. Fallon held his men back, judging his moment then, when the Kottermanis appeared at their most distracted, led them forward again. The Gaelish lines had tightened up as the Kottermani archers switched their aim to Gallagher's men on the roofs and they met the Kottermanis head-on.

For a few moments the Kottermani lines held, both sides snarling at each other over shields, pressed so close that they had no room to swing a sword. But the second and third ranks of Gaelish stabbed with spears and the Kottermanis had none of those – they began to fall, barely able to see the spears striking them in the dark and rain until it was too late, and the Gaelish pushed forwards, stepping over writhing bodies.

Fallon picked out a giant Kottermani soldier who was battering at the Gaelish line with sword and shield. He rammed his borrowed spear forwards, feeling it sink deep. The Kottermani fell, ripping the spear out of Fallon's hands, and he let it go, pulling out his sword instead.

The footing became treacherous as blood, bodies, bowels, shit and brains combined with the rain to make a kind of human mud. And if you slipped, you became a fresh part of this mud. The stench filled the nose and was enough to make you vomit.

"Keep going! Push them back into the sea!" Fallon shouted. He felt like they could not stop him.

*

After what Abbas had told him, Kemal had expected the Gaelish to attack them from the rooftops and from the side streets. But he had not been prepared for the viciousness of the attacks, nor for the effectiveness of the crossbows. His men's armor could not turn them back, despite the rain affecting their power. Yet he could not accept that the Gaelish were pushing his men back in a straight fight. That must not continue.

"Seal those streets off," he ordered his boluk-bashi Mahir. "I shall go forward myself."

"High one, surely it is better to stay back here, where it is safe," Mahir said worriedly.

Kemal knew he had good reason to worry. If anything happened to the Prince, the boluk-bashi's life would be forfeit, as would be the lives of his family. But that was not his concern.

"Nowhere is safe," he said.

He drew his sword and pushed his way through the soldiers towards where the Gaelish fought his men, both sides spitting and screaming and slashing at each other. Some of the soldiers turned to protest but then saw who it was.

"Soldiers of Kotterman! Why do you retreat?" Kemal roared into the night. "Are we to be humbled by these barbarians? I go to fight them. Do I go alone?"

The men around him howled their answer and, as one, pushed forwards. The Kottermanis being pushed back by the Gaelish ran into the men behind pushing forwards and both sides came to a stop, before the Kottermanis began to edge the Gaelish backwards.

"Do not stop, or I shall have to go forwards and kill them all myself!" Kemal bellowed and his men redoubled their efforts, hewing and hacking at the Gaelish with renewed vigor.

Kemal inspected them with satisfaction and looked around. Nazim should be in position by now. The Gaelish were brave but he had their measure now. Time to tighten the trap. He saw Mahir and beckoned the boluk-bashi over. "Take three companies and the last of Abbas's men and swing around to our left to surprise the Gaelish there. You know the plan."

CHAPTER 55

Devlin led his men in a fast march around the backstreets, aiming to meet up with the Kottermani advance further down and surprise them, perhaps even drive into the rear of their advance. He was more concerned about losing his way in the dark than anything else, so when the mass of Kottermanis poured out of the alleyways ahead, it took him a few moments to recognize them. They let loose with a volley of arrows that knocked over half a dozen of his men and made him realize how many of them there were.

"Back!" he shouted.

He raced away, hating having to leave wounded men behind, but knowing they could not rescue them and survive. Behind him, the Kottermanis poured through the streets in a silent wave, even more men than he had seen back on the main road.

For the first time that night, Devlin felt a touch of cold fear.

*

Gallagher saw the Kottermanis break cover and pointed them out to his nearest groups. "Sound the horns, we have to warn Fallon!" he shouted.

His men turned their crossbows on the new Kottermani advance but they replied with a huge cloud of arrows that forced the Gaelish to take cover. Men were struck and fell screaming. One group of a score or so was exposed on a roof where the

Kottermanis could hit them from two sides. In desperation, the survivors broke and ran, ignoring the long ladders they carried and trying to jump to safety instead. Five made it, two more fell screaming to the street below to hit with a wet thunk that Gallagher heard over all the other battle noise. He leveled his crossbow and loosed, then waved to his men without seeing whether he had hit anything.

"Pull back! Get out of here!"

*

Brendan raced around a corner and into a mob of Kottermanis. In an instant he was in the middle of them, driving them back with huge swings of his hammer. But the men with him were not so lucky, being swarmed under.

Brendan cried out his challenge, daring the Kottermanis to get him, and swords heaved in his direction. He crushed one swordsman, then a Gaelish sword saved him by turning away another thrust. A hand grabbed his shoulder and pulled him back.

"There are too many!" Craddock shouted, then lunged, letting a Kottermani run onto his blade.

Brendan hated to retreat but there was a small square there and the Kottermanis could use their numbers.

"Brendan! Now!" Craddock cried, blocking a sword thrust and then chopping off the wielder's hand with a return blow.

Cursing, Brendan turned and ran.

*

Fallon sheathed his sword when the horns began to blow. He had been trying to shore up his front line, but the Kottermani resistance had stiffened and they were now fighting like maniacs, while his own men were getting tired and losing their spears and, with them, their advantage.

He backed away, not really believing what he was hearing. Another Kottermani force on his left flank? Too many for Devlin and Gallagher to hold back? How many men did they have?

One thing was clear, it was only a matter of time before they emerged from some of these side streets and cut his men apart.

"Back! Fall back!" he cried. "Hold your lines!"

That was easier said than done, because the Kottermanis were pressing close.

"Hedgehog run!" he shouted.

That was one thing they all remembered and the rear ranks took several rapid steps back, allowing the front rank to turn and race away, opening up a gap between them and the Kottermanis. They ran for perhaps fifty yards then turned and reformed the lines, checking the Kottermani pursuit, which had been caught this way before.

"Keep going! Slowly!" Fallon ordered, racking his brain to think of where they could meet up with his friends and hold off this other Kottermani attack.

*

"They are in trouble. There is another Kottermani army coming around the back," Padraig said, his voice going hoarse. "A big one. Worse, they must know their way through the city, for they are sweeping around our men."

Bridgit knew her father's strained voice would not be from the magic use. "The city was our big advantage. If they know it as well, then Fallon is in trouble," she said.

"He needs more men," Padraig confirmed.

Bridgit felt a touch of panic, the old familiar fear that horrible things would happen, then took a deep breath and let it out. Not this time. Not if she had anything to do with it. "Where can we find some? Kerrin, you know."

He looked up at her uncertainly but she nodded and his brow furrowed in thought.

"Casey! He and twenty men are guarding the Duchess Dina in her house!" he exclaimed.

"That foul bitch," Bridgit spat. "That's a start. Padraig, can you send a bird to him? Guide him to meet up with Brendan's men?"

The old wizard sighed. "I can send him the bird but I can't make him understand it."

Bridgit grabbed a piece of parchment off the table Fallon had been using as a desk and, after checking there was nothing more important on the back, scribbled hasty instructions. "I'll say it is from Fallon, to save questions now," she said. "Can you get a bird who can carry that?"

"Can't you make it any smaller? It's a bird, not a messenger. And how will it last in the rain?" Padraig grumbled.

She drew her knife and sliced away the extra parts of the parchment, then ran over to the shelf and grabbed a canvas pouch. "Happy now?"

Padraig took the package and hurried off.

"That will help, won't it, Mam?" Kerrin asked.

"It will but it's not enough." She clicked her fingers. "Aren't Gannon and the rest of Dina's men in the castle cells?"

Kerrin gulped. "Dad said they weren't allowed out."

"He also said Gannon wanted a chance to prove he wasn't part of Dina's schemes. Seems like the perfect time. Come on."

He looked reluctant but she hurried off and he grabbed his crossbow and followed. The Kottermanis had prepared for this, curse them, making sure they knew the city's backstreets. They must have a plan in mind – maybe even a specific place to surround Fallon and the others. She did not know Berry: damn! She could not sit there and wait and hope. She had to save Fallon.

*

Kottermanis exploded out of a side street and were on Fallon almost before he could react. Even as he turned to face them, shouting orders, Bran and his reserve hit the bastards from the side, bowling over the first soldiers and giving Fallon time to send men to help. Shields and spears sealed the Kottermanis away and the retreat could continue.

Fallon nodded his thanks to Bran and tried to think of a way out of this. It wasn't supposed to be like this. For a start the rain had ruined the fiery barricades they had planned to use to slow the Kottermanis down. Everything was sodden and would not light. They were the ones who had the knowledge of the streets, who had spent a moon training on the cobbles and rooftops for just this battle. Yet the Kottermanis seemed to always know where they were going and always had men pouring out of the street where Fallon wanted advance. He was beyond proud of his men. Despite the losses they had taken, the running and the fighting and the incessant rain, they still held their ranks and obeyed him. They would sprint away, form the hedgehog and sting the Kottermanis, throw some more of them back and then pull away again. Yet there always seemed to be more Kottermanis. He could hear horns being sounded but, rather than make things easier to understand, they only confused him. Both Brendan's and Devlin's companies kept announcing they had run into more Kottermanis, while he had heard nothing from Gallagher for what seemed like an age. The battle had shrunk down to what he could control in front of him.

*

"We're going to have to get off the roofs," Gallagher decided. "Make the call."

The two recruits with horns stared at him incredulously and he pointed down at the fighting below. "We can't keep up with them any more, and the Kottermanis are picking us off. We can do more good down there now. Now sound the horns, curse you!"

They hurriedly blew, time and again, and Gallagher hoped all his men got the message – as well as Fallon. He peered through the rain and saw men climbing up onto the roof of a nearby house.

"What are those idiots doing? The horn said go down!" he cried angrily.

But although they could hear the horns clearly, it was obvious the men were ignoring it. Gallagher was about to yell at them when he realized they carried bows over their shoulders, not crossbows.

"They're bogging Kottermanis! Follow me!" he cried.

He grabbed one of the long ladders and swung it around, grunting with the effort, letting it drop onto the Kottermani roof. "Get them!" he shouted and raced across the ladder, heedless of the wet wood and the killer drop below.

One of the Kottermani archers heard him and hurried to tip the ladder off the roof. Gallagher loosed his crossbow from the hip, aiming by hope more than skill. The bolt struck the archer's arm and spun him around. Another archer ran forwards but Gallagher hurled his empty crossbow at the man and then pulled out his fishing knives, leaping the last pace onto the other roof.

The archer ducked under the flying crossbow and straightened up just in time for Gallagher to open his throat with a huge slash of his knife.

The one with the bolt in his arm drew a sword with his free hand but Gallagher stabbed down, driving his other blade deep into the junction of the Kottermani's neck and shoulder. The man shuddered and convulsed and the fisherman was horribly reminded of some of the big fish he had hooked, then he ripped his knife clear, drenching himself in blood, and forgot about fish as more Kottermanis closed in. He was about to sell his life dearly when a shout announced the rest of his men were arriving. They raced into the Kottermanis and the two sides tottered and staggered on the uneven, sloping roof, fighting as much to keep their footing on the wet wooden shingles as they did to defeat one other.

Gallagher locked blades with a Kottermani archer, then head-butted the man, breaking his nose. The archer staggered backwards, then slipped and fell off the roof with a screech and a soggy thud.

Crossbows were loosed close enough to throw them at their foe and proved to be the better weapon in this fight, for by the time the archer could draw his bowstring back, a Gaelish fighter was on him. Gallagher threw himself across the roof to kick the feet out from one archer, knocking him to the cobbles below, then regained his feet to slit the throat of another who was choking the life out of one of his recruits.

He wiped blood out of his eyes with a soggy tunic sleeve and spat the coppery stink out of his mouth. The last Kottermani was down, thrashing and gasping with a crossbow bolt in his stomach, and the Gaelish were panting and looking around.

"Right. Let's get off these bloody roofs and find Fallon," Gallagher said.

*

The Duchess Dina watched her guards race off into the night and smiled. They had left, only two young men left standing outside her front door, trying to shelter from the rain. Munro had at least six of his agents nearby and she had all this beautiful rain and confusion to aid her. Aroaril might reward the virtuous but luck favored those who planned, she decided. It was time to take advantage of this chance. She lit several candles, placing them in the pre-arranged signal pattern in her window, and then began to pack. She had much to do that night and no time to waste.

*

"Are you ready to prove you are on our side, one of Hagen's men and not a traitor to your Lord?" Bridgit announced loudly as she strode into the cells, holding a lantern high. She ignored the one she knew was filled with the real traitors, Keverne and Mika and the men who had killed the Duke.

Most of the other men inside the cells clustered up to the bars, and she liked that. The ones who stayed at the back were the ones she did not want. She guessed there were more than a hundred men in these cells and three-quarters of them were pressed against the bars, trying to see what was going on.

She strode along the cells until she spotted Gannon, the big former sergeant towering over his fellows.

"Fallon's Bridgit. Welcome back," Gannon said. "How did Fallon win your return?"

"I escaped," she said shortly. "But we don't have time for that. The Kottermanis are here and we are fighting for survival. Are you ready to prove yourself?"

"I have been ready all along, but Fallon does not trust me!" Gannon growled, his big hands squeezing on the bars.

"Then rejoice, for I bring you a chance to regain your honor and be hailed as a hero of the night," she said briskly. "Are you willing to fight the Kottermanis?"

Gannon spat. “Of course. But will Fallon want me? Why did he not come himself? Why did he send his wife to speak to us, if not to torment us further?”

She strode up to the bars. “Because he is fighting for his life. He needs saving and you are the man who is going to do it.”

Gannon shook his head. “He said he could not have us behind him. He thought we would stab him in the back. He might turn on us. And he certainly won’t let us serve under him.”

“Fine. You will serve under me. I got more than two hundred of our people out of Kotterman and defeated these bastards once. Follow me and I will defeat them again. And prove once and for all what you are worth.”

“I wish I could believe you,” Gannon said. “But Fallon would rather see us shipped to Kotterman as slaves.”

Bridgit stepped even closer, so close that he could have reached out and grabbed her. But she showed no fear. “You took an oath. I call on you in Hagen’s memory to follow me and save fellow Lunstermen who are fighting and dying out there. And I swear to you that if you fight for me, nobody will ever touch you and I will sail back to Kotterman as a slave before you do,” she said, her voice low and vehement. “None will ever doubt you again and Fallon himself will embrace you.”

He stared deep into her eyes and she matched his gaze, letting him see the determination that had driven her out of Kotterman and across the ocean.

“I can see why Fallon was willing to do anything to get you back,” he said hoarsely. “Get us out of here and give us weapons. I will follow you into the pits of Zorva himself.”

She snapped her fingers at Kerrin. “Get the keys and then get us to the armory,” she instructed. “Are you all with me?”

“I will pick the ones worthy of you,” Gannon said. “And I will kill them myself before they let you down.”

*

Brendan felt dizzy and lost. In the dark and rain, the alleyways began to blur and it seemed that, no matter which way they turned, there were more Kottermanis there. A mass of them poured out of an alley and he was hard-pressed to turn them back. Brendan set his feet and prepared to go down swinging, then the Kottermanis fell apart as someone drove into them from the side. The foreign soldiers dropped back, allowing the two groups to meet up.

"What is Devlin doing over this way?" Brendan demanded of these new Gaelish recruits.

"Brendan! It is me, Casey!" their leader yelled.

Brendan peered through the rain until he recognized the young officer and a score of prime Gaelish recruits.

"What are you doing here?" he asked.

"Fallon sent for us. We have been following a bird that Padraig sent."

"I wish that crazy old wizard would send us something hot to drink and maybe some more light," Craddock said.

Brendan felt his head clear. "Then let's follow this bird of Padraig's back to Fallon. I have had enough of scampering through alleys. Let's join up and send these bogging Kottermanis screaming back home to mama."

"I wish we had your mama here to fight. She'd send them home screaming all right," Craddock said.

*

Fallon had the growing sense he was being herded in a particular direction. But every attempt to push back was met with more Kottermanis. The bastards were even up on some of the roofs now, and it had been ages since he had seen crossbow bolts flying down to slow the Kottermanis. Their pursuit was relentless.

Then Kottermani pressure on their retreat died away as someone attacked them from the side, driving in their front. Fallon saw his chance and turned his men around.

"Get them! Charge!" he cried, his voice feeling raw after all the shouting he had been doing.

They struck the Kottermanis just as they were closing around the other group of Gaelish. Hit from both sides, the Kottermanis held for a moment, then were cut apart. Fallon had stopped using his sword now, for the Kottermani armor seemed to get harder to cut through the wetter it got. His shillelagh was devastating at close quarters and the Kottermanis seemed to have no idea how to block it. He broke jaws and noses and pulped eyes, cracked elbows and sword hands, putting men out of the fight without killing them. He preferred that anyway, for he had seen more than enough blood that night to last him a lifetime.

He broke through to the new group, just as their leader sent a Kottermani flying with a broken neck, courtesy of a huge swing of his hammer.

"Brendan!" Fallon cried, not only delighted by the sight of his big friend but relieved to see him alive.

"These bastards are everywhere. It's like they know what we are doing," the smith said angrily.

"They must have had men watching us training," Fallon said grimly. "But what is their plan?"

"Are they trying to drive us back to the castle?" Casey piped up, stepping out from behind Brendan.

"What are you doing here?" Fallon asked, recognizing the young man. He looked as blood-spattered and rain-soaked as the rest of them.

"You called for me. Sent me a bird with a parchment order and I followed it to Brendan and then to you, just as it said," Casey replied.

Fallon wiped rain out of his eyes. "Padraig. He and Bridgit must have done that. Aroaril knows why and we can worry about that later. Let's find Gallagher and Devlin and get sorted. I have had just about enough of being pushed around by these boggers."

*

"I think they are trying to trap them in Slaughter Square," Padraig announced.

"What in Aroaril's name is Slaughter Square?" Bridgit demanded.

She had pulled on a boiled leather jerkin that stank of men's sweat and old cows. Her skin crawled wherever it touched it but it made her look more warlike, which was all she was aiming for.

As for weapons, she kept only the knife she had brought from Kotterman. She did not know how to use anything else and, anyway, if she had to do the fighting it was all over for everyone. She planned to use her head, not her sword skills, to beat the Kottermanis again.

More than seventy former Lunster guards had joined Gannon and were picking up a motley collection of weapons, old swords and shillelaghs that had been left behind by Fallon's men. None had shields but most had the old leather jerkins that smelled like they had been stored there for too many years. With them were many of the men she had brought out from Kotterman, from Baltimoreans like Dermot to the young thieves Fitz and Arron. More than a hundred were gathered now. Gannon was handing out handfuls of crossbow bolts to them all. She did not know why and did not have time to ask. But he seemed confident enough about it, so she let him keep going.

"It's where the slaughterhouses are, where flocks of sheep, herds of cows and pigs get their throats slit every day," Padraig said. "It only has two ways in and out – one from the gate and one that leads to the main road. If they get pushed down there, there is no way out and the Kottermanis can use their numbers to crush our forces."

"But surely they can just go out the other side?" Bridgit asked.

"That's a locked gate, strong enough to hold back an angry bull. And the passageway from there to the city gate will be filled with animals. It's a dead end. Truly."

"Well, we can't let that happen. Where is everyone?" Bridgit said.

"Rosaleen and her priests are out in the streets, trying to save the wounded – she won't come here while there are men she can save. The Kottermanis have split Devlin and Gallagher's men off from Brendan and Fallon. They think to destroy Fallon first and then will turn on the smaller group," Padraig said. His face was glistening in the torchlight and she did not think it was from the rain. For a moment she worried about the strain the magic was putting on him, then pushed that aside. There was no time to spend on that, or on fears that one or more of Gannon's men were traitors or that she should not be leading men out into a battle. It had to be done.

"Our friends and family are out there fighting and dying. It's time to save them. Follow me!"

*

"I'm out of crossbow bolts," Gallagher said.

"You don't even have a crossbow. You left it on a roof somewhere, you careless bastard," Devlin replied.

"All my men are," Gallagher said. "That's what I meant."

Devlin ripped his sword out of a Kottermani stomach and kicked the shrieking man backwards.

"What was that?" he asked. "Didn't hear you."

Gallagher tugged at his gutting knife, which was jammed in a Kottermani eye socket. He put his boot on the dead man's head and ripped it free with a curse. "I said we're not crossbowmen any more, because we have no bolts!" he shouted.

"You need to draw swords and fight, because I think you're out of bolts!" Devlin called.

Gallagher jumped at a Kottermani threatening to dash his friend's brains out. He crossed his knives to make the block, feeling the impact shake him from his arms to his toes, then Devlin hooked the soldier's legs out and the man fell with a crash and vanished into the press of soldiers.

"We can't break through. We need to pull back!" Gallagher yelled in his friend's ear.

Devlin grabbed at his ear. "There's no need to shout!" he called. "My ear's ringing like a bell now!"

Gallagher would have smiled but he did not have the time. Since meeting up with Devlin the pair of them had been trying to force their companies through to Fallon. They could hear the horn calls and they could reply but they could not find a way through. Every street they tried was blocked by Kottermani soldiers.

"Maybe Fallon can break through to the castle?" Devlin asked hopefully.

"Aroaril, we'll be lucky if we can," Gallagher muttered.

*

"Where in Aroaril's name is Gallagher? Those bogging Kottermani archers are killing us," Fallon cursed.

"What now?" Brendan asked.

Fallon tried to look down the road, through the gusts of rain and wind. Despite his best efforts, people were still looking out to see what was going on and at least the firelight spilling out of the windows was giving some light to the street. As he'd feared, daylight had only turned the sky from black to dark gray. What both revealed was not pretty. A Kottermani force had got ahead of them and blocked the road to the castle. Behind him, his rear guard was fighting off the main Kottermani force and he did not have much time to break through this new blockade.

"Breaking them will not be easy," he said. "Maybe we should go down that street there and try and circle around. Casey, where does that lead?"

The young officer peered down the narrow street, then stiffened. "We don't want to go down there. That only leads to Slaughter Square," he said.

Fallon spat. "So that is their plan. Get us in there, trap us and either kill us or force us to lay down arms. Once we go in there, we don't come out again."

"Can we get over the roofs?" Casey asked.

"Without any ladders, while carrying fifty wounded men? I don't like the chances of half of us making it far enough to get away," Fallon said, racking his tired brain for an answer. There had to be an amazing way out of this. He couldn't let the bastard Kottermanis beat them. That was the thing he came back to, time and again. "Let's break through that shieldwall," he said.

Yet, even as he looked around at his men, he doubted they could do it. They were exhausted and almost all had one or more wounds. Yet it was a better chance than if they went down that ominous, dark street to Slaughter Square. "Follow me!" he shouted, his voice cracking.

*

Kemal was feeling much happier about the way the battle was going than when he had been forced to inspire his men to stand firm. His losses were still terrible and the Gaelish had astonished him with their tenacity. He had never seen a battle before but, from all the histories he had read, no other foe had fought so hard. He was stepping over the evidence of this with every pace.

He watched as a small group of Gaelish were cornered in a side alley. They drove back his men with swords and spears, leaving his soldiers screaming on the ground, until they were brought down by a volley of arrows and left to thrash and bleed in the rain.

Thanks to Abbas and his men, Kemal's companies were hunting through streets they had never seen before as though they had grown up there. Now they almost had the main group of Gaelish, led by the bastard Fallon, in their grasp. Then all the suffering and sacrifice would be worth it. "Pass the word. I want to be there when Fallon is brought to bay," he ordered.

*

Fallon drew his sword slowly. All the fighting had blunted it and he was not even sure if it would cut parchment, let alone Kottermani armor. But he could not lead a charge with a shillelagh. "Brendan, stay to my right, Casey my left. I'll crack a hole in their line and you go through," he said.

"Let me do that," Casey said. "Sir, they'll all target you and kill you!"

"No, let me do it. My hammer will open them up," Brendan said.

"I led us into this. I have to lead us out," Fallon said. "Come on!"

He broke into a shambling run, his men forming a pyramid shape behind him. Maybe it would be enough to break the Kottermani line. Maybe not. For a moment he thought bitterly how cruel it was to have won back Bridgit and then be lost to her. Then he forgot about everything but the Kottermanis.

"Kill them!" he howled and sprinted at the solid line.

The invaders had locked shields and that line bristled with sword points, while he did not even have a shield. But he persuaded himself that was enough. Besides, dying here was better than falling into Kemal's hands for his revenge. Perhaps the Kottermani might be satisfied with just his head, and leave Bridgit and Kerrin alone. He used that thought to fill himself full of fury and he picked out his man, a towering Kottermani with a fearsome moustache. He braced himself for the impact with the Kottermani line – and then it dissolved.

He slowed as another force hit the Kottermani company from behind, turning them from an ordered, disciplined formation into a rabble in an instant.

"Come on!" He sped up again and raced into the fight as the Kottermanis turned to meet their surprise attackers.

Caught between two sides, the Kottermanis were destroyed, the handful of survivors throwing down their weapons and cowering at the side of the road.

Fallon sheathed his sword on the second try, astonished he was still alive. Then he spotted some familiar faces.

"Devlin! Gallagher! Thank Aroaril you got here when you did!" He grinned.

"Don't thank us, it wasn't our doing – it was her," Devlin said, stepping aside and pointing.

Fallon blinked rain out of his eyes and gasped as Bridgit strode forwards, a tall, blood-spattered yet familiar figure guarding her side.

"Bridge? What in Aroaril's name are you doing here? And what is he doing here?" he cried.

"Saving your foolish skin," she said. "I saw you needed every sword we had, so I called on Gannon and his men to prove their loyalty. Which he has just done."

Fallon grabbed her arm and whisked her to his side. "He cannot be trusted," he said. "They lie to your face, you turn your back and they sink the knife in!"

"He has had plenty of chances and not taken them. And he just saved your life," she pointed out. "And if you won't listen to reason, listen to this: he is under my protection."

Fallon bit back angry words. "We can worry about him later," he said. "Now we are together, we can fall back to the castle and fight from the walls there."

"No," Bridgit said softly, so only he could hear. "They will only turn on the people then, slaughter them until we are forced to come out. I have a better idea."

"Since when have you become a war captain?" Fallon asked incredulously.

"Since you got trapped and needed saving. Listen to me and we'll end this without killing most of your men."

Fallon sighed. He was bone tired, soaked to the skin in blood and rain and his rear guard was still fighting furiously to hold off the Kottermanis pushing up the street. "Let's hear it then."

*

"We have them trapped in the square of slaughter!" Mahir announced, the boluk-bashi's voice betraying his joy.

Kemal clenched his fists to contain the surge of joy. Abbas and his men had proved a Godsend. Even in the rain and dark they had led his companies, time and again, right onto the Gaelish defenders, moving them always back and across into the trap. He had worried Fallon would find some fiendish way to slip out of the net closing around him but now all that remained was to make the Gaelish surrender and ensure that bastard peasant did not die before he received the vengeance he so richly deserved.

"I must be there. Hold them until I arrive. Quick now!" The last was to his guards, who formed up around him and pushed him up the street, through the lines of exhausted, wet troops. Yet they were soldiers of Kotterman and all, even the wounded, saluted as he went past, cheering the Prince who had led them to a hard victory in these filthy, sodden streets.

Kemal indulged himself for a moment, imagining how the history scrolls would record this triumph and how his father would thank him for creating this new outpost of the Empire. Yes, their losses had been severe. But the histories never recorded such trivial details. What mattered was the result.

He could see Feray's admiring glance in his mind's eye and could not wait to go and tell her. Nobody could deny he was a man now. Then those warm reflections were brought to a halt, literally.

"What is going on?" he demanded.

Nobody seemed able to answer, so he pushed his way bodily through the crush of people to find a group of Gaelish women blocking the road, trying to pull apart the mounds of bodies, while Kemal's men shouted at them.

"What is this?" Kemal thundered, in Gaelish. "Get out of the way or you shall join these bodies!"

Instantly the nearest woman, a young mother, rushed over to him. "Those are our sons, husbands, brothers and friends out there. They are dying alone, in the dark and rain. What kind of monster are you that you would stop us?" she demanded furiously.

"Get back, woman! Do you know who you are talking to?" Mahir snarled, although as he was speaking in Kottermani, the effect was lost. To emphasize his words, he drew back his hand to strike her.

Kemal, meanwhile had glanced around the street, which was covered in bodies, most of them moving, moaning, thrashing, calling and bleeding.

"No," he told the boluk-bashi. "Let them care for the wounded. They were brave men and fought well. Soon they will be part of our Empire and one day they might even live to serve under you, in another part of Kotterman."

"As you wish, high one." Mahir bowed.

"What is your name?" Kemal asked the defiant woman.

"Rebecca," she replied, glaring at him.

"You are a brave woman. Do what you can to save these men."

He left her looking astonished and hurried up the street, finally reaching the entrance to the road leading to the square of slaughter. His corbaci, Nazim, waited for him there.

"High one, my men are in the square, holding position. The Gaelish are drawn up within in a defensive square and wait for our attack," he said.

Kemal looked up the street to where his blocking force was in tight ranks, their shields held proudly high. The bodies scattered over the cobbles before them showed how hard they had fought to close the trap. They raised their swords and slapped them against their shields to salute him. In return he waved back at them. Even the dawn had brought little light to the street and he could barely see them through the driving rain but he knew they would appreciate the gesture.

"They have secured the victory," Kemal said. "Theirs was the hardest task and we shall honor them for it afterwards."

That company began to march forwards, somewhat raggedly, but he could forgive them that after what they had done.

"Shall I send them to the rooftops, so we can overwhelm them from all sides, high one?" Nazim asked.

"It is not necessary," Kemal said. "Once I speak to the Gaelish, they will give up. Follow me."

He strode triumphantly down the narrow street, his guards ahead of him. In his mind's eye he was seeing Fallon begging for mercy on his knees and that was all he cared about. The square ahead stank of blood and waste and normally it would have revolted him. But now the smell bothered him not at all.

"High one, the company that held the road is following us down. Shall I order them to return?" Mahir asked.

"Let them join in my triumph. After all, they secured it," Kemal said dismissively.

As Nazim had said, the Gaelish were drawn up on the far side of the square, locked in tight ranks. Facing them were Nazim's men, who parted ranks to let him through.

He stood at the front, although Mahir was careful to have men with shields on either side of him, in case the Gaelish still had crossbows.

"Let Fallon come forth! Or does he care nothing for your lives, that he would sacrifice you all to save himself?" Kemal roared.

There was a commotion among the Gaelish and a figure pushed his way out of them.

Kemal felt a pulse of mixed elation and hatred to see Fallon there.

"Time to enjoy our victory," he announced and strode forwards, his guards closing in around him. Behind them, another company marched forwards also, until there was a solid column moving out of the ranks.

Kemal frowned a little. It made him look as though he was afraid of Fallon and that was the last impression he wanted. "Send them back, I only need my personal guards," he ordered Mahir.

But, even as the boluk-bashi snapped out the orders, the company pushed forwards faster. Kemal's guards moved to stop them, shouting angrily but, to Kemal's astonishment and horror, the other company clubbed and stabbed the guards down.

"What is the meaning of this?" Kemal bellowed but the soldiers did not respond, instead pressed forwards faster. Mahir drew his sword, only for a tall man, wielding not the regulation sword but a pair of long knives, to knock it aside and then slam him to the ground.

Kemal fumbled for his own sword, shocked at the sudden turn of events, except two soldiers pounced on him. One, a bald giant, knocked his sword from his hand. The other held a sword awkwardly to his throat.

"What are you doing?" Kemal roared.

The soldier tugged at his ill-fitting helmet and knocked it off, revealing a mop of long blonde hair that was instantly soaked by the rain.

"Winning this battle," the soldier said in Gaelish.

In the gloom and rain, it took him a moment to recognize the face and voice. "Bridgit?" he gasped, an icy fist grabbing his heart.

"The same. And these aren't your men. They are mine. Tell your soldiers to throw down their weapons or you will die," she said harshly.

He stared around in shock and confusion as men he had thought were his soldiers spun around, forming a defensive ring around him – except they were protecting against his real soldiers, under Nazim. The bald-headed giant of a man grabbed his arm and hustled him backwards, the rest of them coming with them, and it was only now, this close to them, that he saw the rents in the armor, the bloodstains that belonged to their former owners, and the clumsy way the Gaelish were marching. How could he have not realized earlier?

His previous exultation was washed away in a tide of horror. This could not happen!

"Tell your men to surrender," Bridgit ordered.

"Never! I would rather die first," Kemal growled.

Bridgit pointed at the tall soldier with the knives. "Bring that officer over," she instructed.

Kemal watched furiously as a dazed Mahir was dragged across.

"Tell your friends over there to surrender or your precious Prince dies," Bridgit told Mahir.

Kemal was about to order Mahir to do no such thing when he was punched in the stomach and, winded, he doubled over, unable to speak.

Mahir spoke little Gaelish but the meaning of what was going on was only too clear. Kemal felt tears of pain and humiliation trickle down his cheeks as the boluk-bashi shouted out what the Gaelish wanted.

There was a pause as Nazim shouted back questions but Kemal was forced upright, a knife against his throat, then Mahir called again, his voice more desperate.

The sound of Kottermani weapons falling to the cobbles was like the chimes of doom.

CHAPTER 56

Fallon enfolded Bridgit in his arms.

"You were right! You did it!" he said.

"Don't sound so surprised," she said tiredly. "I told you it would work. Men see what they want to see, not what really is there, especially when it is dark and raining. Walking down that alleyway with Kottermanis all around us nearly stopped my heart but we knew all we had to do was get to Kemal and we would be safe. And so it proved!"

They had both been working solidly for the past six turns of the hourglass, through the driving rain, which was only now beginning to let up. At least it had cleaned away some of the horror from the cobbles.

Men were out scouring the streets and rooftops for wounded and checking for Kottermani agents, as well as securing the harbor. Wounded men had been found in the strangest of places and, luckily, many would survive. Rosaleen and an army of priests and helpers were doing their best but much of the healing had been begun by ordinary people, who had bound up wounds and tried to stop men bleeding until real help could arrive. There had been extraordinary tales of survival as well, from a crossbowman who had fallen from a rooftop and only broken a leg to the young guard who had raised the warning, found shivering and bleeding but alive in the harbormaster's office.

Above all, however, there had been tales of death. The tally was still being made but more than two hundred young Gaelish were gone, with almost all of the survivors suffering some sort of wound.

Yet it was still a triumph. They had Prince Kemal and the Kottermanis would buy his freedom only once Gaelland could be sure it was free. Fallon mourned those who were lost but it was a smaller price than he had feared he would pay to save the country.

He sat down beside Bridgit and kissed her wet hair. Every part of him ached, while he had three cuts on his arms and chest that stung furiously every time he moved.

"Thank Aroaril that will be our last battle," he said.

"Thank Aroaril I was on your side," she said.

He laughed and then groaned as his wounds pulled at him.

"We'll find a priest to look at those," she said.

He shook his head. "There are too many others who need it more. I can wait." He leaned in to kiss her but she turned her head and he ended up with a mouthful of ear. "What?" he began, only for her to turn his head also.

"I am sorry to disturb you, Captain," Casey said, his hair plastered flat against his scalp by the rain, "but I thought you should know. We went back to the Duchess Dina's house and the two men I left there were dead. She is gone, run into the night."

Bridgit cursed and he looked at her.

"Where did you learn those words?"

"You would rather not know," she said grimly. "But that is ill news on a dark day. I wish I had never summoned them away from there."

Fallon sighed. "But if you had not, then Brendan might have been lost, and then me with him, even before you got to us. No, it was the right decision. Casey, double the guards on the gates just in case but I expect she has got out of the city by now."

"Then we should send men after her. Capture her and bring her back," Bridgit said.

"We will, but it matters little," he said, reaching out to embrace her once more.

"Fallon, you need to listen to me. She is dangerous!"

"So she goes to Swane. It just means we get them both in the spring. What harm can she do us? She cannot create an army for him."

Bridgit shivered a little. She told herself it was only the cold but things did not feel like they were finished. Worse, she was beginning to wonder if Fallon had the foresight needed to run this city.

*

Feray watched the coast of Gaelland slip over the horizon and shivered. She had ordered both crews from the two remaining ships onto the best vessel and sunk the other after stripping it of all supplies.

"Ana, when is our baba coming back to us?" Orhan asked.

She hugged her son. "Your baba is a prisoner with Fallon and Kerrin, as we once were," she said gently.

"But when is he coming back?"

"Soon," she said. "We are going for a little sail now. We need to see baba's baba, your grandfather the Emperor. And together we are going to get your baba back."

Acknowledgments

Even though my name is on the cover, there are many people who helped – either to make this book a reality or to make the story, the characters and the words better. Without them, it would be a lesser work and I thank them deeply for what they added to the book.

To my beta reader Belinda, who always has good suggestions; my agent Jo Butler at Cameron's Management; the team at Momentum – Joel, Ashley, Patrick and Michelle; to copy editor Kate O'Donnell, whose brilliant work made me think about every aspect of this book and made my writing look better; to the fantastic proof reader (Melissa Kemble) whose eagle eyes were very much appreciated.

If you enjoyed this book, then you deserve my thanks as well.